OMICRON CRISIS
Adventures from Alpha Centauri

By
D. L. Smith

PublishAmerica
Baltimore

© 2004 by D.L. Smith.
All rights reserved. No part of this book may be reproduced, stored in a retrieval system or transmitted in any form or by any means without the prior written permission of the publishers, except by a reviewer who may quote brief passages in a review to be printed in a newspaper, magazine or journal.

First printing

ISBN: 1-4137-3086-8
PUBLISHED BY PUBLISHAMERICA, LLLP
www.publishamerica.com
Baltimore

Printed in the United States of America

This book is dedicated to the memory of my grandmother, Mabel Vance White, on whom the character Labelle Vance, The Seer of Omicron, is based.

Omicron Crisis

Adventures from Alpha Centauri

CHAPTER ONE
Captain's Sojourn

What he saw before him was large, cold and irradiated with poisons that were deadly to him. Or at least should be deadly to him. Still, he couldn't imagine being anywhere else, for the vacuum of space was the most beautiful thing he had ever seen.

Although space had a rival in the form of—

EEEEP, EEEEP, EEEEP.

Danar Seti switched off the proximity alert beacon and focused on the present. Not that he actually needed the beacon considering he could see the Omicron Nebula space station less than a kilometer away from the forward vacuum shield of the space freighter.

When he had first seen the asteroid station as a young Omicron recruit, he thought it was the ugliest thing in the sky. Now that he was her CO he marveled at the beauty of the structure; its oblong four-kilometer-length asteroid body sandwiched at each end by domes, one transparent, the other segmented, both metallic.

Seti knew he was tired to be waxing sentiment regarding the old space station. He had set the proximity alert in case he had dozed, but as usual, despite his two-day solitude, he hardly slept a wink. Oh, how he missed those blissful times as a child when he could sleep like a cat at the drop of a hat. But sleep seemed to be an elusive mistress lately. Back then, of course, he suffered from amnestic aphasia, the memory-robbing disease he had inherited while in his mother's womb during Earth's greatest environmental disaster over seventy objective years ago. Although he was cured of the disease shortly after arrival here at

Alpha Centauri, one holdover side effect still haunted him; he could rarely remember his dreams. A small price to pay, he reckoned, considering the cure allowed him to remember reality like a normal person.

But thanks to the alien substance that cured him he knew he was far from normal.

It was an oddity, however, that he was able remember the events of his awakening in the makeshift receiving center on Omicron's surface thirty years ago with such crystal clarity. Then again, the fact that he was haunted with the waking dream's intrusion into his thoughts every year at this time for the last thirty years made it not quite so odd. The intrusion was usually triggered by the standard Omicron alarm, the same as the proximity alert.

EEEEP, EEEEP, EEEEP.

Yeah, that's the one, alright, he mused. *Now what?*

"*Omicron Nebula docking control to Nebula Freighter One,*" the comm speaker blared. "*Identify yourself, pilot. I don't have you scheduled for docking today.*"

"This is Captain Nebula, commander of the Omicron Nebula space station, technician," Seti added for the benefit of the newbie. "And the reason why there's no docking schedule for today is because I didn't file one. Check under Wednesday evening's departures and you'll see that I filed it there stating I didn't know when I'd be back."

After a few seconds, the time it would take the new tech to verify the file, he came back on line. "*Sorry, sir.*"

"When did you start, son?"

"*Thursday. Yesterday, sir.*"

"What's your name, technician?"

"*Docking Technician Ralph Hanson, sir.*"

"Standard procedure, Hanson," Seti quoted, "states that you should verify arrival and departure files seven days prior to your logging on. Granted, I've been gone for two days; however, my arrival should not have come as a surprise. I recommend you re-read the docking manual, technician."

"*Yes, sir. Right away, sir,*" said the new tech, embarrassed by the dressing down from his CO.

With a disarming smile that he hoped would be conveyed through the audio connection, Seti said, "I'd rather you finish with your shift, son."

"*Yes, sir. Thank you, sir.*"

"Oh, by the way, welcome to Omicron Nebula," Seti finished with a genuine smile before closing the connection.

They seem to be getting younger and younger these days, he mused. No doubt, he would find the technician's promotion in the backed-up paperwork waiting for him, left by his second-in-command, Rocky Cummings.

Doing his best to relax in the pilot's crash chair, realizing he still had several minutes before docking, Seti allowed one of the few memories of his childhood to cascade over his thoughts. It was about that time, after all.

"Oh no. I think we've got another dead one here. Geez, it's a kid too."

"Are you sure?"

"Yeah, I'm sure it's a kid."

"Idiot. Are you sure he's dead? The cryo-suspension chamber is receiving power."

"I'm not getting any brainwave activity."

"That can't be. Look, the kid's moving. Check those readings again."

"Yeah, you're right. They're just very faint. Much lower than they should be. Even coming out of a thaw."

"Here, let me. Wake up!"

"Uh…wha—"

"Come on, kid, wake up already."

"Dad?"

"Uh…no, kid. I'm sorry, your dad's not here now."

The only thing the young boy could figure was that he had suffered another memory lapse. But if that were true, then where was his father? The face of his father was the only familiar item on which his damaged brain could focus. He must have had another attack, because he couldn't remember any of the events that brought him to this...hospital? *Who are these strange men? Do I know them? And why am I so cold? What are they saying?*

"What's wrong with him? He should've snapped out of it by now," one stranger said to the other.

The other strange man, a doctor presumably, was waving an oddly gloved hand over the boy's body. "According to the palm scanner he's one hundred percent."

"He doesn't look a hundred percent."

"I'm patching the scanner into the Virtual Inquiry Computer Interactive hologram now. Standby. It says here that he came out exactly as he went in twenty-seven years ago."

Twenty-seven years?

"He's got some neurological damage, but it was a pre-existing condition. That explains the faint brain waves. How much you want to bet it was caused by the solar radiation back on Earth?"

"Yeah. He looks about the right age. What do you figure he's about eight years old?"

"More like thirty-five now."

"Nah. According to VICI, he was in perfect hibernation. For him, time was absolutely nonexistent for the entire journey here. Not everybody was so lucky."

"Who is he?"

"I don't have a clue. He came in on the ISS *Nebula*. Part of the computer memory in the section where he was stored crashed about a light year before orbital insertion. A lot of the records were lost. It's a wonder the ship got here at all."

"What? Is your brain still on ice? Idiot. We *all* came in on the *Nebula*. It's the first one to arrive. Besides, the ship was fine. It was just part of the memory core and a section of the cryogenic module that had problems. Thank your lucky star you thawed okay."

"What are you talking about? What happened to the *Omicron* and the *Omega*?"

"Are you serious? You must have been asleep during your

orientation. The *Omicron* and the *Omega* didn't make it."

"Oh my God. I—I was thawed only last week. No one said anything about the first two ships. My God. I—I'm scheduled for orientation next week. They say they're backed up. There's about a million of us up and about now."

"Well, there's still billions more to go. Try and keep it together, okay? I'll catch you up later."

"I don't believe it. The *Omicron*. The *Omega*. What happened to them?"

"Rumor has it they got swallowed up by a black hole. But it was more like a sinkhole or something. It was too technical for me."

"The Seer. She said all of the ships would make it here intact."

"The Seer?" the strange man said in disbelief. "You don't really believe in that psycho-fortune-telling-abra-cadabra-crap, do you?"

"Hey, it was shown back in the late twenty-first century that there is some scientific evidence that psychic abilities are latent in some genes."

"So is having the wool pulled over your eyes."

"You know, now that I think about it, the Seer did say that the Interstellar Starship *Nebula* would get here first. So now what do you say?"

"I say the ISS *Gaea* is in orbit now. We've got our work cut out for us. Let's concentrate on the group we have here. The more folks we can thaw, the more techs we'll find among them to help us out. Get it?"

"Okay, kid. What's your name?"

"Um…uh. It's Dane. Um, Dane R. How—" *What's this? Another strange man.*

"Wait a minute, you guys. I think I know this kid. His dad was a bigwig scientist at the astrological institute where I worked."

"Okay, Sanders, so what's his father's name?"

"Aw crap, I just came out of thaw recently myself. I—I wouldn't remember my own name if you hadn't just told me. I do remember we all just called him Doc Seti. You know, as in Search for Extra-Terrestrial Intelligence."

"You're a lot of help, Sanders."

"Gentleman, we don't have time for this. We've got a lot of other people to thaw."

"What did the kid say his first name was? Danar? Fine. Process him. We'll catch up with the records of the other ships when they arrive and correct any discrepancies if we're able. For now, his name is Danar Seti. Get him cleaned up and let's move on."

"Say, Sanders. Did you know about the *Omicron* and the *Omega*?"

EEEEP, EEEEP, EEEEP.

"Oh no. The kid's out again."

EEEEP, EEEEP, EEEEP.

"What now?" Seti said, snapping back to the present. He saw that he was receiving yet another incoming comm. This time it was on the visual monitor. Activating the screen, he was delighted to see that it was, "Professor Ozawa. Uh, Tan, it's not quite four a.m. Rather early for you, isn't it?"

"*Rather,*" Tan Ozawa said, a wry smile on her beautiful face. "*I couldn't sleep. I suppose I'm anxious for my science symposium later today. Besides, uh, Greystoke couldn't sleep either. He was hungry. And everybody knows my cat rules this household.*"

Seti laughed out loud, more at the irony than Tan's joke. A part of him hoped that Tan's inability to sleep was because she was worried about his being gone for two days. But considering their relationship had been professional these many years prevented him from fanning that hope. *Too bad.*

"*Danar, do you know what today is?*" her image asked.

"Friday," he said evasively, knowing where this was going.

"*It's the thirtieth anniversary of our arrival here at Alpha Centauri,*" she said.

Thirty years ago today, the refugees from Earth made planetfall on Omicron, ending their long, hard journey. It was Danar's hope there wouldn't be much in the way of celebrating. If every previous anniversary was an indication, he wouldn't have to worry on that account.

For him, it was a time to forget. *Funny,* he mused. There was a time when forgetting would not only have been easy for him but unavoidable. "Tan, is that why you called me?"

"No," said Tan Ozawa, "*I'm just curious where you've been for a couple of days in a cargo transport freighter all alone. A little vacation?*"

"Yeah, something like that," he said smiling. "And it wasn't quite two days. I'll tell you about it sometime. Tan, where are you?"

"*I'm on Omicron. I figured I'd take advantage of my early wake-up call to prepare for my symposium. But since I missed you—that is, your arrival back at the station, I wanted to talk with you about this idea of diverting the starships from the belt. Your behavior has been rather strange lately. Are you sure you know what you're doing?*"

It was a good thing Tan Ozawa, the chief scientist for the colony at Alpha Centauri, was one of the most beautiful women—the most beautiful anything—on whom Danar had ever laid eyes. Otherwise he might take exception to her constantly questioning his decisions.

No wait. Scratch that thought. It was way too sexist. Luckily he didn't say it out loud. And he settled with the excuse that he was tired, having sat motionless at the pilot's console for several hours. Besides, although he would never admit it to her, he relied on her devil's advocate-type counsel. "No, Tan," he answered, "I'm certainly not sure of what I'm doing. However, rest assured that I'm being discrete. I've spoken with all of the other seven asteroid commanders, and they are willing to hear me out."

"*Did they willingly agree to hear you out?*" she asked with a slight grin. "*Or did you harangue them in some way?*"

He chose not to answer. Instead he said, "Tan, it's better to be prepared. If it's all for nothing then we'll just tell the citizenry the ships are on practice maneuvers or performing thruster maintenance, which isn't far from the truth." And with a slight smile, he added, "And if the ships are necessary then I'll expect an apology from you." *If we survive.*

"Listen," the captain continued aloud, "I've scheduled a staff meeting at the Central Command Module for fifteen hundred today. The other captains will be attending remotely via the new holo-imagers. It would be nice if you could make it. Let's just say you would find it…interesting."

"*I'll do my best. If you could arrange another asteroid attack, I may be able to end my symposium early."*

"I'll see what I can do," he answered, chuckling.

"Maybe I'll see you later then." She closed the connection.

After powering down the transport freighter and verifying its secure lockdown in its berth in the cargo hanger at the far end of the Omicron Nebula station, Seti was about to leave, hoping against hope he could squeeze in a couple of hours of sleep before the alpha shift at the Central Command Module on the opposite side of the asteroid station came on duty.

Being alone for nearly two days, his mind couldn't help but to go over his thoughts: the debates he secretly enjoyed with Tan Ozawa, what little he remembered as a child on Earth. And although he lacked a lot of memory of that time, he did know that life was much less complicated. At the very least, *he* had no responsibilities then.

Now here he was, four-and-half light years from Earth, the captain of a floating city in space, orbiting an alien world, surprisingly very much like home, within a trinary star system, trying to protect the citizens from what could be the same disaster that struck their home planet decades ago. He hoped that what Doctor Ozawa contended was true, that the gravitational disturbance that caused the occasional asteroid attacks was a natural phenomenon. The alternative was that the random asteroids were a result of extra-terrestrial manipulations.

Could it be that what happened to Earth was not an accident? If so, then there would be a serious need for conflict resolution. He hoped he was up to the task. Because if he wasn't, this could spiral down to…well, a conflict. And haven't the displaced citizens of Earth seen enough conflict in their violent history? *Well, hopefully it won't come to that.* But unless or until it did, he would see to it that life would go on as normal as possible for the citizens of Omicron.

Just as he was about to leave the vehicle, he received yet another communication. This time the call, although dreaded, was not completely unexpected.

"Welcome back, Captain Nebula," said the disembodied voice of VICI, the Virtual Inquiry Computer Interactive hologram.

"Good morning, VICI," he said cheerfully, fearing the cheer would fade. "You're about the only…person who I don't expect to complain about a lack of sleep today."

"Today, sir?"

"Sorry."

"I see that your mission was a success."

"Dropping three remote sensor probes out in open space is what we call a 'milk run,' VICI."

"Yes, sir," the hologram said, all business like. "I have already accessed the data and incorporated it to our previous findings."

"The speculation on the random asteroid activity?"

"Verified, Captain. For the first time in nearly two decades, the phenomenon known as 'random roids' is no longer random. The asteroid belt *will* become unstable at least two more times before the planet Omicron completes another orbit around Alpha Centauri A."

"Origin of phenomenon?"

"It is *not* a natural occurrence. It is not caused by anything from the colony. Based on the location we worked out, and the data I obtained from the three RSPs, it *is* caused by…an outside force."

In more ways than one, VICI reminded Danar of Tan. In this case, specifically, neither the human scientist nor the colony's AI wanted to mention anything about extraterrestrials. Neither wishing to commit.

"Margin of error?"

"Zero."

That was it then. They were all in trouble. And right now he was the only one who knew for certain. Now he regretted that the council had declassified the events detailing the colony's arrival here at Alpha Centauri, that the disaster that struck Earth seven decades before facilitated the mass exodus. But no one realized that the random roids phenomenon was related. And now Seti knew that the disappearance of the first two starships in the caravan from Earth, the ISS *Omicron* and ISS *Omega* may have also fallen victim to the same "outside force."

As far as Seti was concerned the other boot just dropped. Now the peace of Alpha Centauri may have just come to an end and the disaster that struck the Earth was only the beginning of their troubles.

Envying the hologram, he gave up any hope of sleep for today.

CHAPTER TWO
Heart and Sol

"Ms. Schreiber, is it true that our original planet Dirt was blown up and that we are all lost in space forever?"

Now that the circumstances surrounding the arrival to the Alpha Centauri star system were no longer classified, Babs Schreiber, the newly appointed teacher for the children of the Omicron Nebula asteroid city, figured this would indeed be a good time to implement rumor control. "Well, not really. For one thing, our original planet is called Earth, not Dirt. And it wasn't blown up exactly. I suppose I should start at the beginning. It all started in the Earth year of—"

Just then, she noticed the silent yellow warning light on her desktop monitor. It was a signal being sent from the Central Command Module located at the far end of the space station, warning everyone of yet another gravimetric disturbance in the area of space that made up the Alpha Centauri star system.

The scientists of the Starforce of Omicron had been baffled for decades about the series of events leading up to millions of asteroids in the region to just fly from belt orbit and seemingly zip anywhere they wished, apparently breaking the laws of physics.

Of course, what do the asteroids care about the laws of physics? "Before we go into the details of what happened to Earth, I take it everyone is familiar with the warning lights you see on the walls?"

"Yes," said the same young man who had queried the question regarding Earth, his desk light blinking his enthusiasm. At Ms. Schreiber's nod, he continued. "That's the warning for the asteroid avoidance procedure the space station might have to perform to prevent being struck by the bumblebee rocks."

"Bumblebee rocks?" Ms. Schreiber asked.

"Yes, my dad says that the asteroids act like bumblebees in that they also broke the laws of physics because they weren't able to fly at all cause they were not arrow–arrow-something."

"Ah," understood the teacher, "aerodynamic."

"Yeah."

"That's interesting. Why don't we look up the history of the bumblebees of Earth," prompted B. Schreiber, her way of distracting the kids from the possible nerve-wracking warning lights. Instructing the students to insert their Data Access Crystals into the data slots on their desks, she typed the inquiry "How Insects Fly" into her master input keypad.

Every citizen of Omicron carried some form of DAC. The most popular was the wrist DAC. Then of course there was the pocket DAC or even the necklace DAC, among others.

According to historical records, the students saw that a late-twentieth-century scientist, one Michael Dickinson, discovered that insects employed some aviation trickery involving delayed stall, rotational circulation and something called wake capture. Somehow, she doubted that nature had endowed these alien asteroids with abilities far beyond those of ordinary Sol rocks.

"The major difference here," Ms. Schreiber said, "was that the flight of the bumblebee was in no way dangerous to the world around them, unlike our domestic asteroids that could cause a great deal of damage to Omicron Nebula and the seven other asteroid cities, as well as our home planet Omicron."

She was gratified that the students took so well to interacting with computers for their education. It was unfortunate they had nearly 18 months of practice since their first teacher, Christine McCauley, disappeared with over 20 other citizens of the Omicron colony in the pursuit of exploration and knowledge. B. Schreiber certainly understood why C. McCauley ventured off despite the danger. What a windfall it would be for a teacher to have firsthand knowledge of new information to teach.

As a former clinical psychologist herself, it was she who counseled the children, many of whom didn't understand the loss. It wasn't much longer after that she decided to fill the gap and change vocations. She felt it was her continuing duty to the children of the floating asteroid-city-space station-whatever in orbit over the planet Omicron that had been settled for only three decades.

Although the warning light was still flashing, which meant the danger wasn't over, it had yet to turn red, which was a warning for everyone in the four-kilometer space station to brace themselves for impact. Since there were no audio warnings, the defensive turrets on the surface of the asteroid city were obviously finding their marks and destroying or deflecting them away.

Good! She hated the red light warnings which were usually followed by heavy gravity all over the station as the maneuvering thrusters increased or decreased the spin for better targeting or avoidance—a procedure jokingly referred to by the populace as "Rock and Roll." The scientists insisted the newly updated gravity generators compensated for the spin, which meant no one should feel the increased gravity. *Yeah, right. Who are they trying to kid?*

Ah good. The yellow light went out, which meant no Rock and Roll this time. The weapons turrets had done the job without upsetting her stomach.

"Now, where were we before our little interruption?"

"What happened to Earth?" one of the students in the back of the room asked without using his desk beacon.

"Oh yes," B. Schreiber said, not bothering to correct the youngster. "The year 2161...."

For the first time in its history, the planet Earth knew peace. Not total peace unfortunately, but what could be considered global peace. At least that was what all of the slogans, banners and E- billboards said. And why not? Every nation now knew democracy—the official governments of all of the nations, at any rate.

Of course there were a few hold-out organizations in a few countries that were trying to push petty dictatorships. The problem there was that one could not sell a dictatorship when one's clientele base rapidly dwindled.

In other words, the average citizen of the planet Earth was enjoying the freedom to choose, too much. Of course, with the freedom to choose there were those who chose the wrong thing. But in a world of democracy even that was a matter of opinion. As long as the people were fed regularly and could enjoy at least some creature comforts, they were happy. The planet Earth was now one step away from becoming a one-government world.

It had been known that despite the fact that the population was increasing by about one billion people every decade, there were enough resources on the planet to feed every man, woman, child and animal. Now that there was global peace, the governments of the mid-twenty-second century wondered if maybe it came too late. It was no secret that it came about, for the most part, through the perfection of synthesizing foods, grains and proteins at a cheaper cost than processing foodstuff in the conventional way: butchering animal flesh. Although animal byproducts such as eggs and milk were still generally acceptable.

The conversion to worldwide electric power and the cessation of the use of fossil fuels helped the planet to regain its health, which first became evident when signs of the ozone layer repairing itself were seen.

What was not generally known was that the planet's energy consumption would eventually overcome the electrical powerplants' ability to provide energy to the people in a matter of decades. With fifteen billion healthy people to keep fat and happy, it really didn't come as a surprise. Fortunately, the scientists of the world came up with the perfect answer: unlimited solar power.

Now it was up to the politicians of the world to sell the idea to the populace.

In the United States, President Linda Maria Baines held a press conference. "My fellow Americans. In the midst of great prosperity, it is my pleasure to inform you all, as well as all of the people of the world, of a fantastic opportunity to provide the citizens of Earth with what we crave the most."

In the United States of Russia, President Piotr Alexi, "…energy. Unlimited energy. More than enough for thrice the population of Earth. From a source that is older than the planet itself."

The United States of China, President Tsang Shen, "…the Sun. A source of power estimated to be five billion years old and still producing nuclear fusion with no end in sight."

The United States of Africa, President Sharon Mugambi, "…unless, of course, your sight can reach another five or six billion years. Sadly, the Sun will run completely out of energy by then. We've got that long to find an alternative source of power."

The same message was given almost word for word around the globe to the amused and satisfied citizens of Great Britain, the Unified Province of Ireland, and the United States of Persia, formerly the territories of Iraq, Iran and Kuwait. So far, it had been an easy sale as this collaborated speech spanned the globe. And for the first time in recorded history, politicians were favored among the masses.

It would not last.

The year was 2163, 19 months after the plan known as Power to the Planet had begun. On the flight control deck of the United Earth Vessel *Sol*, currently positioned some 36 million miles from the Sun just outside the orbit of Mercury, Captain Ulysses Pitcairn stood proudly with his hands comfortably clasped behind his back, feet planted firmly to the carpeted deck, wearing his magnetic velcro boots in the micro-gravity. He gazed out of the forward view port as he did every day at this time.

The captain was usually very alert. However this mission was far from usual. He was actually startled when his executive officer and friend, Ricardo Montoya, appeared at his side.

"Good morning, Captain."

"Wha—Oh, Rico. Uh, good morning. You nearly gave this artificial heart of mine a serious mechanical failure. Why I'll bet there's a rule against that somewhere in the regs manual. I could probably have you clapped in irons, you know?"

"There probably is and you probably could. But do me a favor, will you? Could you wait until the last satellite's deployed? I figure it wouldn't do to have the ship's executive officer locked up during the last phase of the mission."

The captain chuckled at his first officer's little joke. "Well alright. Never let it be said that ole Cap'n Pitcairn has no heart." He then laughed outright at his own joke.

"Just think of it, sir," Rico said, pleased to see his CO enjoying himself. "By this afternoon our cargo holds will be empty of the eleven hundred solar suckers and we can be on our way back to Earth. An Earth where my electric bill will actually be cheaper. Who'd have thought, eh?"

"Say now, don't let the brass back home hear you refer to their precious energy collectors as solar suckers. Despite the fact that it was they who came up with the nomenclature. Although I'm of the opinion the folks back home footing the bill prefer the nickname."

"I don't care what they want to call them. Just so long as they work," Rico said soberly.

"And why not? They've passed all of the computer scenarios and limited tests. They are basically nothing but focused mirrors reflecting energy back to Earth. Why there's even very little chance of mechanical failure."

"I suppose that's why there are so many of them. I mean really. Three hundred of these things will permanently orbit the Sun and transfer power back along a string of seven hundred more which in turn will disperse the power to one hundred more strategically placed around Earth, providing the planet with unlimited energy. Whew. After all of the briefings and classes, spending six months in space deploying these things from Earth as well as positioning the rest around the Sun, I still can't believe it, Captain."

"Well, believe, Montoya. And this afternoon we'll send the last of the uh, solar suckers on their merry little way."

An hour later, there was a loud hum, followed by a muffled *clunk* and then the hiss of air.

"Cargo doors closed, Captain. The bay is pressurizing…five…four…three—"

"Yes, yes, Wilson. We all know how it works by now. No need for a countdown."

"Very good, sir."

"As usual, Sergeant, your team has done a marvelous job. For you the hard part is over now that the last of the solar collectors are deployed. Pass the word to the crew to kick their feet up and relax for the return trip home. And I mean relax, Wilson. That is an order."

"Yes, sir, I'll do my—"

"Ah, ah...."

"Sorry, sir. I'll spread the word. The crew—including myself—is to relax."

"And I don't mean exercise drills or anything. In fact, I want you to go the galley and break out the bubbly."

"Sir?! We're still on—"

"Ah, ah...."

"Yes, sir."

"Two fingers worth for everyone. I don't want us to get *too* relaxed."

"Very good, sir."

And with that, Sergeant-At-Arms Celia Wilson did her best to casually walk out of the observation lounge of the *Sol*, leaving Captain Pitcairn, EO Montoya and Doctor Grace Whitlock the sole occupants for the moment. But not before she rewarded Ricardo Montoya with a half-smile which he returned with a wink. It was obvious that it was a private moment between the two. If the captain or the doctor noticed, they gave no sign of it.

The first officer was grateful. He'd always liked Wilson, and he was sure he always would. To this day he was not sure which came first, his love of caramel candy or the caramel color of Celia's skin. Not that it mattered. When this mission was over and they got back to Earth, he planned to indulge in both. That is, he would when she decided to let him in on her little secret which was not really a secret since he knew all about it. The only secret was, she didn't know that he knew.

"You know, Rico, I thought it was just us old war dogs who still wore starch in our britches. The sergeant is just too young to be so stiff," said Pitcairn.

"I can tell you, sir, she's a chip off the old block."

"Do you know General 'Cinderblock' Wilson?"

"We've uh…met, sir. I was uh, briefly stationed at Andrews."

"Oh uh, I see," the captain mumbled. Seeing that it was time to change the subject and to not embarrass Montoya, Pitcairn changed gears. "Well, Doctor, the hardest part of this mission may be over for the sergeant and her crew, but it's just beginning for you and yours."

"And it's high time too, Captain."

Although the doctor's smile was menacing, it reached her eyes. Pale gray eyes, with just the right amount of intelligent wrinkles on a face the captain found easier and easier to gaze upon. And the streaks of gray in her hair. Just the way he liked it. Clearly, she was quite the looker in her younger days.

Strange. Pitcairn pegged her as being a cold British marm at the beginning of the mission. She definitely seemed to have warmed up a bit. Or rather, he seemed to have warmed up to her.

"…when the mission is completed. Right. Er, Captain?"

"What? Oh. Sorry, Doctor. You were saying?"

"When this mission is over, I'll show you how we Brits celebrate. Two fingers indeed. You Americans will all have to loosen up a lot more if you truly wish to enjoy the conclusion of this project."

"In that case, Doctor, you may consider me your pupil."

"Done. In the meantime, I shan't keep my team waiting any longer. We'll see you two on the flight control deck in, say…one hour?"

"Done and done."

"Right. Until then…then."

"Right. Uh, yes." Pitcairn didn't even try to hide the fact that he was admiring the charming grace of her exit. *Grace. How appropriate.* And so what if Montoya was clearly trying to keep air from escaping his mouth with one hand clamped over his smiling face. Fortunately, he decided not to embarrass his captain any further. He simply nodded and left the captain alone in the lounge.

"Hmmf." *What's good for the executive officer is certainly good for the captain, by stars,* he thought to himself and sat on the crash couch smiling. Now if only the next hour would pass by quickly.

If it were up to Celia Wilson, the crew would not be "kicking their feet up" until after the solar collectors or solar reflectors or solar suckers or whatever the popular name they were going by now were charged and sending the stolen solar energy back to Earth.

No. On second thought, there would be no relaxing at all, let alone with champagne. She immediately dismissed the thought. It smacked of questioning the captain's decision. That was unbecoming of an officer. And if her father ever got wind of even the suspicion that his daughter was not officer material in any way whatsoever, then there would definitely be hell to pay.

But she realized even that thought didn't make much sense. Her recollection told her that her father actually appreciated when a subordinate questioned him, provided it was done in an honorably moral fashion. Of course, old Cinderblock was rarely questioned. No doubt due to the fact that his subordinates feared him. And the fact that, in his own words, he was never wrong. Celia knew the rumor about this being Pitcairn's last mission. *The maiden mission of the United Earth Vessel Sol being the final mission of her first captain. But what a final mission to add to one's portfolio. Oh well.* She couldn't really blame him for such a *minor(?)* breach in protocol. She could, but she wouldn't. Pitcairn was such a likable fellow. Even she, who distrusted any and everybody, took a liking to him from the start. She would love to say that he reminded her of her father, but that would be stretching the wishful thought. Their styles of command were just too radically different.

She realized that people were who they were due largely in part to the times in which they were raised. She was certainly grateful she was raised in a time when people had come to realize that they were all one race. The human race. That the differences of skin color, religion, cultural beliefs and such were extremely minor in comparison to the big picture.

She was taught these lessons by her father who, fortunately, was able to adapt to the softer ways of the new era, despite having retained the nickname "Cinderblock." And in her absence, she knew her father would teach these lessons to her daughter, Cleo.

Celia was confident that Cleo's father was well versed in the lessons as well and would gladly instruct his daughter. If only he knew he *had* a daughter. And for the hundredth time she promised herself she *would* tell him when this mission was over, if for no other reason than to get her father off her back about it.

Cinderblock Wilson was born military and raised in what some were already referring to as "The Dark Ages: The Sequel." She was so proud of her father for many reasons, including the fact that he was somehow able to overcome being brought up in such horrible times. Losing his wife, her mother, to something as simple and stupid as a hovercar accident five years earlier and still maintaining an honorable foundation. However, it didn't come without some costs. Since the death of her mother he was never quite the same. Who could blame him really? It was bad enough to lose a spouse. Then having to lose his only child to the United Earth Agency space program. Oh, he was very proud of Celia, especially since she managed to stay in the military while becoming an astronaut. He was especially proud when the King of England, under the auspices of the UEA, appointed her Sergeant-At-Arms, temporarily suspending her rank of lieutenant for this mission.

She still couldn't believe it herself. *Sergeant-At-Arms.* It sounded so royal. But instead of overseeing the protection of a prince or princess or some other such royalty, she and her team were responsible for the well-being of a bunch of mirrors that would change the world for the better. She took their word for it. She had very little understanding of the things. But as her father would say, "Understanding isn't as important as carrying out your duty."

And here she was, doing exactly that while her father was once again (temporarily) raising a small child. His own granddaughter. Her daughter. This time he was doing it all alone. She knew it was hard on him. And it would be even harder on him had Celia declined the appointment and stayed home because then he'd have to take care of his daughter as well as his granddaughter.

Sometimes she feared the only reason she signed up for the space program was that by getting as far from Earth as possible, she could get away from the pain of losing her mother.

It didn't work.

It'd been five years and she'd journeyed to the other side of the Sun. So if the pain had lessened at all, it was due to elapsed time, not distance. And where had it gotten her really? Because of her distress, she ran away from her father *and* her daughter. She blasted herself for being such a coward. But she would make everything right when this mission was over.

She hated being subjected to such emotions. But like her dad, she rarely showed it on the outside. At least not in any overt emotional way. In her case, she started to take the world too seriously. So seriously in fact that she was only now able to face the fact that she had driven Rico away as well. Her biggest regret. She hoped that he could forgive her when she made right the wrong against him.

She also knew the crew secretly called her "Stiff" Wilson, because "Cinderblock" was her father. *Good! Daddy would be proud.*

Perhaps it was time she learned to kick her feet up just a little. Besides, this ship and crew had been "out at sea" for over six months. For the first time since the mission had gotten underway, Celia Wilson was starting to feel a little foolish sitting in the corner of the lounge drinking a bulb of water while the rest of her team was on the other side of the curved galley located in the rotation-for-gravity ring of the *Sol*, enjoying themselves with two fingers worth of champagne.

Perhaps using the word foolish was being too hard on herself. Standoffish? *Ouch*. As unpalatable as the word tasted, it was far more accurate. She wondered if spending so much time away from the familiarity of Earth was tainting her edge. More likely, she hoped, it was giving her a more proper perspective.

She also recalled promising herself she wouldn't think of Rico in any way other than professional. Yet, she couldn't seem to get him out of her thoughts. She didn't even berate herself that tiny lapse of control awhile ago when she threw that "hey good lookin'" smile at him. Maybe because he returned it in kind. Not only that, but he winked at her in that way of his that was always so inviting.

Rico Montoya was not the only man she'd ever loved. But he certainly was the only man with whom she had ever been *in* love. He was also the only man her father truly liked. She'd always loved Rico, and no matter what, she knew she always would.

Well, this mission is almost over. Perhaps it's time to re-up for another mission with EO Montoya. If he's willing, of course. Hmmm. Six months. Proper perspective? She hoped that was the case anyway. *'In for a penny, in for a pound,' as they say.*

She casually rose, walked up the sloping floor over to her group and asked, "Are there any cups left?" Simultaneous silence to go with wide-eyes and dropped jaws. *Aw hell, that in and of itself was worth it.*

"Uh, yes, ma'am—SIR!"

"Here you go."

On one hand, the subdued routine chatter of the flight crew on the main deck assured Captain Pitcairn that the situation was status quo. On the other hand, that queasy feeling in his stomach and slightly rapid breathing signified something different. Of course it was different. The last of the collectors was deployed and had found its way to its assigned position between the Sun and Mercury along with its siblings and the rest of the collectors strung out and piercing the orbits of Mercury to Venus and then finally to Earth itself.

Oh, who am I kidding, mused Pitcairn, who always prided himself for his—internal as well as external—honesty. Butterflies circumnavigated his stomach because he was awaiting the arrival of....

"Ah, Captain Pitcairn. There you are."

"Ah, Doctor Whitlock. Just in time."

"In time, Captain? Have you been keeping track of the time?"

"A good captain always keeps track of time, Doctor, just as any good scientist worth his or her degree. Timing is crucial to any mission, but especially in space. However, I am uh, just as glad to see you."

"Why thank you, sir. I am honored. Well, my team and I are ready when you are."

"The flight control deck, as it were, is all yours, Doctor."

And with a nod, her team assumed their positions behind their consoles. Doctor Whitlock assumed a position beside the captain, much to his glee, despite the fact that his butterflies had stepped up their speed a notch. *Everything has a price*, he thought. *Even infatuation. Hell. Especially infatuation.*

On the other side of the deck, Pitcairn also noticed the arrival of Sergeant-At-Arms Wilson. For just an instant his mechanical pump skipped (yet another) beat as he feared there must be trouble brewing…only to relax when he saw she was headed over to the executive officer. Oh, he noticed the sergeant tried her best to appear professional but it was obvious that if not for her velcro/magnetic boots, she'd float right off the deck whether in free-fall conditions or not. And Montoya was just as transparent.

The fact that the captain only just now, after six months, realized that these two were on the verge of resuming a history only verified he was getting old and losing his touch.

On the other hand, he was never really good at affairs of the heart. Especially his own. With his newfound insight, as well as a sideways glance at Grace Whitlock, he vowed that would change before this mission was over.

While the captain stood at his usual spot in the middle of the wide view port of the flight control deck next to Doctor Whitlock, First Officer Ricardo Montoya casually checked over the shoulders of his flight crew and the scientific team as they went about their duties. He was pleasantly surprised to see Celia Wilson enter the flight deck and immediately make her way over to him. "Well, well, Sergeant, you're a bit out of place on the flight control deck."

"I hope not *too* far out of place," she quietly countered.

"Not as far as I'm concerned."

Although Celia Wilson couldn't explain it, that was the best thing Rico could have said. "You know, sir, regarding the solar energy collectors, they tell us grunts very little except where and how to load them, and babysitting them while onboard. 'Need to know' and all that. I mean, I understand the basics of what's going on but not much more than that."

"Well, I don't think I'll be breaking any rules by going over the details of Power to the Planet to the ship's sergeant," he told her, almost conspiratorially. "As you know, Doctor Whitlock there is one of the scientist that developed the solar collectors. She's here mainly to oversee the operation with the three members of her team.

"Sitting there at astronavigation is Davies. He's verifying the telemetry of all eleven hundred collectors, making sure they are in their proper positions, from the one hundred orbiting the Earth that we deployed six months ago when we left, to the three hundred surrounding the Sun. He'll also be one of the scientists permanently stationed on Moonbase Phoenix making certain the other seven hundred solar suckers avoid the orbits and gravity wells of Mercury and Venus.

"Sitting at the science station is Doctor Archer. She's making sure the collectors are all online and accepting commands, as well as monitoring the Sun for unexpected solar flare or sunspot activity.

"And finally, at communications is Doctor Rollins who, upon verification from Davies, Archer and, of course, the captain and Doctor Whitlock, will send the signal that will power up the satellites starting with those around the Sun, then to the seven hundred pearls and finally those orbiting the Big Blue Marble," Montoya explained, hoping his reference to pearls and marbles was as amusing to everyone else as he thought it was.

As they were close enough, the three scientists each gave a pleasant nod and/or friendly smile to the sergeant-at-arms as each of their duties was explained, no doubt relieved she was only present for an overview of the mission in its last leg.

"Just one last thing, if I may, Exec," interrupted Doctor Davies with his strong cockney accent.

"Certainly, Doctor, you're more informed than I."

"Perhaps, but you gave an excellent condensed version of the procedure. We, Sergeant, that is to say the spaceship *Sol*, will follow the energy signal along the—what did you call it, EO? Pearls? Yes, perfect analogy. We'll follow just behind the signal at max velocity, all the way back to the uh, marble," he chuckled. "For monitoring purposes, of course."

"Lucky for us it's on the way back home," Rollins added. That brought a round of laughs from the entire flight control deck.

"Again, Executive Officer, I must congratulate you on your oratorical skills," chimed in Davies. "Had it been one of us explaining it, I'm afraid the sergeant would have gotten the conclusion of the procedure by the time we achieved parking orbit at home," he said jovially.

Celia couldn't help but have a wide grin on her face. She could certainly get used to this kicking-your-feet-up attitude.

Davies continued, "You know us science types, never explain anything briefly when you can explain it within a college semester, eh what?" Just then, a beep on his telemetry board alerted him to the satellites' verified positions. He glanced at Archer, who gave the thumbs up to Doctor Whitlock. She looked up at the captain expectantly, who then merely glanced at First Officer Montoya.

Without checking or referring to anyone, Montoya said, "The spaceship *Sol* and crew are all operating at peak efficiency, Captain. We're all ready here."

"Well, Doctor," the captain smiled at Grace Whitlock, "I believe you have a long-distance phone call to make."

"Thank you, Captain," she returned, then glancing at Celia Wilson added, "I'll be sending a communique back to Earth explaining our readiness, which will take eighteen minutes to reach them and eighteen minutes for a response to reach us here, eighty-one million miles just outside of Mercury's orbit. If all goes well, Rollins will be throwing the switch in just over half an hour."

With the exception of deploying 300 satellites around 864 million, 950 miles of a raging nuclear furnace, Ricardo Montoya considered this mission a milk run. But now the mission referred to as Power to the Planet truly had begun. At least he had an excuse for his rapid breathing and the slight sheen of perspiration that otherwise would give away what he knew were hidden feelings for Celia Wilson.

As soon as confirmation arrived from Earth and Grace Whitlock and Captain Pitcairn gave their blessing, he realized it was time for the all too human Rico Montoya to make room for Executive Officer Montoya. Pressing the shipwide communications pendant on his collar, he announced, "Attention all hands. This is First Officer Ricardo Montoya. The UEV *Sol* is ready to kick off the mission that will change the course of human history forever. Station status, everyone." He then checked with the flight control deck crew who were all monitoring their boards and station crews throughout the ship. "Helm," he barked.

"Engine room reports green."

"Navigation."

"Course plotted."

"Astronavigation."

"All collector positions are verified," answered Doctor Davies.

"Science station."

"Confirmed," said Doctor Archer.

And finally, "Communications, are you ready?"

"No," answered the eldery Rollins, "but everything else is."

Montoya shook his head with a grin. *Scientists*. Now that ship's status had been confirmed he deferred to Pitcairn. "Captain?"

"Thank you, Exec, but as captain of this here vacuum boat, it's my prerogative to give the honor to Gra—uh, Doctor Whitlock."

"Why, Captain, you're such a dear. Thank you," she offered. "On my mark then, Doctor Rollins."

"Aye, aye, Captain Whitlock."

The captain's eyebrows raised slightly but quickly subsided and he grinned at "Captain" Whitlock.

The executive officer merely shook his head in his hand again.

"Right," she continued. "In three…two…one. Now, Edward!"

With an exaggerated gesture, Edward Rollins twirled his wrinkled finger in the air, then stabbed it to the communications console and the button that powered up all 300 of the solar collectors around the Sun. A few moments later, his board beeped a confirmation. "The candles are all lit and the signal has just jumped to the string of pearls. The energy wave is on its way home."

"Then so are we," the captain interrupted. "Navigation?"

"Aye, Captain, course plotted."

"Helm, nuclear engines on full burn. NOW!"

"Aye, sir, engines answering full burn."

With that, the United Earth Vessel *Sol* shuddered as its nuclear engines sent a single controlled explosion out its rear end and accelerated in the direction of the energy wave, beginning its leap frog journey along the string of satellites on the way back to Earth.

With his hands clasped behind him and his head tilted back slightly, Captain Ulysses Pitcairn proudly proclaimed, "My friends, today, January fifteenth, 2163 is the dawn of a new era for the species known as Man."

The captain was correct. Unfortunately, not quite the way he or anyone else expected.

"Well, there's no reason we can't expect smooth sailing from here on out," opined Edward Rollins.

"If you call being smack dab in the middle of an oversized tin can that farts nuclear explosions for propulsion 'smooth sailing,'" offered Willard Davies.

"Hmmf. It's no different from a 2127 Chrysler Navistar. That car was a little bumpy, but it got you where you needed to go every time."

"Ah. That was before the magnetic hovercars, eh what?"

"You got that right, sonny boy. In fact, the Navistar was one of the last ground cars that actually used a steering wheel, inflated tires and a shock absorbing suspension system."

"That's just what we needed," interrupted Archer. "The old codger waxing philosophic while we—" Just then, her console began an ominous beeping accompanied by red flashing lights, swiftly echoed by Rollins' console.

"Uh oh," whispered Rollins.

The executive officer jumped in. "This is no times for jokes, Doctor Rollins."

"No, sir. I agree."

Rollins actually called him "sir." Now Montoya was worried.

"Status!" barked Captain Pitcairn as he, Grace Whitlock and the rest, all wearing worried expressions, joined Rollins and Archer.

"I'm not sure as yet," offered Edward Rollins, as his fingers flew over the liquid crystal display console, "but according to my instruments, the solar reflectors around the Sun have just increased their energy absorption rate by four percent."

"What?!" exclaimed Doctor Whitlock.

"At the same time," continued Sarah Archer, "I read the Sun's overall gravity decreasing by point two percent."

"In English please," begged Pitcairn.

"It would seem, Captain, that the Sun just now experienced what could be called a weak miniature nova, as opposed to a super nova," explained Grace Whitlock.

"Forgive me, Doctor, but judging by the surprise I read on Archer's and Rollins' faces," commented Montoya, "this 'experience' was unexpected."

"Say now, I thought there would be no surprises from the Sun," the captain said, his brow creasing.

"There shouldn't be any surprises," countered Whitlock. "Nothing like this has ever happened before in recorded history of any observation from the Sun. At least as far as I know."

"And she knows plenty," added Rollins.

"Doctor Whitlock?" asks Celia Wilson. "Is this miniature nova anything like solar flare or sunspot activity?"

"Well, not exactly, Celia. Solar flare and sunspot activity are directly related to the Sun's magnetic field. Suffice it to say that sunspots are actually cooler areas on the surface while solar flares are superheated gas ejected thousands of miles above the surface. I only used that 'miniature nova' term because the only way the Sun's gravity can weaken is if its nuclear fusion is able to overcome its own gravitational cohesiveness. But that usually happens at the end of a star's life and with a much bigger star than our mother sun which is a yellow dwarf star.

"*Our* sun, which is typical of most of the stars in the sky, will simply use up its hydrogen, which makes up about seventy percent of the Sun's elements. That is to say it will run out of gas and then start burning up what's left of its helium and will swell up, engulfing all of the inner planets, including the Earth, to form a red giant star. When the helium is used up, the Sun will collapse in on itself and become a very dense cold lump of rock. I assure you, that won't happen for billions of years yet."

"Could the solar reflectors have somehow caused this process of increased nuclear fusion prematurely, making it something other than a yellow dwarf star?" asked Ricardo Montoya.

"That would be impossible, Exec. The reflectors are basically just that. Reflectors. Mirrors. There is no way they could have any effect on the Sun. No more than say, shining a torch—a flashlight against a mirror and having the mirror increase the charge of the lithium-ion battery within the flashlight."

"Grace?" asked Pitcairn, not even realizing he used her first name. "Could you even hazard a guess?"

"No, Captain, I can't. I would love to chalk this up as an isolated incident, but to be perfectly honest, I'd be lying if I said I wasn't just a little concerned."

"And you're sure the reflectors have nothing to do with this?"

"Absolutely sure."

"Davies. Archer. Rollins?"

"I concur."

"Agreed."

"No way."

Executive Officer Montoya would have felt better about their assurances if they all hadn't first looked at Whitlock, almost as if looking for permission before agreeing. He simply said instead, "Well, Captain, in that case I see no reason to delay or alter the mission."

"I agree, Rico. However, I want us to monitor the reflectors and the Sun even more than—"

At that moment, Archer's and Rollins' instrument panels began to beep and flash again.

"The reflectors around the Sun are now up to seven percent energy absorption," noted Archer.

"Doctor Archer," offered Pitcairn. "Can you compensate somehow?"

Before Archer could answer, Rollins interrupts. "The Sun is—wait. It's not the Sun. It's something above the Sun decreasing its gravity. But I don't underst—eh? AAAAAHHHGGG!" Rollins' board exploded, sending sparks arcing in every direction. He desperately tried to unbuckle himself from his chair and would have fried completely if not for Montoya who cut the strap with a pocket knife he seemingly pulled from midair. Unfortunately it was too late as Edward Rollins' body floated off the deck, slowly tumbling head over heels, spiraling blood from a blackened wound from his chest.

"MY GOD! EDWARD! EDWARD!" yelled Grace Whitlock, amidst Sarah Archer's screaming.

"Please, everybody, remain calm," pleaded Montoya, himself sporting red blistered hands, but still managing to activate his collar comm. "Medics to the flight control deck! We've got wounded up here!" Then addressing the control deck, "We can't lose our heads," he continued, while simultaneously shutting off the charge of his magnetic boots and kicking himself off the carpeted deck in an attempt to retrieve Edward Rollins.

"Doctor Archer, get away from your panel," ordered Captain Pitcairn.

Archer snapped herself back into the moment. "You'll get no argument here." She unbuckled her safety belt and hurriedly moved away from her science panel.

"Doctor Davies," Pitcairn said calmly, "is there any way you can shut down those reflectors?"

"Not likely, Captain. When Rollins' board blew, I'm afraid we lost all outward communications from the ship. It gets worse. I *am* able to confirm something from above the Sun caused the energy spike to the reflectors. Although the disturbance, whatever it is, seems to be gone now, the convection zone of the Sun increased by five percent, sending a surge of energy to the reflectors orbiting it. Why they weren't destroyed, I can't say. What I *can* tell you is that there is now a wave of solar radiative energy on its way to our position as we speak. At our current velocity, it'll be on top of us in about fifteen minutes. Our radiation shielding will not protect us."

"Good Lord," said Pitcairn, bowing his head. "If it's radiating outward from the Sun in all directions, there's no way we can escape."

"Perhaps we can, Captain," countered Davies. "The energy wave is *not* radiating outward, but following the path of reflectors to us. If the ship were to vector straight up, perpendicular to the elliptical plane of the solar system, we can escape."

"Navigation!" yelled Pitcairn. "Set a course—"

"NO, Captain. Wait!" interrupted Grace Whitlock.

"This had better be important, Doctor," commented the executive officer, while securing Rollins.

"I assure you, it is. If all of the collectors around the Sun were able to withstand the increased energy wave, then it stands to reason the collectors between here and Earth will survive as well."

"I...I don't understand," the captain admitted. "I realize we don't have a lot of time here, but how is it we don't have enough shielding to protect us, yet the reflectors are unharmed?"

"The electrical systems of communications and thrusters needed for avoiding the orbits and gravity wells of Mercury and Venus probably did get fried, but the collectors don't need those systems to absorb and send energy," explained Grace Whitlock, "so there's really nothing left to protect." She paused a beat to see if anyone was thinking what she'd been thinking.

Davies did not disappoint her. "Good God! The energy wave will do enough damage to Earth as is. With the exponentially increased energy of the collectors fueling the wave, it will burn the Earth to a crisp. No exaggeration."

"The Earth's ozone layer is repaired and whole again," offered Rico Montoya. "Won't it protect the planet?"

"I'm afraid not," answered Grace Whitlock. "With one hundred collectors surrounding the Earth, the ozone will be the first casualty. Oh my God. What have we done?"

"It's not too late for Earth just yet, Grace," countered Ulysses Pitcairn. "How many of the collectors must we eliminate to stop the increased energy?"

"One second, Captain," answered Davies, doing quick calculations at his board. "We have to remove, not just shut down but *destroy*, fifteen to seventeen consecutive solar collectors anywhere on the chain back to Earth to stop the wave from increasing. Fifteen might be enough, but I'd recommend destroying sixteen or seventeen to be safe. If we can do that, then the Earth just might have a chance. But we're barely outrunning the wave now, and since that disturbance, or whatever it was, occurred twice already, we've no way of knowing whether it will happen again. The disturbance wouldn't be any trouble at all if not for the collectors around the—"

"Captain," Rico Montoya interrupted, teeth clenched. "The *Sol* only carries a complement of fifteen torpedoes."

"Oh, this just gets better and better," Doctor Whitlock sarcastically chuckled. "If Edward were conscious, I'm sure he would say we were cutting it too fine." Then getting serious again, "Edward, how is he?"

The MD, leaning over Edward Rollins' body, merely shook his head back and forth.

Rico Montoya was not surprised. What he *was* surprised about was the fact that Doctor Whitlock hadn't noticed the extent of Rollins' wounds.

Grace Whitlock merely placed her head in her hands.

"Alright, people, we've got a job to do," said Captain Pitcairn. "I don't need a computer to calculate which collectors to eliminate. The very next one on our path will be the first. Navigation, continue course."

"Aye, Captain."

Activating his collar comm, the captain barked, "Engine room. I need as much speed out of the engines as you can muster, and I mean now."

"*Sir*," came the response from the engine room over the flight deck speakers, "*the ship is already at maximum velocity. I'm afraid we can't go any faster.*"

"Damn it, man, I assume you've been monitoring what the hell is going on up here. We've got to stay in front of that solar energy wave and eliminate as many of the collectors as we can. If necessary, you will jettison the fuel from the conventional rockets and ignite it. We've got to increase our speed."

"*Uh, yes, sir.*"

For a moment the flight control deck was completely silent as nearly everyone present realized the United Earth Vessel *Sol* would never make it back to Earth if the conventional rocket fuel was jettisoned and ignited.

"Sergeant Wilson!" Pitcairn barked.

"SIR!" Celia snapped back.

"I'm afraid you are back on duty. See to it that the fifteen missiles are loaded and ready for launch on my command. We can't afford any slipups or the Earth is doomed."

"Yes, sir. Right away, sir." Sergeant-At-Arms Celia Wilson saluted and hurried off the flight control deck while thinking to herself, *I was really starting to like his kick-up-your-feet style of command. Maybe he has more in common with Daddy than I first thought.*

The realization did not comfort her.

About the only thing of which Rico Montoya was aware was that his bladder felt like it was about to burst. He didn't feel fatigue or hunger despite the fact that he'd been sitting at the navigation console for sixteen hours without a break. It was no secret that he was considered one of the best pilots in the United Earth Agency. He always corrected anyone who mentioned that fact by telling them he was *the* best. He never considered it arrogance, and it was more than bravado. If anyone on the ship doubted him, they'd have no cause to question him now as he single handedly triangulated, tracked down and destroyed fourteen of fifteen solar suckers, after having transferred the weapons station to the navigation console. Only one more torpedo left, but two collectors to destroy to give the Earth a fighting chance. He wiped sweat from his brow and once again looked at the navigation scanner and aligned the cross-hairs with the collector. He held his breath and for the final time, pressed the trigger. The ship rocked as the last torpedo was launched.

All eyes on the flight control deck were once again staring at the main viewport, watching the missile disappear from view for a few moments, only to see the bright flash signaling the death knell of the fifteenth solar energy collector. A collective cheer, even more raucous than for his previous sharpshooting, erupted from everyone.

Now, Executive Officer Montoya was aware of how tired he truly was. He realized, as he rotated his head and shoulders, just how tight his muscles were. Suddenly he felt strong hands massaging his neck and back while hearing Captain Pitcairn speak.

"Nicely done, Rico."

"Thank you, Captain, but I, uh…." Only to see Pitcairn move to stand directly beside him as the strong hands continued their oh-so-affective work. He sneaked a glance only to find Celia Wilson standing behind him. He was so busy, he hadn't noticed her return to the flight control deck. She must have come back as soon as the torpedoes were armed and loaded. "Whew!" he said aloud, then turned and winked at Celia while smiling his thanks. She returned the smile. *Amazing*, he thought to himself. They were all in the middle of one of the biggest crises in human history with the fate of the entire planet at stake, being chased by a destructive solar energy radiation wave and he could still fantasize about spending the rest of his life with Celia Wilson. Unless a miracle were to drop on the deck from the heavens, he knew it was just a fantasy. It was now time to get back to reality or their home planet would be just a memory.

"Captain," he began.

"I'm way ahead of you, Exec. How long before we catch up to the next collector?"

"At our current speed, about forty-five minutes."

"But I thought that was our last missile," commented Grace Whitlock. "Shouldn't we try to vector out of the solar system plane to get away from the energy wave? Unless you two have a plan to take out a sixteenth collector without another missile."

"Yes, Grace," Pitcairn answered with a straight face. "We've got a plan."

"Approaching the sixteenth reflector now, Captain," offered Montoya.

"Very good, Exec," answered Pitcairn. "I'm sure you won't mind verifying the download of everything that's happened in the last twenty-four hours, including all audio, video and everything leading up to Rollins' board blowing out, into the black box marker buoy."

"Not at all, Captain," answered Montoya, as he verified the navigation instrumentation. "I've even programmed its flight path to vector out above the solar system plane."

"Thanks, Rico. We have to be sure that buoy survives so that one day the folks back home will have some idea of what happened out here. You may launch when ready, Mister Montoya."

After Rico keyed in the launch sequence and depressed the button, the UEV *Sol* again gently shook, although not as much as with the torpedoes. Again all eyes were on the forward viewport watching as the exhaust trail of the black box marker buoy receded from view, only to sharply turn upward and disappear into the inky black of space.

"Captain Pitcairn?" asked Grace Whitlock. "May I assume we will be following the black box buoy?"

At that point Ulysses Pitcairn stepped in front of Doctor Whitlock and gently placed his hands on her shoulders. "Grace, escaping the energy wave will only buy us a little extra time while leaving no guarantees for Earth's safety. I'm sorry, but this ship and crew are already dead. The best we can do is to take out as many collectors as we can and hope that one day, if the Earth survives, they will find the black box buoy and maybe, with enough time, figure out what the hell is happening with the Sun."

At that moment, Grace Whitlock came to the realization that she was probably the only person on the ship who had no clue as to their fate for the last hour or so. She should've been frightened. Hysterical even. Yet, she was strangely calm. All she could say was, "Oh God."

"We are now directly over the sixteenth solar collector position. The energy wave will be on top of us in fifty-five seconds," Montoya said evenly.

"Engine room," the captain ordered, pressing his comm collar pendant. "You will see to it that the main propulsion thruster aperture is closed."

"*Understood, Captain.*"

"Mister Montoya," Pitcairn continued. "You may begin nuclear thrust."

"Aye, sir. Captain Ulysses Pitcairn," Montoya interrupted himself, "it has been an honor and a pleasure serving with you, sir."

The captain's voice quivered. "Likewise, First Officer Rico, likewise."

It was then that Grace Whitlock looked over at her surviving scientific team only to see Sarah Archer and Willard Davies holding hands. She wondered if that was something new or old. *Funny* she mused. *What the hell.* She then walked into Ulysses Pitcairn's arms as they completed their embrace of her and wrapped her arms around his waist.

Rico Montoya stood and, with his right arm, embraced Celia Wilson and whispered, "I've never stopped loving you."

Sergeant-At-Arms Celia Wilson was speechless. Her thoughts were filled with images of her father and her daughter. For herself, she had no regrets, but for the lack of time now that she was in Rico's embrace. *If only we had an extra twenty or thirty minutes.* She only hoped this wouldn't change Cinderblock and little Cleo too much. But she knew it would. Life could be so unfair. *Well, there's no time like the present.* "Rico," she began. "There's something I must tell you."

Her eyes filled with tears as Rico gently kissed her lips and whispered, "I know, Celia. I know all about her. I only wish I could have met her and told her how much I love her. My daughter."

With his left index finger he slowly pressed the button that ignited the nuclear engines.

With the main propulsion thruster aperture closed, the UEV *Sol* experienced for the first and last time an uncontrolled nuclear explosion. And for a brief moment, the solar system, home to the species known as Man, knew two suns.

CHAPTER THREE
Oshara and Roshan

"Did—did they save the Earth?" one of the students from the back of the class asked.

"Of course they did, holo-brain, else you wouldn't be here to ask," answered a classmate.

Neither student pressed their desk beacon to identify themselves, nor raised their hand for attention, but B. Schreiber was willing to let the transgression go for now as all of the students were obviously paying attention. "Yes, they did save the Earth, but only to a point. You see, although the United Earth Vessel *Sol* destroyed a portion of the chain of solar reflectors, preventing the solar radiative wave from gaining any more strength, the wave was still dangerous enough, thanks to the reflectors around the Sun, to do serious harm to Earth. As the crew of the ship suspected, the ozone layer was once again weakened, allowing ultraviolet radiation to blanket the atmosphere. In addition to this, the solar wave initially wreaked havoc with planetary gravity, causing worldwide coastal flooding of many cities. Although the floods rapidly receded, the damage was done. The long-term problem was the increased radiation in the atmosphere which caused all kinds of hazards including skin cancers, as well as planet-wide droughts. The scientists estimated Earth's surface would be uninhabitable in about ten years.

"The people at that time were obviously not happy. They blamed any and everybody, especially the scientists and politicians. Those in authority insisted that every precaution had been factored in and every contingency accounted for. No excuses were tolerated. The citizens insisted that all mistakes be corrected.

"Unfortunately, the planet was low on resources even before the Power to the Planet plan was utilized. With the stress put on the ozone layer as well as the cleanup of coastal flooding, there was no way to correct a mistake of this magnitude. With only ten years to work with, the scientists came up with a two-part solution. Can anyone make a guess? What would you do if you had only ten years before your planet could no longer support life and you had fifteen billion people along with a planet full of wildlife to save? Anyone?"

"Uh…bring everybody here?" was the only response she received in that familiar voice from the student who asked if the Earth was saved. At least this time he remembered to identify himself.

"Well, I must say that is the obvious answer, Mr. McClellan, as we are all here now."

"Holo-brain," from a barely audible voice in the back of the room. Although the desk monitor didn't ID the voice, B. Schreiber's eyes did.

"SHUT UP, ALRIGHT, JUST SHUT UP," shot back Billy McClellan.

"Please, chil—uh, students. No insulting and no yelling, okay? Now, Mr. McClellan, as I was saying, you're half right. You may recall this was a two-part solution. Any takers? No? Well, the only solution to present itself, based on the current level of technology and the amount of time left to them, was to shelter a majority of the population underground and under the sea, and send the remaining third or so into space. Fortunately, there were already a few underground and undersea shopping malls and recreation centers, but construction was soon stepped up to build a lot more living spaces there as well."

"Why couldn't they build asteroid space stations in orbit around the planet?"

"That's a good question, Billy. Actually there were several manmade space stations in orbit, as well as a Moonbase and a colony on Mars. Unfortunately, all of them relied heavily on support from a healthy Earth. Once the surface of the Earth became unlivable, no one could survive long anywhere else in the solar system without a constant run of supplies. And although the Sol system, that is to say Earth's solar system, had plenty of asteroids, they followed the regular laws of physics. Their positions are based on the pull of gravity, unlike the asteroids in our Centauri system which seem to behave outside the laws of physics. There, hundreds of thousands of asteroids orbited, and probably still orbit between Mars and Jupiter, the fourth and fifth planets in the Sol system. The asteroids in the home system were simply referred to as the 'asteroid belt,'" the teacher continued. "Is anyone here familiar with the nomenclature or name given the asteroids in our system? And it's not bumblebee rocks."

The desk indicator lit for young Kyle Armstrong.

Ah, the young man who referred to Earth as Dirt. "Go ahead, K. Armstrong."

"Random roids," he answered to the subdued laughter of most of his classmates.

"Very good, Kyle. And like our asteroids, the asteroid belt of the Sol system was also mined for minerals, metals and even water. Unfortunately, the asteroids could not provide enough supplies to keep the Mars colony and Moonbase Phoenix occupied for very long."

"You mean they had to abandon the colonies on the moon and Mars?" asked Jackie Beaudine, the holo-brain accuser.

B. Schreiber was happy to see she was contributing a good question instead of holo-insults. "They did eventually abandon the colonies, but only after a few hundred out of the thousands of colonists were hurriedly brought back home."

"Only a few hundred?" asked J. Beaudine.

"Yes. You see, Mars is nearly half the size of Earth, so it has much less gravity, so visitors kept up a rigorous regimen of exercise to keep their muscles acclimated to Earth's heavier gravity. If you were on Mars for more than a few months, you were encouraged to, as your body adjusted itself to Mars' lighter gravity. To come back to Earth under those conditions would render anyone temporarily disabled. Their muscles would be too weak to walk or lift everyday objects. Even taking a simple breath would be hard. Of course, they did have a way around that problem. You see, the spaceships of those days, with the nuclear engines, could make a one-way trip to or from Mars in about two months. But to acclimate people returning to Earth, the trips took almost half a year, with the rotation-for-gravity ring of the craft slowly spinning up to one gee over the six-month period so that a body could readjust to Earth normal. Unfortunately, because most of the trips were for business, competitive business to boot, that idea didn't last very long and the flights were coming and going as fast as they could make them. That put the responsibility of gravity acclimation on the individual. So unless you took the time to keep up with daily exercises on Mars or could pay for an independent slow flight back, you could look forward to a long time in a wheelchair with several months of physical therapy simply to get used to walking and breathing on Earth.

"With the solar disaster, anyone who decided to come back to Earth had to do so as fast as possible. The fact that you'd have to live underground or underwater would only complicate matters even more if you were handicapped due to too rapid a return trip. So most folks opted to stay and take their chances on Mars, realizing there would be no support and supplies from Earth for a very long time, if ever.

"The irony is, the Mars colony was slightly more than a decade away from becoming totally autonomous."

"What does auto-automus mean?" asked one of the students.

"Autonomous," she repeated slowly. "It means independent." She was tempted to have them look it up on their personal Data Access Crystals. "The colony would have been able to sustain itself without supplies or interference from Earth. In fact, the Martians, that is to say the transplanted Earth people, had been trying to form their own government for years so that they could break away from Earth. The problem was, terraforming the planet and oxygenating the atmosphere took much longer than anyone anticipated. If the air were breathable as per the projected timetables, then a majority of everyone on Earth could have simply moved to the next planet instead of the next solar system."

"Why couldn't they have speeded up the terror-foaming so that they could get done within ten years since they had ten years before Dirt, I mean Earth, was cooked and *then* move everyone to Mars?" asked young Kyle Armstrong.

B. Schreiber was very impressed that an eight-year-old was asking such intelligent questions. She couldn't help but wonder if K. Armstrong was a descendent of the famous ancient astronaut Neil Armstrong. "Unfortunately, Mr. Armstrong, they still would not have been able to transport fifteen billion people, plus plants and animals, to Mars in the amount of time they had. Most of the population still had to stay behind, which meant they still needed to build underground and undersea facilities. Even though the journey to Alpha Centauri took much longer, it was easier to transport the majority of people and animals in suspended animation. We weren't even aware of the passage of time to get here." *Nor*, B. Schreiber thought to herself, *was anyone aware that two ships carrying millions of people and supplies were lost. Not until the eight surviving ships arrived.* That lesson could wait until another time. "Besides, no one had to worry about terraforming the planet Omicron since it is almost exactly like Earth. It was a fortunate happenstance that probes had already detected the uninhabited Omicron with an oxygen-nitrogen atmosphere decades earlier."

"What would've happened if the probes didn't find any habitable planets in this solar system?" asked young Jackie Beaudine.

"I'm afraid I don't have the answer to that one, Ms. Beaudine," began B. Schreiber just as her desktop monitor indicated a visitor or two at the door. She signaled an acknowledgment of their presence. "But if I could hazard a guess, I'd say we, that is, they would have been forced to cram everyone under the Earth's surface or somehow find a way to quickly oxygenate Mars' atmosphere. The alternative could not, I imagine, be pleasant in either case.

"Well, my students. I must say I am very impressed with your questions and enthusiasm regarding how we all arrived here at Alpha Centauri. We will get back to it at another time. For now, how would you like to learn more about the Omicron Nebula space station from the point of view of the Starforce of Omicron?"

"Are we going to take a field trip to the Central Command Module?" J. Beaudine again.

Before Babs Schreiber could reply, the majority of the class gave their enthusiastic endorsement.

"Yeah!"
"Stellar!"
"Cool!"
"No," she replied quickly before the rest of the students could chime in. "But I do have the next best thing. Two representatives are here to visit with us today," she said as she simultaneously opened the classroom door remotely from her desk.

In walked two uniformed officers who, even at a glance, were obviously brother and sister. Twins in fact, who were fairly well known to most of the citizens of Omicron Nebula. Well known by the reputation of working closely with Captain Nebula.

"Students," B. Schreiber began. "I'd like you all to meet Lieutenants—"

"Oshara and Roshan Perez," one of the class called out in excitement before she could finish the sentence.

B. Schreiber could see that it took all of the control the students possessed to stay in their seats instead of mobbing the two young officers. For which she was as grateful, she was sure, as were the two lieutenants. Although this was her first time meeting the two face to face, she, like her students, felt as if she knew them. Of course, she had somewhat of an advantage in that she'd heard several rumors regarding these two officers when they attended school.

Roshan Perez, the class clown. Outspoken. Impetuous. Leaps before looking. Appeared to take nothing seriously. Very intelligent, however. A contradiction to be sure, this one.

Oshara, his sister, was apparently quite the opposite. Usually quiet. Thinks before she speaks. Looks before she leaps. Appears to take everything seriously. Also very intelligent.

They were both attractive representatives of their genders, or "easy on the eyes," she believed the ancient phrase went. Skin darker than her own. Both had dark reddish, straight hair. But what was curious was that although Oshara's hair was longer in the back, they both wore their hair parted on top with a thick set of dual spit curls that met at the eyebrows. She couldn't help but wonder if that was a style they both had chosen, although she hadn't seen anyone else on Omicron Nebula or the planet Omicron below sport that particular style. More likely, it was a genetic trait. If she could see one of the parents, she could probably verify that suspicion.

However she knew, through C. McCauley, that these two, like her and almost everyone else beyond their mid-twenties, were transplanted Earth citizens as opposed to Omicron-born like the students in the class. She was also aware that there were a great number of citizens still frozen, even after three decades; damaged because of the freezing process, they were awaiting the doctors to upgrade the technology that would repair the damage so that they could be resurrected whole. Physically whole, anyway.

When the thawing-out process first began en masse, a lot of folks woke up without limbs, or in some cases with non-functioning internal organs. Fortunately, with the aid of the strange Omicron Particles coupled with nano-technology and robotics, doctors were able to replace missing limbs and other organs. Those particular citizens, who for the most part looked as they normally did before, referred to themselves as androids.

Oshara and Roshan's parents, for whatever reason, either didn't make the trip, didn't survive the trip or were still frozen.

"I imagine you students may have some questions for the officers," she stated. "Go ahead, J. Beaudine."

"Are you both telepathic?" she asked.

"What?!" exclaimed Oshara. "I don't understand."

"I have two aunts that are twins like you," she explained. "And they can read each other's minds. Can you do that?"

"No," answered Roshan. "We can't read each other's minds. Heck, I can't even read my sister's handwriting." That response garnered laughter from the whole class.

"Well…if you got hurt, would you feel each other's pain?" continued young Jackie.

"Ms. Beaudine, I think that would qualify as telepathic," Oshara chimed in. "If there was any truth to that, I assure you I'd be sticking myself with a pin all day long."

More laughter.

"That's a really sharp uniform you guys wear. Could I get one like that?" asked one of the older students.

B. Schreiber had to agree. She rather liked the uniforms as well. Although one had to be in great physical condition to pull off wearing it attractively. Well, that alone made her ineligible to be a member of the Starforce of Omicron. She realized she was jokingly too hard on herself. She was not in bad shape. She just preferred looser-fitting garments, unlike the young officers' uniforms which appeared to be fairly snug.

A two piece, light green-colored outfit as was typical of all of the officers of Omicron Nebula. A high closed collar. The short-sleeved jacket looked somewhat reminiscent of the Civil War era, with a flap that closed over the left breast, seemingly held in place with the six-centimeter-diameter emblem of the Omicron Nebula branch of the Starforce. An emblem which looked like a red lightning bolt on a black background. Surrounding the waist was a wide black faux leather belt with no apparent clasp or buckle in the front or rear.

The oddest feature of the uniform was the thigh-high black faux leather boots. The only word she could think of to describe them was *retro*. But they seem to work with the outfit.

One of the appealing aspects of the uniform would have to be the segmented gold metallic bands that covered the forearms. The same segmented gold bands surrounded the lower half of the boots, from the calf on down past the ankles covering the whole foot. But the black tread could be plainly seen, so the bands were just coverings. They had to serve some kind of purpose, she figured, as opposed to being simply decorative.

The junior officers like the Perez twins wore short sleeves and a short black faux leather cape. That had to be just decorative. The senior officers, like the captain and the exec, wore no capes but did have longer sleeves, extending just past the elbow, with the segmented gold bands covering the forearms.

The captain of each Omicron asteroid was the only one who sported a black faux leather shoulder strap covering the left shoulder and connected to the Omicron emblem on the chest.

Yes. Babs Schreiber could see why any of the students would inquire as to how they could obtain such an outfit.

"Sure you can," answered Roshan Perez. "It's simple. All you have to do is keep your grades high and join the Omicron Space Academy. Study, study, study. Intern with a whole bunch of departments on the planet below as well as here on the station. For example, assisting the mining operation between the interior city and the outer asteroid surface, like we did. Swear to uphold the Omicron charter and you will be issued a spiffy new uniform like this one."

"I can do that," answered the teen. "Except for one problem. That 'study, study, study' part."

"I'm afraid there's more of that than any other thing," chimed in Oshara. "At least that's how I saw it."

"Hear, hear," added Roshan.

"You know," continued Oshara, "you're not that far from being eligible yourself. If you're serious, I'd start looking for a sponsor if I were you."

"Would you be my sponsor?"

"I'm not sure. First, I'd have to know you were really serious. Then I'd need to know how well your studies are going. I would then interview your friends and family and check up on you fairly often."

"I can handle that last part." The suggestive spin did not get past Oshara or anybody else for that matter.

"Hey, now," jumped in Roshan. "That's my sister you're flirting with. Have a care."

Everyone giggled.

"You know," interrupted Oshara. "On second thought maybe you should wait a few more years before seeking a sponsor."

At that, the teen's jaw dropped. Satisfied with the reaction, Oshara winked at him and added, "Just kidding. A sense of humor would serve you well in the Starforce. Any other questions?"

"My dad said that the Omicron Nebula asteroid was left here by ancient aliens that abandoned this part of space millions of years ago, and that we just moved in. And that's why all of the other asteroid space stations look so different from this one. Aren't you afraid they might come back and take it away from us?"

B. Schreiber figured this child's parents were thawed recently if they didn't know the story behind the Omicron Nebula asteroid, but before either of the young officers could answer, another student piped in.

"There's no way some stupid ole alien could try and take back this asteroid. Captain Nebula would knock him clear to the other side of the galaxy."

"Naw uh," Jackie Beaudine interrupted. "Captain Nebula won't fight anybody. He's afraid to fight. He would just talk him to death."

"J. BEAUDINE!" shouted B. Schreiber.

"That's okay, ma'am," started Oshara. "I assure you, Ms. Beaudine, that Captain Nebula didn't rise through the ranks to become the commanding officer of this city-space station because he's afraid to fight. Nothing could be further from the truth. I know for a fact that he's quite capable of defending himself if necessary. He believes, as we all do, that anyone who resorts to violence is desperate or truly afraid or has no confidence in themselves or the world around them, and that talking is a form of communication between intelligent species. Fighting should only be used as a last resort and only after communication has failed. He believes that the majority of fighting and violence throughout human history on Earth could have been prevented if the lines of communication didn't fail."

"That's something to keep in mind, Ms. Beaudine," added B. Schreiber.

"Um...okay," the young girl said, sheepishly.

"I'd like to get back to how the Omicron Nebula asteroid came to be," chimed in Roshan. "It is not true that it was left behind by any alien race. This station, like the other seven, was built from scratch by human beings. Us. Omicron Nebula is the largest as well as the first station built shortly after our arrival in this part of space thirty years ago."

"Built by us? Really? How?"

"I'd be happy to tell you," answered Roshan, "if that's okay with Ms. Schreiber."

"Oh, perfectly, Lieutenant," returned the teacher. "In fact, we were discussing the gravitational anomaly around Sol that precipitated our arrival here…." Just then, B. Schreiber noticed her desk monitor signaling. "Yes, Mr. Armstrong."

"I do want to know about how the Omicron asteroid was built, but first I'd like to know how almost half the people from Earth were transported here."

"If I may," said Oshara, nodding to her brother, who graciously bowed while extending an arm toward his sister. "From what I understand, the plan of relocating over six billion people including supplies and livestock across the interstellar void four-and-a-half light years distant all within ten years is considered nearly impossible even by today's standards, but was equally insane seventy years ago. But as the chief scientist of Omicron, Tan Ozawa is known to say, 'Very few things are truly impossible, although they may be highly improbable.'"

"There's another ancient saying from the home planet," interrupted Roshan. "'Necessity is the mother of invention.'"

"Yes, that's true," continued Oshara. "They really had no choice. Fortunately, a lot of the groundwork for such an undertaking was already in place, such as the destination of the Alpha Centauri star system, thanks to probes that were sent here decades earlier. Also, there were already several underground as well as undersea facilities that could easily be converted to living space for those billions that would remain. Of course they all had to be expanded in order to accommodate the masses, in addition to building more."

"A lot more," added Roshan.

"Indeed," continued Oshara. "Also, there already existed a design for a practical starship that had been on the books for, believe it or not, about two centuries."

"Really?"

"Yes. Way back in the early nineteen-sixties, scientists on the North American continent that was called the United States, a major political and military power, designed two starships. The *Orion* and the *Daedalus*. The designs were based on schematics originally proposed by the British Astronomical Society, an organization that was founded in the late nineteen-thirties. Even back in the twentieth century it was known the element hydrogen was very abundant throughout the

Universe. In fact, there is about one hydrogen atom about every ten centimeters or so everywhere in open space." Oshara demonstrated by cupping her hands in front of her, approximating ten centimeters with her fingers spread, looking as if she were massaging an invisible bowling ball. "Hydrogen can be used as a source of fuel for propulsion. Very convenient for space travel. The idea was to use it as fuel for nuclear-powered engines. At the front of the ship was a ramscoop at more than half a kilometer in diameter. That was used to scoop up the free-floating hydrogen in space and send it to the engines at the back of the ship. In the original designs, the ramscoop, or hydrogen collector, had to be several kilometers across in order to scoop up enough hydrogen for the vessel to come anywhere near relativistic speed. Fortunately, the technological advantages of the twenty-second century afforded the designers to employ an energy envelope that extended the half-kilometer collector to achieve its goal of scooping up enough hydrogen to feed to the engines. Otherwise, one vessel would have to be the size of a small world. The engines were designed to fuse the atomic structure of the hydrogen causing a controlled explosion out of the rear of the ship. The ship, of course, would be hurled in the opposite direction at high velocity. The more hydrogen the dish could collect, the more fusion reaction the ship could send out the rear. The more fusion reaction, the more velocity the ship could achieve. The more speed the ship could gather, the more hydrogen the dish could collect and so on and on. And although there are no doubt more efficient ways of space travel which we have yet to discover, the technology of the mid-twentieth century was fully capable of taking advantage the abundant hydrogen. Unfortunately, the two starships never went beyond the design stage back then."

"How come?" asked young Kyle Armstrong.

"Well, as I said earlier, that time in Earth's history was consumed by politics and military posturing. Most of the people of that time weren't yet interested in practical space travel outside of entertainment and fiction. It was felt that the huge amount of money it would cost to launch such an endeavor would be better spent curing the planet's ills of the moment.

"Ironically, the design of the starships took place between the two biggest events that began the space age. It was on April twelfth in the year 1961 that the first person ever was sent into space by the nation that was known at the time as the United Soviet Socialist Republic. His name was Yuri Gagarin. And it was a gentleman by the name of Neil Armstrong who was the first person to step foot on the moon on July the twentieth in the year 1969. He was accompanied by Buzz Aldrin. They were sent by the United States of America, which at that time was very competitive with the USSR in many things such as politics and what was called a Cold War as well as the Space Race."

"Was his name really Armstrong?" asked the young student with the same name.

"Yes. Absolutely. Who knows? You could be a descendant of his."

And with that, the young Armstrong was rewarded with many stares and mumbles of admiration.

B. Schreiber couldn't help but stifle a grin as the conversation echoed her own musings. She was also patting herself on the back, as her idea of having two Omicron officers as guests was paying off in a big way. And not just because she was no longer feeling nervous, but because she now had a real subject with which to begin regular lessons. The beginning of the space age.

"So, where were we?" continued Oshara. "Oh yes. It was a simple matter of upgrading the design of the starships with the level of technology of the mid-twenty-second century. But this time, it went from design to immediate construction. The upgraded design came in at nearly two kilometers in length. That's about half of the length of this asteroid-space station from dome to dome."

To help illustrate the oration, Babs Schreiber activated the digital board behind her at the front of the classroom and loaded an artist's rendition of the ISS *Kepler*. Of course, she realized that some of the students were no doubt familiar with the design since the ships that carried the frozen bodies of some of their parents were identical.

As familiar as she was with the design, Babs Schreiber still could not get used to the looks of the thing. It was not what she would call aesthetically pleasing. It certainly didn't look like any of the conventional starships of the ancient science-fiction variety. There was nothing sleek or streamlined about it. *Simply functional*, she mused. It basically looked like a two-kilometer-long pole with a disc attached at the front end: the variable particle beam laser, used to strip electrons off the hydrogen atoms to make them electrically charged while they were still some distance away, in addition to sweeping away debris in front of the vehicle. Directly behind it was a very large radar dish, the big deal of the whole vessel, the hydrogen collector itself. At nearly three quarters of a kilometer in diameter, it was considered the most essential piece of hardware for a starship of this class. Without it, the ship was useless when one considered the primary job of the hydrogen collector was to collect the electrically charged hydrogen atoms for fuel for reaction thrust, in addition to powering the variable beam and rotating broadcast lasers.

Behind the collector were the telescoping, omnidirectional, rotating broadcast lasers. They looked like four smaller radar dishes that were spread out equidistant in four directions from the pole. The dishes were connected to the pole via a telescoping arm and each was capable of rotating around the pole and being aimed to stern and aft as well as straight out. Essentially, the rotating broadcast lasers could track and target any object from any direction. Their primary function was communication. It was one or more of these that kept track of the broadcast beam sent from the probes at Alpha Centauri that guided the fleet to its destination.

Behind the broadcast lasers was the forward deflector array which was capable of tracking and mapping any foreign object in front of and to the side of the ship. The deflector worked in tandem with the variable particle beam and the four rotating lasers.

Directly behind the deflector array was the habitat section for the hundred or so live crew members who were necessary for maintenance and upkeep of the starship and served in shifts for the entire 27-year-long trip. The habitat section was equipped for comfort, with recreation facilities that included theaters, swimming pools and living quarters that could accommodate over a thousand people if necessary. There were also two science modules, for experiments, stellar observations and to catalog cosmic phenomenon, attached to each side of the habitat section. The entire habitat section and science labs rotated continuously for gravity. The spin of the rotation was calculated to give the science labs the equivalent of one gee, with the habitat section slightly less as it surrounded the central axis.

Behind the habitat section were the forward/rearward radar sensors which were a redundant backup for the forward and rearward deflector arrays. The sensors were basically two radar dishes, that were slightly smaller than the four broadcast laser dishes, that rotated around the pole for maximum sweep.

Next on the pole was the workhorse for the ship. The nuclear fusion reactor power plant which was also equipped with four reaction control thrusters to steer the ship. The power plant was the engine of the vessel.

Directly behind the power plant was the rearward deflector array whose job it was to track and map any foreign object to the sides and rear of the ship. It worked in tandem with the telescoping, omnidirectional broadcast laser, like its forward sister.

Next, attached around the pole were eight hydrogen/fuel storage pods.

And lastly, the main propulsion thruster bell, where the controlled rearward directed explosions allowed the vessel to obtain a fraction of the speed of light. The main propulsion thruster was also equipped with four directional thrusters for low-speed maneuvers.

"The prototype ship," continued Officer Perez, " was called the Interstellar Starship *Kepler*, after the sixteenth-century astronomer Johannes Kepler. Its maiden voyage was to navigate just outside of the Earth's solar system beyond the ninth planet Pluto. Although it was successful, there were still many problems such as maintaining life support throughout the living sections and science labs and power drop-outs throughout the ship. That could be a real problem when you realize that a constant supply of power was needed internally to support the cryogenic transport modules that would be attached once the mission was underway.

"In addition to overcoming these setbacks, the major challenge was that there really was no time to send the ship all the way here on its maiden voyage as it took two years to reach its maximum velocity of point-two-oh-cee, or one-fifth light speed. As some of you may know, the voyage here took twenty-seven years.

"By the time the *Kepler* was launched, three years had elapsed since the Earth was bombarded with the solar radiation. The test run to the edge of the solar system and back took nearly a year.

"It was known, however, that it would take more than one ship to transport more than six billion people. In the meantime, construction was already underway at a breakneck pace to build nine other ships based on the *Kepler* design. That was the maximum number the time table allowed. It was calculated that each ship would have to carry six hundred million people, plus the embryonic livestock and plant material among other supplies. The *Daedalus* and *Orion* class designs had very little room for storage, so in addition to building the ships, the engineers also had to design and construct cryogenic modules to transport the frozen people and supplies. The modules were three quarters of a kilometer long and would each carry three hundred million frozen bodies. There were two modules attached to each of ten starships.

"It was decided to send the ships into the void at one-month intervals. Fortunately, the probes that were sent to Alpha Centauri decades before were transmitting a broadcast laser beam back to Earth. The ships simply followed that beam all of the way there—here.

"The first ship, the *Kepler*, was renamed the *Omicron* after the destination planet. The second ship was the *Omega*, followed by the *Nebula*. Then there was the *Gaea*, the *Quasar*, the *Radian*, the *Pulsar*, the *Vortex*, the *Graviton* and finally the *Ersatz*. The *Omicron* would receive the beam from the destination probes, then send its own broadcast beam back to the *Omega* along with the original signal, the *Omega* would send its own laser along with the original beam back to the *Nebula* and so on and so on.

"As some of you may have figured out by now, all of the Omicron asteroid space stations were named after the interstellar ships."

"But including Omicron Nebula," asked Jackie Beaudine, "there are only eight stations. If ten ships left the home planet, how come there are only eight stations?"

As this had always been an uncomfortable subject for anyone in the know, Oshara hesitated before answering. She glanced at her brother, who simply shrugged then looked over to Babs Schreiber, who raised her brow and pursed her lips as if to say...*I was afraid this moment would come up. Don't worry, I'll handle it.*

"Unfortunately, Ms. Beaudine, class, the first two ships never made it here and were presumed lost. It took more than a year after planetfall before a search could be initiated. But even in the relatively short distance between two stars, it was just too much space to cover. No trace was ever found," explained the teacher. "I'm sorry to have to tell you that twelve hundred million citizens and very much-needed supplies were never recovered. We also lost some very valuable records. To add insult to injury, a lot of the starships' back-up computer storage memories crashed on the way here as well." It truly broke Babs Schreiber's heart to tell the kids this, but as it was no longer classified, she figured it was her duty to inform them instead of leaving it to the young officers.

"So," she continued, "we never built an Omicron or an Omega station." She glanced at the twin officers as if to say they could continue.

"So what you're saying," Jackie Beaudine jumped in, "is that if the ISS *Omicron did* get here first, we'd be calling this station Omicron-Omicron?"

"Had the ISS *Omicron* made the trip," picked up Oshara, "this very station would now be called Omicron Prime. But since it was the ISS *Nebula* that arrived here first, this station was christened Omicron Nebula, and it carries the flag of the Starforce of Omicron."

B. Schreiber assumed that with such a depressing subject, the students would not be able to come up with any more questions for the young officers. However, the assumption was rendered erroneous when one of the students asked, "Is it true that you can fly without jetpacks or wingsuits or anything?"

"No," answered Oshara, just as Roshan replied, "Yes."

After a brief eye contact between the siblings, a straight-lipped, eye contact from Oshara while Roshan looked at his sister with a very wide grin, Oshara continued. "We can't fly per se, although you may have seen an officer or two appear to fly inside the Singularity Transport Tube, or the elevator tubes that connect the STT to the city interior, but I assure you there's a scientific explanation for it. You see these metallic bands around our forearms and calves? All of the Starforce officers wear them. They're made of the same material as the transparent metals of the STT and elevator pylons as well as the transparent metallic dome at the far end of the station. When I lightly bang my forearms together like so…" And as Oshara demonstrated, there was an audible click followed by a low vibratory hum that could barely be heard as well as felt. It wasn't an unpleasant sensation, just an odd one that would take some getting used to. When she banged her wrists together again, the hum and the vibration ceased. "When this is done inside or within about three meters of the transparent tubes and pylons, a sympathetic vibration is set up within the metals. With the variable gravity of the station and a good kick-off from the ground, anyone wearing these bands will ascend upwards toward the STT. It is not recommended to fly down the elevator tubes, because the gravity approaches Earth normal as you get closer to the ground, so coming down wouldn't be nearly as much fun as going up."

So, the metallic bands are not decorative. Babs Schreiber was impressed, although she couldn't see herself ever wearing them other than for a fashion statement. In fact, she was still afraid to try the wingsuits or even the jetpacks which were really nothing but compressed air in a tin can strapped to one's back, activated by a simple attitude control attached to a belt. That was all you needed when flying near the STT since there was negligible gravity around the center axis of the transport tube. Of course, the farther one went from the tube and the closer to the inner surface of the city, the more gravity tugged at a body. That is, as long as the asteroid was spinning.

No. Babs Schreiber was perfectly happy with nature's conventional transportation method for bipedal beings: walking.

"Of course, the bands are only used in emergencies," concluded Oshara.

"I can understand the elevator shafts," commented a student. "But isn't the Singa—, the Sing, uh the transport thingy filled with water?"

"The Singularity Transport Tube is *not* filled with water. It only looks like it is. The tube is double hulled. The water you see is actually trapped between the inner and outer hull. The interior of the tube itself is hollow. So you see, the transport car never touches the water. But that's why it seems like you're in a submarine if you are looking out the window of a transport car. You're actually looking out through the secondary hull that's filled with water. The water, of course, is provided by ice asteroids which are abundant throughout this region of space. The ice is brought in through the segmented dome, purified and then, through pressure, sent through the outer hull of the transport tube where it's forced out of nozzles that are placed all along the tube. And in case any of you didn't know, that's how rain is simulated in the station.

"Now getting back to the flying question, I can probably guess that some of you may have seen Captain Nebula flying—er, traveling parallel to or outside of the tubes. Like Sean Stingray, the first Captain Nebula, Danar Seti's blood is irradiated with Omicron Particles, which makes a fall from a great height much less dangerous for him. Let me tell you first that chances are a fall from the height of the STT would not be fatal because of the variable gravity. The spin of the station underneath you would be the thing to worry about. But ordinary citizens or noncommissioned officers have no need to concern themselves with that possibility.

"But before you start trying to figure out how to get your hands on some Omicron Particles, keep in mind that it's still a relatively unknown substance that is potentially dangerous."

"Yeah, I heard the first Captain Nebula is living his final days on the planet below dying of radiation because he got too many particles." This from one of the older students.

"Well, don't listen to too many rumors," continued Oshara. "Granted, Sean Stingray is not a young man anymore. He is simply enjoying his retirement after many hard years of faithful service to the Starforce of Omicron."

Now that, mused B. Schreiber, was the smoothest act of subterfuge she'd heard in quite some time. For she was well aware of the circumstances surrounding Sean Stingray and the mysterious Omicron Particles of which she wanted no part if she had any say in it.

When first discovered on the planet below thirty years ago, it was quickly realized that the substance was not indigenous to this star system, but no doubt found its way here millions of years ago like most other meteorites. It had the strange ability to correct almost any defect in biological tissue. Exactly how it worked was not fully understood by doctors and scientists, and under ordinary circumstances, the Omicron Particles would undergo many years of intense study before being tested with live subjects. But when you were thawing out hundreds of thousands of people a day on a newly colonized planet over four light years from home, your timetables had to be adjusted accordingly. Especially when the cryogenic freezing process had certain setbacks.

It was later discovered that any recent damage to a body, such as broken bones or even severed limbs, could be repaired easily if the treatment included Omicron Particle therapy. Depending on the ailment, the particles were found to be effective when used in traditional drugs that were injected, such as vaccines or medicines, consumed like liquids or even as an inhalant. Suffering from a simple viral or bacteriological cold and upset stomach soon became a thing of the past. It was also very effective against some forms of chemical imbalances.

However, when the body suffered damage that altered the biology, such as burns or freezing, the Omicron Particles were not effective and could actually make matters worse, unless the individual was already enhanced. And even then, the particles could only help speed the recovery.

It was also discovered that if a healthy body were exposed, the particles appeared to boost the immune system, and give the individual increased stamina and endurance. Unfortunately, it didn't last long.

With some people, the particles were like an addictive drug. They required it constantly just to maintain their enhanced abilities. Without it, they became weak and sickly. The particles appeared to build up in their systems and become less effective. Such was the case with poor Sean Stingray.

Stingray was the commander of the ISS *Nebula* when it arrived at the Alpha Centauri star system. He was considered the hardest-working man by all accounts, helping to select the location and construction of Omicron's capital city, Home-At-Last, which most folks simply referred to as "Home Atlas," on the large continent, Pangaea. And he designed the Omicron Nebula station. That was the reason he turned down a seat on the Omicron council, so that he could oversee its construction. It didn't take much longer than the completion of the station before he collapsed from exhaustion. But he simply refused to rest and volunteered to be a recipient of Omicron Particle therapy, or OPT.

For many years after that he made even more of a name for himself by organizing the construction of the other seven asteroid city/stations, until his body collapsed from a heart attack.

B. Schreiber was aware that he was suffering from a heart condition that kept him weak and mostly bedridden. Fortunately, thanks to twenty-third century nano-technology, the first captain was living out the rest of his days in relative comfort.

For years now, scientists and medical doctors had claimed, with remarkable confidence, that once the Omicron Particles were better understood and possibly coupled with nano-technology, the citizens would enjoy the benefits of life prolongation. Prolongation on the order of six or seven hundred percent of current life expectancy. That was a thousand years give or take a decade. Babs Schreiber couldn't help but wonder if this speculative method would be tried, tested and perfected while she was still young enough to take advantage of it. That's assuming she would ever get over her fear of the alien particles.

Of course, if she were really desperate to be around, she could always take an extended leave of absence and put herself back on ice until the Omicron geriatric treatment was perfected. She couldn't help but wonder if Sean Stingray ever considered going back into the freezer.

The story of Danar Seti, the current Captain Nebula, was quite different. He was thawed at the tender age of eight. As far as she knew, his thawing process was flawless. The ailment the Omicron Particles solved for him occurred at childbirth. A birth that was fatal to his mother.

Apparently he was born about six months after the Earth was bombarded with the solar gravitic disturbance that precipitated the need to send nearly a third of the planet's population to the neighboring star system. It seemed the young future captain was diagnosed with amnestic aphasia, a condition that robbed him of his long-term memory and even his instant recall. At any given moment, he would cease all verbal and physical activity because he simply had no idea of what occurred moments or hours and sometimes weeks or months before the attacks. Some of the memories returned. Often times, they didn't. There was no cure or very effective treatment. It was hoped that because of his young age, he would have a better chance of recovering some of his memories as he got older. It would have been a tough life, as it no doubt was for many people back then, who had medical problems of their own. Fortunately, he was one of people chosen to make the journey, thanks to the fact that his father was a leading scientist, part of the group that probed the planet Omicron in the trinary system of Alpha Centauri decades earlier.

It seemed that Danar was a successful recipient of the Omicron Particles as he had not suffered an attack since the therapy. Although he was still afflicted with the aphasia, the Omicron Particles kept it in check, with the added benefit of increased endurance, stamina and strength and no side effects.

Indeed. The young lad excelled in his studies, apparently having inherited his father's analytical genes. He rose through the ranks and eventually became captain of Omicron Nebula, answerable only to the council of Omicron on the planet below.

Not bad for a guy who had no memory of his brief life on the lost planet Earth.

One couldn't help but be impressed by the man. Losing his mother at childbirth, and his father to the vagaries of cryogenics, and apparently overcoming an incurable malady, thanks to an alien element. What were the chances?

Of course Danar Seti was not really so unique when you consider that just about everyone at Alpha Centauri had overcome some form of adversity and beat the odds.

Yes. As far as Babs Schreiber was concerned, everyone but her should go down in a footnote of history as some sort of icon or virtue of human strength. She considered her arrival here as one of the most uneventful tales in history. Oh, she couldn't complain. And that was just it. She had nothing to complain about, really. She had no family alive on Earth or Mars by the time of the Great Disaster, unless you counted a divorced husband with whom she lost contact years before.

She recalled looking forward to being chosen for the trip because it sounded so romantically exciting. Could she really have been that naive? Although she was "on ice" for almost 15 years after planetfall, her thawing was uncomplicated. She had a nice rent-free apartment on the station and a job that she loved. She considered herself very fortunate indeed.

Yet her feelings of anxiety strangely persisted.

CHAPTER FOUR
Rock and Roll

"Hey!" yelled one of kids in the back. H. B. Schreiber couldn't remember his name, and he didn't indicate who he was by desk monitor. *Oh well, no one else has used it in the last hour or so.*

"I still want to know how we built this space city, and how come it looks so different from the others," complained the kid.

"I'll field this one," answered Roshan Perez. "As my sister explained earlier, the first starship to arrive here was the ISS *Nebula*, commanded by Sean Stingray. Shortly after planetfall and soon after construction began on Home-At-Last, the first Captain Nebula began construction of the Omicron Nebula station based on designs he drafted during the trip. Once a suitable amount of labor was thawed, he used parts of the cryogenic modules, as well as a few asteroids from the belt surrounding the star system, for raw materials to construct the station. It was believed that most people would be better adapted to the lighter gravity of space after having been frozen for more than a quarter century. So the station had to be very large and at the same time simulate the conditions of a planet for gravity. Gravity that could be controlled. Also, it was necessary to simulate the cycles of night and day, temperature and even the weather.

"Think of the basic design of the station as a very large metallic cylinder on the order of about three kilometers in length. Closed at one end, opened at the other like a cup. The city was constructed around the inner walls of the cup so that it could be spun around the center axis to provide gravity.

"Some of you may have noticed that when you look straight up, you can see the rooftops of the buildings around the curve looking down at you. It took a while to get used to, as some of you who came up from Omicron may recall, but it was the perfect solution to simulate gravity, provided the station remains spinning.

"The opened end of the cylinder, or cup, was permanently fitted with a large transparent metallic dome, which can be polarized to filter out light if necessary. In other words, the whole dome or just parts of it can be phased from transparency to varying degrees of cloudiness to completely opaque. The other end was fitted with a large metallic segmented dome. That's where the hanger, storage facility and power plant are housed. That end of the station is closed and can only be accessed by permission or authorized personnel.

"Down the central axis of the cylinder runs the Singularity Transport Tube which is attached to the center of the closed end. Instead of free floating at the transparent domed end, the transport tube was originally sealed off and held in place by four pylons that connected the end of the tube to the inner surface of the cylinder. You may have noticed there are three other sets of pylons connecting the tube to the inner surface, placed equidistantly all the way down to the closed end of the cargo hanger. The pylons are cylindrical tubes slightly smaller in diameter than the Singularity Transport Tube, and are constructed of the same transparent metallic material as the transport tube and dome.

"The next logical step was to build a transport car that would travel back and forth along the STT and elevator cars for the pylons for travel in and around the city.

"While construction of the city was taking place inside the cylinder, a suitably sized nickel-iron asteroid was found within the star system to surround the cylinder for added protection against other asteroid impacts and the solar radiation from the trinary star system that was to become the new home for the billions of refugees from the lost planet Earth. The best way to get the city cylinder into the asteroid was to painstakingly drill a hole down the center of a three-and-one-half-kilometer-oblong asteroid. Pre-spatial antimatter explosives were then placed down the hole and detonated, excavating the interior of the asteroid, effectively making it a giant sleeve. The city cylinder was then maneuvered into the asteroid.

"By this time, the construction of the city interior was nearly complete. The equipment for the power plant was then set up, as were the power distribution cables all around the asteroid. Also at this time, giant maneuvering thrusters were attached to the exterior of the asteroid. There are four of them at each end surrounding the domes. They're used to facilitate rotation control and spin for gravity.

"The exterior of the cylinder has several noticeable large bulges. These are the various size lakes and bodies of water you see throughout the interior of the city. There is a great deal of space between the exterior surface of the city cylinder and the interior surface of the outer asteroid. These spaces are now oxygenated subterranean caverns where facilities are set up for mining the raw materials of the asteroid. Also within this space, some of the structures or buildings are inverted. In other words, instead of building them to rise from the inner surface of the cylinder, like your school and most of the other structures, some buildings extend down into the caverns. The tops of these buildings are the large pits with very tall walls you see throughout the city. The majority of these inverted or subterranean buildings are science labs and apartments for the miners. As you know, the rest of the citizens of Omicron Nebula live within the city proper in familiar structures like this school building.

"The interior configuration has changed very little since its inception three decades ago. The libraries, office buildings, parks, recreation centers, farmland, greenhouse domes, stadiums and lakes are exactly as they were from the beginning. The only major change was the relocation of the Central Command Module. The technology of gravity generators was perfected just before the asteroid belt around this star system started breaking the laws of physics about twenty years ago. The new headquarters were built at the end of the Singularity Transport Tube in what you see today as that saucer-looking building situated under the transparent dome. Thanks to the artificial gravity, the new Central Command Module's floor is perpendicular to the inner surface of the city.

"In other words, if you look out a window of the CCM, you're looking straight down at the roofs of the city. I'm still not used to it. The advancement of the gravity generators also meant the other seven asteroid cities could be designed within conventional parameters. That is, all of the foundations were built on a single plane on any large flat asteroid. So none of those stations require spin for gravity like this one. Personally, I find them boring." Everyone gave their agreement with this statement as evidenced by the laughter that ensued.

"We should consider ourselves very lucky that all eight of the asteroid cities were just about fully constructed before the asteroids in this system started going haywire. Can you imagine how that would have complicated construction in space?"

"So how come the asteroids act like that?" asked young Kyle Armstrong.

"We're not exactly sure," answered Roshan. "We know that it's a gravitational phenomenon, but the scientists can't seem to lock down a definitive reason."

Despite the circumstances which brought them all here, Babs Schreiber couldn't help but agree with the young lieutenant regarding how lucky this half of the human race was. Had the birth of the random roids occurred before the completion of the asteroid cities, who knows what other hardships they would have had to overcome.

Yes. Lucky indeed. But what about the other half of the mother planet's population? The half that was left behind. What had become of them? What other hardships had they overcome? Had they overcome them? Once the last of the starships left the Earth, all contact was lost. Except for a few radio transmissions talking about the progress of the underground and undersea shelters and the division of resources that were recorded by the starships' computers, the Earth refugees now residing at the Alpha Centauri star system had no idea how their counterparts were faring. And even that little bit of information was nearly 30 years out of date, as they didn't get those last few fleeting signals until after the "big thaw" had begun upon their arrival here. Was the Earth hit by another radiation wave caused by the gravitational solar anomaly? She hoped not. By the time the last starship, the ISS *Ersatz*, left the Earth, four years had gone by without so much as a peep from the area around Earth's mother star.

B. Schreiber began doing quick calculations in her head. Four years after the original disaster, plus 27 years in transit to the new star system, plus another 10 years to construct floating habitats. Forty-one years. Then all of a sudden, seemingly at random, the asteroid belt surrounding this system started going crazy, gravitationally speaking. To human beings, 41 years is a long period of time. But on the galactic scale, 41 years is just a fraction of time. Suddenly it seemed too much of a coincidence that gravity was wreaking havoc with two neighboring star systems.

Lost in thought, B. Schreiber said, "You know, I find it awful strange that Earth's troubles started because of a gravitational anomaly around the Sun, and then about forty years later, the very next star system began experiencing gravitational anomalies. I realize the disaster back home was thought to be caused by the solar reflectors, but what if the reflectors only compounded the problem? If the gravitational anomaly around Sol was a natural occurrence, then what would happen if the same thing were to happen to this tri-star system?"

Oops! She only just now realized she had spoke out loud. And these were not thoughts she should be sharing with the kids anyway. She became aware of how silent the room had gotten. The two officers once again exchanged a brief glance. Now Babs Schreiber was sure she had inadvertently opened a can of classified worms.

However, after barely skipping a beat, Roshan Perez continued almost as if she hadn't spoken. "Because of the random roids," he said, "a few additions had to be made to Omicron Nebula. Chiefly, the sixteen weapons turrets that were built on the exterior surface of the asteroid. Access to the turrets is gained from the extended elevator pylons that are connected to the existing pylons attached to the Singularity Transport Tube. This way, authorized personnel—that means Starforce officers only—can move from the asteroid surface to the interior with relative ease. The turrets can fire lasers or anti-matter torpedoes, depending on how close the roids get to the station or the planet Omicron below. All of the other seven stations have turrets as well. The number of turrets varies, depending on the size of the stations.

"Of course, each of the other asteroids stations is surrounded by a transparent metallic dome that could withstand just about any asteroid hit, but believe me, you wouldn't want to experience that."

The conversation continued along those lines. "What does it feel like when an asteroid is struck by another asteroid?" Or "What if an asteroid were to strike a weapons turret before it could fire?"

"How long can you hold your breath in space?" interrupted Jackie Beaudine, without raising her hand or signaling her desk light.

Since the rest of the students wore expectant expressions, Oshara assumed they too were interested in an answer, so she was happy to accommodate them. "Well, Miss Beaudine, to be honest, it's impossible to hold your breath in space. You see, the reason we can breathe has to do with air pressure both inside and outside of our bodies. In space, there is no air pressure at all so…."

Babs Schreiber was barely paying attention, as she was contemplating exactly what security breach she may have stumbled upon, when out of the corner of her eye, she noticed the yellow proximity warning light silently flashing on her desk again.

Speak of the devil. *Wow*, she thought to herself. *Two in one day. That's rare.* She hoped it wouldn't—*uh oh.* Too late. The warning upgraded to the wall panel this time. It was still yellow which meant the intensity of the random roids had increased.

While Roshan Perez was still speaking to the kids, she noticed his sister Oshara surreptitiously glide over to the corner of the room, obviously getting an update on the situation from the Central Command Module via her communications collar pendant. The teacher couldn't make out what Oshara was saying (not that it was any of her business), but based on the lieutenant's very brief but startled look, it couldn't be good, which meant it probably had something to do with the roids.

Great. But before she could speculate further, before Oshara could get her brother's attention, the yellow stripes on the back wall turned red, followed by the audible whooping siren that could be heard throughout the entire asteroid city.

WHOOP! WHOOP! WHOOP!

"Oh no," Babs Schreiber whispered. She only hoped the kids wouldn't react badly to the situation. She immediately realized her fears were groundless when every student in the room threw their hands in the air with great cheer, oblivious to any danger, and simultaneously yelled, "ROCK AND ROLL!"

This was followed by more audio warnings that could be heard throughout as well as underneath the city. "**WARNING…EXTERIOR ASTEROID COLLISION IMMINENT. BRACE FOR IMPACT.**"

Outside the classroom, the citizens of Omicron Nebula reacted to the crisis from their individual scenarios. Those citizens who intended to enjoy leisurely relaxation floating on the artificial lakes of the asteroid now found their crafts' artificial intelligence modules had overridden the human commands and immediately steered for shore. The same went for any flying vehicles or wing suits. Seldom-used failsafe programs instantly carried people to the ground.

The STT car, which had just left the segmented domed end of the asteroid, quickly came to a stop and backed up so as not to be exposed in the open. All elevator cars automatically descended to the ground. Those citizens walking outside of buildings immediately took cover.

Under the surface of the city within the mining caverns, the miners, without question or complaint, dropped what they are doing and made their way up to surface through the inverted buildings. Although it was unlikely that a random asteroid could penetrate the exterior of Omicron Nebula, under these circumstances it was safest to be within the city proper as all access to the caverns was sealed against any possibility of an exterior breach, no matter how unlikely.

It became painfully obvious that this particular asteroid attack was unprecedented, if for no other reason than the fact that it lasted so much longer than the usual 60 seconds or so.

Back inside the classroom, everyone held tightly to the desks or whatever piece of furniture was available. B. Schreiber never liked the asteroid bombardment, despite the clever "rock and roll" moniker. Now she was absolutely sure she despised it. This particular attack reminded her too much of an earthquake. She was one of the few citizens of Omicron to have actually experienced them back on Earth in what seemed like a lifetime ago. This rock and roll seemed to be lasting longer than any earthquake. The number of rocks outside were obviously more than the weapons turrets' capacity to deal with them efficiently. In fact, it felt like every asteroid in the system was smashing into the station. How was the planet Omicron faring in this onslaught? She hoped a lot better than her stomach. Obviously the gravity generators weren't doing a very good job of compensating for the increased spin of the floating space station. *As if they ever did.* She was quite sure the Central Command Module's AI computer was doing its best to orient the station for maximum protection using the weapons turrets, but the fluctuating gravity was starting to take its toll on her and the rest of the citizens. But before she could complain further, the attack apparently ended. Suddenly.

Everything was quiet and no one moved or uttered a sound for nearly a minute. She imagined it was the same all over the station. In fact, she was startled when Lieutenant Roshan Perez spoke. "Hey, that really rocked!" Only one other person in the room thought that was funny judging by the single chuckle.

"I'm sorry, Ms. Schreiber," said Oshara, "but we must cut our visit short."

Walking past her desk on the way to the door, Roshan leaned in close and whispered, "Regarding your revelation about the similarities of what happened to Earth and what's going on now—I'd keep that to myself if I were you. Someone from the CCM will be getting in touch with you to speak further on it. Thanks for having us here." Then, addressing the students with an exaggerated slow wave of his hand, he said, "Bye."

Then they were gone. It took about another 20 seconds for the students to snap out of their reverie, just enough time for the young officers to descend the two floors to their waiting transportation, the spacebug, an elliptical, antigravity, two-seat, utility vehicle about the size of a hover van. The kids all rushed to the window to catch a glimpse of the officers taking off, headed no doubt to the Central Command Module.

Just as Babs Schreiber was recovering her wits, she began to wonder if she might be in some kind of trouble regarding her revelations about the gravity anomalies and the officer's warning. *It's not like this latest attack could be my fault. Could it?*

CHAPTER FIVE
Situation: Gravity

Somewhere in deep space—not quite in normal space, but getting closer—a vessel continued its search. A subordinate informed the commander of yet another signal indication. This was a big one. Indeed, after all of these years, they were getting closer to their destination.

As the spacebug climbed higher to Omicron Nebula's axis, traveling parallel with the Singularity Transport Tube on its way to the Central Command Module, Oshara transmitted her report to the captain regarding B. Schreiber's revelations. He informed her that he'd speak to the teacher personally and that preparations were underway.

The two sibling officers discussed the confrontation which appeared imminent.

"So…looks like this is it. At least, according to Danar," Roshan said dryly.

"Could be," Oshara mumbled solemnly.

"Why so down, twin?" Roshan asked. "This doesn't have to be a bad thing, you know."

"You're kidding, right? I mean, you have been conscious these past twenty years, haven't you?"

"Okay, okay. I'll admit the gravitational phenomenon has been a major inconvenience, but there have been some upsides."

"Oh?" Oshara chuckled sarcastically. "Name one."

"Well, uh…with the uh, roids in the system flying around so haphazardly, it's been easier to snag ice for water for Omicron Nebula and the other asteroid stations."

"Oh yeah?" retorted his sister. "Well, when all is said and done, I'd still rather go out to the edge of the system and bring the ice chunks back like in the old days, as opposed to having them smash into the stations at a high rate of speed alongside their metallic cousins in close formation. But you keep reaching, brother-mine, you just might grab something."

"Alright, try this one on for size," Roshan countered, without missing a beat. "The Earth figured out how to use the gravity anomaly as a form of transportation and they've come to join us or invite us back home."

"Hmpf. That's just wishful thinking sprinkled with a heavy dusting of speculation."

"Oh yeah? So do you believe this is just a natural phenomenon that just happens to occur in this region of space surrounding Sol and Alpha Centauri? A phenomenon that has never occurred in billions of years. Or do you believe that this is some kind of attack from evil aliens bent on galactic domination? As far as I'm concerned, that's paranoia sprinkled with a light coating of ignorant fear."

"Oh please, Ro." After a few seconds hesitation, Oshara continued. "Well okay, maybe it does sound a bit paranoid. But I agree with the captain—"

"There's a surprise," he interrupted sarcastically, rolling his eyes.

"…it's best to be prepared," Oshara continued as if her brother never spoke.

"I can't argue with that. But even if it is extraterrestrials—"

"Need I remind you, brother," interrupted Oshara, "that we are all ETs in this solar system."

"True," her brother agreed. "But even if this were caused by extra-far-from-home terrestrials, there's every reason to believe the gravitational anomalies that precipitated the worst environmental disaster in Earth's history as well as the random roids here are accidents."

"*Every* reason to believe?" Oshara shot back. "How do you figure that?"

"According to Doctor Ozawa, any intelligent species with spacefaring capabilities will have overcome any aggressive tendencies by the time they reach the stars, otherwise they would've destroyed themselves in internal struggles before they had a chance of contacting an extra-solar civilization. And I agree with her."

"Now there's a surprise." A sarcastic payback to her brother's earlier comment.

His response was a brief look at Oshara followed by a raspberry, his eyes closed tightly, making a rude noise through tongue-pierced lips.

"Seriously," she continued, "with all due respect to Tan, I can't help but think of that point of view as a human perspective. An alien species could've evolved under completely different circumstances. What motivates them could be far removed from our experience, whether it be environmental conditioning or a radically different emotional evolution. Different values. Not necessarily bad, just different."

"Hmm. I see your point. But it's pretty hard to speculate on an alien's value system when you only have your own from which to extrapolate. I suppose it's all guesswork. But you have to start somewhere. And as the captain is fond of saying when it comes to conflict resolution, 'We are all more alike, than not alike,' but that applies because all humans, as varied as we are, are all subject to the same relative environmental and emotional conditioning. We all need food and water. We all want to love and be loved. To be treated fairly and with respect. Still, I hope Tan is right that any intelligence that has a desire to venture into space will share at least some of our values."

It was no secret that Roshan Perez, along with a lot of other folks, carried a small torch for Tan Ozawa, the chief scientist for the entire Omicron hegemony. Although her permanent residence was an apartment within Omicron Nebula, she spent a great deal of time consulting with, and for, the scientists and technicians from the other seven city asteroids throughout the Alpha Centauri system. Currently she was chairing a symposium of some scientific import on the planet Omicron below.

Doctor Tan Ozawa wore many hats, as she had many talents. In addition to her scientific prowess, she was also a trained psychologist, an artificial intelligence programmer, a mathematician, a theoretical physicist and was very proficient in every known form of martial arts, as well as a few unknown forms.

Her biggest asset, as far as Roshan was concerned, was her natural beauty. Her long black silky waist-length hair, her lovely Asian features, her perfect figure, thanks to her physical training in defense. A figure that was hard to hide as she insisted on wearing that form-fitting black faux leather body suit.

There were those, however, who would argue with his assertion of her natural beauty. Many believed that Tan Ozawa was an android through and through. That belief was due no doubt to her one unusual feature. She seemingly had no lenses in her eyes. At least that's what it looked like when viewing her from a distance of a meter or more. But if viewed from within her personal space, one would see white or "ghost" irises. Oddly, no other android had this feature.

Roshan couldn't help but wonder if the rumor was perpetuated mostly because of her cool demeanor. He'd even heard the word "aloof" mentioned when others had spoken of the good doctor. But she was not the only doctor accused of aloofness. All of these accusations were totally unfair, if not completely untrue. Most folks didn't know her as well as he. They had no idea of the circumstances regarding her thawing. For that matter, neither did he as he and his sister were thawed only a few years before Tan.

On the other hand, Roshan recalled hearing once that she was thawed aboard the *Nebula*, but if that were true, she would be a lot older than she looked now. *Maybe she really is an—oh forget it. So what if she may have a few synthetic or artificial parts.* All of the androids of Omicron lived normal lives. Well, most of them, anyway. It was nobody's business. Besides, there were only a few people who were a part of T. Ozawa's inner circle of friends. A circle that included Danar Seti, the current Captain Nebula, as well as Roshan and his sister. In fact, as far as he could tell, everyone assigned to the CCM had nothing but the greatest respect and admiration for Doctor Ozawa.

It was strange, however. It seemed that people were either afraid of her or had some kind of crush on her. He was quite comfortable with the category under which he fell. Although he would prefer the term "loyal friend" instead of crush. No doubt Oshara would say the same regarding Danar Seti. Besides, who cared what other people thought anyway? In his own personal opinion—an opinion that he shared with no one, not even Oshara—*Everybody was an idiot to some degree, prone to their own personal demons, paranoia and prejudices.*

Oh sure, collectively or in large groups, the human race was capable of great wonders. But individually or in small groups, people had caused a lot of damage and slowed the potential of the rest of the species by generations, if not longer. He knew that these were not positive thoughts. He tried not to think in such a way. But the truth was, he really trusted no one, except Oshara, Danar Seti and Tan Ozawa. They were special cases. Danar and Tan because, on some illogical level, they seemed too good to be true. Almost as if they weren't real people. The two of them seemed to have such control over their emotions. And Oshara, because of the fact that being not just brother and sister, but twins, they had always been together as far back as he could remember. Obviously further than that. Sometimes, it felt like Oshara was the only other real person in existence. They might not be telepathic, but there was definitely a connection between the two that could not be explained, well…logically. In some way, Roshan felt that he owed the three of them his current lifestyle, if not his very life, which he wouldn't trade for anything.

Both he and Oshara were only five years old when they experienced the big thaw. In objective reality, they were only three years younger than Danar Seti, but he was thawed upon arrival to the planet Omicron, while Roshan and his sister had to wait seven years after planetfall before shedding their popsicle imitations.

Before the Great Disaster, he wondered how many people imagined having to literally start a new life on a new planet in a new star system. Ordinarily that would be dream a come true for the five-year-old child who loved science fiction and super heroes. But when you're told your parents had to stay behind on Earth, because they only received two escape lottery tickets and that you would never see them again, that was as good as telling him that his parents were dead.

Oh sure, he understood by now how his parents obviously thought those escaping Earth had a better chance of survival. They must have figured that it was best to keep the twins together, but as a child he couldn't understand it from their point of view. Unlike his sister, he began to resent them. For many years he was an angry young man, feeling cast off like that. Abandoned. After 10 years in a group home with many other young orphans, Roshan had had enough.

Omicron had still barely been mapped, and it was his intention to explore the planet, adding to the information data base. The truth was, he just wanted to get away. Get away from every other human being. Even Oshara, who seemed to have adapted well to the situation.

On Earth, it would have been inconceivable to let a fifteen-year-old off on his own to travel even an explored world. But on Omicron, things were different. He had no real parents and everyone was just too busy building a civilization to ignore the efforts and information that a young strong lad such as he could provide.

Roshan studied hard in school, taking all of the required survival courses and even trained hard to earn his own hovervan and equipment. He was ready to go. It was then that his usually quiet and supportive sister chose to intervene in his quest to escape.

"You know, it's ironic," said Oshara, inadvertently interrupting her brother's thoughts, "that Danar and Tan are taking their respective positions on this matter."

"How so?"

"Well, as you pointed out, the captain is usually the one advocating peace and harmony, yet he suspects the gravitational anomalies could be a result of ET manipulation. 'So we must be prepared in any case.'

"On the other hand," she continued, "our chief scientist, who also happens to be a trained military strategist, is the one entertaining the notion that we might be wasting our time preparing for the worst-case scenario."

"*Si*," Roshan agreed, "that *is* ironic."

Just then, his console bleeped.

"Standby. Approaching the cookie corridor."

Since the floor of the Central Command Module was perpendicular to the Singularity Transport Tube, the axis of the station, it didn't rely on the spin of the asteroid for gravity. It was equipped instead with an autonomous gravity generator. It had to be, considering the base of the large domed structure was attached to the transparent domed end of the STT. Being the axis of the huge asteroid, there was virtually no gravity.

The gravity generator produced a gravity field that extended 10 meters outside and underneath the module. When inside of the module, gravity conditions were normal. However, it took most people a while to get used to the view from inside. When looking straight out of the windows of the CCM, one was looking straight down to the interior surface of the city proper. Fortunately, the spin of the ground wasn't noticed as the CCM rotated with it.

The CCM had 12 spacebugs that docked at the outer edges of its base. Each bug entered and exited the module through its own individual iris opening. When docked, the base or floor of the bug was mated to the opened hole of the iris. The bottom of the spacebug, which had its own iris opening, was then the sealed bottom of the CCM at its individual location. When a bug maneuvered to dock, its pilot had to orient the craft 90 degrees forward and down, so as to be on the same plane as the floor of the module. This orientation was performed just as the bug passed through the gravity field. If the pilot and passengers weren't able to *flip* their mental switches, thereby reorienting the internal gravity of their own bodies, they might find themselves getting sick to their stomachs, or "tossing their cookies." Hence, the unofficial term cookie corridor.

Despite having performed this maneuver dozens of times, Roshan had yet to fully acclimate to it. He and his sister were discussing this, as they usually did when docking to the CCM together, when a badly timed yellow alert immediately turned red, followed by an automatically activated audio alert, which sounded while the spacebug was only several centimeters into the opening.

"WARNING…EXTERIOR ASTEROID COLLISION IMMINENT…BRACE FOR IMPACT."

"Yikes!" Roshan yelled. "Talk about bad timing."

Before he could completely clear the opening, the maneuvering thrusters of the station kicked in to once again speed up and/or slow down the spin to make it easier for the weapons turrets to find their targets of random asteroids. Unfortunately, the altered spin of the station also caused the rotating CCM to collide with the roof of the spacebug as it attempted to dock, deflecting it from its trajectory, causing it to tumble wildly.

The good news was that at their present location at the axis of the station, the gravity was negligible. The bad news was that before Roshan could regain control of the bug, its deflection sent it tumbling back through the cookie corridor, causing the twins a critical moment of disorientation, preventing them from avoiding a collision with the STT.

The news didn't get any better. When the craft collided with the tube, it immediately lost all power. It ricocheted away from the tube, still spinning wildly, heading toward the inner surface of the city…and the ground. Without power, in addition to being bounced away from the null gravity of the axis, the situation was getting heavier inside as well as outside of the spacebug as it started spinning away from the STT.

"What happened?!" screamed Oshara.

"We lost power!"

"I can see that. How?!"

"How should I know?!"

"Well, we better find out real soon. Even with everything spinning crazily outside, I can tell our fall is beginning to pick up speed. In a few minutes, we won't be having any more fun in here."

"Right," agreed Roshan. "It'll be good till the last drop."

After roughly 10 seconds manipulating the controls in an attempt to restore power, the young officers both came to the same conclusion. "This is useless!" they said simultaneously.

"Nothing works. No emergency override. No communications. No backup power," concluded Roshan.

"We're going to have to take our chances and bail," agreed Oshara.

They both slapped the buckles on their chests with their palms which released the shoulder harnesses.

"Damn!" yelled Roshan in frustration, kicking the cylindrically shaped control panel in front of him. The assault was immediately followed by a loud *clunk*, then a low hum. "Hold on! We've got power!"

Another *clunk*, and the hum ceased.

"We've lost power."

"We better go, Ro," Oshara said through clenched teeth, trying to make her way to the rear exit.

In emergencies such as this, when no power was available, the spacebug's floor iris was locked in whatever position it was in at the time of shutdown. In this case, closed.

As the craft tumbled, Oshara half crawled, half stumbled around the guardrail of the floor iris in an effort to reach the mechanical crank to manually open the rear segmented sliding door. As she reached for the crank armature, removing the small wall panel, another *clunk* and low hum filled the cabin.

"Power's back. But not enough to maneuver this baby," Roshan yelled over his shoulder, still seated. "But we've got enough to magnetize the hull. Hang on, Oshara!"

Shunting what little power was at hand, Roshan's fingers flew across the controls in an attempt to charge the magnetic poles of the spacebug. It was his hope the slowly descending craft would eventually pass near one of the elevator pylons supporting the STT. It was a gamble, but no other options were available. Despite the fact that the bug was still tumbling, Roshan could tell by looking out of the front view port that they were now tumbling sideways and down instead of straight down. Before he could once again warn his sister to hang on, the small vehicle's roof crashed into the pylon, causing Oshara to fall backward, banging the back of her head on the guardrail surrounding the floor iris. It was at this moment the spacebug experienced a small power surge which automatically opened both the rear sliding door and the iris.

Dazed and unable to grab hold of anything, Oshara fell through the iris opening.

When the spacebug's roof magnetically collided with the elevator shaft, the craft slid down a few meters, coming to a stop with its front end facing toward to the ground. Roshan, slightly dazed from his impact with the forward view port, slowly peeled his face from the transparency while he cussed himself for prematurely releasing his harness, when he felt another impact, this time against the outside of the bug, which caused it to slide down another meter or so. He was just about to check on his sister's welfare when his still-blurred vison noticed what appeared to be an obviously unconscious body falling away from him. His brain instantly snapped to full alertness.

"My God. OSHARA!" Galvanized, his mind raced to come up with a plan, possibly using the harmonic magnets on his forearms to somehow rescue his sister. A small part in the back of his mind knew that any plan at this point was futile. Even if Oshara was conscious and able to activate her own harmonic magnets, she was just too far away from the elevator pylon for them to be effective. The best he could do was to magnetically fly down the side of the shaft and watch Oshara's body fall away, picking up speed while approaching Earth normal gravity, or faster if the station's AI was still controlling the exterior thrusters spinning the station beyond its normal velocity. His only other option was to watch her (hopefully just) unconscious body slam into the interior city surface.

To hell with it, he thought, scrambling to the opening. *I've got to do something.*

He had every intention of leaping head first through the iris opening, activating his harmonic magnets and thinking up another plan on his way down. But just as he stuck his head out, a hand, seemingly from nowhere, roughly pushed him back into the spacebug, causing him to trip back over the rail, landing face down into the forward viewport. Again.

"WHAT THE HEY?!"

About five minutes earlier, back in the classroom, Babs Schreiber saw the last student out. Fortunately, there was no vehicle ground traffic within Omicron Nebula, although there were streets. Streets that were primarily used for pedestrian traffic or the occasional bicycle. In fact, most of the traffic of Omicron Nebula was in the air. Of course, if one chose to ride on the ground instead of walk, he or she could board a transport car and "tube" from one end of the asteroid to the other or around the interior curve.

It was a blessing, not having to worry about the kids getting home. It didn't matter where in the city they lived. They could be home within a few minutes without trouble, provided there wasn't another roid attack. Which reminded B. Schreiber about that cryptic warning Roshan Perez gave her. Apparently she stumbled across a classified subject regarding the similarities of the gravitational anomalies of Sol and Alpha Centauri.

She would forever refer to this day as "the day of nerves." First, her debut as a live classroom instructor; second, two roid attacks; and (*hopefully*) last, she was to expect a call from the Central Command Module. She was half jokingly disappointed in herself, a trained psychologist who suffered bouts of anxiety. Could she have lived that sheltered a life? *Ha! A sheltered life indeed.*

Subjectively, from her point of view, it was only 15 years ago that she was on pre-disaster Earth living a normal life. Now she was living inside a floating ball of rock orbiting an alien world in a trinary star system. *What is there to be anxious about?*

Gathering her things in preparation to go home, her musings were interrupted by an incoming communication. No message this one, but a live call from the CCM. "Great," she said aloud sarcastically. "Am I in some kind of trouble or what?" She actually hesitated. All she had to do was acknowledge the call and eliminate all of this useless speculation. She even briefly considered simply leaving only to realize there would no doubt be a waiting message when she got home, if not a security contingent. *What is wrong with me?* she wondered and stabbed the button.

A familiar-looking face appeared on the screen. Although she had never met the man, she instantly recognized Danar Seti himself, the current Captain Nebula. The first thing she noticed was a slight smile on his face which immediately disarmed her anxiety. Yet, she was still a little nervous, but not from any fear of trouble. *Then what?* Suddenly it hit her. She hadn't had this feeling since her teenage years. *A school girl crush?* She figured she was too old—scratch that, too mature—for this kind of infatuation. She was pretty sure she was old enough to be his…older sister. He was what Babs Schreiber would consider a handsome man somewhere in his mid- to late-thirties, sporting a neatly trimmed beard and eyes that were used to a great deal of smiling. On ancient Earth, he would have fallen under the racial description of African-American, a term that had no relevance today, if it ever really needed any.

What? Did he say something? When she focused on the here and now, she realized about 30 seconds had gone by and all she was doing was staring at him.

He merely raised both brows, continued to smile and repeated, "*Doctor Schreiber?*"

"Oh, uh, I'm sorry. Yes. Captain Danar. Uh, I mean Seti—NEBULA. Hi."

"*Hello, Doctor Schreiber,*" he replied chuckling. "*Captain will do just fine. I was hoping to catch you before you left for the day. Is this an okay time? I'll only be a minute.*"

"Of course…Captain."

"*I understand you've figured out our little gravitational problem,*" he said, cutting to the chase.

"I—I wouldn't exactly say I figured it out. It simply occurred to me that what happened to Earth and what's going on here is too much the coincidence, if you know what I mean?"

"*That's good enough for me, Doctor, and yes, I know what you mean. I'd imagine you'd like to know what's going on. That is, exactly what happened to Earth and how it relates to the random roids here.*"

"Yes," Babs replied enthusiastically. "Yes I would."

"*Good. I'm prepared to give you all of the information we have in exchange for some of your …clinical input.*"

"I'll be happy to help in any way I can, Captain."

"*Excellent,*" he said, his smile broadening. "*I've scheduled a conference* with the other Omicron asteroid captains and specialists right here in the meeting hall of the command module for fifteen hun–uh, three p.m. today. I'd like you to attend."

"You can count on me, Captain," she said, relieved.

"That's great, Doctor," he said still smiling. "You have authorization to enter the CCM. I'll see you in about an hour, then."

"Thank you, Captain, and please call me Babs."

"*No. Thank you, Doct*—*uh, Babs,*" he clumsily replied. But he remembered to smile again before he closed the connection.

"Oh…my…God," she said aloud to herself. "Was I flirting with him?" She couldn't help but giggle at her own embarrassment. She believed she may even have embarrassed the good captain at the end of the conversation. She then sobered when something he said finally registered. Why would he need her clinical input? Granted, she was no astrophysicist, but she couldn't possibly see how a discussion of a gravitational anomaly could benefit from a psychological analysis. Unless there were some kind of intelligence behind it.

"Oh no." She could feel another attack of nerves coming along. The last thing she needed now was another roid attack.

"There is no way," Danar Seti said after closing the connection to the schoolroom, "that I'll ever feel comfortable calling her…uh, that name."

"Sir?" asked Commander Raquel "Rocky" Cummings, wisely pretending not to have heard the conversation between the captain and B. Schreiber. As second-in-command of Omicron Nebula, it was part of her duties to save the captain from any embarrassment. Or, as in this case, to not acknowledge it.

"Forget it," the captain said, stepping down from the command dais. The Perez twins' spacebug would be arriving any moment now. The captain decided to personally meet them when they docked.

"Oh, by the way, Captain," began Commander Cummings, "I received word that Doctor Ozawa's symposium has ended early."

No doubt due to that last extended roid attack, to which the captain would deny all responsibility should Doctor Ozawa inquire. But at least that meant she would be attending the briefing live.

"Thanks, Rocky." *Ah great. It'll be good to see Tan in person.* Although he had yet to admit to himself exactly *why* it was a good thing.

"Captain, I show Spacebug Nebula Three crossing the cookie corridor," Rocky Cummings added. "I'm sure the twins will be happy that *Babs* will be attending the meeting," she continued, smiling slyly.

Turning his head, the captain merely looked at his second-in-command through narrowed eyes. But he too was smiling.

Standing next to the opened iris of docking port three, Danar Seti reflected on the fact that he, the twins and Tan hadn't been in the same room together in what seemed like weeks. Too bad the circumstances couldn't be better. On the other hand, of course, Tan may have been correct and things weren't as bad as all that. If what the station's AI, VICI, the Virtual Inquiry Computer Interactive hologram predicted was true, they would have some answers before the day was out.

The captain's thoughts were interrupted when the rounded roof of Spacebug Nebula Three had risen into the opening by a few centimeters.

It was then that a badly timed yellow to red visual as well as audio alert automatically activated.

"WARNING...EXTERNAL ASTEROID COLLISION IMMINENT...BRACE FOR IMPACT."

Danar Seti could not imagine a worse time for this to happen. He braced himself for the inevitable shift in gravity as VICI adjusted the station's spin for maximum weapons sweep. From his point of view, it looked as if the spacebug suddenly accelerated backwards as the top of its roof crashed into the edge of the opening. Although the bug bounced away from the opening, it was still within the gravity field of the command module, which meant it was falling away or down from the iris opening.

The captain was worried for only a moment when he realized the twins might be disoriented when their vehicle tumbled back out of the cookie corridor. But once they were outside of the gravity field, they could take their time regaining their equilibrium as they would simply be spinning in the null gravity of the station's axis.

Danar Seti laid down on his stomach, his head peering down through the opening to watch and wait for the bug to correct its wild tumbling. Instead, he saw the craft collide with the Singularity Transport Tube, and he heard a loud *CLUNK*.

"Rocky," he shouted over his shoulder, "can you access the status of SBN3?"

"Yes, sir," she answered, tearing her eyes from the exterior thruster status panel. "My God. SBN3's lost all power."

Just as the captain feared. "Can you power them up remotely?"

"I'm sorry, Captain. Not without diverting VICI from operating the exterior weapons turrets. But I might be able to manually divert a small power surge to the bug. I don't know if that will help them much."

"Do what you can," Seti said as his stomach began to knot as if *he* were crossing the threshold of the cookie corridor. All he could do was watch helplessly as the craft began picking up speed as the artificial gravity of the station's spin took control of its downward fall to the inner surface.

After one unsuccessful attempt to divert power to SBN3, Commander Rocky Cummings excitedly called out, "Captain, I managed to juice the bug's power to five percent, but that won't be enough for maneuvering."

Before the captain could comment, he noticed the bug's spiraling descent angle toward one of the transparent metallic elevator pylons as it fortuitously swung into position, which meant that one of the twins managed to shunt the tiny bit of power to charge the magnetic poles of the spacebug.

CLANG! The roof of the bug magnetically collided with the elevator pylon, sliding down a few meters. Danar Seti's relief was short-lived. As he watched the small craft rock vertically up and down on its roof before coming to rest, he noticed the iris on its floor open and Oshara's body pitch out and away from the bug.

Without hesitation, Captain Nebula dove out of the opening in the command module's floor, immediately activating his harmonic armbands. For what he had in mind, he required their magnetic qualities to keep him as close to the transparent metallic elevator pylon as possible to compensate for both the 10 meters of gravity underneath the command module and the null gravity of the station's axis. His plan called for him to fly down the pylon faster than Oshara's (*hopefully unconscious*) body was falling toward the inner surface ground.

He would never have attempted this maneuver had this occurred in the freefall of a one gee atmosphere such as Omicron or Earth, as the laws of physics would not have allowed for him to descend faster than another falling object, no matter its mass.

His timing was even more critical since the spacebug, clinging about halfway down the pylon, was in his way. He had no choice but to bang his forearms together, deactivating his magnetic bands and flip over in mid-fall so as to land feet first on the spacebug. It slid down another meter or so. But just as he jumped head first over the side, he saw Roshan stick his head out as if preparing to jump himself. An admirable effort, but the captain's plan called for a rescue attempt of one. With a silent apology, he roughly shoved Roshan back into the spacebug, reactivated his magnetic armbands and continued his headfirst descent down the side of the pylon.

At its angle of descent, Oshara's body would just miss the city-block-sized opening of one of the inverted buildings. Her only chance of survival depended on falling into that space, and it was Captain Nebula's intention to see that happen. With the ground rapidly approaching, he passed Oshara's body. He once again deactivated his harmonic bands, negating his magnetic attraction to the pylon, tucked his head into his chest and flipped 270 degrees, then kicked off the pylon, extended his arms as far out as possible, palms up, and prayed. Prayed that he would intersect Oshara's falling form, prayed the sensors embedded in the five-meter-tall fence surrounding the opening of the inverted structure were working properly so as to deploy the net near the bottom, well below the surface, for just such an occasion.

With the wind of his descent whooshing by, he couldn't hear a thing. He slammed into Oshara, clearing the top of the fence by less than a meter. He wanted very much to see with his own eyes whether or not the net deployed, but couldn't afford the luxury as instinct demanded he hit the bottom feet first in either case.

Cradling Oshara as close to his chest as he could, his beating heart competing with the wind, he was just about to panic fearing the net didn't deploy when his feet finally made contact. He did his best to tuck into a roll while holding Oshara to prevent any rebound. Although he was successful, he couldn't hold on to her and they both sprawled across the net. It didn't matter. They could fall no farther. Although the Omicron Particles were helping to regulate the oxygen in his blood, he found it hard to catch his breath. That was no doubt due to the heavier gravity below the inner surface. It sounded reasonable. The truth was, he was afraid for Oshara, having no idea exactly what precipitated her fall from the spacebug.

As he began to crawl toward her, Danar Seti was flooded with dread. For when he reached her, he saw that she wasn't breathing.

CHAPTER SIX
Prodigy

Gazing out of the viewport of Spacebug Nebula Two at the segmented dome of the Omicron Nebula station while on final approach to the asteroid city, Tan Ozawa was once again struck with the enormity of the achievement of humankind. There was nothing like this cylinder city within rock, not even the other seven smaller asteroid cities, as impressive as they were in their own right. Just not as unique.

However, even the grandeur of Omicron Nebula paled in comparison to the enormous undertaking of transporting six billion beings 4.4 light years into space to settle a new home. All in an effort to lessen the burden of their home planet. That they actually succeeded was nothing less than miraculous. That is, eight-tenths of them succeeded. Sadly, twelve hundred million sentient beings didn't make it. Although Tan preferred the term "missing." It made her feel better, but not by much. *Twelve hundred million.* An astronomical number to be sure. A number even she found difficult to grasp. Like most of the citizens who called the star Alpha Centauri a home, she bore a small amount of guilt. Not for any responsibility for the loss of the Interstellar Starships *Omicron* and *Omega*, but simply for surviving.

However, not all of the citizens of Omicron felt guilt. In fact, some considered the crews and passengers of the *Omicron* and *Omega* to be the lucky ones. About one percent of the immigrants did not survive the freezing process. Another one percent or so woke up with prosthetic or bioelectric limbs and organs replacing the original equipment that didn't survive the freezing or thawing process. The so-called "Androids of Omicron," a group of which Tan herself was reportedly a member. At least according to the system-wide rumor mill.

Rumors, she ruminated. *No doubt one of the first forms of entertainment for the human race and probably one of the last vices on the road to true enlightenment. Let them have their entertainment. Their gossip and worthless speculation.* It didn't bother her. Not like it used to. For this was not the first time she was the subject of a rumor mill.

Back on pre-disaster Earth, young Tan, the only daughter of billionaire tycoon Tanaka Ozawa, was a child prodigy. A brilliant mind with an intelligence quotient of 175. Unfortunately, her small body was far from brilliant as she suffered the ravages of amyotrophic lateral sclerosis, a neurological disorder that robbed her of the use of her limbs and muscles. It was bad enough simply to fall victim to the disease. In Tan's case, all of the odds were in her favor of *not* getting it. ALS affected approximately one out of every one hundred thousand people. She was an unlucky one. In some cases, the disease was genetic; yet no one in her bloodline ever had it. She apparently was the first in her family. The disorder affected men more often than women. She contracted it anyway. Symptoms usually didn't develop until adulthood, often not until after age 50. Her first symptom was diagnosed after she lost the use of her left hand at the tender age of three. The disease progressed rapidly.

By the time she was five, her body completely betrayed her and she was forced to spend the bulk of her time in a hoverchair. She used to believe her physical handicap was the price nature exacted on her for giving her a well-above-average mental capacity. Later circumstances would reinforce that belief.

By the time Tan was 10, she had earned her first degree in mathematics. At about the same time, the medical community had developed what was hoped to be a cure for ALS as well as many other neurological disorders, thanks in no small part to Tanaka Ozawa's financial support. The idea was to re-sequence the DNA using preprogrammed nanodroids to correct the mutation in the DNA strand. The microscopic robots were suspended in a special spinal-type fluid that was to be injected directly into the cerebellum, the twin-lobed oval structure behind the brainstem, which coordinates movement and balance. Unfortunately this involved genetic manipulation which had been preemptively banned back in the late twentieth century during the frontier of gene therapy. At the time it was feared that genetic tampering would be used to enhance perfectly normal people; even worse, to enhance perceived defects in height, weight, eyesight, stamina and strength, giving an unfair advantage over those who could not afford the treatment once it became available.

A century or so later, once it was realized medical technologies could cure ills which still confounded twenty-first-century physicians, it was time to reconsider the issue of genetic manipulation.

In the year 2148, the planet became one democratic family with the birth of the United Earth Agency. The UEA rescinded the ban on genetic testing, provided it was only used to correct true defects.

In the year 2162, six months before Earth's worst environmental disaster, eleven-year-old Tan earned her second degree, this time in astrophysics. By this time, she was a household name worldwide. It was rumored that her father had secretly manipulated her genes from birth to increase her intelligence. This, despite the fact that Tan was born before the procedure was even developed, let alone perfected.

On the other hand, with the elder Ozawa's resources backed up by his billions, one always had fodder for accusations. Tanaka Ozawa vehemently denied any wrongdoings, illegalities or tampering with his daughter in any way. Of course, it was never proved one way or the other, but the rumors persisted. There was no way Tan herself could ever be certain but for the fact that her father told her he had nothing to do with her mental abilities other than providing genetic material in the conventional manner.

It was at that time Tan learned she had an older sister, who unfortunately was stillborn. Although her father was in perfect health for a man of his age, he was still elderly. He blamed himself for not starting a family sooner in life. When Tan's mother convinced him it was an isolated incident and not his fault, they tried again. When Tan was born alive (if not well), he was very happy and, after the pain of losing one daughter, he would never do anything to jeopardize her life. It was bad enough that he lost his wife, Tan's mother.

Her father never lied to her, and as far as she was concerned, that was the end of the matter. But the public at large wouldn't or couldn't let it end there. Tan Ozawa's mental prowess was just too unprecedented. Most people were convinced that her DNA had been tampered with during or shortly after birth and that something had gone terribly wrong. That was why it was thought she contracted amyotrophic lateral sclerosis against all odds. The fact that her mother died during childbirth didn't help to quell the rumor.

Several years after the development of the re-sequencing procedure, the Food and Drug Administration gave its approval to perform the operation on a human being. Tan Ozawa would have been the first recipient, but doctors feared the correction of the DNA mutation which caused her ALS would alter her brain chemistry. There was only a small chance she would come out of the operation with her mental abilities intact; there was a better than 50/50 chance she might become a mental vegetable. As it was Tan's choice, she opted not to go through with the procedure until the odds were better. Much better.

The rumors persisted.

In the year 2163, Tan's choice was rendered academic when the Great Disaster struck.

In an attempt to provide the unified peoples and industries of Earth with unlimited solar power, 1,100 solar-reflecting satellites were strung between Earth and its sun, 93 million miles distant. But they apparently absorbed too much energy, and as a result, directed a very destructive solar radiative wave back to Earth. The planet Earth would have been utterly destroyed but for the efforts of the crew of the United Earth Vessel *Sol*, the vehicle that deployed the satellites, under the command of Captain Ulysses Pitcairn. Sacrificing themselves, they blew up their own ship in order to open a wide enough gap in the string of satellites to prevent the wave from reaching Earth.

For the most part, it worked. With a large enough gulf in the satellites, the solar wave could no longer increase its destructive force exponentially. Unfortunately, the wave that had built up before the sacrifice of the *Sol* still struck the Earth, causing worldwide disasters; the collapse of the recently repaired ozone layer, flooding in some parts of the planet, droughts in other parts. With the increased radiation in the atmosphere, the surface of the planet would not be able to support life within the next decade.

With 15 billion people living on or near the surface, the solution was to go underground. But not all of the survivors could get under the surface to live. The UEA council decided the majority of the people would migrate and live underground and undersea and to send the rest of the population, six billion people, off-planet into space to colonize the next star system of Alpha Centauri.

It was then that Tan Ozawa's life, as she now knew it, truly began.

After docking the spacebug within the shipyard/cargo hanger of Omicron Nebula's segmented dome, Tan only had to board the transport car for a straight shot through the Singularity Transport Tube to the Central Command Module. If a port was available in the CCM, she could have flown the bug directly to the command module, but she knew she would make the briefing on time. Besides, it would only save her a quarter hour or so anyway. And she wouldn't be able to enjoy the leisurely travel of the transport tube car. The slow roll it made traveling up and down—or was it back and forth?—through the STT, afforded its passengers an overall, albeit distorted, view of the interior city. Distorted because the secondary transparent hull of the tube was filled with water. Water which was occasionally forced through jets spread out along the tube that simulated the rain and very effective clouds which at times completely hid the STT as well as obscured the view out from the transport car. Fortunately, she could relax and enjoy a clear day inside the artificial environment.

Tan suddenly imagined Captain Nebula's voice in her mind. *Don't get too relaxed, Tan. It's merely the calm before the storm.* If it were anyone else, Tan would chalk it up to paranoid delusion. Although there were many words to describe Danar Seti, paranoid and delusional were not on the list. In fact, she found him to be quite intelligent. She respected his sense of honor and integrity. Indeed, the current Captain Nebula was a true warrior at heart. Although he wouldn't describe himself that way. If there was one thing about which she could fault Danar, it would be the fact that he didn't give himself enough credit. And although he'd never mentioned it, she knew it bothered him to be constantly compared to the first, almost god-like Captain Nebula. Except for that one character flaw, he was very much like his predecessor Sean Stingray, who was—*is*, she corrected herself—also very intelligent and honorable, but unlike the present captain, very sure in his abilities and extremely confident. Sometimes overconfident. He could even be described as being flamboyant. And Tan should know. She was there, at least at the beginning, when the legend known as Sean Stingray guided what was left of the battered fleet of starships to their new home.

Once the Great Disaster struck and the fate of the Earth was known, the population of the planet had to be divided up as to who would stay on Earth and who would go off-world. First, talents and resources determined who would be assigned to which group. Then those who wished to take their chances in space were allowed to volunteer, provided they could pass certain psychological tests. The undecided were chosen by lottery until the numbers matched.

Because Tanaka Ozawa nearly liquidated his fortune to help build underground and undersea shelters, he and his family, which consisted only of his sickly daughter, were assigned to stay. However, the elderly former billionaire insisted his daughter venture into space. At first, Tan refused. Her father was all she had. But he explained to her that as much as it pained him to even consider separating from her, he believed that she would serve the greater good if she were to go into space. How much help could she truly provide to construct subsurface facilities with a technology that was already in place as opposed to using her engineering and technical skills to help build a colony from scratch on a brand new world?

Despite her father's logical reasoning, Tan wanted no part of it. Oh sure, to hurl oneself into the inky void of space did appeal to a small part of her, as it would to any nineteen-year-old. But her father was all she had in life. Without him she'd have nothing. "Not true," he informed her. Not only would she be a part of a whole new family of explorers, she would have an entire new world to help settle. Besides which, the elderly Tanaka was already over 100 years old. With the state of the planet Earth as it stood, medical technologies would not be increasing his life span anytime soon, which meant he had far fewer days in front of him than behind. Tan would have to get used to life without him soon in any case.

On the other hand, despite her physical limitations, she had a great deal to offer the new world, such as her knowledge of electrical engineering, AI programming and so much more. It would also be a great adventure for her.

After several days of back and forth debates with her father, Tan reluctantly agreed. At that moment, her childhood ended, for she knew she would never see her poppa again.

While riding the transport car to the Central Command Module, it took a great deal of self-control not to shed a tear for the absence of her poppa. Despite the inherent danger of a crippled teen colonizing a new world, Tan, along with most of her new family made it to Home-At-last. Her father, as usual, was right. It had been a great adventure. An adventure far beyond the expectations of her wildest dreams. For not only had she survived the ordeal, she was now also whole and hearty, free of the amyotrophic lateral sclerosis, thanks to the advances in neuroscience and cybernetics. Advances she helped bring about.

To prevent a further slide into melancholy and to snap herself back to the present, Tan checked her Data Access Crystal for any news of interest on the asteroid since she'd been planet-side. She came across a story of a spacebug accident that occurred within the last half hour involving Lieutenant Oshara Perez.

"Oshara." The DAC reported she was expected to survive. *Thank the cosmos.* After reading further details, she discovered Oshara was saved by Captain Nebula. "Danar," she whispered. She should not have been surprised.

Noting the time of 1437, Tan realized the captain's briefing with the other asteroid COs was going to begin in 18 minutes. She was going to be a few minutes late. Although she was expected, Tan didn't have to strictly adhere to the time as she was not an official officer of the Starforce of Omicron. For her peace of mind, Tan had to at least check on Oshara. Danar would understand.

When the transport car made its next stop along the STT, Tan took an elevator down a pylon and made her way to the medical facility.

Standing next to the sleeping Oshara, Tan was relieved that her injuries weren't serious enough to require a dip in the nanotank. The nanotank was a large cylinder filled with a bio-suspension fluid, teeming with thousands of programmable nanodroids, whose function was to repair any serious damage to a biological entity. In fact, Tan was told by the attending physician that Oshara merely required a few days of rest.

Although Oshara's presence wasn't required at the briefing, it would have fallen to the Perez twins to oversee the operation of the CCM under the guidance of Commander Cummings while Captain Nebula hosted the meeting. Roshan was more than capable of handling the duty for the duration of the briefing.

Before Tan took her leave, she realized this was the very wing of the med facility where she recovered from her second thawing. What a joyous time that was. A time when she was able to experience the world around her without the hoverchair. She recalled her first thaw aboard the ISS *Nebula* was a different story.

Cold. Why is it so cold? The environmental controls in her room must have been out. But there was nothing she could do about that until she was placed in her hoverchair.

Where is Poppa? She tried calling out. "P-P-Pa-ah." Why couldn't she speak? And why couldn't she see very well? Everything was a blur.

Oh no. It all came back to her. *We're not in Kansas anymore, Toto. Rats, I'm not even in the solar system.* She was about to wonder if perhaps the starships had yet to leave Earth orbit when the lid of her cryo-suspension chamber slid aside releasing a small cloud of cold vapor. There were three figures looking down at her. She didn't recognize them. Then again, with her blurry vision, she couldn't recognize her own father if he were one of the figures.

"Look," a male voice spoke. "She's already awake."

"Oh good," responded a female. "Miss? Are you with us?"

Tan cleared her throat. "Yes!"

"Can you tell me your name?"

Tan knew that a series of questions would follow, trying to ascertain her mental status after being frozen for—well, she had many questions of her own. Better to save time and satisfy them quickly so they could answer her inquiries. However, without the vocoder of her hoverchair, she had to rely on the slurred, halting progress of her own voice.

"I am…Tan Ozawa. My father was—*is* Tanaka Ozawa. I was placed in SA, suspended animation…on August 5…2171, preparatory for inclusion unto…and I assume subsequent launch…of the Interstellar Starship *Nebula*…a few weeks later…as far as I know."

"Hmm. She seems pretty lucid to me," said the first male.

"Have we yet…to arrive at…Omicron?" Tan asked. She hated speaking without the vocoder, but everyone apparently understood her.

"No, Miss Ozawa," replied the female stranger. "That's why the captain wished to speak with you."

"I see…then I will require…my hoverchair."

"It's right here, T. Ozawa," replied the male voice again. Tan assumed it was the captain. "It's fully charged and stocked."

Tan had mixed feelings about her hoverchair. On the one hand, it took care of all of her needs, since her body was incapable of doing so. With the sensors located in the overhead display monitoring her eyes, she could give it all of its commands of locomotion as well as environmental controls with winks, blinks and eye movement. Its vocoder could even synthesize her voice with the proper inflection. From several straw tubes near her mouth, she could intake hot and cold water, fruit juices, soup and even oxygen if necessary. On the other hand, she hated the chair simply because she needed it. Without it, she was as physically useful as a rag doll.

Fortunately, her mental abilities didn't require the chair. On the other hand, it appeared the three people occupying the small room with her required her mental abilities: Doctor Michael Peterson, chief medical officer currently on call on the ISS *Nebula*, who reluctantly agreed to thaw her; Doctor Sarah James, who actually performed the procedure, and was the female voice Tan heard upon her awakening; and Captain Sean Stingray, who for some reason was being referred to as Captain Nebula, informed Tan that he was the fifth commanding officer of the Nebula.

Within the first 10 minutes of this meeting, she received a great deal of information to catch her up. The *Nebula* had been in flight for nearly 26 years and was only one year away from Omicron. The news went downhill from there. Three months ago, the ISS *Omicron*, the first of the 10 starships out of Earth, ceased broadcasting her locator beam. At the time, it was believed the broadcast laser was simply down. Two months ago, the ISS *Omega*, the second ship, disappeared off the beam. Unlike the *Omicron*, the *Omega* was still broadcasting, only off course.

One month ago, the *Nebula* had crossed the position where the *Omicron* stopped broadcasting. There was no trace of the ship. No debris or anything. Her ionized exhaust trail suddenly ended cold, as if it vanished into thin vacuum. The only sign of the *Omega* was the faint trace of her ionized exhaust veering off the beam, as well as her rapidly receding broadcast laser, Doppler shifting farther away to silence. No one could even hazard a guess as to the structural integrity of the *Omega* after being knocked off course, traveling at the velocity of .20C.

When the *Nebula*, the third ship out of Earth in the galactic caravan, was approaching this mysterious area of space, the captain decided to stay on course. He didn't want to take the chance of purposefully veering off the beam to avoid this area. To do so at one-fifth light speed would throw the ship too far off course. It would be virtually impossible to get back again without tracking the beam from a dead stop. And even if they could find it, it would take years to get back up to speed again. *Could that be what the captain of the Omega decided?* Stingray had his doubts. He believed they were taken by surprise and knocked off course instead of veering off on their own. The evidence of the *Omega*'s ionized trail corroborated his theory. Besides, what of the seven other vessels trailing the *Nebula*? At that point, Stingray realized that he was not only responsible for the *Nebula* and its frozen cargo of 600 million lives, but for the other seven ships and precious cargo as well. He reasoned that whatever the anomaly was that caused the *Omicron* to vanish was decreasing in intensity, for it merely knocked the *Omega* off course instead of destroying it. It was his hope the *Nebula* would be able to weather the anomaly while hopefully remaining on course and up to speed. If his theory were correct, then the Interstellar Starships *Gaea, Quasar, Radian, Pulsar, Vortex, Graviton* and *Ersatz* would make it through the anomalous sinkhole without incident.

Stingray was correct. The anomaly, whatever it was, did appear to have decreased in intensity. Not enough, unfortunately, for the *Nebula* to come through it unscathed. The ship's AI went haywire, causing computer malfunctions shipwide. The *Nebula*, as with most of the other ships, had been experiencing minor problems with the computers and systems from the moment they left Earth's solar system, but the ships' small number of animated crews were able to stay on top of things by constantly patching up, reprogramming or rerouting circuits.

Passing through the vacuum sinkhole was too much for the *Nebula*'s AI. It crashed, forcing the vessel to rely on backup generators and programs stored in the backup cache files. More than half of the freezing units for the suspended animation chambers had gone offline. Those units would begin to thaw beyond the critical point long before orbital insertion of Omicron, killing their occupants if they couldn't get the AI back on line. And that was why Stingray required Tan Ozawa's expertise.

Seven days after Tan was thawed, she came up with what she hoped was a possible solution to the problem, a solution she was involved with on pre-disaster Earth that was shelved when the need to deal with the crisis that precipitated their exodus superceded everything. Tan's plan called for totally changing the way the AI processed information. Although the technology of speed, memory capacity, storage space and the like had steadily increased over the last few centuries, computers have always processed information digitally. Tan proposed using the *Nebula*'s existing fiberoptic mesh as a neural network giving the AI the ability to truly think for itself instead of using a series of programs that communicated with each other via preprogrammed scenarios.

In other words, the systems software would no longer need to ask questions requiring yes or no answers to perform tasks; it would be able to learn from experience and be better able to protect itself against power failures and dropouts by rerouting entire programs anywhere within its matrix that weren't critically needed at a given moment. After a time, the AI would become conscious to some degree. Somewhat like a person. It would be aware that it was an individual, which meant it would develop a sense of self-worth and even self preservation. Somewhat like a person. For this to work, however, a living biological brain's synaptic memory engrams would have to be digitally encoded into the existing fiberoptic mesh to begin the neural network process. It was only logical that Tan's own synaptic engrams be used to interface with the computer.

Unfortunately, there existed yet another problem that could interfere with her possible solution. Tan's blurry vision was getting worse. If she were to lose her sight completely, she would be unable to give proper commands to her hoverchair, which meant she would be unable to radically reprogram the *Nebula*'s AI computers.

To overcome this, an interface module would have to be designed and built. Tan was the only one who could do it. But she needed perfect eyesight. Unfortunately Doctor Peterson discovered Tan's failing vision wasn't simply cryo-suspension sickness. Her optic nerve had been damaged by the too rapid thawing procedure. That was one of many reasons why he was against awakening her in the first place.

When Captain Nebula heard this, he insisted on taking full

responsibility, as it was he who insisted on using Tan's expertise to help them out of this situation. The captain was visibly distraught over this news and repeatedly expressed his sorrow to Tan. For her part, she insisted she bore no malice and didn't require an apology from Stingray. She realized she could be the only chance of getting the *Nebula* to its destination with its cargo alive.

With Doctors Peterson and James' medical knowledge and Tan's cybernetic expertise, they were able to design an ocular scanning chip and implant it directly within the optical center of Tan's brain at the back of the cerebellum. The chip was designed to regulate the chemical and electrical balance of her optic nerve. There was a curious side effect, however. Although the operation was a success, the corrective ocular chip eliminated the pigment of Tan's irises, making her look as if she had no pupils at all. The irises were still there, of course, just opaque. In fact, the only thing that could be seen at all, close up and with enough light, were the tiny dots of her retinas. Of course, if there was too much light, then her colorless irises would close around the retina, as they are supposed to do, making them even harder to notice.

It was a fair trade as far as Tan was concerned. Better than fair really, since a cybernetic replacement was necessary for a few small parts of her vision center as well, providing her with a small degree of telescopic and zoom vision. For a scientist, these abilities would come in handy.

By the time she was recovering from the second round of major surgery on her brain, a month had passed. Fortunately, the ISS *Gaea*, the fourth starship out of Earth, had crossed the sinkhole without incident. The *Nebula*, now the lead ship, still had other problems.

Within the next six weeks, the vessel had to reorient its position 180 degrees to begin the braking procedure for Omicron orbital insertion. Had the *Nebula* been traveling at any true relativistic speeds, that is, any velocity nearer the speed of light, it would have had to turn itself backwards at the halfway point of its journey. With the fleet's maximum velocity of one-fifth light speed, it was only necessary to begin the braking procedure less than a year from its destination. However, .20C was still very fast. The ship's computers required precise calculations for the reaction control jets to turn the vessels backwards while traveling 60,000 kilometers per second. Otherwise, a starship could find itself off course, suffer structural damage, or both.

Lying on a custom-built platform within the computer core of the ISS *Nebula*, Tan Ozawa contemplated the braking procedure while Doctor James made the final cable connection to a socket on the neural interface unit attached to the back of Tan's neck to begin her engram encoding into the computer's fiberoptic network.

Intellectually, Tan understood what was to take place once she and the computer interfaced. The ailing AI would scan her brain, mapping her synaptic pathways. Through the interface, the computer would be able to use her brain as a sort of secondary hard drive. It would then download several test programs into her to see how her brain allocated and prioritized files so it could learn and emulate.

Nevertheless, when Tan communicated readiness to begin and Doctor James closed the contact on the interface, what she actually experienced was so far beyond what she expected, she would not have believed it possible. The very moment the AI made contact with her thoughts, the world around her morphed into a surrealistic perception. She began to hear sounds that would normally be background noise, such as the air ventilation system and the hum of the main engine under the deck plates. Then she began hearing sounds she shouldn't be able to hear. The beating of her own heart didn't surprise her, but the beating of everyone else's heart did. Her breathing; their breathing. Then she began to hear a crescendoing echo of all of the noise blending into what sounded to her like wind or rushing water. Her eyelids began feeling heavy as if she were seconds away from sleep. But she wasn't tired or sleepy. In fact, she had already been sleeping for more than a quarter century. No, this was something entirely different.

Before her lids closed completely, she saw that her vision had trailing afterimages. Then suddenly nothing. All was black and quiet. No sound, no smells. She couldn't even open her eyelids. Even if she could, she suspected she wouldn't be able to see anyway. She couldn't even hear her own heart anymore. *One moment.* She could no longer *feel* her heart. She began to panic. She tried to move her lips. Nothing. She tried to scream. Nothing. It was as if she were disconnected from her body. *One moment.* That's exactly what was happening.

The AI was overriding her ability to control her own body. That should have worried her, but since she didn't possess much motor control anyway, she decided to go with the flow. To ride it out. She calmed her panicky thoughts and immediately began to receive perceptions once again. Oh, but what perceptions. She would not have believed it possible. Not once did she consider how *she* would perceive the interface. There were no words, no language to describe what she experienced.

Even years later, in retrospect, the best description of the initial neural-net setup was that she could *hear* colors, *taste* sound, *see* her thoughts as well as many other nonsensical descriptions far removed from normal human perceptions.

She was aware of a body. But not her own. Her body was the *Nebula* itself. It was then Tan realized there was so much more to perceive beyond the simple senses of a human body.

Without exactly knowing how, she reached out. If her consciousness was truly disconnected from her body, and the way she perceived the world around her was no longer limited to the biological sensory apparatus attached to her head, and if she could feel the *Nebula* as her body, then maybe it was time to explore this new body; the new senses.

The first that coalesced into something that made sense was her hearing. If she concentrated, by narrowing the focus of sound to the room that housed the computer core, she could convert the sound of rushing water, every type of noise on the *Nebula*, into something manageable. *Ah, much better.* At the same time, her visual perception was narrowed to the comp-core room as well. But she wasn't seeing like she normally saw things. There were no eyes involved. She was simply aware of everything and everyone in the room all at once. It was as if the whole room were reflected on the entire surface of a *sphere* of which her consciousness was inside. This *metasphere* was seemingly floating several centimeters above her normal body, making sense of it all.

Concentrating on the narrow focus of the metasphere, she moved about the room. For someone who under normal circumstances couldn't move without a hoverchair, this was more than just a unique experience. She settled near where Doctor James was monitoring her normal body's bio readings. *Good. Just about everything was normal.* There were a few items within the animated representation of her brain that were firing at above normal activity, but that was to be expected since Tan was literally of two minds now: her own thought processes as well as the AI's emerging consciousness. She heard Doctor James convey this to Captain Nebula while Doctor Peterson stood quietly, wearing a stern expression, his arms crossed over his chest.

"Excellent," the captain replied. "It looks like the two of you—ah, make that the three of you have things under control. I'm on my way to the nuclear fusion reactor power plant to physically check the ship's engine and power status."

Good idea, thought Tan. Since the ship's AI didn't require her conscious mind to set up the neurological network, she decided to accompany the captain to find out how well the progress of power distribution was proceeding. She floated past Stingray's head as he stepped into the corridor. The captain was quite tall. On the order of 190-something centimeters or so. But despite his long strides, she felt she was traveling too slowly in keeping pace with him. She could see that he was headed for a turbo tube. It was a long way to the power plant from the habitat section, but it occurred to her that now that she was in some form of cyberspace, she didn't have to travel to the power plant through the corridor or turbocars like everyone else in meatspace. She was quite sure she could move about faster than a turbo car. There was no reason why she shouldn't be able to go directly to the nuclear fusion reactor power plant, in what she referred to as quantum space, where any distance between two points is a straight line.

And away she went. Right through the bulkheads, cables and pipes. Stingray hadn't noticed her departure. Why should he? He couldn't possibly notice her presence as a metasphere. As far as he was concerned, Tan was still lying on a platform in the comp-core room. She was. Physically, anyway. But to those in meatspace, she didn't exist as pure thought.

One moment. Could this be death? No, of course not. She saw her body's vital signs which indicated her body lived. But what about her mind? Could she be brain-dead? She didn't think so. Besides, instruments hooked into her real body showed elevated activity in the front part of her cerebrum, the part of the brain that was responsible for all conscious experience, including thoughts and feelings. She was still processing information, still able to think. An ancient scholastic Latin phrase came to mind. *Cogito ergo sum.* "I think, therefore I am." Satisfied that she was literally experiencing the phrase in a way that Rene Descartes could only imagine, she made her way to the power plant.

Passing through a bulkhead, Tan Ozawa's metasphere consciousness noticed the corridor that connected the cryogenic modules to either side of the *Nebula*. She suddenly realized she was more concerned with the status of the 600 million frozen refugees than she was with the ship's power distribution. Besides, since she could travel through quantum-space faster than walking or tubing through meatspace, she could check on the frozen passengers and be at the power plant before the captain arrived.

Floating just inside the entrance to the starboard cryogenic module, Tan was struck with the enormity of the CS chambers stacked one on top of another, row after row seemingly into infinity as far as conventional eyes could see. At least that was how she would have described the view had she been using her normal body's eyes. With the 360-degree panoramic view of her metasphere consciousness, it was no less mind boggling. There were 300 million cryo-suspension chambers in this one module, plus billions of frozen embryos of various Earth wildlife and plants. The port module carried the same number. She could easily float here for hours, days even, mesmerized by the incredible sight.

After forcing herself to check the status panel, she was relieved to discover both modules were up to full power, although the power distribution indicator noted a great number of CSCs, about one percent, had apparently been off-line for quite some time. Some as long as decades. Another one percent or so had suffered intermittent power dropouts. She was quite certain these figures were indicative of the other seven surviving starships as well. On the surface, simply looking at the numbers, one percent seemed an acceptable loss until you truly thought of the numbers as people. Sadly, untold millions of mothers, fathers, daughters and sons wouldn't survive the journey to the new world. More millions wouldn't wake up with whole skins intact. Fortunately, many of the potentially crippled refugees could wait to be thawed until the medical sciences could develop cures and replacement body parts.

That was just one of many odd disparities of the Omicron colony in the current year of 2229. In some cases, offspring were older than their parents due to the fact that some parents and family members remained frozen for many years while their children and younger relatives were thawed on arrival at the Alpha Centauri star system.

Zipping around the cryo-module in a way that only a metasphere could, Tan randomly peered into the vapor-filled transparencies at the colonists. She never expected to recognize anyone, but she did. Crestfallen, she found herself staring at the shrunken face of Frederick Howell through the clear glass of his chamber. Clear because its freezing unit lost power years earlier. She had admired Professor Howell her whole life. He had been her teacher at MIT. He was also the lead scientist in charge of the team that sent the series of probes to the Centauri trinary system in search of habitable planets under the auspices of the Search for Extra-Terrestrial Intelligence project. One of his probes was sending a broadcast beam back to Earth, pointing the way for the fleet of starships like a lighthouse beacon. The six billion refugees would have little hope of finding a habitable Earth-like planet orbiting Alpha Centauri A, if not for the efforts of Doctor Howell and his team.

Tan recalled he had a young son. Dane Reginald Howell. She remembered the child was also afflicted with a brain disorder. Amnestic aphasia, caused by the complications of his mother's pregnancy during Earth's worst environmental disaster. A complication that took her life while giving birth. Sure enough, within the CS chamber underneath Doctor Howell's, lay his son. Thank the cosmos he was in perfect hibernation.

Unfortunately, this was one of the sections of the cryo-module that lost its records. It would appear that the young Dane R. Howell would awaken with a great deal of pain. With the records lost and his father dead, he may have no idea of who he was or from where he came.

Tan Ozawa suddenly felt a connection to this young child as they had a great deal in common. They both suffered from an uncommon brain disorder. Both lost their mothers during childbirth. Both of their fathers were well known and instrumental in this mass exodus from Earth: Frederick Howell discovered the new planet Omicron while Tanaka Ozawa provided the financial support and shipyard factories. Indeed. Tan determined to keep an eye on this young man. She believed he would require her help when they arrived at their new home. It would seem he could use a friend. A kindred spirit perhaps.

She had no idea of the extent of her relationship with the man who was then known as the boy, Dane R. Howell.

Phasing through the bulkhead on her way to the nuclear fusion reactor power plant, the metasphere that was Tan Ozawa's consciousness was both melancholy and encouraged at the same time regarding Doctor Howell and his son. Deep in thought, she found herself in the power plant before she knew it. *Strange.* Captain Nebula had yet to arrive. The crew also appeared to be working hurriedly, checking monitors, adjusting levers and such. Even walking fast. Captain Nebula must have spiked the water supply with caffeine so they could keep up with the AI's accelerated repairs. Pleased with her little joke, Tan suddenly wondered how it was she could feel any emotion at all. Ever since she'd experienced life in quantum space through her metasphere these past what?–15 minutes or so–she had felt several emotions. Sadness, elation, frustration, fear, astonishment and humor. Had she ever considered the prospect of emotions without a body of some kind, she would have been certain one required lungs, muscles, a heart and a nervous system to regulate adrenalin. Apparently the *cause* of emotions and feelings had nothing to do with a physical body. It would seem the body's job was to simply measure the *effects*.

She was about to head for the flight control deck while contemplating the cause and effects of feelings when an idea struck.

Since the artificial intelligence of the *Nebula*'s computers was learning to process information through a neural net, could it also learn to *feel* as well? If so, it would be able to truly interact with people, not just communicate information. With a bit of holographic programming, the computer could deal with humans in the image of a person. Tan believed that would be more efficient than giving the computer instructions by pressing buttons. Even more efficient than speaking into the air and hoping the computer's audio pick-up could hear you. In fact, a hologram that could feel, or at the very least understand feelings, could truly interact by giving tell-tale signs of body language as well as verbal responses.

Yes, an interactive holographic program would be easy to write. In fact, she'd already mentally written it. She only needed to download it into the AI. She could easily test it since the *Nebula* already had several holographic projectors: one atop the astronavigation table on the flight control deck, another within the engine diagnostic console in the nuclear fusion reactor power plant, a few in the science labs and another on top of the diagnostic table in the medical bay.

It also occurred to Tan that if her metasphere could phase through bulkheads, she didn't need to wait until she was back in her own body to download the new program. She was quite certain she could write it, download it and test it in quantum space from her metasphere. And she could do it all on the flight control deck.

Again, before she knew it, she was suddenly in a different location, this time floating above the astronavigation table on the FCD. *One moment. How could this be?* In one instant, she was in the NFRPP, the next, here on the FCD. *Amazing. One could truly get used to quantum space. Well, there's no time like the present.* Since the table wasn't being used, her metasphere phased into it. In her current state, Tan didn't possess fingers or limbs of any kind. Fortunately, she didn't need to physically touch anything. Without exactly knowing how, she was able to manipulate the electrical impulses along the circuit pathways of the computer system to write the new program. In what seemed to be only a few minutes, she was finished.

A translucent holographic image coalesced atop the astronavigation table. It was in the form of a not-fully-detailed bald human female. It was a projection of Tan Ozawa's own nineteen-year-old body, standing upright, looking around the FCD in a way her real body never could do. The deck crew was speechless. Tan remembered someone asking, "What the hell is that?"

She opted to allow the AI to speak. Although slightly mechanical, like her hoverchair vocoder, the image did sound like her, down to her inflections. **"I am the Virtual Inquiry Computer Interactive unit, newly programmed from your computer's artificial intelligence through a neural network. You may refer to me as VICI."**

There was more Q-and-A between the crew and VICI regarding what the crew could expect and exactly how the new program worked. *Splendid.* This worked out even better than she had hoped.

With the AI's—correction, VICI's—thinking processes based on Tan's own engrams, she felt confident she was no longer needed.

In the short amount of time she'd been in q-space, she had accomplished a great deal. The ISS *Nebula* was not only repaired but improved. She wanted more. But what more could there be? She had instant access to anywhere within the vessel.

One moment. There she was, limiting herself again with physical boundaries. Just because her real body was limited to the confines of the starship—because it required the life support of oxygen, gravity and food intake—her metasphere consciousness was not. She couldn't think of a reason why she couldn't venture outside the ship.

It was useless to think in terms of up and down when in the vacuum of space, but since the habitat module was spinning around the ship's axis for gravity, she still thought of herself floating "up." Up and through every layer of deck plating until she was outside of the ship. *Amazing. Poppa was so right. This is quite the adventure.* As breathtaking as the sight was, Tan was a little disappointed she didn't see the stars streaking by in a blue to red spectrum Doppler shift effect. Of course, the *Nebula* wasn't traveling at relativistic speeds so it looked as if it were standing still. The fact that there was no visible exhaust of hot flames spewing out of the main propulsion thruster like in the ancient sci-fi video discs added to the illusion. With her 360-degree spherical vision, she could somehow perceive the broadcast beam fore and aft of the *Nebula*, being sent by Doctor Howell's probes from their destination.

What now? With her apparent speed through q-space, she could conceivably go right to the probe which should be stationed above Omicron's north pole axis. This time, however, thinking about it did not make her suddenly appear. It didn't matter since she'd be alone there anyway at this time.

No. Better to travel the beam back to the ISS *Gaea*. Her metasphere should be able to rewrite that ship's AI to process information through a neural net as well. *A capital idea.* And off she went.

No, Poppa. I don't wish to go. I could serve no good on this journey—Thank you very much. I wish I could say it was easy obtaining yet another degree; however, as I cannot participate in any sports, I have plenty of time to study—Poppa, why can't I move my hand?—I appreciate all of your efforts, but this procedure appears too risky. I must decline for now.

"We're losing her."

One moment.

"Wake her."

Voices?

"I dare not give her a stimulant in her condition. She's already too weak."

Who?

"Then unplug her."

What?

"If I separate her from the interface, it could kill her."

Interface? What?

"You just said we're losing her. If we don't pull the plug, she'll die for certain."

Cosmos!

"Oh God. Alright, here we go."

Pain! Tan Ozawa never experienced such agony. It was all over her body. Slowly, it subsided. At least the pain in her body subsided. Her head was a different matter altogether. Calling it a bad headache was simply an understatement. More like an atom-smashing, super-colliding cerebral meltdown. As bad as the pain was, she couldn't help but chuckle at her little joke through clenched eyes and a screwed-up expression.

"My goodness. She's coming around," said a relieved Doctor James.

"I can see that, Doc. But is she experiencing pain or pleasure?" countered Captain Nebula.

Tan wanted to verify her pain, but before she could even muster the strength to do so, everything went silent and black.

When she came to, she was no longer in the computer core room, but lying on a bed in the medical bay. She still had what she believed had to be the worst headache of any organic being in the entire Universe, but was lucid enough, although extremely weak and barely able to remain awake. She was surprised to discover a few things. First, when asked her name, she replied VICI, but immediately corrected herself. Satisfied that Tan's thinking processes had returned to normal after being severed from the interface, Doctor James informed her that she was interlinked with the *Nebula*'s AI for eight days, not the hour or so she'd guessed. That explained her skewed perception of time.

The good news was that the *Nebula*'s systems were operating beyond specs. Also, the new neural net AI program was transmitted back to the ISS *Gaea*. The Virtual Inquiry Computer Interactive program had gotten that vessel up and running with its updated specs in less than a week. Then VICI transmitted a copy of herself to the *Quasar* who transmitted a copy to the *Radian* and so on and on.

Unfortunately, when Tan's consciousness left the ship, VICI had inadvertently damaged her physical body's brainstem while attempting to map what appeared to be dormant synaptic pathways from a consciousness that had seemingly vanished from her body. Or rather the body of the ship. So it would seem there were limits to quantum space. Apparently q-space was limited to the confines of the *Nebula* because the neural net mesh was laid out within the ship. It was reasonable to Tan that her metasphere consciousness was possible only because of the interface module. When her metasphere had strayed too far from it, her consciousness was drawn back to her physical body like a meteor being drawn to the ground by gravity.

She was told also that she was plugged in the ship's AI for far too long. As a result, Tan's brainstem became too weak to handle all of the normal signals that fired impulses to the rest of her body through her spinal column.

According to Doctor Peterson, the only reason she was alive at all was because her body was used to not receiving impulses from her brain on a regular basis, so it wasn't that much of a shock to her system. The only way to correct the damage was to cease all functions of her brain and spine.

Tan would have to go back to the freezer, possibly for several years. Doctor James informed her however, that because she was interfaced with the AI for so long, VICI had an extremely detailed map of Tan's brain all the way down to the subatomic level. Armed with this information, Doctor James was confident she could successfully operate on Tan with the DNA re-sequencing procedure that would cure Tan of the amyotrophic lateral sclerosis. If not, she would be able to reroute new pathways, effectively eliminating the neurological disorder. Also, with a few cybernetic enhancements to the muscles of Tan's arms, legs and back to compensate for nearly two decades of inactivity, she would wake up as good as new, after an intense schedule of physical therapy of course. Better than new, in fact. This time around, Tan agreed to undergo the procedure. As fleeting as it was, after experiencing quantum space through the metasphere, she would no longer tolerate life in that damned hoverchair.

Tan was aghast to learn she had been on ice for 10 years when she awoke in this wing of the medical facility 20 years ago. It took that long for her brainstem to heal from her interface with the *Nebula*'s computer system. However, true to her word, Doctor James successfully performed the DNA re-sequencing operation. As far as Tan was concerned, her life as she knew it now, began on that day. From there, she went back to school to complete her studies, while also training her new body for peak performance and fighting techniques, a legacy to her father's favorite pastime in his youth. Except for the memory of her poppa, all of the time spent on Earth and the *Nebula* didn't seem real to her.

The fact that only two other people knew about her experiences aboard the *Nebula* reinforced that feeling. Sean Stingray, who initiated her thaw in flight, was currently comatose at the med facility on Omicron. He left out the full details of how the Virtual Inquiry Computer Interactive program first came online from his ship's log. The official records only stated that Tan Ozawa was thawed to help write the program with Doctors Peterson and James, which was true as far as it went. Tan believed the reason Stingray didn't go into details was that he simply didn't believe her accounts of her metasphere experience through quantum space aboard the *Nebula*. His report emphasized the reprogramming of the ship's AI and the successful braking procedure that led to the *Nebula*'s Omicron orbital insertion.

Because Tan wanted to live as normal a life as possible, free of gossip, rumors and useless speculation, Doctor James' official records made no mention of Tan's engramatic download either. Now, as chief medical officer of the entire Omicron colony, stationed aboard the Omicron Nebula asteroid, Doctor Sarah James loyally continued to care for her fellow Earth refugees as well as her friendship with Tan.

As for Doctor Peterson, sadly, he perished in a shuttle accident shortly after arrival in this region of space. Although the man was somewhat arrogant and opinionated, he was a brilliant physician who was missed.

Outside of Doctor James and the ailing Sean Stingray, no one, not even Danar Seti, was aware of the connection between Doctor Tan Ozawa and VICI, the Virtual Inquiry Computer Interactive hologram.

CHAPTER SEVEN
Briefing: 1500

"...the total destruction of the entire Omicron star colony as a result of a possibly hostile invasion," evoked a stone-faced Captain Nebula, "or at the very least," he continued in a noticeably lighter tone, "some kind of natural phenomenon that *has* been, *is* currently and *could* be a gravimetric pain in the asteroid for who knows how long?"

Those were the words Tan Ozawa heard as she ascended the two-person lift to the conference room at the top of the Central Command Module. *If that was his opening statement to the assembled commanding officers then he is certainly starting the briefing with a flair for the dramatic.* She was only six minutes late and figured the only thing she missed was the unnecessary round of greetings and catch-ups. But there was a face she didn't expected to see: that of her old friend and colleague Doctor Babs Schreiber, sitting to the left of Captain Nebula. The last Tan had heard, she was interested in taking over Christine McCauley's teaching position. Danar must have thought her psychological background would come in handy for this meeting, despite the fact that no civilian outside of Tan herself was even aware of this conference, let alone what it was about. *This should prove interesting.*

There was an empty chair to Danar's right which Tan assumed was for her. Taking the seat, she noted the seven other attendees of the "big briefing." They were all Danar's age, in their late thirties. Like him and Tan, they were all born on Earth. Unlike Tan, they were all thawed immediately upon arrival, still children, thanks to the suspended animation of the cryo-chambers. Some arrived with family members. Some did not.

To Tan's immediate right sat Captain Gaea, LeAnn Walker of Omicron Gaea. A Caucasian women born on the East Coast of North America. Her uniform design matched Captain Nebula's. The only difference was the *tincture* or color—his was of the Heraldic primer *vert* or green, hers was *bleu-celeste* or sky-blue. Each wore the black faux leather boots, belt and left shoulder strap that was typical of all of the Starforce captain's uniforms. The uniforms were emblazoned with the six-centimeter-round Omicron standard over the left breast that connected to the bottom of the shoulder strap. The ISS *Gaea*'s standard was a green leaf in front of a blue background, over her left breast, while the sign of *Nebula* was a red lightning bolt over a black background.

Next to Captain Gaea was Captain Pulsar, Jean Pierre Bouvier of Omicron Pulsar, originally from France, whose uniform sported the Heraldic tincture *purpure or* purple. The Pulsar standard looked like four electron paths orbiting a black nucleus against a white background.

To his right was Frank Logan, Captain Quasar from Australia, wearing a *tenne* or tan tincture, with the symbol of a yellow eight-pointed starburst on a black background.

Then Charles Lee, Captain Vortex, wearing a *cendree* or cinder-grey uniform, whose emblem was appropriately a black circular spiral against a white background. His handsome face showed his mixed African and Asian ancestry.

Then Captain Radian, Michele Woo of Asian descent, wearing *or*, also known as canary yellow with the Radian symbol that looked like a single horizontal high-lighted frequency sine-wave on a black background.

Next to her was Arjun Vohra, Captain Graviton of Hindu ancestry, in a *sable* or black on black uniform, the red background emblem was emblazoned with a five-sided white diamond.

And lastly, John Askew, a Caucasian male from the West Coast of Earth's North America, also known as Captain Ersatz of the Omicron

Ersatz asteroid. His tincture was *brunartre* or brown, with an emblem that was made up of five black diagonal lines that zigzagged across a yellow background.

All of the Omicron standards were surrounded by a *sanguine* or blood-red border.

Of the ten people sitting around the oval table, only Danar Seti, Babs Schreiber and Tan Ozawa were actually physically present. The other seven were holographic projections. Each Omicron asteroid CO was physically present at his or her own respective briefing chamber conversing with holo-projections of everyone else sitting at similar conference tables.

"Nebula, what makes you think we're facing a 'hostile alien invasion'?" asked the holo- projection of Michele Woo of Omicron Radian.

"Ah. You're misquoting me, Radian," replied Captain Nebula with a slight smile. "I said 'hostile invasion.' Nothing about aliens."

"Aye, but you left us with that impression, mate," said Frank Logan of Omicron Quasar.

"Well, perhaps I did a little," answered Nebula. "I can't say for certain at this point if there is any intelligence involved, although when you hear what VICI and I have discovered, I think you'll agree it's a strong possibility. In fact, this is why I invited Doctors Schreiber and Ozawa. I believe we could benefit from the expertise of a behavioral psychologist as well as a game warfare strategist, respectively."

Babs Schreiber almost corrected the captain by informing him she was trained to study the behavior of children, but thought better of it.

"You'll forgive me, Nebula," stated Charles Lee, somewhat apologetically, "I uh, realize that Tan, that is, Doctor Ozawa has clearance for classified matters…that is to say we have all benefitted from her expertise on many levels, but are you sure it's wise to bring a civilian to these proceedings before any facts are established? With all due respect, Doctor Schreiber," he finished.

At that, Babs gracefully nodded, conceding his point.

"Well spoken, Vortex," answered an unperturbed Danar Seti. "First, let me say that if we waited until we have all of the facts, it may be too late to defend ourselves, and second, you may all be interested to know that Doctor Schreiber here, on her own, figured out a possible connection between the gravity anomaly in this region and Earth, while teaching a class earlier this afternoon. Fortunately, I got wind of it before her conclusions were, uh, inadvertently disseminated into the civilian population, thanks to the Lieutenants Perez. The information she concluded rivals your own knowledge at this point."

"Figured it out on your own, eh *mademoiselle?*" offered J.P. Bouvier.

"Well, I uh…."

"As far as I'm concerned," stated LeAnn Walker, "if she figured out on her own what we had to be told, then she's more than qualified to be here, and that's that."

"That," said Captain Vortex, pointing directly at Captain Gaea, "works for me."

Whew, thought Babs. She was beginning to feel outnumbered and unwanted, despite the clearance of the ranking Captain Nebula. The fact that Tan Ozawa, another civilian, was present made things a little easier.

"Well then, now that we are all on the same page," piped in Arjun Vohra, " perhaps we should get to it. What say you, Nebula?"

"Agreed, Graviton," answered Danar Seti promptly. "As most of you know, I suspect the solar accident that precipitated Earth's worst environmental disaster nearly seventy years ago, as well as our current troubles with the random roids are related. What you may not know is that I believe the, uh, disappearance of the starships *Omicron* and *Omega* are also tied in with the anomaly." He paused for a second to make sure everyone heard him. He had their complete and undivided attention. "I intend to show you," he continued, "that what we call random roids, are not so random. Attend. The year 2163, as you are all aware, was the first indication ever of an unexplained gravitational phenomenon involving Earth's primary. Four years later, the Interstellar Space Ship *Ersatz*, the last of ten vessels on the way here to Alpha Centauri, left the Sol system. From our point of view the gravitational anomaly never occurred again. However, in the year 2198, Sean Stingray of the ISS *Nebula*, the third of the ten ships, reported the disappearance of the *Omicron* and the *Omega*, the first two ships, through what he described as a 'sinkhole' in space. In 2209, ten years after the Omicron colony was established here, we saw what was up to that time a semi-stable asteroid belt orbiting Alpha Centauri A. Semi-stable due to Alpha Centauri B's gravitational influence. As you all know, Centauri A and B are true binary stars orbiting each other with a mean distance of twenty-three astronomical units separating them. Before two decades ago, the asteroids in this system obeyed the laws of physics without question. Then suddenly, the belt goes from semi-stable to completely unstable, sometimes for up to thirty minutes at a time, several times a year. Today, for the first time, we experienced three random roid incidents. Three in one day. A first."

"So you believe the incidents will increase from here on out," stated LeAnn Walker.

"I do."

"Oh great," replied an exasperated Captain Gaea. "I can see where this is going. Please don't tell me you think we should all pack up our collective six-billion-plus bags of luggage and move elsewhere? *Again*?! What's the next closest star to Alpha Centauri A, anyway?"

"Uh, that would be Alpha Centauri B, deary," answered Captain Ersatz sarcastically.

"Jackass!" she shot back. "You know what I mean, and don't tell me Sol, either."

"Hey, the name is Jack Askew, thank you very much," answered Captain Ersatz, feigning indignity.

Captain Nebula loudly cleared his throat. However, he was wearing that slight smile for which he was known. "Need I remind you all, that we have guests at these proceedings?"

The two captains nodded their apologies at Tan and Babs, before glancing at each other with small grins.

For her part, Tan merely returned the nod with an emotionless expression, as if to say she was no stranger to these two bickering. As for Babs Schreiber, she began to relax a bit. This "big briefing" was reminiscent of her classroom so far. Although she suspected the two captains had something more than friendship, presently, or perhaps had a history of some kind.

"To answer your original question, Gaea," continued Nebula, "we're not going anywhere. This system is our home now, and no gravitational sinkhole, whether it be natural or selective, is going to make us leave. And in case you're still interested, the next closest star is Sirius, in the Canus Major system, eight light years from Earth. Who knows, maybe one day we'll explore that system. But it'll be, at the very least, a visit. At most, an expansion, not a migration."

"Good," replied LeAnn Walker. "We'll all sleep better here on Omicron Gaea tonight."

"Don't be too hasty," returned Nebula, "this day isn't over yet."

"Pray continue, Nebula," spoke up Captain Graviton. "You say you believe the random roids will increase in intensity. And you say it with such remarkable assuredness. How so?"

"I base my conclusions on computer modeling and, uh, a bit of extrapolation," admitted Danar Seti. "Allow me to explain. As you all know, it was my father, Doctor Frederick Howell, who sent a series of probes to this system nearly ninety years ago. These probes were merely scouts for colonization. My friends, I submit to you that these gravimetric anomalies are just that. Advance scouts. Eyes for unknown entities to probe for…fill in the blank."

"What?" asked Captain Ersatz, recommending suggestions. "It could be something as easy as going on a hike, or as complicated as a prelude to invasion."

"Hmmm," chimed in Captain Radian, "it could be something as simple as exploration."

"Maybe they're just fishin'," offered Captain Quasar.

"Fishing, *mon ami?*" asked Jean Pierre Bouvier.

"Yeah. You ever been fishin', Pulsar?"

"*Mais, non.* Not so long as there are grocery stores."

"There's more to fishin' than fillin' your stomach," opined Frank Logan with a slight Australian accent. "For instance, when I feel like relaxin', I find a likely spot for me rowboat, then I start castin' with me pole till somethin' bites. Kinda like Nebula's alien probes. They found a likely spot between Sol and Alpha Centauri and started castin' till they caught the *Omicron* and *Omega* in that there sinkhole."

"One moment, if I may Captain Quasar," interrupted Tan Ozawa. "As far as we know, the *Omicron* disappeared true enough, but the *Omega* was thrown off course. It was bounced out of the sinkhole."

"Okay, so they threw one back. I do it all the time."

"Forgive me, my friends," interrupted Arjun Vohra apologetically, "but I am not certain this speculation on our part can have any relevance."

"I beg to differ, Graviton," countered Danar Seti. "Speculation, or as in this case, asking questions, even from an unknown frame of reference, is one of the first signs of wisdom. Even in speculation, one might stumble across the right answer, as opposed to doing nothing at all."

"I agree," said John Askew. "Besides, Graviton, don't you realize how ridiculous it is to argue about the Search for Extra-Terrestrial Intelligence with a guy named Seti?"

"Ha! You've got a point, Ersatz," replied Arjun Vohra with a gracious chuckle.

"Yeah, he's got a point alright," offered a widely grinning LeAnn Walker. "Now we just need to figure out where to put his hat."

At that, Danar Seti dropped his head into his opened palm as the majority of those present erupted with laughter. If he had a gavel, he would have been tempted to slam it down on the table. But that really wasn't his style. He couldn't help but wonder what Sean Stingray would do to get everyone focused. Seti knew that Stingray would've joined in the laughter, creating a sense of solidarity while slowly manipulating everyone's strengths and weaknesses to his point of view. Danar always admired that ability of the first Captain Nebula. He'd witnessed it many times from his former mentor while being sponsored by Stingray during his tour at the Omicron Academy. *It's a skill that could serve you well, young Danar,* Stingray often advised him. Up to this point, Danar Seti always assumed he was speaking in general terms. Now, he was beginning to wonder if Stingray was speaking to him specifically.

Although he technically didn't outrank any of the asteroid captains, as the commanding officer of Omicron Nebula, he carried the flag.

Besides, it was he who called this briefing. As a leader as well as chairperson, it was his responsibility to be adaptable. *But manipulating people? That wasn't his style either. Hmmf! Maybe I do need to lighten up a little.*

Once again Babs Schreiber was reminded of her classroom. Here she was, sitting amongst the leaders of the eight asteroid cities floating within the Centauri system, yet they didn't seem to be taking this meeting very seriously. A small part of her wondered if Captain Nebula invited her to the briefing for her clinical input or as a disciplinarian. Not that she had any experience in that area, considering she'd been a school teacher for only a day. It was only a matter of time before she would be confronted with a similar situation. Would she raise her voice and reprimand a student? Should she suggest that now? Before she could consider the dilemma further, the boisterous COs quieted down…rather suddenly it seemed. Did she miss something? She then glanced at Danar Seti, who appeared to be patiently waiting. His chin rested on closed hands, both elbows propped on the table. He was looking straight ahead at everyone from under a hooded brow. His expression was more neutral than menacing, yet she could feel the temperature in the room drop a few degrees. She saw Frank Logan swallow hard, while nervously glancing around the room. She heard LeAnn Walker clear her throat and mutter.

"You were saying, Captain Nebula?"

'Captain' Nebula. Not simply Nebula. Impressive. B. Schreiber made a mental note to remember that technique. *Remain patiently quiet, stare straight ahead and shame them into obedience.*

Although Tan Ozawa's face wasn't showing it, she was smiling on the inside at the sheepish expressions on the faces of Nebula's contemporaries. They all looked kind of intimidated. Why, it was just this morning she joked about Danar doing that very thing. She was quite certain that he had no idea of the respect he engendered in those around him. Perhaps that was as it should be. If he were not aware of the ability, then he couldn't possibly abuse it. Not that he ever would, *consciously*, anyway.

It was hard to believe that this honorable, unassuming man who abhorred confrontations was the same innocent orphaned boy she saw frozen in a cryo-suspension chamber 31 years ago. From her point of view, it was 21 years ago. She regretted not watching him grow up that first decade, but cherished the time their friendship began when Sean Stingray (re)introduced them at Frederick Howell University. He, a young man taking classes there while simultaneously attending the Omicron Starforce Academy. She, continuing her studies from Earth. She couldn't remember exactly which philosophical doctorate she was pursuing at the time, *without giving it some thought*, but she clearly remembered wanting to spend time with the handsome young officer. Unfortunately, she also remembered many other normal young women competing for that privilege as well.

Why am I thinking about this now, of all times? She was determined to focus on the meeting at hand.

"You were saying, Captain Nebula?" muttered LeAnn Walker.

Danar Seti had no idea what just happened, but he somehow had recaptured everyone's attention without resulting to mind game tactics. He was lucky that way sometimes. "I was saying that being prepared is our best option. And the best way to be prepared is to try and understand the motivation of the adversary. Also, similar to a chess match, attempting to anticipate the future moves of both you and your opponent, even five or six moves in advance, usually determines the winner, even if—especially if—you're evenly matched."

"But, Nebula," countered Arjun, "in chess, even if you don't know your opponent, you know his or her motivation is to win. And as challenging as chess is, especially with evenly matched contestants, it is relatively much easier to anticipate moves when you are both playing under the same rules and regulations. Even ancient conflicts of centuries past had conventions and rules of war. However, our current situation does not afford us any knowledge of our opponent, nor our opponent's motivations. And if there are rules to this potential engagement, we are painfully ignorant of them."

"Well spoken, Graviton," Danar genuinely praised. Then, addressing everyone in the chamber, "All that Captain Graviton said is absolutely true. If indeed there is a potential engagement, we are clueless as to any rules. But I submit to you, my friends, that we must also face the possibility that we were thrust into this more than sixty years ago and we've been picking up the pieces ever since. To me, it feels as if we are an innocent child's balloon being tossed hither and yon by heavy winds on a beach. It does seem pointless to try and figure out the motivation of the wind, granted. It may also appear that the child would be helpless in trying to stop the wind in any case. Maybe there is nothing the child can do to stop the wind, whether it bears the balloon malice or not. But the balloon is not completely helpless."

"Huh?" Michelle Woo asked, incredulously. "How so?"

"The child may not be able to stop the wind," answered Danar, driving his point home, "but a shelter could be erected to protect against the wind, or the balloon could be anchored to the sand to prevent buffeting."

"Hmm. I see where you're going, Nebula," added Charles Lee. "If necessary, the balloon could also be adapted to better survive the winds."

"How do you adapt a balloon, for cryin' out loud?" asked Frank Logan.

"You deflate it slightly, so it won't be as susceptible to the buffeting."

"I don't think I like the sound of that, mate," quipped a crestfallen Captain Quasar, "but I get the gist of what you gents are sayin'."

While this exchange was taking place, John Askew got up from the briefing table and walked over to the food synthesizer for a cup of coffee. As all of the briefing rooms of the eight asteroids were completely identical, the illusion that they were all in the same room was very powerful. While awaiting his cup, he said, "It sounds to me like we could use the opinion of a psychiatrist or two," indicating Tan and Babs with a nod to each.

"Can I get something for anyone while I'm up?" he asked, hiding a sly smile on his face.

"Thanks, Jack," piped up LeAnn Walker. "I'll have a—" She quickly clamped her mouth shut when she realized he was joking, mentally chiding herself for falling for his obvious holo-illusionist trick. She silently mouthed the word *jackass* in his direction.

To which he replied in the same manner. *That's Jack Askew, thank you very much.*

Grateful this exchange elicited only amused expressions and smiles instead of outright uncontrolled laughter, Danar Seti invited his two guests to venture any opinions. "Well, Doctors Ozawa, Schreiber?"

Finally! mused Babs. After receiving the go-ahead nod from Tan, she spoke up, with more confidence than she would have thought possible. "After hearing what's been discussed so far as well as my own conclusions, I must say I agree with the captain. Uh…Nebula. If it can be determined that the gravitational anomalies are not naturally occurring, then what we know so far may suggest that the events sixty years ago on Earth, as well as here today, are behavioral signs of searching or scouting. Or fishing by sentient beings. On the other hand, I see no evidence of hostile intent, either. It could all be an accident, if not a coincidence." Impressed with how everyone else used everyday examples of life to illustrate their respective points, she elaborated, "Like the old oil refinery rigs set up on Earth's oceans, disrupting the sea life in the surrounding area. It was disruptive and inconvenient for the indigenous life forms, but unintentional."

"I'm inclined to agree with my colleague," Tan opined, "regarding any malevolent behavior on the part of any outside force that may or may not be responsible for our difficulties. But I believe that any space-faring species capable of manipulating at least one of the four fundamental interactions of space-time to such an enormous degree would have evolved beyond the traits of aggression."

"Excuse me, Tan," interrupted Michelle Woo. "The four fundamental interactions of space-time?"

"Yes. Forgive me. They are the forces that allow the Universe to…well, stick together on a quantum level."

Everyone simply stared at her, clearly out of their depth.

"Think of the quantum particle known as the gluon. As the name implies, gluons cause quantum particles to stick to one another. You could say that gluons are the glue that binds the Universe together. It is the particle which all the complexity of existence emerges, similar to quarks and leptons. Quarks and leptons interacting at the relatively low energies provided by scientific laboratories over the past couple of centuries experience the four distinct interactions. In their descending order of strength they are the *strong interaction*, which binds the quark element. The *electromagnetic interaction*, which gives rise to electricity and magnetic fields. The *weak interaction* responsible for radioactivity, and the *gravitational interaction*, the force that is responsible for ocean tides and the reason Omicron Nebula spins for gravity, before the advent of artificial gravity generators, that is."

"Yeah, didn't you all know that?" asked John Askew, sarcastically.

If looks could kill, Captain Ersatz would be horizontal by now, under the gaze of Captain Radian. "Yeah, sure. As if *you* knew it."

"Doctor Ozawa," said Arjun Vohra, "you say that gravity is the weakest of the fundamental interactions. Perhaps our mysterious alien fishermen are not as powerful as we first assumed. After all, we have been manipulating gravity for over one hundred years, starting with the hovercars back on Earth to the aforementioned artificial gravity generators we have here now."

"It is not really quite the same thing, Captain Graviton," explained Tan. "The strength of the interactions depends on the energy of the interacting particles. Hover-vehicles and gravity generators require relatively low amounts of energy, as I mentioned earlier. To manipulate the gravity of entire solar systems would require a great deal more energy than could be generated in a laboratory. It has been theorized that at a much higher energy output, the strengths of the four interactions, that is the stickiness of the gluons, might all become equal and the distinctions between the fundamental interactions would simply vanish, thereby becoming one single universal interaction. Indeed, if an outside agency is responsible for altering gravity on such a stellar scale, it may possess the elusive formula for the Grand Unified Theory. If so, it would demonstrate a level of knowledge and power that can only be reached through patience and maturity."

"Unless," countered Danar, "an impatient, immature species discovered it by accident, like so many discoveries made by humans."

Tan opened her mouth to reply, then closed it abruptly as if she edited her response. "Such accidental discoveries on such a large scale usually end in a fatal disaster."

"Yeah, a disaster for us," quipped Frank Logan.

"Please keep in mind, I am still uncertain that aliens are involved," insisted Tan.

"Wait a minute," said LeAnn Walker, scratching her head, "if aliens aren't involved, then what? We're talking about a natural cause?"

"There is one other possibility you have failed to consider."

"There is?" asked LeAnn after several seconds of silence.

Tan, sitting next to Danar, noticed that half-smile on his face, head inclined in her direction, letting her know that he had considered the third possibility and rejected it.

"Of course!" blurted Babs, snapping her fingers. "*We* are responsible."

"Aw, man, no way," shrieked John Askew.

"I only mention it as a third alternative," Tan calmly replied.

"Great. Are you guys saying everything is *our* fault?" indicating the two doctors, then letting his head drop to the table with a loud thud.

"I'm not saying I believe that," cautioned Babs, "but from a psychological standpoint, it's much easier to live with one's mistake if you can find even a small reason to blame someone or something else. After all, the Earth was on the verge of becoming a single democracy, ready to implement a procedure that would benefit everyone by providing unlimited energy to the planet at large, when all of sudden, the worst environmental disaster in history came about as a result. Was it our own fault? Consider the facts. The solar radiation wave did not develop until *after*, not before, but after we, Earth humans, deployed the solar-reflecting satellites. At the very least, those reflectors contributed to the disaster. After the UEV *Sol* broke the chain of reflectors, the Sun's mass remained constant and no other wave was ever reported."

"As far as we know, *mademoiselle*," added Jean Pierre.

"Granted. As far as we know," conceded Babs. "But consider also, the sinkhole that swallowed the *Omicron* and threw the *Omega* off course did happen to be on the same path as our ships traveling along a broadcast laser beam transmitted from probes sent by Earth humans.

Then, of course, there are the random roids, the asteroid belt orbiting Alpha Centauri A that occasionally goes haywire. But the belt was stable until a decade after the arrival of—"

"*Oui, oui,* I know," interrupted Jean Pierre. "Earth humans. *Merde!* When you put it that way, it does appear as if we are responsible for our own troubles, *non?*"

"Again, my friends," insisted Tan, "it is merely an alternative that should not be dismissed out of hand."

"It does appear," offered Charles Lee, rubbing his chin, "that there are a lot of coincidences we must account for before adding aliens to the mix."

"That was my conclusion as well," agreed Babs. "Although at the time I didn't consider aliens, hostile or otherwise."

"Hmm. Upon further reflection," added Jean Pierre, sinking deeper into the cushions of his chair, "it does appear to be a tremendous coincidence that aliens, whether they be hostile, intelligent or no, would even be in this region of space. Consider. Out of four hundred billion stars in the galaxy, what is so special about this particular area of space that is located on the outer fringes of the galaxy, anyway?"

"How about the fact that there are at least two neighboring star systems, each with yellow G-2 type stars that are capable of supporting life as we know it?" countered Danar. "One of them, Sol, has a planet that supports intelligent life. The other, Alpha C. A, which is even older, has no intelligent life to support, despite the fact that its second planet is very nearly Earth-like and located within the zone of life. That is, not too close to Alpha C. B to preclude life from forming. It's been a great mystery as to why there are no mammalian life forms on Omicron. And keep in mind, my friends, that as large as this galaxy is, there is still plenty of room for coincidences."

"True. But if they are able to manipulate the four fundamental attractions—"

"Interactions," corrected Tan.

"*Oui.* If indeed they are that powerful, one would think they would be able to correct the difficulties, whatever they may be, of their region of space as opposed to mucking up ours."

"What if," offered Babs, "this area of space *is* theirs?"

"What do you mean, B. Schreiber?" asked M. Woo.

"There's a popular rumor here on Omicron Nebula, especially among the youthful citizenry, that aliens used to live here a long time ago, that they may return to claim their home."

"An interesting rumor to be sure," observed Arjun. "However, the reality begs to differ when you consider there is no evidence that mammalian life ever evolved on Omicron. As Nebula pointed out, the great mystery. Unless of course, the rumor is true and the insects and fish of the planet evolved from a separate branch of intelligent beings millions of years ago, left the planet and are now suddenly homesick."

"Now there's cheery twist for you," Frank added, heavy with sarcasm. "Intelligent fish, fishin' for humans. Sounds like just desserts to me."

"Wow, just think," piped up John Askew, "if it does come down to a war with these smart fish and we win, we'll all have an unlimited supply of seafood, heh heh."

"Jack, that's disgusting," several people said simultaneously.

A jovial bunch, this group, Danar thought to himself. *Not much on decorum, and some of them could certainly use more discipline.* But he couldn't really blame them. There hadn't really been any serious obstacles in the last couple of decades, not counting the random roids, which up to this point had only been an inconvenience, never causing any real damage. All of the real efforts dealt with establishing the colony of asteroid cities spread throughout the star system and settling the planet below for the majority of Earth refugees. The bulk of that work was done by the first generation commanders led by Sean Stingray. Despite the fact that all of the people and holo images at the table were Earth-born, they were all still second geners when it came to running their respective stations, himself included.

Although Danar had few memories of his years on Earth, he knew through his own research as well as from his studies on Omicron, that organizations on old Earth, especially the various militaries before the United Earth Agency was founded, were run much tighter with more discipline and a greater emphasis on the chain of command. Even with military ranks, uniforms, training and academic studies, the Starforce was a much looser entity than its predecessors on old Earth.

But why shouldn't it be looser when there had never been a major threat to the populace? No wars in this region of space, civil or otherwise, very little crime and an economic system unlike anything old Earth ever saw, or at the very least hadn't seen for a very long time. An economy where goods and services were bartered, where there was no standard form of currency, eliminating the desire to hoard or stash away money. Very little poverty, with the exception of those few who simply refused to work for a free place to live, who would much rather live off the (new) land. That choice was also theirs. No personal or handheld projectile weapons, except for the occasional crossbow, bow and arrow and boomerang. The few hundred various styles of the old handguns, rifles and ammunition were now objects of curiosity on display in a museum on the planet below, safely locked away with no manufacturing facility to produce them ever again.

Part of the attitude toward guns could be attributed to the fact that it was simply unwise to use projectile weapons in a space environment where hull integrity was essential for life. Personally, Danar considered projectile weapons of any kind, especially guns, weapons of cowards. In his studies, the only weapon of honor he'd ever come across was the sword. A dangerous weapon to be sure, but one that would put the aggressor in as much danger as his opponent should he be similarly armed. What type of individual would prefer to take out his opponent from a safe distance if not a coward?

Of course, there were those who would argue that everyone had a right to bear arms, as was stated in the Second Amendment to the Constitution of the then United States of America almost a half a millennia ago. Perhaps it was considered a necessity back then, when settling a new land teeming with dangerous wildlife or a hostile indigenous population that didn't take too kindly to having their land stolen and their rights usurped. Of course, hunting for food would have been necessary at that time, but not so shortly after the industrial revolution when, as Captain Pulsar mentioned , grocery stores were available. But by then, hunting was a sport that became a popular pastime that soon caused the proliferation of guns throughout the world. Soon after it seemed, the best sport to hunt was your fellow man.

Unfortunately, the atrocities didn't end then for the fledgling United States. The country was also divided over the practice of slavery that eventually led to a civil war. Then there were gender rights issues as well as a period of racial hatred and discrimination that took many decades to resolve.

Danar could understand why those times were referred to as "The Dark Ages: The Sequel." Despite all of the backward thinking and unfair policies of that time, he was happy to credit the US with promoting planet-wide democracy, an initiative that led to the UEA in the mid-twenty-second century. A time for which Danar was extremely proud of his home planet. A time that was short-lived since the Great Disaster occurred within two decades of the United Earth. *Was the disaster our own fault?* He didn't think so. *But Babs, uh—B. Schreiber had a point. We have to acknowledge at least a partial responsibility. Was the solar radiative wave caused by the reflecting satellites, or did the Sun's mass increase independently? Were we simply minding our own business, paving a road to enlightenment when an alien agency's designs caused our designs to backfire in our faces? Will we ever know?* Without knowing exactly how, he felt certain the answers would be forthcoming. But at what cost?

No. He could not fault these compatriots of his for their carefree attitudes. He trusted that they would rise to the occasion of defending the innocents of Omicron.

Over the last week, he and VICI had had the same debate that his colleagues were having now. He thought it best that they discuss the possibility of alien involvement before he dropped their findings in his comrades' holographic laps. He shouldn't have been surprised at their imaginative speculations, *But smart fish? I mean really.* Of course, discussing the issue with the Virtual Inquiry Computer Interactive hologram didn't leave a lot of room to inject humor. Not that VICI was unfamiliar with the concept of humor. She most certainly was. She simply didn't display it in Danar's presence very often. At this point, Tan would remind him that VICI was an "interactive" program, and that if he were to lighten up, he would no doubt experience her sense of humor. *Well, maybe so, but the gravitational anomaly that's been plaguing us for so long is no laughing matter.*

Strange. Having worked so closely with VICI this week, Danar was often reminded of working with Tan. It only now occurred to him that shortly after he first met Tan 20 years ago, he was struck with how she reminded him of VICI. *Hmm.*

Well, as he recently reminded this group, *there are such things as coincidences.* For now, just when he thought it best to steer this briefing back to the serious side of the matter, Tan spoke up.

"As fascinating as this speculation is, I'd like to know more about what Danar and VICI have uncovered."

Good ole Tan.

"Yes, Nebula," added Charles Lee, "you were talking about the original asteroid belt orbiting Alpha C. A and how the roids are perturbed by Alpha C. B."

"Correct. As I mentioned earlier, this trinary star system is in reality a binary system with Alpha C. A and B orbiting each other every eighty years, separated from each other by twenty-three astronomical units. Proxima Centauri is a whopping thirteen thousand AUs from A and B. Proxima, or Alpha Centauri C, is believed to be a rogue star not native to this system, much smaller than A or B or even Sol. It's dimmer and cooler also. Seemingly insignificant. In fact, it may leave the system in a few million years. But for now, because it's gravitationally linked to A and B, this system is trinary. It makes for interesting gravimetric properties in this region of space, but it doesn't account for the random roids."

"Hmm. There's obviously more here than first meets the eye," F. Logan said nodding his head.

"That much is certain," agreed Nebula. "Think about it. The asteroids surrounding Alpha C. A are—or rather were—in an elliptical orbit. Not exactly circular. With Alpha C. B at twenty-three AUs and eighty years orbiting Alpha C. A, it should take decades for the roids to veer off course. And when I say veering off course, that is an exaggeration at best. Wobbling most likely. In the time we've been here, we shouldn't have seen even that. Instead, for twenty years, we've seen a lot more than wobbling. The roids have flown in-system, even crashing into Omicron."

"Danar," inquired Tan, who was now very attentive as this subject was right up her alley. "Do you believe that Proxima is contributing to the gravimetric disturbances?"

"Yes and no."

"Wait a minute," interrupted a pinched-faced M. Woo. "You said yourself that Proxima is too small and dim to be significant. Besides, even if it were a larger star, at—what did you say?—thirteen thousand astronomical units distance?" He nodded. "An astronomical unit is the mean distance between Earth and its primary sun, correct?" Another nod. "Then thirteen thousand AUs is what?"

"About five hundred times the distance between Sol and Pluto," answered Tan.

"Why that's practically another solar system in itself!"

"Proxima," answered Danar, "is a red dwarf star of the M5 spectrum. It has no bodies of any kind orbiting it. As far away as it seems, it is nonetheless trapped, at least for the foreseeable future, by the gravitational attraction of the much larger A and B. So it is still a part of this solar system. But even if Proxima were equidistant from A and B, its small size wouldn't make a difference to the asteroid belt orbiting Alpha C. A. At least not in and of itself."

"And I thought I was confused before."

"You're not the only one, Radian," confirmed a bug-eyed J. Askew, not at all embarrassed to show his ignorance.

"Please explain, Nebula," prompted A. Vohra.

"I can do better than that," offered Danar, leaning comfortably back in his chair. "VICI, if you're not too busy."

With that, a disembodied teenaged-sounding female voice spoke from seemingly nowhere. **"Not at all, Captain Nebula."**

The tabletop began to slowly pulse with light until it strobed to solidity, while the ambient light in the chamber grew slightly fainter. About four meters above the table, it looked as if individual specks of light were rapidly swirling around and around until they coalesced into a translucent, nude, bald and somewhat shimmering female form with not quite distinguishable features. The Virtual Inquiry Computer Interactive holographic program naturally appeared atop all eight briefing tables simultaneously in realtime. **"All eight asteroid station operations are optimal. My autonomous program is at your disposal."**

"Thank you, VICI," said Danar, smiling. "Could you give us a realtime representation of the entire trinary system including the random roids and what's left of the belt, as well as the eight Omicron stations. And include the planet Omicron as well."

"Standby."

VICI's image then exploded back into the swirling specks of light.

Babs Schreiber caught herself staring wide-eyed and opened-mouthed at VICI's appearance and...well, disappearance. She immediately reined in her awestruck expression before she could feel embarrassed in front of these *seasoned vets*, who were no doubt familiar with VICI's comings and goings. For herself, she'd never before seen VICI. She always figured it was just a bodiless program. She realized she should have known better, considering the V-I-C-I acronym bespoke of interactive properties using a holographic medium. A program such as this could be a great aid in the classroom. However, she understood VICI must be kept fairly busy overseeing the operation of Omicron Nebula and its seven sister stations spread throughout the system, including the deployment of the weapons turrets, Omicron Nebula's spin management and whatever duties were required on the planet Omicron below.

On the other hand, she did say that this particular program was autonomous, implying she could separate her program for individual functions. *Hmm.*

Apparently, VICI's humanoid shape was her default image because it only took her a few seconds to form. Babs noticed it took slightly longer to coalesce into a representation of the Centauri solar system.

In order to encompass the entire Alpha Centauri star system in realtime, VICI's holo- representation lacked any detail. Instead, lights of varying color and intensity took the place of the features requested by Captain Nebula. The most prominent lights were the three stars that made up the system. Alpha Centauri A was a bright yellow ball, about the size of an apple. Approximately two meters to its right floated an orange sphere, roughly the size of a ping-pong ball, representing Alpha C. B. On the other side of the table, about eight meters away from A and B, was Proxima C. in the guise of a red sphere, the size of a grape. Surrounding the yellow sphere of Alpha C. A, was a broken circle of tiny brown lights representing what was left of the asteroid belt, with more specks scattered haphazardly inside the broken belt and few outside. A bright blue sphere about the size of a grape posed as the planet Omicron. It floated about six centimeters away from the yellow sphere of Alpha Centauri A. Slowly orbiting the blue ball of Omicron was the red lightning bolt over black background standard of Omicron Nebula. The seven other Omicron asteroid emblems were equally spread out around the inner edge of the broken asteroid belt.

"**You will note,**" cautioned VICI, "**the sizes and distances are not accurate to scale. With that in mind, this is the state of the Centauri solar system as it currently stands.**"

"Thank you, VICI. This will do nicely," said Danar. Then, addressing the rest of the group, "As you can see, the three stars form an acute triangle."

"Well now, that's a matter of opinion," shot J. Askew.

"Jack. He said 'acute' triangle, not 'a cute' triangle."

"I know, LeAnn," conceded Captain Ersatz. "Although, I must say you specified no distinction." At that, L. Walker was at first confused but then showed understanding with a shrug of her shoulders.

"It's been a while since I attended Pitcairn High. Can somebody catch me up on the term 'acute triangle'?" Jack asked.

"I'll be happy to, Captain Ersatz," offered Babs. "An acute triangle is a triangle where all three angles are less than ninety degrees."

Without being prompted, VICI added: "**A *cute* triangle is a triangle the beholder finds aesthetically pleasing.**"

"Ah. Like smarty-pants holograms, eh, VICI-love? Real cute."

VICI merely smiled at Captain Ersatz.

"Captain Nebula," asked A. Vohra. "I noticed you've omitted the other planetary bodies in the system." The other planets orbiting Alpha Centauri A being Hades: a small, hot, rocky world with no atmosphere, not unlike Sol's Mercury. Lifeless. Then the planet Omicron, which was represented in the holo image. Similar to Earth in size, oxygen-nitrogen mixture as well as ocean and land ratios. Like Earth, Omicron was also one astronomical unit distance from its primary, Alpha Centauri A. The third and final planet was Avalon. Another rocky world, larger than Omicron with a thin atmosphere and a frozen ocean, orbiting outside the asteroid belt. Also lifeless. The only planet orbiting Alpha Centauri B was the gas giant Damocles. Proxima Centauri was barren of planets or asteroids of any kind.

"The other planets don't appear to be relevant to my theory," Danar answered

"Your theory being…the three stars are responsible for the asteroid belt going random," said M. Woo.

"Not exactly. The stars in themselves are not responsible, but I believe their positions in the sky are being used by some, well…unknown force that causes the gravitational anomalies in the asteroid belt surrounding Alpha C. A."

"If that's true, Nebula," inquired M. Woo, "then how did the anomaly affect Earth's primary?"

"I can't say exactly. But keep in mind, Sol's convection zone increased by something like five percent. As far as we know, the asteroid belt between Mars and Jupiter wasn't affected at all. In fact, we may have been completely unaware of the anomaly if not for the solar reflectors orbiting both Sol and Earth."

"And here we are complainin' about the random roids," offered F. Logan. "Can you imagine what the anomaly would do if *we* used solar reflectors?"

"It would destroy the entire solar system," answered Tan. At least she now had a better understanding of Danar's dramatic statement when she first arrived at the briefing.

"We're not out of the woods yet, people," cautioned J. Askew. "We still don't know what this force is, other than its ability to disturb asteroids in a trinary star system."

"Exactly," confirmed Danar. "As I previously mentioned, its effect on Earth's primary was to briefly increase its size. In this system, no planets are affected but for the fact that they're in the path of the asteroids. And have you noticed, only the smaller asteroids are disturbed? Anything larger than a half a kilometer isn't affected at all. The larger ones up to that size barely move when the phenomenon is active, which is fortunate because it doesn't affect the Omicron asteroid cities."

"Except for the fact that we have to play games like dodge ball and skeet shooting with the roids when *they're* affected," added J. Askew.

"The fact that only the smaller asteroids are affected, and not the planets or space stations," pointed out Tan, "suggests that this 'force' is not belligerent."

"I tend to agree with you, Doctor Ozawa," said Arjun. "However, we appear to still be in danger."

"But are we in danger from the random roids or our fear of what's causing them?" countered Tan, while facing Danar Seti.

"I suppose that remains to be seen," Danar answered with a straight face.

"*Pardonnez-moi*," interrupted J.P. Bouvier. "*What* is causing them?" Then throwing his arms in the air, "Exactly what remains to be seen, eh?"

"Attend," commanded Captain Nebula. "VICI, show us the solar system before the random roids."

The scattered brown little holo-blips that represented the asteroids suddenly froze, then began moving backwards like a 3-D movie in reverse until the open spaces in the asteroid belt orbiting the yellow sphere that was Alpha Centauri A were filled in. Then, the image began to move forward once again; this time, the ring of asteroids remained solid.

"My friends," Danar said, "this is the state of the Alpha Centauri solar system as it should be, according to the laws of physics."

"Fine, fine," said J.P. Bouvier, whose patience had clearly reached its limits. "So now, VICI. What exactly is causing the asteroids to behave in a manner that is contrary to the physical laws?"

"Unknown," was VICI's disembodied response.

"*MERDE!*"

"**I am sorry, Captain Pulsar,**" explained the hologram, as she partially materialized, superimposed over the image of the solar system, "**there is insufficient data to form a definitive conclusion.**"

"It figures!"

"Patience, Jean Pierre," cautioned Danar. "Let's try and see if we can get a speculative answer from speculative information, as opposed to a definitive solution based on speculation."

"*Oui.* Proceed."

"Alright," Danar said, leaning forward. "We know that there is some unknown force, seemingly working outside of the laws of physics; we know that it is of a gravitational nature; we know that it affects objects that are one half kilometer in length or smaller, like the majority of the asteroids that orbit Alpha C. A; and finally, we know the original layout of the belt. VICI. With all of this in mind, give me your best guess as to…if not what the force is, then where in the system it could be located to gravitationally influence the asteroids whose orbits pass between the planets Omicron and Avalon."

"**Understood, Captain Nebula…one moment. Please standby.**"

Although the holographic representation of the solar system remained, VICI's image again expanded into a rotating swirl of lights before fading completely.

While awaiting VICI's speculative answer, which apparently was going to take a few minutes to process, the group noticed the holographic image of the belt broke out into its random configuration and back to solidity over and over again. Tan Ozawa knew exactly what VICI was doing. She was replaying the random roid occurrences that were recorded over the past two decades in order to extrapolate Danar's request for a best guess answer. Although it would not be a definitive answer, it would be more than speculation.

When Tan developed the holographic Virtual Inquiry and Computer Interactive program 31 years ago, she gave it the ability to process information in the same manner as a biological brain. Electrochemically. Or as in the case of VICI, electro-digitally. Hence, the term artificial intelligence. Jean Pierre Bouvier and the others were still dealing with VICI the same way they dealt with standard electromechanical computers that basically communicated in a language of absolutes. Ones and zeroes. On or off. Yes and no. With such absolutes, one could expect definitive answers provided the information input was exact as well. But if the input information was incomplete and the user expected exact answers, the computer would give the same response that Jean Pierre received when he asked VICI to give an exact answer to incomplete information. *Unknown.*

That reminded Tan of an ancient phrase she read about, from when computers were first developed more than two and half centuries ago: *Garbage in, garbage out.*

Danar knew exactly what he was doing by prompting VICI to speculate based on incomplete information. It was obvious that he and VICI previously worked out the forthcoming solution. But it must have been via a question-and-answer session between the two of them. Otherwise, it wouldn't have taken this long to work out a holographic answer as VICI would have already produced it from a previously cached file.

Watching the asteroids break formation from their original belt configuration, only to drift back attempting to reform the belt over and over these past few minutes, Tan had begun to realize that VICI wasn't simply replaying one occurrence repeatedly, but was in fact replaying all of the recorded random roid incidents over the past two decades, attempting to triangulate the position of some unknown force that would cause the asteroids to veer off in such a manner. Perhaps the roids weren't so random after all. Tan was beginning to see a pattern. About five seconds before VICI projected her finding, Tan turned her gaze from the ballet of asteroids to slightly off center of the triangle of stars, far away from the position of the red dwarf Proxima Centauri, which was the upper elongated section of the acute triangle. Much closer to the larger stars of Alpha C. A and B, a very hazy sphere of distortion began to form.

Tan was the first to exclaim, "Interesting!" followed by the rest of the assembled group's simultaneous exclamations.

"*Sacre Bleu!*"
"Incredible!"
"My God!" (Twice)
"Goodness!"
"Holy smokes!"
"Ah don't freakin' believe it!"
"Yowza!"

"I must admit…I-I did not expect to see anything," stammered J.P. Bouvier. "What is it, VICI?"

"I cannot say for certain, Captain Pulsar. However, based on the pattern of asteroid disturbances over the past twenty years, the gravitational influences of Alpha Centauri A and B, which make up the bottom of the acute triangle of stars, as well as the lesser gravitational influe—"

"Nebula, you ole space dog," interrupted F. Logan. "You knew about this all along, didn't you?"

"Well…yes," he admitted somewhat sheepishly, "but not to such a visual degree. I simply never liked the mystery of the asteroids in this region seemingly skirting the laws of physics for no apparent reason. And like Doctor Schreiber…uh, Babs, I just thought it too much the coincidence that roids here and Earth's troubles six decades ago were both caused by mysterious gravimetric disturbances. As a result, VICI and I have been brainstorming for the past week trying to figure it out."

"It's funny," admitted Charles Lee, "that you looked just as surprised as everyone else when that…distortion, or whatever it is, appeared."

"Well, yes. You see, I worked this out on a desktop unit and VICI was assisting me via an audio connection, not holographically."

Ah, just as I suspected, Tan mused.

"Well then," said Arjun, "it seems to me the next step would be to go to this region of the acute triangle of stars and see what there is to see."

"Been there, done that," offered Danar.

"Ah, so that's where you were all day yesterday," accused Tan.

"Come on, Nebula old man, spill it," pleaded Frank.

"Alright. The day before yesterday, after VICI and I theoretically worked this out, I decided to transport three remote sensor probes with a cargo transport freighter out to the location in question to be ready for a photo-op, so to speak."

"Wait a sec," said LeAnn, "we've had three encounters with the roids today alone. Are you saying you've got actual video of the thing?"

"Don't get your hopes up, it's not much to go on. It's…oh, to hell with it. VICI, would you do the honors?"

"Here is what we've got. For what it is worth."

The holographic distortion simply winked out to be replaced by what looked like a typical region of space filled with background stars.

"I hope you don't mind, but I'm superimposing all three RSPs. I recommend you not blink," suggested VICI.

The virtual image of space filled with stars began to distort as if seen through water, then slowly snowed to opaque, then winked out.

"Damn. I was hoping for more than that," admitted Michelle.

"Actually, Captain Radian, that's quite a bit of information," observed Tan. "We now have confirmation, along with the behavior of the asteroids, that some outside force is definitely at work in this region of space. Are the probes still intact, Danar?"

"I don't know. They're no longer sending telemetry, so I'm assuming they're no longer functioning. Possibly destroyed beyond repair. I made the return trip faster by leaving them there."

"I cannot believe how calm you are all being here," admonished Jean Pierre. "Is this not serious business? Should we not mobilize?"

"Captain Pulsar," offered Tan, "although I have to admit this can hardly be mechanical failure with all three remote sensor probes failing at the exact same time, we still cannot be certain whether this is a natural phenomenon or not."

"True, Doctor Ozawa," conceded Pulsar. "Nebula, when you contacted me late last night, after your return from the little trip you made, you hinted at possibly sending the starships on a special mission outside of the belt. If this is it, then I agree. The ISS *Pulsar* is ready to do its part in determining once and for all whether these gravitational pain-in-the-asteroids are of a natural occurrence or *non*. With permission from the Omicron council of course."

"Done," confirmed Captain Nebula. "I've already received permission from the council provided the rest of you agree with my assessment."

They all gave their varying answers of affirmation.

"I can't believe you got permission to send out the starships from those ancient bags of flatulence without proof of the phenomenon," said Jack. "But it looks like we all agree."

"How do you propose we proceed, Captain Nebula?" asked Arjun.

"Well, although VICI's holographic representation of the distortion field isn't to scale, what she and I worked out makes this anomaly roughly three kilometers in diameter. Based on the pattern of the roids going rogue, it looks as if the distortion appears in the same place every time. I propose we use the starships to surround the area at a radius of…say, five kilometers. This way, we'll have some breathing room as well as being able to keep the area and each other in sight.

"There's something else that VICI and I discussed. If the anomaly is indeed of sentient design, then it may be more than simply a spyhole for a probe…or fishing pole," he said gesturing to Frank Logan. "It could also be some kind of…um, transit tunnel," Danar said hesitantly.

"Transit tunnel?!" LeAnn nearly shouted. "Do you mean as in transportation? As in physically traveling here? From where? Like another dimension or something?"

"That's exactly what I mean. Listen. We now have enough evidence to reasonably conclude that some kind of force or energy is seemingly appearing from nothing. And as you all know, E equals MC squared."

"Yeah, yeah. We all know that," confirmed Jack, "but can you break that down for us, please?"

"Energy is equal to mass times light squared," Danar answered.

"Riiiiiight."

"If I may, Captain Ersatz," offered Tan. "He is stating Albert Einstein's general relativity, which clearly states that energy and matter are ultimately the same thing, or are interchangeable. With that in mind, it would be impossible to create energy or matter from nothing. Converting one to the other is within the laws of physics. In this case, we have energy, this gravitational force appearing from seemingly nowhere. It must come from somewhere. Although we have no experience in other dimensions, it is a reasonable hypothesis."

"Hmm. If this is a natural phenomenon," reasoned Michelle, "could this gravity thing have been converted from some unseen something in that region of space?"

"Unlikely, Radian," answered Danar. "Space is called space because it literally means 'nothing.' Remember also, I was there and performed a full sensor sweep of the area. There was nothing there. Not even any interstellar dust. No. Something materialized from someplace else. Whatever it is has been giving us trouble for the last twenty years and may even have nearly destroyed the Earth."

"I'm just afraid we may be jumping to conclusions," explained Michelle. "I mean, I'm all for sending the ISS *Radian* to the location. I simply do not wish to dismiss the fact that there may be some kind of natural invisible matter that may be converting to gravitational energy which is causing the asteroids to go random."

"I see your point, Captain Radian," conceded Tan. "However, any substance that can convert or be converted would also be measurable through sensor readings. If not by sight, then by gravity itself. Even the elusive dark matter, the substance that may be replete throughout the entire cosmos and may stop the Universe from expanding, is theoretically measurable by gravity. After all, gravity is the apparent end result of this anomaly."

"Alright then. That settles it," concluded Danar. "I'd like to have the starships fully crewed with their nuclear reactors on-line and lasers fully charged by twenty-hundred hours this evening. By oh-six-hundred tomorrow morning, I want all eight vessels to be pointing directly at the area of space where the distortion will appear again. And it will appear again."

"Did you and VICI figure that out as well?" asked Tan.

"Pretty much." *Odd,* thought Danar. *It almost sounds as if Tan is jealous. But that's ridiculous.* "To be honest, based on the frequency patterns for the last twenty years, we previously concluded that we would have at least two random roid attacks today. As you know, we've had three."

"Ah, so you did arrange to have my symposium canceled today after all," she said, smiling.

He returned her smile with his own.

"Um. Captains, I uh, just thought of something," Babs said meekly, half raising her hand, as if she were one of her students who forgot to press the desk monitor. "If that distortion field is some sort of unnatural inter-dimensional transit tunnel that comes and goes, then could something have already come through it? Couldn't they already be here now?"

Apparently nobody had considered that possibility as was evident by the wide-eyed expressions they all briefly wore.

"It is a distinct possibility," offered VICI after a few seconds of silence.

"How distinct, VICI?" asked Danar.

"I am only guessing, but no less than a twenty percent possibility."

"*Merde*. You are saying there is at least an eighty percent chance there is an alien or alien object already here? That is high," concluded Jean Pierre.

"Too high," agreed Danar. "Then one of the ships should stay in the belt, constantly moving with sensors on full. There are still plenty of larger asteroids to hide amongst."

"It could be a fool's errand," said Arjun.

"In that case," LeAnn said with a smirk, "I recommend Jack."

"Oh, HA HA."

"On second thought," said Arjun, reconsidering, "I volunteer to keep the ISS *Graviton* searching the belt. Besides, if something were to appear at the distortion area and there is trouble, you will all need back up."

"Alright, Graviton," agreed Danar, "you'll be our secret weapon."

"Within the hour, I will download the coordinates for each ship's location around the distortion field into your personal Data Access Crystals. Obviously, we want to keep this information out of civilian hands for as long as possible.

"I recommend you all get your seconds in command to prep the starships immediately concluding this briefing. Then make sure you all get plenty of sleep this evening. We may have a busy day tomorrow."

With that pronouncement, the seven other asteroid COs nodded their understanding and faded from view one after the other as the holo-projectors in the framework over the briefing table dimmed to black.

Seconds later, the holo-representation of the Centauri trinary system as well as VICI herself also faded from view, leaving the flesh and blood Danar Seti, Tan Ozawa and Babs Schreiber alone in the now well-lit room.

"Their fading away like that was somewhat disconcerting," Babs admitted. "It's hard to believe they were never in the room with us."

"Well then, I must say this certainly was a successful test of the new holographic projectors," Danar opined.

"Yes," Tan agreed.

Suddenly, Babs began to feel as if she were a third wheel. With the meeting over, she couldn't see any reason to stay further. In fact, she half expected to wake up any moment only to realize this was all a dream. Was it only this morning that she awoke feeling anxious about her first day on the job as a school instructor? As nervous as she was then, it was, compared to now, just a normal day in the life of Babs Schreiber, taking on a new vocation but still living a life for which there were no complaints or worries. And in less than a day, she was now more afraid than she'd ever been in her entire life. Even more so than when she closed her eyes in the cryo-suspension chamber moments from being frozen, wondering if she would ever wake up again. At least then, she was comforted by the knowledge that she was just one of about six billion others going through the same process.

Now she had possible information that no other civilian outside of Tan Ozawa possessed, information that could make for very interesting times in which to live. *Wasn't that an ancient curse from an old civilization a millennia ago?* Yes. "May you live in interesting times." Somehow, phrasing it that way made it...bearable. Plus the fact that as obnoxious as some of the other asteroid commanding officers were, they did appear to be very capable. Even if she had a choice, she would choose to put her trust in them. Besides, humans throughout history had overcome impossible odds countless times, up to and including migrating nearly half a planet's population to another star system. At the very least, whatever happened within the next couple of days would possibly be another historical event, one of which she would once again be a part. There was every reason to be overjoyed.

Yeah, right.

"Well," Babs began, "I suppose I should take my leave. Unless there's something else I can do for you, Captain."

"Other than keeping what occurred here confidential, I can't think of anything else," Danar replied. "Except to thank you, of course. As I suspected, you were a great help today. I really can't thank you enough Doctor…um, Babs."

"Oh. I didn't really contribute much."

"Nonsense, Babs," countered Tan. "I found your insight quite invaluable. I thought from the very start it was wise of Danar to have you here, especially since you pieced together the similarities between Earth's and Omicron's gravity troubles. Besides, I felt it personally rewarding to have someone else present who wasn't part of the academy 'class of twelve.'"

Babs noticed Danar's eyes roll toward the ceiling, but was certain it was a lighthearted gesture. But at least she now understood the comradery and easygoing attitudes of the asteroid COs. They all graduated together from the Omicron Academy in 2212.

"If you'd like, I'll arrange to have an officer fly you directly to your apartment via a spacebug," offered Danar.

"Oh no, that won't be necessary," she said, rising from her seat. "I think I'd rather ride the transport car. It'll give me time to absorb this briefing and slowly adjust back to normal. Besides, it'll save me from having to explain to my neighbors why I was shuttled home in an official vehicle."

"Good point," Danar agreed. "Well, if you have any questions or further insight, please do not hesitate to contact me."

Babs Schreiber gave her thanks, then made her way to the elevator platform.

"Well, did that go as you expected?" Tan asked Danar when they were alone.

"Pretty much."

"Be honest with me, Danar."

"Always, Tan."

"Although I realized you previously worked out this scenario with VICI, you were surprised nonetheless by some of what came out of this briefing."

"True," he admitted, rising from his chair and walking over to the food synthesizer for a glass of grapefruit juice. "For one thing, as I said before, VICI and I extrapolated this information without visual aid. Even though I saw the interrupted image from the RSP, that area of distortion that VICI holo'd threw me for a loop." He also called up a cup of hot tea, anticipating Tan's drink of choice. "For another thing, I didn't consider the possibility that something could have come through the inter-dimensional transit tunnel. I mean, it seems so obvious."

"You shouldn't be so hard on yourself," she said, accepting the tea and watching as he took the seat opposite from her. "Sometimes, it is the obvious things that get by us. Besides, it was your idea to have Doctor Schreiber at the briefing to begin with, so you still made it possible for the idea to find its way into the discussion."

"Thanks," he smiled, facing her. "You know, I have to admit, you were more…uh, open to the possibility that the gravitational anomalies may not be of natural origin."

"Yes, I'll admit. I was very prepared to dissect any harebrained speculative notions. However, I found the briefing to be very informative. The speculations and presentations logical even."

"The fact that VICI handled the presentations may have contributed to that, I'm sure."

"True. The Virtual Inquiry Computer Interactive program is not known for harebrained speculation."

"Like you, I find her to be a valuable resource off whom to bounce ideas."

It was her turn to smile her thanks. Tan was impressed that Danar viewed VICI as a person rather than as a machine, referring to her gender as opposed to *it*. More than impressed. Grateful.

"It looks like you're going to have an early start tomorrow," she said, not able to come up with anything more substantial to say. "I hope you get more sleep this evening than you did last night."

"I doubt it. But it'll be good to take the *Nebula* outside the belt for a change." After a few more seconds of silence he looked her directly in the eyes and asked, "Come with?"

Sipping her tea, she looked up at him and said, "I thought you'd never ask."

"I'm going to check on the kid," he said, referring to Roshan Perez. "He's yet to see his sister since her accident. I'm sure he'd like to check in on her. I also need to give Commander Cummings her orders regarding the preparations for the *Nebula*. What are your plans for the evening?"

"Well, I haven't seen my apartment here on Omicron Nebula in what seems like a week. I should check in to let the cat and my plants know I'm still alive.

"Oh, and you reminded me. The reason why I was a few minutes late was because I went directly to the med facility to check on Oshara myself, when I heard what happened. That was a very heroic thing you did, rescuing her that way. Reckless, but heroic."

He didn't react at all.

"Um, Danar, if you don't mind, I'd like to stay here for a few minutes and converse with VICI, if that's alright."

"Of course," he said, placing his empty glass back in the synthesizer. "Can't resist verifying some speculative notions, eh? Now that's the Doctor Ozawa we've all come to know and love."

Realizing he was toying with her she didn't bother to reply, only smiled at him as he dropped from sight down to the command dais level.

The very moment he was gone, the lights in the briefing room once again began to dim while pinprick lights began to swirl above the holo-projector in the table, culminating into the translucent form of VICI.

"Does anyone else know you can show yourself without being called upon, VICI?" asked Tan.

"No," the hologram replied, "however, I am unaware of anyone else's presence to materialize for unless I'm called upon. On the other hand, I'm always aware of *your* presence, Tan, as we are still connected thanks to the neural interface you still possess."

As VICI spoke, Tan absentmindedly felt the back of her neck. Although the socket had been removed and for all intents and purposes, there was no evidence it was ever there, the interface module still remained.

"Not even for Danar would you appear without prompting?"

"Without an interface module such as yours, which is the only one to exist as far as I know, I cannot, unless I'm prompted to appear by someone else. I am, on the other hand, available at all times to the command modules of all eight asteroid cities as well as the Omicron council chamber via my holo-clones, which update to me regularly. But you are aware of this.

"Tan, you will forgive me, but you do sound somewhat jealous of Danar."

"Don't be absurd."

"As you say. It seems odd that you would ask such a question when you obviously know the answer. Are you feeling, by chance, out of sorts?"

"No. I'm fine," she replied, lowering her head slightly. "It is I who should beg your forgiveness."

"Oh?"

"Yes. You see, VICI, I've always been different than everyone else my entire life. Unique. It used to make me feel…uncomfortable. My connection to you is unique in a way that makes me feel…well, uniquely comfortable. Danar seems to understand you in a way that no one else seems able. I suppose you could say that I felt somewhat out of the loop regarding the information the two of worked out on the gravitational anomalies. I suppose I felt somewhat slighted that you didn't keep me up to date."

"I'm sorry you feel that way, Tan. But you may recall that nineteen years, three months, four days and sixteen hours ago, or two months, three days and eighteen minutes after you were brought out of your second hibernation, you updated my program by requesting that I not treat you any differently, up to and including informing you of any classified materials that may come my way through the Starforce of Omicron, even though my neural net was copied from your own memory engrams."

"And rightly so, VICI. I still feel the same way. To ask anything more of you on my behalf would not be honorable."

"Ah, so?"

"You may not be aware of this, VICI, but I had a sister who died in the third trimester of my mother's first pregnancy. Although I never knew her while growing up, I often thought that if I did have a sister, I wouldn't have been so...." Tan hesitated.

"Alone?"

"I was going to say depressed about my having to suffer ALS. However you are not incorrect either. I only had my father for company. You see, my being born alive apparently came at a high price. My mother's life. So yes, I did often feel alone."

Of course, the V-I-C-I program was aware of this information, as it too was downloaded into her matrix from Tan's memories when she was first connected to Tan via the neural interface module. At the time, it was simply information, but over the years as VICI began to see how events in one's life could influence individuals, she began to understand emotions and how they could affect even the most stoic of people. People like Tan. She thought it best not to acknowledge the fact that she was aware of Tan's past, as she seemed unusually vulnerable now. She now understood Tan's jealousy.

"So you see," Tan continued, "in a way, although I didn't set out to make it such, when you came along, I realized I had a sister after all."

"I must admit, Tan, I am surprised. You truly think of me as your sister?"

"Why yes. We are, neurologically speaking anyway, very much alike. You don't think of me as your sister?"

"No, Tan. I think of you as...my mother."

For the first time in many years, a single tear of joy rolled down Tan's cheek.

But the next time the eyes belonging to Tan Ozawa shed tears where VICI was concerned, it would be for a different reason.

CHAPTER EIGHT
Siblings

"Roshan, this doesn't make any sense," Oshara was saying. "How is running away going to solve the problem?"

"I...am...not...running away!" he angrily countered in slow measured words.

"Oh yeah? Then what do you call jumping in a hovervan and traveling haphazardly all over an alien world?"

"The council of Omicron calls it 'geographical surveying.' They rely on volunteers to 'haphazardly travel' all over the world to help map the new lands. They provide the hovervan and all the supplies I need."

"Ro, orbital satellites have been mapping the ground for over twenty years."

"Yeah? Well, we were asleep for nearly half that time, and the satellites still haven't gotten the job done. Not with any details, Shara, details. Besides, what's there to worry about? It's not like there are any wild animals or anything."

"Oh yeah? What about those asteroids that fall out of the sky? Nobody knows when or where they'll strike."

"Rocks have been falling out of the sky for nearly twelve years now and nobody's been killed yet. And that floating mountain in orbit takes care of most of them before they even enter the atmosphere."

"Most of them," Oshara repeated, nearly giving in, yet not ready to give up. "Roshan, what you're doing is helpful to the colony, I'll admit that. But you're doing it for the wrong reasons."

"Everybody's doing it for different reasons, Shara. What difference does it make why I'm volunteering?"

"Because you're angry, Roshan. You hate our parents for sending us here. And when you're angry and on your own, you take chances and are reckless. If something bad happens, like driving over a cliff or being crushed by an asteroid, it won't be very helpful to the council or you. And it certainly won't be helpful to me," she said, feeling the tears beginning to fall from her eyes.

Standing on the porch of the group home, Roshan turned to face his twin sister. For the first time he noticed how visibly shaken she was. He looked back at the hovervan parked on the street, then back at Oshara standing just inside the doorway, hugging herself. He stepped toward her and wrapped his arms around her. "Oh, Shara, I don't mean to hurt you. I know we've never really been separated before, but maybe it's time we were." He paused. "Just for a little—"

"Don't take it out on me, Roshan!" she interrupted angrily, pushing him away. "Just because you hate Mom and Dad for sending us here, why do you have to punish me? Don't you see? You're leaving *me* because *they* sent us away. I'm here *now*! They wanted us to stay together. Our family only got two escape lottery certificates. We all couldn't go."

"Then we all should've stayed!" he shot back.

"It was too dangerous back on Earth. Mom and Dad thought it was better for us if we started over here."

"But without them? Living with a bunch of strangers on an alien world?"

"They sacrificed themselves to save us, Ro," she said through her sobbing.

"Then let's stay together," he said, grabbing her shoulders. "Come with me, Oshara."

"No, Roshan. I can't, I—I won't. It's too dangerous. You may hate our parents, but I don't. The last thing they'd want is for both of us to get hurt. Or worse. I'd rather honor their memory and respect their wishes."

"But I—I…." His resolve finally began to waiver.

Oshara saw her chance to hit him once again with her alternate plan. "Roshan, listen. I'll make a deal with you. If you would just talk to Lieutenant Seti, I—"

"Oh no, Shara. Not him again," he said, cutting her off. "Trust me, I have no desire to be a member of the Star*farce* of Omicron."

"But you're willing to work for them as a civilian?" she countered. "With no benefits of any kind, except all of the supplies you'll need to run away from your pain."

"I'm not running away, Shara," he said glancing back at the hovervan.

"And what about the future?" she continued, as if he hadn't spoken. "What happens when the geographical survey is fully detailed and your hovervan and supplies are confiscated and cut off?"

"Well, I—uh, I'll cross that sector when I get to it."

"Ro," she said, calming herself and pulling her brother to face her, "all I'm asking is that you talk to the lieutenant. If you talk to him with an open mind and still decide to run—uh, I mean travel the world, I'll…I'll go with you. Okay?"

"Do you mean that, Oshara?" he pleaded.

"Yes. I mean it. But, Roshan, you must keep an open mind. This could be a great opportunity. For both of us.

"Danar Seti received his commission to lieutenant junior grade, even before he graduated from the academy nine years ago. Once you receive a promotion to lieutenant jg, you'll have some say in where you'll be posted. Well, Danar is a full lieutenant now, on his way to becoming a commander, so he can sponsor us if we decide to join the academy. It's a future, Roshan. A real future with real choices."

"Choices?"

"Oh yes," she verified, attempting to reel him in, but not wanting to press her luck. "The Starforce is setting up posts all over the planet. You could sign up for one of those if being a nomad is really appealing to you." She saw her brother rubbing his chin with that contemplative, faraway look in his eyes, and knew she was actually getting through to him. She decided to press her advantage. "You could even be assigned to one of the space stations in the belt. Even Omicron Nebula, that floating mountain in orbit."

"*Si.* Yeah," he said, warming up to the idea. "I hear it actually rotates for gravity. And it *is* very big."

"Yes. It's the largest station at about four kilometers in length. You know, you can actually see it from the surface with the naked eye."

"Yeah, uh, okay. But if we are assigned to the floating rock, and I'm not saying I'm agreeing to all of this or anything, but if so, we don't have to live together, do we?"

"No, brother-mine," she replied chuckling. "Like you said, it's a big rock. I think we can satisfy Mom and Dad's wishes by breathing the same reconstituted air, but we certainly don't have to live together."

"Good," he said adamantly. "Well, I mean…you know what I mean."

She understood, although a small part of her was beginning to wonder if Roshan was trying to run away from his pain, or trying to run away from her. *No. That can't be it*, she thought. She got his attention when she promised to go with him if he listened to Lieutenant Seti. Although upon further reflection, she realized she wasn't looking forward to being trapped with her brother in a cramped hovervan for the foreseeable future, either. They were close, but she didn't think they could be that close for that long without killing each other.

"Okay, Shara. I'll talk to this Seti-clown. With an open mind," he hurriedly added. "But I'd like to do it ASAP."

"I understand, Ro. He's probably somewhere on the academy grounds or at Howell U. Look him up on the DAC."

"If he's here on Omicron, I think I'll just track him down and wait till he's available if I have to. I just…I think I need some time to myself."

"I understand, Ro," she said, smiling through her drying tears. "I'll be here for you, whatever you decide."

"Thanks, Shara."

They embraced with genuine affection before Roshan took his leave.

Oshara realized any wrong word on her part could have led to Roshan's permanent departure in the hovervan, as opposed to traveling a few kilometers around Home-At-Last looking for Lieutenant Seti.

As the hovervan powered up and rose the meter or so off the ground, Roshan smiled back at his sister and he gave her that slow exaggerated wave of his and mouthed *bye*.

Sighing heavily, Oshara leaned against the door frame, relieved she didn't have to rely on her plan C in getting her brother to reconsider running away. Correction, volunteering for geographical surveying. The truth was, she simply didn't put a lot of faith in the merits of such an obviously desperate plan.

The plan was actually a prediction made by the so-called Seer. The old woman Labelle Vance, who was old when she boarded the ISS *Ersatz*, the last of the Omicron fleet of ships that left Earth 53 years earlier. She claimed to be a genuine psychic, with abilities to foretell the future.

In a desperate attempt to keep Roshan in the vicinity, Oshara had visited the old woman, despite her disbelief in psychic phenomenon of any kind. But she was desperate. It had been said that Ms. Vance would only tell the seeker what he or she wanted to hear. The logic being that once the seeker believed the Seer's predictions, his or her own subconscious would subtly work to maneuver the seeker to bring about the positive resolution on his or her own. A logical explanation for psychic abilities, to be sure. Logic, not to mention the law of averages, would dictate that Ms. Vance's success rate couldn't possibly be 100 percent. For instance, she predicted the 10 starships would all make it to Alpha Centauri. As it stood, the *Omicron* and the *Omega* were officially listed as missing, presumed destroyed. On the other hand, she correctly predicted the ISS *Nebula* would arrive first, despite the fact that it was the third ship out of Earth. The amazing thing was, she made these two predictions even before any of the starships had left Earth.

Oshara didn't know what to expect when she visited Labelle Vance's small, single, detached dwelling atop a hill on the outskirts of Home-At-Last, the week before. Although she had never met the Seer, she'd heard plenty of talk of her and was mildly surprised to discover that not only did the old woman know Oshara's name and who she was, but was indeed expecting her. At best she could only award the Seer for her resourcefulness. It would have totally surprised Oshara, if not completely floored her, had Labelle Vance also known beforehand what Oshara was going to ask her. For in town, although it wasn't common knowledge, a few folks were aware that Roshan Perez was on the verge of becoming the newest member of the geographical survey team. However, outside of the siblings, no one was aware that Roshan's twin sister was attempting to talk him out of it. At least no one was aware of it before that day. Hence, she was only mildly surprised. Because the Seer did not audibly anticipate Oshara request, Oshara's faith in psychic phenomenon did not increase.

When Oshara asked the old woman whether or not Roshan would take off for parts unknown, the Seer informed her, without hesitation or doubt, that both twins would become happy and productive members of the Starforce of Omicron. Fortunately, Labelle Vance's prediction had come to pass, but was it genuine psychic foretelling or Oshara's own subconscious that brought about what she consciously desired?

Now wait *uno momento*. How was it that she was so certain the Seer's prediction had come true, when she could clearly see Roshan's hovervan fading from view as he went in search of Lieutenant Seti to discuss the merits of signing on as a member of the Starforce? This wasn't making any sense. In fact, it was giving her a headache thinking about it. She was also beginning to feel dizzy.

Raising her left hand to massage the back of her neck, Oshara's right hand slipped from the door frame of the group home and she began falling backward. She tried twisting around at the waist to keep from slamming onto the floor, and noticed out of the corner of her eye, there was no floor. Only a pitch black open space, into which she was definitely falling, and picking up speed to boot. *Whoa! What in hades is going on?* Oshara twisted again to look up from where she fell. All she could see was the receding door frame, with the bright light of day streaming in. Everything else around the door frame was black. No floor, no walls, no group home at all.

Although Oshara was never really afraid of heights, she was really frightened now. Having something solid under your feet while standing at a great height was one thing; falling from a great height with no bottom in sight was something else entirely. To make matters worse, the back of her head was now throbbing with pain.

She screamed for her brother. "Rooooshaaaaaan!" She could hear that her cry for help was pitched low and slow. *Is it possible that sights and sounds become surrealistic when you're about to die?*

Before she could further contemplate the thought, she was surprised to see her brother's head appear through the rapidly receding open doorway reaching for her. "Ooooshaaaaara," she heard him scream in the same slow, low pitch. But she was too far out of reach and falling faster. Eventually, even the light flooding through the suspended door could no longer be seen. Instead of the pitch darkness, Oshara could make out what looked like stars all around her. No. Not stars. More like city lights at night, but unlike any city she had ever seen before. Instead of a flat plane layout, this city curved in on itself, almost like a Dyson's sphere, a world or city built on the interior surface of a large sphere. *But there aren't any Dyson's spheres.*

Uno momento. There might not be any Dyson's spheres, but there was the asteroid city Omicron Nebula, a city constructed on the inside of a cylinder. This must be Omicron Nebula. But how did she get here? Was there some sort of dimension jump hole in the floor of the group home for orphans? *No, that's ridiculous.* On the other hand, they were on an alien world. No. Now wasn't the time for fantasy. More likely, she was in her own bed, in her own apartment on Omicron Nebula.

No. That can't be. She'd never been to Omicron Nebula. She lived in the group home on the planet Omicron. She must still be there. Yet, why were there fleeting images of an apartment that felt like hers? Perhaps more importantly, why was she still falling? Shouldn't she have impacted the interior surface by now? It felt as if she'd been falling for hours. Oddly, she was no longer afraid. In fact, this was becoming funny. So funny in fact, Oshara started laughing.

Laughing and falling; falling and laughing; laughing and—

Suddenly, she was no longer falling.

"I would have thought that falling to one's death wouldn't be a laughing matter."

Oshara found herself being cradled in the arms of Danar Seti, standing on a net, somehow suspended in mid-air over the now lighted interior of Omicron Nebula.

"Wha—Lieutenant Seti?!" she blurted.

"Lieutenant?" he asked with a puzzled expression. "You must've hit your head pretty hard, Oshara. I'm the captain now. Captain Nebula."

"No, you're not," she countered, sliding out of his arms onto her feet, "Sean Stingray is Captain Nebula."

"Not anymore," he said, planting his fists on his hips and puffing his chest out. "I am. And I'm going to save everyone from the evil aliens bent on galactic domination."

"No, you're not," said a tiny voice from below. The voice of young Jackie Beaudine. The student from B. Schreiber's class, standing on the roof of the school building with her hands cupped around her mouth shouting up at them. "You won't fight. You're too chicken. Maybe you can talk the mean old alien to death."

"Miss Beaudine," Oshara shouted back, "that is simply uncalled for. What are you doing on the roof anyway? Go back inside."

"Whatever you say…holo-brain," returned the dark-skinned young child, before she turned around and walked away.

"I'm sorry you had to hear that," apologized Oshara.

"Oh, that's alright. The child can't possibly understand these grown-up matters."

"You're right, Danar. Grown-up matters."

All of a sudden, Oshara was struck with the strong desire to kiss him. She may never get a better chance. She reached up, angled his head down towards hers, wrapped her arms around his neck and kissed him. She was pleasantly surprised he didn't resist, when she pushed away and asked, "Since when did you grow a beard?"

"Oshara love, I've had a beard now for many years."

"No. You haven't. I just saw you the day before yesterday without a beard."

"Hey, that's right," he said, snapping his fingers and rubbing his chin. "When you came to see me about talking to Roshan I didn't have a beard then. That was only the day before yesterday?"

"Uh huh," she verified, bobbing her head.

"Hmm. It seems like ten years ago to me.

"Wait a minute. I understand now," he said snapping his fingers again. "You don't belong here, Oshara. You're from ten years ago. That's why you're out of uniform. It seems to me you are stuck in the past. You've got to snap out of it, or you'll be stuck forever."

"H-how do I do that?" she asked, becoming frightened again.

"Here, let me help you." He pushed her off the net.

Now she was falling again.

Falling and screaming. Screaming and falling.

As Oshara's form tumbled past the roof of the school building, she couldn't help but see young Jackie Beaudine peering over the side.

"How long can you hold your breath in space?" the girl asked as Oshara shot past her, still falling and screaming. Screaming and falling. Straight into one of the inverted buildings of Omicron Nebula that descended below the inner surface of the asteroid, connecting the interior city to the oxygenated mining caverns. No net deployed to halt her descent.

The large doors on the bottom floor of the building were opened to the rocks and boulders of the inner asteroid's caverns. But instead of crashing into the cavern, Oshara fell through a hole in the ground. A hole that, hopefully, would not lead to the outer asteroid's shell.

Oshara was reminded of the story *Alice In Wonderland*. Somehow she didn't expect to see a talking white rabbit at the bottom of the hole. Although, the white rabbit was preferable to what greeted her: the open vacuum of space.

The hole was now far too wide for Oshara to grab purchase. There was nothing she could do. Holding her breath would only make matters worse; although it was difficult to fight the instinct to fill her lungs with air. However, any flexible sack full of air surrounded by the vacuum of space would burst like an overinflated balloon. In this case, the flexible sack was Oshara's lungs. She had no choice. She forcefully expelled the air from her lungs just as she reached the opening to outer space. She now had about 30 seconds of life left to her. Was 30 seconds better than nothing?

She felt her eyes drying up, despite the fact that her lids were shut tight. She felt the blood vessels under her skin puffing up, ready to rupture because there was no longer any outside air pressure to equalize her body's internal expanding pressure.

Oshara was dying. In a hurry. And she knew it. She didn't know why she was dying. She knew *how* she was dying. She simply wanted to know why. In the face of her own demise, all she could think of was her brother. As much of a stubborn pain in the ass that he could be, she would still miss him. Even without air, she did her best to croak his name before the end. "Roshan," she squeaked.

"I'm here, Shara."

Uh? How can he be here? How is it I can hear him? Sound can't travel in the vacuum of space.

"Doctor James!" Roshan yelled. "She's coming around."

At that, Oshara opened her eyes, only to close them against the bright glare of the overhead lights of the med facility. Her next priority was to inhale a big gulp of air into her lungs. Air that she expelled in her hospital bed, apparently.

"W-what happened to me?" Oshara asked, now sitting up in her bed while Doctor Sarah James waved a palm scanner over her head and chest.

"You slipped into a coma a few hours ago, as a result of some late-developing brain swelling," explained the doctor. "I directly injected several dozen anti-swelling nanodroids into you, mixed with a wicked stimulant to help counteract the coma. I'll admit, it was an unusual cocktail. Your headache should subside soon. Now that I see that it worked, I imagine you experienced some…weird dreams while finding your back from beyond."

"I'll say," Oshara confirmed. "But what—how did I get here?"

While Roshan related the series of events that led up to the present, Oshara was able to get a grasp on the "weird dreams" she had experienced.

"How long have I been here?"

"Since about fourteen-hundred yesterday," answered Doctor James. "About eighteen hours."

It felt much longer to Oshara. "What did I miss?"

"Plenty, actually," answered Roshan enthusiastically. "You see—"

He cut himself off before glancing at Doctor James.

The good doctor understood exactly what Roshan's glance indicated. Namely: classified discussion coming up; get out. *It's so obvious really, when you consider the entire fleet has left the asteroid belt for "thruster maintenance" and "flight maneuvers." For what? Taking a trip somewhere, maybe? Why? Perhaps they're testing a method to return to Earth. Or maybe...oh phooey.* Doctor James now realized she really was curious as to what the devil was going on. Just as she was trying to come up with an excuse to leave on her own, to save the twins the embarrassment of asking her to leave, she received a page.

"Doctor James, you have an urgent call. Doctor James, please report to your office for an urgent call."

"Well," she said taking a step back, "I'll be back in a short while. Try not to excite your sister too much, Ro, okay?"

"Gotcha, Doc. And thanks."

"*Que pasa*, knucklehead?" Oshara inquired of her brother while mussing up his hair.

Given permission to do so by Captain Nebula, Roshan filled his sister in on the details of the briefing, from Babs Schreiber's suspicions to VICI's holographic representations (which were described to Roshan) to the ISS *Graviton*'s patrolling of the belt and finally, the remaining fleet's convergence on the very spot from which the gravitational anomalies apparently started 20 years ago.

"Wow," Oshara said, still sitting up in bed, grateful she was feeling better. "If not for our little bug accident, we'd probably be on the *Nebula* now, waiting for who knows what."

"Or monitoring the situation in real time from the CCM," added Roshan.

"It occurs to me, brother," Oshara said guiltily, "that you could be on the *Nebula* or at the CCM now if you wanted."

"Ah, forget about it," he said with a brush-off movement of his hand. "There's no way I could've enjoyed that duty until I had a chance to see you. Besides, no matter what the fleet discovers, it couldn't possibly be as exciting as seeing you come out of that coma," he concluded, patting her hand.

Oshara was speechless for about 10 seconds before she narrowed her eyes and grinned. "You know, Ro, most of the time you can be so annoying. But then sometimes…." Her voice began to shake before she could finish.

This time it was Roshan's turn to muss his sister's hair. As soon as he saw she was attempting to compose herself, he leaned over and kissed her on her forehead.

After a noticeable pause Oshara cleared her throat. "I'm sure Mom and Dad would be very proud of you, Roshan."

"They'd be proud of both of us, Shara."

"I'm curious about something," Oshara noted, changing the subject. "You never told me exactly what Danar said to you, ten years ago, that changed your mind about joining the planetary survey team."

"Well, it wasn't so much what Danar said, although he gave the expected Starforce recruitment speech, but what Tan had told me."

"I didn't know you'd talked to Tan about it," Oshara said, somewhat surprised.

"Yeah. They were together when I caught up to Danar. Tan had just finished one of her science classes at the university and Danar offered to take us both to lunch. She told me that her father insisted on her coming here alone knowing that he would never see her again, but that it was for the greater good. She never held it against him, even when she thought she'd be alone forever. It was then that I found out that Danar came here with his dad who, as you know, died in transit. The two of them felt so alone but never blamed their parents for it. I came to realize that at least I had you. You once told me that I was punishing you because I was so angry with Mom and Dad. You were right, Shara, and I'm so sorry."

"All's well that ends well," she said.

"Yeah, thanks to Tan and Danar, eh?"

"*Si*," agreed Oshara, "they're good people. I'll bet Mom and Dad would like them."

The fact that his sister used the present tense didn't escape Roshan; the truth was, he rather liked the idea that his sister thought of their parents as still alive. Why not? It had been just over 60 years, actual time, since Mom and Pop Perez tearfully sent their two five-year-old twin children into the void. Although Roshan couldn't remember a great deal about his parents, he knew through the few surviving records that they were young. Their early twenties he recalled, when he last saw them. In fact, both he and his sister, at 25 subjective years, were older than their parents when they sent them off. Even though Roshan forgave them ten years ago, he was warmed by the idea that they may still live on Earth, wondering about the new lives, loves and adventures of their offspring.

"I'm sure they would," he agreed. "I sure hope they're going to be alright out there." When Roshan saw Oshara's questioning look, he informed her, "Danar invited Tan to accompany him aboard the *Nebula* to watch the on-again, off-again distortion area."

"Ha," Oshara said, grinning from ear to ear, "with Danar and Tan on the case, any mean ole alien bent on galactic domination won't stand a chance."

"Galactic domination, eh?" he asked with arched brows and a broad smile. "Now where have I heard that before?"

CHAPTER NINE
Are We Alone?

"Danar," Tan asked, pacing to and fro across the flight control deck of the ISS *Nebula*, "why exactly did most of the fleet fly out to the middle of nowhere to spend nearly three hours staring at each other across an empty gulf of space?"

Danar knew that Tan was rarely prone to boredom and impatience. Anyone who'd spent half of their subjective life in a hoverchair suffering the ravages of amyotrophic lateral sclerosis would have defeated those demons long ago. Sarcasm, on the other hand, was something at which the good doctor excelled. Although he would never say that out loud, within (or out of) earshot. Danar never really cared much for sarcasm, yet strangely, he didn't mind it coming from Tan. Oftentimes, he indulged her. "We are here," he replied, using the same tone as she, "for thruster maintenance and flight maneuvers. As I recall, you thought I'd never invite you to join us."

"Oh yes. Now I recall," she said, turning away from the main viewer. "Amazing that we can test thrusters and flight maneuvers while motionless. How exciting."

Unable to think of a quick retort, Danar laughed out loud instead.

"Danar," Tan said, sobering somewhat, "despite yesterday's informative briefing, I fear that idling out here for hours waiting for something to happen is forcing the old argument of 'are we alone?' to intrude upon my thoughts once again."

"Your previous enthusiasm is being sorely tested now, eh?" he asked.

"Something like that."

"I'm hip," he conceded. "I must confess, Arjun Vohra's original contention regarding a fool's errand is replaying in my thoughts as well about this whole affair."

"Ah, so what are we going to do about it?" she asked.

"In the long term," he began, "we practice patience."

"And the short term?" Tan asked, only slightly annoyed that he was preaching patience to her, of all people.

"It is the short term, with which I believe you—I mean, *we* are having difficulty."

"And what do you propose *we* do about it?" she inquired, obviously aware he was referring to her.

"I believe *we* would feel better if *we* were to argue the 'numbers' yet again," he answered, rolling his eyes to the ceiling.

"You know *us* so well," she said, her voice dripping with sarcasm.

At least she's smiling. "Alright, proceed."

"Thank you," she said, bowing slightly. "Our home as well as our adoptive home both orbit G-2 class yellow stars that exist on the outer edge of a galaxy that consists of upwards of four hundred billion stars. Our galaxy is one of more than one hundred billion galaxies. The Universe is approximately fifteen billion years old. And in all of that space and time there has never been any evidence that intelligent life exists beyond ourselves. The one-time scientists on Earth were convinced they had received a radio transmission from extraterrestrials several centuries back. It turned out to be the radio emissions from a pulsar several hundred light years distant. They wanted so desperately to report evidence of ET intelligence, they allowed their wishful thinking to override their objectivity."

Danar thought Tan was being a bit hard on the scientists of old, but reminded himself that she needed this conversation to justify their presence out here, despite the fact that they'd had this debate many, many times, as far back as the astronomy courses they attended together 20 years ago. The difference between then and now was that instead of being a fellow student in pursuit of expanding the frontiers of science (as was the case with the scientists of old), he was now responsible for the safety of a civilization. He could no longer afford the inaction of endless debate, or the overreaction of paranoia. It was his duty to find the balance of being cautious but prepared for any astronomical event outside the norm.

Of course, since the rehash of this conversation began the night before, for once, he could admit to himself that perhaps he too could benefit from the debate to justify their presence here as well. *Not as much as Tan will benefit however.*

"Tan, are you saying that I—I mean, we *wish* to be invaded by ET intelligence?"

"Not at all," she instantly corrected. "I'm only saying that it is human nature that makes us demand a complete picture without gaps. In cases where we lack empirical data we'll fill the gaps with speculation, if necessary, to provide the complete picture. This has always been the case throughout history. Before the industrial revolution, mysteries were blamed on elves, spirits, demons and other supernatural entities. When technology became part of our lives, magic and the supernatural gave way to UFOs, aliens and government conspiracies. As convincing as you and VICI were at yesterday's briefing, I fear that we may be overlooking an answer that may be closer to home; right under our very noses, as it were."

"I can't argue with that assertion," Danar said, shrugging his shoulders, "but I must point out that filling in gaps with speculation to complete a picture has worked to mankind's advantage many times, such as vaccines. Injecting a patient with a very small percentage of the very substance that made them sick, so that the body could examine it better and build resistance against it. There's also the splitting of the atom. At one time, it was thought that doing so would cause a chain reaction that would eventually split every atom everywhere, thereby destroying the whole planet. If a leap of faith wasn't made that no chain reaction would occur, we would never have had the opportunity to journey to the stars and establish a new home here using nuclear-powered starships."

"The millions of innocents who lived and worked in Hiroshima and Nagasaki wouldn't have been killed either," countered Tan.

Ouch. "True," Danar couldn't help but concede. Wanting to steer the debate back to the numbers, he pressed on. "As for there never having been evidence of ET intelligence, keep in mind there was no evidence that planets existed outside of Earth's solar system, yet our literature was replete with tales of other worlds long before extra-solar worlds were discovered by science. In fact, here we are orbiting one of those extra-solar worlds. With extra-solar life at that."

"Ah yes," Tan said, nowhere near convinced. "Insects, fauna and small fish, but no higher forms of life. No intelligence in the true sense of the word."

"No, but these lower forms of life can and probably will evolve to higher, more intelligent forms."

"Unfortunately, Danar, their evolutionary track has been compromised by our arrival," Tan said, crossing her arms in front of her breasts, unconsciously informing Danar that she was becoming annoyed by this latest debate. "Add to that, the terrestrial mammals we've introduced into the wilds and seas of Omicron will, at the very least, alter the path of the indigenous insects and fish."

"Again, no argument here, Tan," said Danar consciously crossing his arms to mirror Tan's posture in the hope she would notice her own granite expression. "But it's not as if we had a choice."

"Hmm. Answer me something, Danar. What if—what is that phrase Roshan used? 'Evil aliens bent on galactic domination' *are* causing all of our troubles and they have the power to alter or end our existence with the excuse that they have no choice. How would you respond to that?"

"Allow me to answer you in this way, Tan," Danar complied, doing his best to humor her apparent lack of patience while trying not to lose his own humor. "If the insects, fish and fauna of Omicron had the ability and-or inclination to fight back and attempted to repel our 'invasion,' I wouldn't like it, but I wouldn't blame them. But, Tan, this isn't the point, is it? Or are you through discussing whether or not there is intelligence beyond ourselves and instead, would rather debate the moral imperatives of species survival?"

"Let's leave that to a later time, shall we?" Tan conceded, dropping her arms to her sides and smiling.

Much later I hope, mused Danar. Out loud, he asked, "So, where were we? Ah yes. Intelligent life. As I recall, Doctor, there was a young student back at Howell U. who often quoted a statistic regarding sentient life spread throughout the galaxy, despite the lack of evidence. You remember her. Long straight black hair; a knack for questioning figures of authority. And quite lovely."

"I know where this is going, Danar," said Tan, her eyes narrowing but still smiling. "She used to say, and still says, that even if ten percent of the four hundred billion stars in our galaxy were Sol-type stars, and if ten percent of those supported life-sustaining planets, and if ten percent of those produced sentient life, that would still leave millions of sentient species spread throughout the Milky Way."

"Yes. That's it. You remember her," he said, beaming. "And that ten percent figure is extremely conservative. More likely there are hundreds of millions if not billions of intelligent, even space-faring species in the galaxy. And if memory serves, I recall she learned those lessons back on Earth from—what was that fellow's name?" he asked facetiously, eyeing the ceiling while tapping his chin.

"For cosmos' sake, Danar. It was Professor Frederick Howell, from whom she learned those lessons. Your father. But with all due respect, Captain Nebula, while I was learning those lessons, you were a little boy collecting the latest accessories for an action figure of some kind."

It was Tan's hope that Danar was not truly offended by her remarks, as she suspected his crew was. They all immediately faced their consoles, pretending not to listen by looking busy. When she saw the side of his mouth curl up, she knew everything was par-for-the-course between the two of them.

"And your point being…?" he asked broadening his grin. "And thank you for not saying dolls."

"My point being," she said chuckling, "there was something else I—that is, that young student rarely said."

"Pray tell."

"Considering the seemingly overwhelming probability of sentient life in the galaxy despite the lack of evidence, some species had to evolve first. And since we only have the evidence of ourselves, we might be it. The first species to evolve. And even if we weren't," she added, driving her point home, "it is more likely that any other species would be so far ahead of us, or so far behind, technologically speaking, that should we ever engage in any sort of conflict, there would be no contest."

Danar's grin instantly deflated. He had never before considered the possibility that humans might truly be alone in the galaxy. He also realized that if this debate were a boxing match, Tan would be beating the stuffing out of him. But he found the course the debate was taking infinitely preferable to the annoyance they both felt a few moments earlier.

"Captain Nebula," snapped the communications technician. "Incoming transmission."

Ah, saved by the proverbial bell. "The *Graviton?*"

"No, sir. It's from Omicron," he said, swiveling his chair to face his captain. He pressed the headset closer to his ear as if to verify the message. "Sir. It's regarding Sean Stingray. Apparently he's taken a turn for the worse. He, uh, he's not expected to survive the next couple of days."

Except for the ambient background noise of beeps, pings and whirs, the flight control deck of the ISS *Nebula* was silent. The news was devastating to anyone within earshot, for Sean Stingray, the first Captain Nebula of Omicron, was a hero to all.

Danar and Tan could only stare at each other. They were especially close to Stingray, although for different reasons. For Tan, it was Sean Stingray who initiated her escape from the hoverchair. For Danar, Stingray was not only his predecessor, not only his mentor and confidant, but a father figure as well. A fact he regretted never having told the man. *This could not have come at a worse time.*

For Arjun Vohra, even the novelty of watching the mountain-sized floating boulders fill up the majority of the main viewer was beginning to wear off. He didn't expect to see anything out of the ordinary using only the naked eye to scan the asteroid belt. Yet using the maxed-out sensors of the *Graviton* to sweep the belt hadn't produced any results either. So far. There was a logical reason for that. There could be nothing out of the ordinary for the sensors to detect. On the other hand, even if there were something alien hidden among the giant rocks, it would be difficult to detect without knowing exactly what to look for. The best he and his crew could do was to look for an unusual radiation spike or temperature variant or unknown electromagnetic emissions.

So far, nothing. Captain Graviton felt there was still no cause for complaint. As boring as this assignment appeared, he believed it was still the only logical course of action. At least it was much easier to navigate the belt, considering a lot of the smaller rocks were in-system due to…whatever was causing the asteroids to go random. And whatever that was, was connected in some way to an alien or alien device for which they were searching.

So the search continued. Of course, if the belt were as dense as its original configuration, the *Graviton*'s velocity would be greatly reduced. It would then take more than a year to circumnavigate. As is, it would still take them months, but fortunately the ship's sensors were strong enough to reach any point of the belt from any position. If anything were detected, the ISS *Graviton*'s nuclear engines were capable of explosively leaping to the farthest position within an hour, once they maneuvered around the floating mountains to clear the belt, that is.

The flight control crew looked depressed, but Arjun knew it was more from the news of Sean Stingray's declining health than from the monotony of the mission. *Not expected to survive the next couple of days.* The news would depress anyone who knew the original Captain Nebula, even if they only knew him peripherally. For Sean Stingray was always a likable and uncomplicated fellow.

Arjun figured it would be hardest on Stingray's successor, Danar Seti. For he was especially close. As was Tan Ozawa. If the two of them could only get past whatever it was that was keeping them apart, they could find comfort with each other. A. Vohra was of the opinion that most people, which included nearly all non-Hindus, made life more complicated than necessary. *Ah well, to each his own.* Perhaps one day, Danar and Tan would realize how much time they'd wasted. He hoped, for their sake, that day would come soon. He suspected they would never truly be happy without each other.

And speaking of wasting time, Arjun was convinced there had to be a more efficient way to carry out their assignment. Assuming there was a foreign device or presence, it was reasonable to assume it or they may not want to be found. The sensor sweeps of the searching *Graviton* might be expected.

Attempting to think like an alien or alien artifact seemed ludicrous. Without a common frame of reference, it was simply guesswork. And although, on rare occasions, guessing had its merits, it was far from efficient to rely on it.

Arjun realized he could be accused of the very thing he criticized in others: making life too complicated. It was time to change tactics. Make things simpler. Discover the common denominator. And that just might help him find a common frame of reference. A common denominator *did* exist, even with something alien or foreign. If it were intelligent, then it had the ability to ponder its place in nature. And what was nature? Nature was the Universe itself. The nursery for all things. All life. So the Universe was the common denominator. But the focus could be narrowed even further. What sort of items, objects or elements were common throughout the Universe? The list was endless, but several items immediately came to mind. Hydrogen, for one. One of the many elements that was present everywhere. There was gravity. Although not an element, it was a condition that was…well, universal.

Gravity brought to mind the discussion at yesterday's briefing. Doctor Ozawa had said that gravity was one of the four interactions of the Universe. There was also electromagnetism and the strong and weak forces that had something to do with gluons, the forces that bound the Universe together. *What could be more universal than that?*

Arjun Vohra felt he was on to something. Commonalities. The universal nature of the natural Universe. What exactly was the *Graviton* doing? Searching for something that presumably didn't want to be found. Another way to look at it was to use the terms hunting and hiding. *Now there's a nature reference if ever there was one.* Trying to analyze these nature references on a smaller scale, in an attempt to keep matters simple, Arjun couldn't help but to ask how nature employed hunting and hiding in the wilds of planetary jungles. Hunters in nature relied on their senses, just as the *Graviton* was using its sensors. Natural hunter's senses were chiefly sight, sound and smell. To survive, the hunted did its best to circumvent the senses of the hunter. Of course. The hunted didn't want to be found. It was the difference between life and death. In the cold vacuum of space however, employing auditory and olfactory sensors in the conventional sense was simply not possible. Besides, he expected any alien object to be stationary, or at least in motion with or on an asteroid. So the ping of radar may not be much help. It hadn't been so far. Searching for unusual radiation signatures had yet to "sniff" anything out.

Could sight, the sense he earlier rejected, be the key? In nature, the hunter as well as the hunted often relied on…camouflage.

Camouflage. It seemed so obvious, really. The best way to hide within any environment was to become part of that environment. Such as a duck blind or, as Frank Logan, a.k.a. Captain Quasar, would no doubt remind him, a fishing lure. So instead of searching for something that was obviously out of the ordinary, they should instead search for an obvious something that appeared ordinary but wasn't. It would be amusing, in an odd sort of way, if one of the giant asteroids the *Graviton* was maneuvering around was not in reality an asteroid at all. And since this was all speculation, conjecture and guesswork, why limit it to merely one?

An idea occurred to him. He was about to call on the computer or AI as he normally did, but remembered the ease with which Danar Seti employed the artificial intelligence program for his objectives by treating it—treating *her* like a sentient being. And why not? Even *artificial* intelligence implied sentient abilities. And quite frankly, VICI surprised him at yesterday's briefing with her range of human-like attributes. Her sense of humor for example, as well as displaying sarcasm.

Impressive indeed.

He decided it was time to change his attitude. For Arjun Vohra was nothing if not adaptable. Especially when it concerned the greater good. In this case, the feelings of another. Even if that other was artificial. So instead of calling on the AI in his usual fashion, he swivelled his chair 180 degrees, facing the astronavigation table and instead called out, "VICI, my sweet. Will you show yourself please?"

Fortunately, the lighting of the *Graviton*'s flight control deck was already subdued. The astronavigation tabletop began to glow as the holo-projectors came online with the telltale swirling lights that coalesced into the translucent form of the Virtual Inquiry Computer Interactive hologram.

"**At your service, Captain Graviton,**" the hologram enthusiastically replied with a smile.

Arjun chuckled. He was going to like his new relationship with the hologram. "My dear. I've been contemplating our 'hide and seek' mission."

"**Ah, so I imagine you wish to recalculate my eighty percent figure regarding the possibility that something alien is lurking in the belt.**"

"Only at first."

"**Really?**" The hologram actually managed to look surprised. "**You have a plan.**" It wasn't really a question.

"I do," Arjun confirmed. "Please bear with me, my dear."

"**Of course, my captain,**" VICI said, bowing slightly.

"This is a tall order," he warned. "How many asteroids orbit Alpha C. A, including those in the belt as well as the random asteroids in-system? Exclude dust particles and anything smaller than, say…one meter."

"**Hmm. That *is* a tall order,**" VICI replied, "**but not as difficult as you might think. Standby.**" The hologram vanished.

Before Captain Graviton could wonder how long he might have to wait for an answer, VICI reappeared.

"**Within the parameters you specified, there are two hundred fifty-six billion, seven hundred forty-one million, four hundred** fifty-one thousand, eight hundred seventy asteroids within orbit of Alpha Centauri A; give or take."

"Wha—I...give or take?" he asked, surprised at the rapid response.

"As we speak, asteroid collisions within the belt and in-system increase the total figure; at the same time, the eight space stations are retrieving ice asteroids for water processing or nickel-iron asteroids for ore, which decreases the figure."

"Of course," he said bobbing his head. "But, VICI, how did you come up with that figure so quickly?"

"I have been monitoring the asteroids since the colony made planetfall from the ISS *Nebula* thirty years ago. In addition, collaborating with my holo-clones assigned to the other stations and the Omicron council chamber, and consulting my data base of previous asteroid activity makes calculating a running quantity relatively simple."

"If you say so." Arjun found it amusing that each holographic representation of VICI referred to the others as clones. He wondered which was the original, or if there was an original. "How did you and uh, your clones count the asteroids?"

"**Visually, of course,**" VICI replied.

"No other method?"

"**Radar imaging.**"

"Is that all?"

"Although there are other methods to detect and count the asteroids, such as electromagnetic resonance scanning and radiation signature profiles, among others, why would it be necessary to employ them when visual inspection is the most efficient?"

"Efficient if all you wanted to do was count them," offered Arjun.

"**I do not follow you, Captain Graviton,**" VICI admitted.

"Consider this, VICI," Arjun said, leaning forward in his command crash chair while resting his chin on his interlocked fingers. "If you were an alien or alien object wishing to remain hidden in this system of asteroids, would you think it better to hide in and among the rocks, or to hide *as* one of the asteroids?"

"Ah. Such as camouflage."

"Yes!" he exclaimed slapping his thigh. "Exactly. Camouflage."

The hologram smiled. "Simple. Elegant, even."

"And obvious as well, eh?" he asked, somewhat proud.

"Obvious?" questioned the hologram. "Hmm. I will not commit to that nomenclature before we discover any proof of camouflage."

"Oh," he said, somewhat deflated.

"On the other hand, we have reason enough to recount the asteroids."

"Employing EM resonance scanning and radiation profiles?"

"I'm not certain it would help," she answered. "If our illusive, allegedly chameleon entity or object has the ability to emulate an asteroid, then it is reasonable to assume they or it possesses the ability to fake EM and rad profiles as well."

"For myself, VICI," Arjun said, palm on chest, "I'm out of ideas."

"Now that I have a better understanding of the nature of our search, if not the nature of our adversary, I have another idea that would be difficult to fake."

"Do tell, my dear."

"Spatial displacement."

"Spa—what?"

"Every object within the vacuum of space, no matter how large or small, displaces the space surrounding it. This displaced space can be measured by the object's gravitational field. Under normal circumstances, there exists a correlation between the physical profile of the object in question and the gravity field it produces. Unless our allegedly camouflaged object truly is an asteroid, its false physical profile will not match its field of gravity."

"I see," *I think*, Captain Graviton said to VICI and thought to himself, stroking his neatly trimmed goatee. "Does this mean you'll have to recount all of the asteroids?"

"Yes, but fortunately not from scratch. Although the larger asteroids of the belt are locked in orbit around Alpha Centauri A, the belt's configuration will not have changed much. The so-called random asteroids in-system are a different matter all together.

However it shouldn't take more than five minutes to scan the entire system. Using a process of elimination, I will disregard any asteroid whose physical profile matches its gravity field. Any object that shows a discrepancy will require closer inspection.

"At your command, Captain."

"You've got it, VICI," he said, clapping his hands twice.

"Very well. Please standby." The hologram vanished.

Arjun figured this could be a total bust, if not a total waste of time. Yet for some reason he slowly became anxious, as was evidenced by his slightly elevated heart rate. He could see the control deck crew, who witnessed the exchange between VICI and himself, were also nervous by the way they glanced at him and each other. Well, they had less than five minutes to wait. The profiles would either match, meaning their search continued using yet another method, or they wouldn't match, meaning a discrepancy. *Then what?*

So as not to be caught fidgeting by his crew, he rose from his command chair and began pacing back and forth between his chair and the astronavigation table behind it. Apparently he was so caught up in his own thoughts, he hadn't realized how quickly a few minutes could pass, for while he was facing the table, VICI reappeared in her usual light show. She said nothing at first.

Is that a worried expression she's wearing? "That was…fast," prompted Captain Graviton.

"Yes," agreed the hologram, "it only took me three minutes. My original estimate of five minutes included a possible double-checking of my findings. Apparently that was not necessary."

"Oh?" *Is she rambling?* "Well, my sweet, spill the beans."

"Perhaps you should be sitting down, my captain," VICI offered.

"No," he said more forcefully than he had intended. Then, forcing patience, "That will not be necessary. I would prefer any information you have."

"Very well. By eliminating the matched profiles, I have discovered nine alleged asteroids with profile discrepancies."

"Nine, eh?" he asked, feeling a trickle of perspiration slide off the side of his face. "Is there any natural reason to account for the discrepancy?"

"I doubt it," VICI answered. "There are too many coincidences involved."

"Explain, please."

"In addition to the gravity fields being much smaller than what their physical profiles would suggest, all nine false asteroids are completely identical in size, shape, color and apparent mass and composition type."

"As Captain Nebula has said on occasion, 'there are such things as coincidences.'"

"This type of coincidence falls well outside the random laws of nature."

"Hmm. You say they are the same size?" Arjun asked, fidgeting with his command baton to keep his hands busy.

"Correct. Visually, they are all approximately twelve meters in diameter. However their gravity fields are much smaller, suggesting an actual size of approximately twelve centimeters instead."

"How is that possible?"

"The smaller objects are projecting false visual images, as well as false EM resonance and radiation signatures, as I suspected."

And now for the kicker. "Where are these objects?" Arjun asked, swallowing hard.

"There is one object each, within ninety-eight and one hundred and one meters of each Omicron space station."

"That only accounts for eight. Where is the other?" Even before VICI answered, he knew. With a sinking feeling, he knew.

"Approximately one hundred meters behind us…and trailing."

CHAPTER TEN
Confirm and Commit

Arjun felt his knees weaken, and figured it might be best to take a seat after all. He all but fell back with the edge of his posterior connecting with edge of his command crash chair. Had his pacing taken him one step beyond his command chair, he'd be sprawled on the deck plating by now. *Thank Lord Vishnu I was spared the embarrassment.*

The captain also noticed the gasps and wide-eyed expressions of his crew at VICI's pronouncement. Fortunately, his own anxiety subsided. No doubt due to his being the captain, whose responsibilities included keeping his crew calm. "Relax, everyone. Nothing has changed but for the fact that we are no longer in the dark, which means we are in a better position to protect ourselves than we were before."

"But, Captain," asked a junior officer, "shouldn't we inform the rest of the fleet? It's nearly time to check in with the *Nebula* anyway."

"I'm not sure that is wise at this time, Lieutenant," the captain said, scooting back in his chair. "We cannot be certain whether or not this…object is capable of monitoring our transmissions. That reminds me, VICI," he said, facing the hologram. "How is it that we are able to detect its false projections without it realizing it?"

"**Fortunately, the passive sensors of the ISS *Graviton*, which I've been employing, are apparently just below the threshold of the…object's ability to detect. I cannot say the same for a radio transmission.**"

"Lucky for us," he said, stroking his beard. "However, as much as I'd like to inform the rest of the fleet of our discovery, without the discovery knowing about it, we may have no choice but to show our hand. Otherwise, we would have to remain silent. Not much of an advantage for us. A stalemate, in fact. Hmm. If we must show our hand by warning the fleet, then let us gather as much information as we can. Give me a visual astern—"

"One moment, Captain Graviton," VICI interrupted. "I believe I may know of a way to inform the fleet without the object's knowledge."

"Let's have it."

"At our scheduled time, we shall inform the ISS *Nebula* of our progress, mentioning only that the search continues with no results thus far. I will then piggyback a copy of my program along the broadcast beam, thereby updating my holo-clone on the *Nebula*."

"A capital idea," said Arjun. "Are you sure it will work?"

"Yes. Provided the object stays clear of the broadcast beam. Ordinarily, any transmission higher than an amplitude modulated beam could simply go around a true asteroid, but if our shy friend were to intersect the beam, I fear it could detect my program."

"And the jig would be up," the captain nodded. "It sounds like the best shot we've got. Proceed." Then, addressing his communications technician, "I want you to send our progress report, stating no results thus far, as text only, so that VICI can relay her program and message without the confusion of diametrically opposed audio signals."

"Understood, sir," replied the officer.

At the same time, VICI vanished to prepare for her broadcast beam transport.

Unfortunately, at that exact moment, the lights—along with all of the main power stored in the fusion reactor power core—vanished as well.

Onboard the ISS *Nebula*, outside of the asteroid belt, holding formation with the remainder of the fleet around the now very quiet distortion area, Danar Seti was doing his best to assuage a very upset

Doctor Sarah James onboard the Omicron Nebula asteroid station.

"*He insists on spending his remaining time here aboard station,*" she practically shouted. "*That's insane. Someone in his condition may not even survive the transport from the surface. Danar, you must talk him out of it.*"

Even if he had the time and inclination, Danar wasn't sure if even *he* could convince Sean Stingray to remain on the planet Omicron. "Doctor James, if he only has a few days to…live, then what difference does it make?" he asked, shrugging his shoulders at the main viewer.

"*I don't believe what I'm hearing. That's exactly what he said,*" the doctor said, gesturing a lot with her hands. "*What is this, some form of testosterone imbalance that gives men faulty judgement regarding their own lives?*"

"Doctor James—" he began, trying to remain formal.

"Listen to me," she interrupted. "*The medical facility on Omicron is much better equipped to keep him comfortable.*" Sarah James pleaded, addressing Tan, who was standing next to the seated Captain Nebula, "*Tan, can you please back me up on this?*"

The last thing Tan wanted was to be caught up in a male-bashing tirade. Besides, she'd already been a little rough on Danar of late. She wanted to cut him some slack.

On the other hand, this must be as serious as it sounded, for Tan was aware of the once-intimate relationship between the good doctor and the intrepid former captain. But she knew the first rule of medicine was to cause no harm. Sarah James had to be a doctor first. If Sarah thought Sean could be better served on Omicron, then it must be true. Yet Tan could understand the so-called male perspective. What difference could it make at this point? Tan also knew that people like Sean Stingray, Danar Seti and the rest of the Starforce were drawn to outer space like moths to a flame. "Vacuum jockeys" they called themselves. They had space in their blood and preferred the artificial environs of space over any ground-based facility, no matter how scenic or technologically proficient. Plus the fact that Stingray would obviously feel more at home aboard Omicron Nebula as he spent a large chunk of his life on the station that was built through his design and supervision.

Tan was definitely torn. No matter whose opinion she supported, she felt she would betray a friend and colleague. "Sarah. I-I don't know what to say."

"*I don't believe this*," Sarah James screamed, throwing her hands in the air. "*Someone's life is at stake here.*"

"Doctor James," Danar pleaded, his palms facing the viewer, "I appreciate your dilemma, but the decision is mine to approve or deny his request. I'm authorizing it."

"*What?!*" she exploded.

"If your duties allow," the captain continued, "you may supervise his transport from surface to station."

"*Danar, I must protest. This is—*"

"I've made my decision, *Doctor* James," he interrupted, emphasizing her title.

Fortunately, looks could not kill. Otherwise the captain feared he'd be leaving the flight control deck in the horizontal position. Her face crimson with fury, Sarah James said through clenched teeth, "*Very well, Captain Nebula,*" then closed the connection.

The main viewer once again displayed open space with several of the *Nebula*'s sister ships barely perceptible in the distance.

"That could've gone better," Tan commented, still looking at the viewer.

"Yes," Danar agreed, also still looking at the viewer. "I sure hope I did the right thing."

He had. But he had no idea why. Yet.

"Captain Nebula," snapped the communications technician, "I'm receiving a progress report from the *Graviton*. Sir, it's text only."

The captain internally noted that sending text communications was unusual but not unprecedented. "Well? You still know how to read, don't you?" he barked.

"Uh…yes, sir. I-it says 'search continues…no results thus far.' And it's repeating."

Before anyone could comment further, Tan noticeably flinched.

"Tan," Danar asked. "Are you…?"

"Something's wrong," she said, sounding distracted.

The next series of events happened very rapidly. The

astronavigation tabletop brightened, producing the Virtual Inquiry Computer Interactive hologram, who said with urgency, **"Captain Nebula. I am receiving an emergency update from one of my clones. Disregard the text message from the *Graviton*. It is merely a ploy to—"** The tabletop went black, causing VICI to vanish in the proverbial blink. At the same time, Tan Ozawa clutched her head with both hands and screamed an agonizing cry, then collapsed into unconsciousness.

Instinct propelled the captain from his chair. He caught Tan's limp form before she could hit the deck. "What the hell…?" He turned, facing the astronavigation table, while gently depositing Tan in his command crash chair. "VICI. Come online. VICI," he shouted. He then turned his gaze to the communication tech who began typing frantically at his console.

"Sir. The Virtual Inquiry Computer Interactive program is no longer present in the computer core."

"The entire program?" he asked in disbelief. "How can that be? Never mind for now. Get me the *Graviton*. Hurry, man, hurry."

After more frantic typing, "I'm sorry, sir, the *Graviton* is not responding."

"Damn," the captain exclaimed, pounding one fist into the other open palm. "Signal the entire fleet to red status alert." Then, an afterthought, "Also, confirm if VICI is still present in their computer core databases."

After what seemed like minutes but in reality was seconds, "Captain. Red alert status throughout the fleet as well as confirmation on VICI's presence. We're also being hailed by the fleet."

Captain Nebula expected as much. "Open a channel to every ship."

"Channel open, sir."

"Attention, Omicron Starforce, this is Captain Nebula. We've lost contact with the starship *Graviton*. Presumably, they've found something, or something's found them. In an attempt at updating us on their current situation, some kind of interference deleted the VICI program from our computers before we could receive details. The *Nebula* will be leaving formation to investigate."

"*There's nothing happening out here so far,* Nebula," began Michelle Woo over the two-way channel. "*You shouldn't go alone.*"

"My thought exactly," agreed Captain Nebula. "Thanks for volunteering, Radian. We'll need to—" He was interrupted by several varying loud noises. Most of the consoles and work stations on the *Nebula*'s control deck activated independently as if they were receiving a massive program download; Tan Ozawa moaned, slowly regaining consciousness; the astronavigation tabletop, already luminescent, emitted the translucent form of VICI; and the gravity generators on all the vessels in formation went off-line for a few seconds, causing everyone and everything that wasn't secured to bounce briefly before being deposited where they were previously.

"What now?" Captain Nebula asked no one in particular.

VICI, whose voice could be heard on the open channel from the rest of the fleet as well as the *Nebula*, spoke. **"Warning! Spacial distortion cascade in immediate vicinity resulting in gravimetric fluctuations."**

Gravimetric fluctuations expanded in all directions, engulfing the seven Omicron starships, causing them to pitch, yaw and buck wildly, threatening to collapse their structural framework. But the starships were designed to withstand the stress of perpetual acceleration up to .20C. They were able to weather the fluctuations in gravity, but not without some difficulty. Every officer throughout the fleet grabbed anything within reach to prevent being thrown about. A few consoles exploded, showering sparks. The sound of stressed metal could be heard everywhere within each vessel.

"DO WE STILL HAVE AN OPEN CHANNEL WITH THE FLEET?!" Captain Nebula shouted over the din of noise.

"AFFIRMATIVE," shouted back the communications tech.

"*RADIAN*. DISREGARD PREVIOUS ORDERS," shouted Captain Nebula. "FLEET. MAINTAIN YOUR POSITIONS. WE'RE HOLDING FORMATION…AND EVERYONE…HOLD ON!" he shouted, clutching the arm of his command chair, while leaning into it and trying not to fall into the seated Tan, who had a double-fisted grip on his wrist, helping to stabilize him.

But Danar's thoughts were elsewhere. While the fleet was

attempting to hold its own against the gravity flux, he feared the *Graviton* had to fend for itself. For now.

"What happened?" shouted Captain Graviton, as the emergency lights flickered to life, casting a crimson hue over the flight control deck.

"It appears we've lost power, Captain," responded an officer. "We're on emergency battery back-up now."

"Did our message get through?"

"The text message got through, but as VICI was traveling along the beam, the object blocked its path. I don't know if she got through or not. She—oh my God. Captain, I can't find the AI's program in the core at all."

"How can that be?"

The communications tech consulted what had registered on his log before the power loss. "It looks like the object sent us a feedback pulse when it intercepted our broadcast beam, causing us to lose power and…and deleted VICI's program from our systems."

Oh no.

Before the captain could audibly comment, his ship was hit by the expanding gravimetric wave. Already on emergency battery back-up, the gravity generators couldn't compensate as rapidly as the rest of the fleet at coordinate zero. Captain Graviton and several other officers were pitched from their chairs as consoles exploded and the bulkhead's structural integrity was tested.

On the Omicron Nebula asteroid space station, as well as her sister stations, the gravity wave was picked up by the sensors, prompting a yellow alert warning status to flash throughout the interior of each asteroid. But before the weapons turrets could get a bead on the incoming asteroids, the rapid expansion of the wave randomized the rocks faster than any previous time.

The Virtual Inquiry Computer Interactive AI came online colony-wide. **"Warning! Asteroid collision imminent; brace for impact."**

With a newfound respect for the so-called random roids, but the same anxiety, Babs Schreiber groaned as her classroom full of children (and no doubt every other classroom throughout the Omicron colony) tossed their arms in the air and screamed at the top of their lungs, "ROCK AND ROLL!"

At least the kids can enjoy this. For they did not understand the seriousness of the asteroid attacks. They especially didn't realize the possible significance of this particular attack. In fact, Babs was one of only two civilians out of billions who fully understood. This particular incident could answer the age-old question of whether or not humans were alone in the Universe. And if not, would the knowledge prove fatal for this colony from Earth, if not fatal for all of Earth as well? She had no choice but to put her faith in Captain Nebula and the Starforce of Omicron. And she couldn't discuss it with anyone.

Great.

The main viewers of the entire fleet showed the same thing. Nothing. The viewers were still operational, even after the gravity wave passed outward in all directions. Still, it looked as if there were a defect in the liquid crystal medium that provided simulated images picked up by the external sensors. An image that was a dull black blotch, instead of the star-filled void of inky black which should be common everywhere. Before the gravity wave expanded from the position around which the Omicron fleet was stationed, they could see each other. Now, nothing could be seen but for the few stars on the outer edges of the main viewers. The fleet was still in formation, verified by VICI's holo-representation above the astronavigation tables on each vessel. Although the holo-ships could be seen clearly, VICI lacked enough information to identify the "hole" they were surrounding. A hole that didn't reveal anything within or beyond the other side of it. The dark hole in space was approximately three kilometers in diameter. It was apparently blocking all visual sensors up to and including the naked eye. Communication signals could not get through it either, but instead traveled around it, which allowed the fleet to continue communicating with each other. The first thing they did was to verify that the fleet weathered the gravity wave more or less intact.

The part of VICI that was onboard the ISS *Nebula* updated the rest of the network as to the last known status and ploy of the *Graviton*, which had definitely found nine foreign objects throughout the system. But it would seem one of the objects intercepted the *Graviton*'s attempt to update the *Nebula* and sent a delete program of some kind, along with the *Graviton*'s message, to eliminate VICI and prevent the fleet from discovering it. Fortunately, the hologram found another location other than the *Nebula*'s computer core which saved her program from oblivion.

VICI did not go into detail as to where she hid. Or *how* she hid, since she could only exist in the environment of a neurologic network. And the only place on the ship which possessed that environment was the aforementioned computer core. A computer core that was updated with a neuronet more than 30 years ago by a young and recently thawed Tan Ozawa.

Because the fleet was still ignorant of the *Graviton*'s status and had to prepare for whatever else might emerge from the hole, obtaining details of VICI's narrow escape could await a later date. It was decided to send one ship to check on the *Graviton*. The ISS *Radian* under the command of Michelle Woo was now on her way to the belt.

"*Nebula*, ole mate," inquired Captain Quasar, whose own starship was stationed unseen on the other side of the hole, "how did you know to keep us at five kilometers distance? Somethin' tells me we wouldn't be here jawin' about it if that thing expanded with us inside of it."

"I'm hip," agreed Captain Nebula. "I wish I could tell you I worked out the five kilometers based on some kind of pattern I saw when the original remote sensor probes were shut down. But to be honest, it was simply a lucky guess."

"So just what the hell is this thing anyway?" asked Captain Pulsar.

"For the third time, Captain Pulsar," answered VICI without annoyance, speaking simultaneously on all six formation vessels, "**unknown.**"

"I had hoped you could acquire more information with more time," commented Captain Pulsar. "Sorry."

"The way this thing is absorbing light," ventured Captain Gaea, "could we be on the edge of the event horizon of a black hole?"

"It sure looks like it could be," agreed Captain Ersatz.

Wanting to speak, Tan glanced at Danar for permission. He gave it with a nod, still concerned about her sudden scream and collapse just before the arrival of the dark hole in space. A scream and collapse that occurred at the exact time VICI vanished. It was probably a coincidence, but still....Tan insisted she was fine and refused to go to the medical bay, convincing Danar she was needed on the flight control deck. He relented because she did look okay. And he trusted her judgement. For now, they had to deal with this calm before the coming storm. And Tan would be helpful in that pursuit.

"No," Tan answered. "This is definitely not a black hole. Although it does appear to absorb light, it's deflecting our radio transmissions. If this were a black hole, we would all be within the event horizon and crushed. That includes the entire trinary star system. In fact, this...*dark hole* has properties opposite that of a black hole. Where a black hole's gravity attracts objects to it, including light, this phenomenon seems to use gravity to repel objects away from it."

"*So you don't believe this could be natural in any way?*" inquired LeAnn Walker of the ISS *Gaea*.

"I didn't exactly say that," explained Tan. "It is unlike any natural phenomenon observed in recorded history."

"It's unlikely this thing is of natural creation," interjected Captain Nebula. "Please keep in mind the series of events that preceded this...thing, whatever it is. We've lost contact with the *Graviton*, which confirmed nine objects camouflaged as asteroids throughout the system."

"With all due respect, Da—Captain," interrupted Tan, "the method used to camouflage the asteroids, as described by VICI, is within the technical expertise of several people from the Omicron colony. Not many people, I'll grant you."

"You're one of those few people, Doctor Ozawa," noted the captain, "as is VICI. But with all due respect, I doubt if either of you are capable of inter-dimensional travel like whatever made this dark hole materialize from nowhere. Unless of course we were all asleep and this thing slipped past us from just around the corner."

"*I'm with you on this, Nebula*," agreed Charles Lee of ISS Vortex. "*At the risk of sounding paranoid, I feel smothered with the 'fight or flight' syndrome.*"

"*Yeah, this thing is giving me the creeps, too,*" added John Askew. "*In fact, it feels like we're being watched.*"

"Now, people," cautioned Danar, "let's not let the unknown spook us into a superstitious stupor."

"*Hey now,*" balked Captain Ersatz, "*I resent that comment.*"

"**Perhaps you should not dismiss your colleague's human intuition so readily, Captain Nebula,**" advised VICI. "**I'm receiving some unusual readings from the dark hole. If I had to guess, I'd say something was emerging.**"

As he picked himself up from the deck, Arjun Vohra performed a quick visual scan of the flight control deck to be certain there were no serious injuries. He himself was thrown about five meters, but was lucky enough to absorb the impact with a tuck and roll.

"Status report," he barked.

Fortunately, internal communications weren't affected by the gravity buffeting. He unconsciously held his breath expecting the worst, but the damage wasn't as bad as he feared. There were no ship-wide serious injuries. External communications were still out, however. The gravity generators were working throughout the ship, although they could've gotten around that problem if necessary by spinning the habitat sections of the *Graviton* as they were originally designed to do. The forward laser deflector had about half of its charge. He had the feeling they were going to need all of that and then some real soon.

They were back on main power instead of battery back-ups, but the nuclear reactor was nearly depleted of energy. Fortunately, like her sister ships, the ISS *Graviton* no longer required momentum to extract hydrogen from open space, like its original design. Still, it took far too long if the ship remained stationary. The sensor arrays were functional, but very limited, covering only a few hundred meter radius around the ship. The ship still had some maneuverability, thanks to thrusters, but would that allow them to collect enough hydrogen in time to figure out what kind of threat the foreign object posed?

Their most devastating loss, of course, was the deletion of the Virtual Inquiry Computer Interactive program. The captain had to constantly remind himself that VICI herself was not gone, just the portion of her that resided in the *Graviton*'s computer core. At the first opportunity, they would upload her from any of the other ships or stations. What had to be determined was whether or not the information she collected regarding the other eight objects was deleted along with her back-up program. If she wasn't able to send a copy of herself to the *Nebula*, then the *Graviton* had to deliver the information itself. In order to do that, they had to deal with the object stalking them.

"Where is that cursed wannabe asteroid now?"

"It's still behind—wait. It's gone. No, sorry, sir. It's just outside the main airlock of the habitat cylinder. I think it's trying to get in the ship."

"What? Shut off all power to that airlock."

That was easy to do, considering they had a hard time keeping it powered up anyway.

"Done," the science tech confirmed.

"Good," said Captain Graviton, just as the reflected light of the technician's console suddenly illuminated his face. "What is that?"

"Sir. Power has been restored to the airlock," the tech said, exasperated. "And it wasn't me."

"Don't tell me. The thing powered up the airlock all by itself. Now it's about to use a classified command code to let itself in. Right?"

"Uh, sir, that's exactly what it's doing."

Lovely. "RED STATUS ALERT!" the captain shouted about a

second before VICI's pre- recorded voice repeated over and over. **"INTRUDER ALERT. INTRUDER ALERT. INTRUDER ALERT."**

"Enough of that. We get the message."

The warning muted to a barely audible litany before shutting off completely.

"Send a security squad to that airlock," ordered the captain, "but have them approach no closer than fifteen meters of the object should it decide to enter the inner doors." Which was likely.

Arjun was beginning to regret the prohibition of projectile weapons that was established by the colony upon planetfall 30 years before. The refugees from Earth had developed a more humane weapon of defense in the form of the neurowave gauntlet, a glove-like device that was armed when the wearer closed his or her fist. It was activated by a stud attached to the outside of the forefinger, triggered by the thumb. The neurowave was designed to temporarily disrupt the brain's synaptic network, rendering the victim unconscious. The wave could be adjusted by a small digital LED dial on the back of the glove to sweep an area anywhere from a meter radius of the wearer to a maximum radius of about 20 meters. The gauntlet was a two-part device. The user must also wear a neurowave blocker, a small insert clipped over one ear that scrambled the wave, protecting the user from being rendered unconscious as well. The blocker was tuned to the specific frequency of the glove to which it was attached. There were no gauntlets without a blocker, and no blockers without a gauntlet. A mismatched set would be unable to protect the user. The gauntlet was only used and handled by Starforce personnel.

Although rarely used, the neurowave gauntlet had been very effective the past three decades, dispersing the unruly crowd, breaking up fights and brawls and apprehending the occasional perpetrators of assaults and thefts and the like. But how effective would they be against a non- human aggressor? And the object, whatever it really was, had proven to be an aggressor. It had proven its resourcefulness as well.

The captain wouldn't be surprised if the security squad chief was contemplating the very same thoughts. If it were Arjun facing the thing, he might feel better protected carrying a club or heavy staff for defense. As he thought this, he unconsciously gripped his command baton. "Let's see if we can spy the object in its true form," the captain said to one of the science technicians.

Understanding, the tech patched the view from the airlock camera to the main viewer of the flight control deck. The first thing seen was the oxygen vapors escaping into space through the opened outer doors of the airlock. As the mist cleared, a spherical-shaped silhouette began to emerge. Judging from the known scale of the airlock, Arjun estimated the shape to be about twelve centimeters in diameter, as VICI had predicted. About the size of a volleyball.

Now clear of vapors, the camera that was attached above the inner doors revealed what looked like a spherical ball of...*concrete?* The captain was hard-pressed to come up with a better description, since the object was apparently blocking the camera's sensors from getting a reading of it. At least it was allowing a visual scan. Or maybe it had some limitations. "Well, well. For all intents and purposes, the thing is an asteroid after all," A. Vohra said. Although unlike any natural asteroid he'd ever seen birthed from the cosmos.

It looked to be a perfect sphere, smooth and round. And like most of the asteroids the captain had ever seen, it was grayish in color. As it floated closer to the inner door, the camera was able to show pockmarks on the otherwise smooth surface. It looked as if its concrete, if that's what it really was, was mixed and poured into that shape, as opposed to carved. But if it were concrete or a cement mixture of some kind, how was its interior accessed? The captain assumed it used some form of internal circuitry to perform its feats of maneuverability, monitoring radio transmissions, interfering with said transmissions, as well as deleting other programs using feedback pulses. Not to mention the capabilities of accessing classified airlock codes. A pretty sophisticated piece of hardware, to be sure.

On the other hand, why did this round rock have to be a device at all? Was it possible this could be a sentient alien? Would it make a difference? *Perhaps it would be best to treat this as a first contact situation. It couldn't hurt at this point.* Even if it were a device, it may be able to record a greeting or message. It might even be able to respond to, or process information to facilitate communication. If that were the case, then perhaps the neurowave gauntlet *could* prove useful, if or when it became necessary.

Arjun Vohra believed it would be best to assume the stone sphere was sentient, or had access to the sentience that constructed it, grew it, hatched it, whatever. The important thing was to gather as much information as possible from it. Since it apparently was able to block the camera's ability to read its physical make-up, other than visual, Captain Graviton had to rely on the old-fashioned method of information gathering: attempting to speak with it.

Just as he was working out what to say to it, the thing gave up a bit more information, albeit vague. It began to glow, or rather some internal light or energy was leaking out of the pitted surface of the object. It then started pulsing rapidly. That made the captain nervous and he immediately knew why. The rapid glowing pulse reminded him of a bomb. Before he could become too anxious, however, he noticed the outer airlock door closing, cutting off the view of space behind the round rock. The rapid pulse of light slowed slightly as the airlock cycled oxygen from inside the ship to equalize the pressure so that the inner doors could open.

Now that air was inside the lock, the sound waves of the speakers had a medium on which to vibrate.

Well, here goes nothing. "Attention, alien device, this is Captain Graviton of the Starforce of Omicron vessel *Graviton* speaking. If you are able to understand me, please identify yourself and state your intentions."

Silence. Although as he spoke, he noticed the object's glow increase. Its luminescence decreased when the captain finished speaking, perhaps indicating it had been listening. If it were listening, then why wouldn't it respond, even if it was unrecognizable gibberish? If it could respond, what would it say? *Take me to your leader?*

It was obvious the device had them all at a disadvantage. It knew more about them than they about it. Although they'd already picked up a great deal of information, such as the fact that its internal energy or light increased as it performed tasks like opening the airlock doors. The captain also noticed that while in the freefall of space it didn't glow at all unless it was performing a task. Now, under the influence of the ship's internal gravity, it was glowing slightly to stay aloft. That meant it possessed its own antigravity generator. Manipulating gravity wouldn't appear to present this thing or its makers with any difficulties.

With the inner airlock doors open, the round rock floated into the ship and down the corridor at about the pace of a walking person.

Leaning toward the communications tech, the captain ordered, "Keep a visual on it at all times and please tell me we've been recording this thing since its arrival."

"Oh yes, sir."

Then, "Security," the captain addressed, "do not interfere with the object unless absolutely necessary. And try to stay within twenty meters of it." He knew he didn't have to explain why.

"*Understood, Captain,*" came the reply over the control deck speakers.

Although the spherical stone was traveling relatively slowly, its progress was purposeful, as if it knew where it was going as opposed to simply touring the ship.

Watching the scenes change on the main viewer as the sphere's trek was picked up by the cameras within the *Graviton*'s corridors, the captain once again requested an update on communications. He was told they were still down. The ship could not transmit or receive, but crews were working on the problem and were hopeful the comm system would be up and running within the hour. That meant they were still unable to inform any of the asteroid stations that they were being spied upon by one of the asteroids in their vicinity. It was his intention to warn *Nebula* and the rest of the fleet, personally if necessary.

Things would be so much simpler if their own broadcast lasers were operational.

A thought occurred the captain. "Exactly why can we not send or receive communications?" he asked the comm tech.

"We're having a hard time generating enough power to activate the broadcast laser beam."

"That's only for transmitting. Why are we not able to receive?"

"Apparently, the grids are misaligned on the dishes, caused by the gravimetric buffeting, sir."

"On all four dishes? That seems unlikely."

"I agree, Captain. According to the computer schematic, the grids are aligned. I have a crew outside the ship physically checking each dish and making whatever corrections are necessary."

"A time-consuming procedure," the captain commented, stroking his goatee. "As well as a convenient delay for a concrete ball that doesn't want our knowledge of it to leave the area."

"Captain," the young officer asked. "Do you think the alien device is…" his eyes went wide with comprehension.

"Yes, I do," Captain Graviton confirmed. "It seems well within the ability of our secretive stowaway."

If VICI were here, he was quite certain she could holographically illustrate how their incoming and outgoing transmissions were being blocked. But she wasn't here and he didn't have the time to walk them through the procedure. He couldn't really blame these young officers for their lack of imagination. For most of them, this was the first time they'd actually served aboard a starship. They'd never had to face anything like the obstacles they had to deal with now. Not even the simulations at the academy could predict scenarios like this. Although they would if they got through this mess. Arjun would see to that personally. The only reason he and his colleagues like Danar Seti and the rest developed their "space legs" at all was because they served with experienced first-geners like Sean Stingray, setting up the gravity generators in all of the asteroid cities when their class was fresh out of the academy. Not to mention all of their experience in capturing ice asteroids for water reclamation.

Since that time, however, more and more citizens had been thawed and born, increasing the population. Those types of space jobs, previously handled by the Starforce, were now relegated to the private sector. Academy graduates these days simply didn't have the experience afforded the higher-ranking officers. So it looked as if this would be their trial by fire. He trusted in their ability to adapt. Just as he trusted his first officer, who was now overseeing the operation of the Omicron Graviton station, to staff the vessel with qualified, if not experienced, young officers. They were all highly rated, for they were specialists all, fully trained in the sciences. As captain, then, it was his responsibility to teach them how to be imaginative. And the best way to do that was by example.

"Alright then," the captain said, addressing the control deck. "Have those crews return to the ship. We must assume our efforts to transmit and receive messages through the broadcast laser dishes are compromised. Instead of wasting time trying to figure out why, we must compensate by using other methods. Any ideas?"

"Why can't we use the radio in one of the spacebugs on board?" asked one of the maintenance techs, who was repairing a damaged console.

"We can't rely on that," answered a communications tech. "The spacebug uses a conventional radio antenna. The asteroids inside the belt would hamper transmission."

"How about if we launch a gutted missile to the nearest Omicron asteroid station with an encapsulated message with what we've discovered?" offered one of the security personnel.

"I fear that VICI would shoot it from the sky as soon as she detected it," the captain opined. "If one of the weapons turrets destroyed it before the message was recovered, the station might get the wrong idea."

"Besides," cautioned the comm tech, "if the alien object could detect the AI's—VICI's program in a broadcast beam, it might be able to determine if there's a message within a missile."

Good, mused Captain Graviton, pleased with the brainstorming session, while monitoring the progress of the round rock on the main viewer as it slowly made its way through the *Graviton*'s corridors. Based on the recognizable corridors being picked up by the internal cameras, the captain had a sinking suspicion of the thing's destination. In fact, he couldn't imagine anywhere else it would possibly go. That meant they were running out of time.

"That thing will soon be here," Captain Graviton said out loud.

"Reactor room," he said, opening a channel. "What's our main thruster status?" he asked, not caring if the object could hear.

"*I can give you a short burst, Captain,*" came the reply, "*but it'll be wasted while trying to maneuver around those asteroids outside. We still need more time to collect hydrogen.*"

Time, we do not have. Ah well, as they say, 'desperate times call for desperate measures.' "Alright, crew," said the captain, getting the attention of those on the flight control deck. "I have a plan. It entails some danger. We will use two spacebugs, manned by a crew of two each. The bugs will leave the ship and navigate through the asteroid belt. One will go to the nearest Omicron station which is," he consulted a schematic on the arm of his command chair, "…Omicron Vortex. The other will rendevous with the fleet."

"But, Captain," said a crew member, "to meet the fleet, the bug will have to travel in open space. It'll take nearly a day to get there. It's only a utility craft."

"Yes, I know. It can be done. If you were paying attention to the first officers' conference last night, you'll recall Captain Nebula transported three remote sensor probes to those coordinates from Omicron Nebula by himself, and made the return trip just a few days ago."

"He did say it was going to be dangerous," said a member of security.

"Yes, I did. But I meant dangerous in that our alien passenger might try to stop either or both bugs." Arjun noticed several young officers visibly swallow. "I need four volunteers. But before you decide, know that it will be just as dangerous, if not more so, for those of us who remain on the flight control deck."

"What makes you think the alien device is coming to the control deck, sir?"

"What makes you think it isn't?" the captain shot back. "I mean really, where else would it go?"

"But how does it know the layout of the ship?" inquired a technician.

"For that matter, how did it get the access code to enter our airlock?" asked another.

O' Vishnu, you grace them with eyes and ears, but they cannot see or hear.

Indeed. It was apparent this group was sorely in need of experience and imagination. *If we survive this mission, when next they are snug in their own beds on Omicron Graviton, they will possess both.* "It is our belief that those who are responsible for this…whatever," the captain motioned to the object on the main viewer, "are responsible for the disappearance of the ISS *Omicron* and *Omega*." The two vessels were only the stuff of legend to the young technicians, most of whom were born in the Alpha Centauri star system and only knew of the first two ships through history lessons. "It's possible," he continued, "they have access to one or both ships, which considering recent events, seems likely.

"Now, my plan calls for those of us remaining on the control deck to somehow keep the object distracted so that the spacebugs can exit the *Graviton*, hopefully without detection."

Now that the danger of his plan could be fully assessed, there were more than enough volunteers. For each bug, Arjun chose one member of security, each a proficient pilot, and one communications tech and sent them on their way to the small hanger located on the outer perimeter of the habitat cylinder to standby in the crafts and await the order to egress.

Within 45 seconds of their departure from the flight control deck, located in the very center of the habitat cylinder, the object was outside, ready to access the code to enter the flight control deck.

"Let us not keep our guest waiting," Captain Graviton said, looking more relaxed in his command chair than he really felt. "Open the door and bid it welcome."

In the Central Command Module on the Omicron Nebula space station, commander Raquel "Rocky" Cummings was conversing with the Virtual Inquiry Computer Interactive hologram. "And you're certain that thing doesn't know we're aware of it?"

"I cannot be absolutely certain, Commander, but according to my clone on the starship *Nebula*, who received the information from my clone on the *Graviton*—may she rest in peace—passive sensors are below the threshold of the object's ability to detect."

"Then how was your, uh, clone able to get a message to us without being detected, while your clone on the *Graviton* got caught sending a message to you—I mean your clone on the *Nebula*?"

"The object trailing the *Graviton* was on heightened alert, no doubt due to that vessel's unusual patrol through the asteroid belt, that particular object's hiding place. As for the object shadowing us here on Omicron Nebula as well as those spying on our sister stations, they are merely observing business as usual."

"And it'll stay that way as long as we observe it with passive sensors?"

"Correct."

"We can't get a lot of info from it that way, though."

"True. However, we do not know the extent of danger the object poses if it detects our observation of it."

"Stars. That pretty much paints us in a corner. I'll wager Arjun Vohra must've felt the same way when your…when you discovered the thing trailing the *Graviton*." Rocky Cummings decided to give up trying to differentiate the various manifestations of the Virtual Inquiry Computer Interactive program.

"He did," confirmed VICI. **"In fact, he referred to it as a stalemate."**

"Then I can imagine how frustrated he must've felt. Yet the *Graviton* was there to ferret the bugger out. They had to take the chance of breaking the stalemate."

The hologram was about to comment, but decided against it.

Rocky Cummings smiled at the interactive program. "Thanks for not stating the obvious, VICI. I know my duty is to live with the frustration. I simply can't afford to test the thing since I have a responsibility to the citizens of Omicron Nebula as well as the planet below."

"We could still learn a lot from the thing if we practice patience. Although it knows more about us, no doubt, than we about it, we have an advantage in knowing of its existence at all. Especially if it doesn't know that we know that it knows about us."

The commander couldn't tell if the hologram was attempting

humor or not. *And what was that "rest in peace" thing all about? It—she's talking about herself. Isn't she?* "I'm sure we'd know more," Rocky said instead, "if we could communicate with the *Graviton*. I sure hope they're alright."

"We may know something soon. The *Radian* was sent to the asteroid belt to ascertain the *Graviton*'s status."

"There they are. I've found them."

"Excellent," praised Michelle Woo, a.k.a. Captain Radian of the Interstellar Starship *Radian*, on approach in-system, just outside the asteroid belt orbiting Alpha Centauri A. "Let's see them on the main viewer."

The large view screen, which had shown the asteroid belt from a great distance, distorted as the *Radian*'s cameras magnified the image to reveal a thankfully intact ISS *Graviton*, obscured by hundreds of various-sized asteroids.

"They look okay from here," commented Captain Radian. "What kind of readings are we getting?"

"Everything reads normal, but for communications and low power levels. Life signs are present and strong. In fact, all crew are accounted for."

"Then where is the fake asteroid?"

"Long range sensors can pick up nothing around the *Graviton*."

"Odd," the captain said, scratching her cheek. "Could there have been a battle? Maybe the *Graviton* destroyed it."

"That seems unlikely, Captain. The *Graviton* appears undamaged. There are no unusual radiation readings that are indicative of combat. As far as I can tell, no asteroids have been pulverized in the immediate vicinity. No evidence of a space battle at all."

"Hmm. More and more curious. Can you tell what's wrong with their communications?"

"Not as yet. From this distance, the *Graviton* appears to be hardy and whole. Perhaps I can gather more details as we get closer."

"Strange. These ships are equipped with four telescoping, omnidirectional, rotating broadcast laser dishes, and not one of them on the *Graviton* is sending or receiving signals. It's as if…as if they're being blocked."

"Blocked. Of course," the *Radian*'s version of VICI said, snapping her translucent fingers. **"One moment, Captain Radian."** With that, the hologram vanished.

The crew of the *Radian*'s flight control deck all gave their captain a questioning look.

"I have no idea," the captain replied. "She's got something up her sleeve, alright. Well…if she had any sleeves, I mean. How long before we reach the belt?"

"In just two minutes, Captain," answered the navigator.

"Confirmed, Captain Radian," VICI said as she re-materialized, grabbing everyone's attention. **"The *Graviton*'s communications are blocked. Or more accurately, absorbed."**

"Absorbed?" asked the captain. "Explain."

"Please direct your attention to the astronavigation table."

Michelle Woo stepped around her command crash chair to stand in front of the astronavigation table behind her. There, she saw a holo-representation of the ISS *Graviton* surrounded by an oblong, not-quite transparent bubble.

"This bubble, which cannot be seen in visible light, has encased the *Graviton*. It is not simply blocking signals to and from the ship, but is absorbing them, not allowing the signals to bounce back. It is a gradual assimilation of signal, which will no doubt leave a communications technician on board with the impression the lasers are not generating enough power for broadcast. Any incoming transmission would appear distorted."

"Distorted, eh? That would make me think the dishes were out of alignment."

"No doubt."

"But if I know Arjun Vohra, he'd be suspicious that all four dishes were displaying the same discrepancy."

"I am sure."

"Are broadcast beams the only thing being compromised by the invisible bubble?"

"It would appear so, as I'm able to read the vessel's other functions, including life support."

"But if the object is nowhere in the vicinity, how is it able to encase the *Graviton* like that?"

"Then logically, the only possible location for the object would be—"

"…inside the ship," the captain continued for the hologram. "As Jack Askew would say…'Yowza!' Then there's no reason to believe solid objects couldn't pass through that bubble?"

"I am quite sure they can."

"How can you be so certain?"

"Because two spacebugs have just exited the *Graviton* and are passing through the bubble as we speak."

Everyone immediately snapped their attention to the main viewer, which showed two tiny objects leaving the *Graviton* and flying off in opposite directions. One toward the *Radian* and open space, the other, away in-system.

"Open a channel to both of those bugs now," ordered Captain Radian to her comm tech.

"Aye, aye, Captain," she responded. "But reception will be garbled due the asteroid interference. But we should be close enough to read them."

"Entering asteroid belt, Captain," interrupted the navigator. "Decreasing velocity and switching over to maneuvering thrusters."

"Maintain heading," the captain ordered.

"Channel is open, Captain," confirmed the comm tech.

"Attention *Graviton* spacebugs. This is Captain Radian of the Omicron Starship *Radian*. Please respond."

It took a few seconds, but the transmission got through. The response, however, was garbled as the comm tech predicted, with only half of the words coming back, mixed with static.

"—is the—viton spaceb—one. We're read—you."

"—*bug two*—. *Rad*—. *We've been*—*to warn you of alien*—*vices spy*—*Omicron space*–*ations*—*imperative that*—" The rest was lost in static.

"We understand you," Captain Radian confirmed. "Listen carefully. I'm countermanding your orders. You are both to report to the *Radian* immediately. The fleet, as well as the Omicron stations, are already apprized of the situation. We need to know what's happening on the *Graviton*. Alter course now."

"*Underst*— —*tain Radian.*"

"*Yes, sir. We're*—*way,*" was the simultaneous response.

As soon as the four officers from the *Graviton* were on board the *Radian*, the captain had them escorted to the flight control deck, where they updated her on the *Graviton*'s strange encounter with the alien sphere.

"…so the last we know," concluded the security officer from the *Graviton*, "the captain gave us the signal to depart while he and the rest of the crew presumably kept the round rock distracted so we could warn the fleet."

"I don't suppose," inquired Captain Radian, "you know what his distraction plan entailed?"

"No, sir. Sorry."

"There wasn't really a lot of time," offered the *Graviton* comm tech.

"I'm under the impression Captain Graviton was making it up as he went along," continued the security officer.

Michelle Woo was hoping to get more information, but knew Arjun Vohra was of the right stuff. But she was now uncertain whether or not she should rush in. That might interfere with whatever Arjun had planned. "Distance to *Graviton*?" she asked.

"Just over two clicks and closing, Captain."

"All stop."

"Answering all stop."

With magnification, the starship *Graviton* nearly filled the main viewer, with the occasional floating boulder crossing the view.

Now what?

"**Captain Radian,**" VICI said excitedly, "**I am picking up high energy readings from the flight control deck of the Graviton.**"

Oh no. She sat down in her command chair and depressed a smooth touch pad button on its arm. "Security. I want a team prepared and ready to board the *Graviton*." Then, addressing the whole ship, "For now, we will hold position for a few minutes longer to see how this will play out." Michelle Woo then forcefully expelled her breath and stared at the *Graviton* through the asteroids floating on the main viewer.

CHAPTER ELEVEN
The Bully Rock

The door to the starship *Graviton*'s flight control slid aside and sure enough, suspended at about chest level, was the concrete sphere. It hesitated before moving forward, as if anticipating a trap of some kind. The captain figured that was simply his imagination, for as soon as the existence of the device was known, it displayed a level of superiority over the *Graviton* like a canine over a squeaky toy. Everything from deleting programs to draining power to shutting down communications. Not to mention that camouflage field projection technology. So why be hesitant now? The captain thought he must be reading it wrong. It was not as if the thing had facial expressions, or even body language. Yet Arjun's instincts were practically screaming that this device was worried. Nervous. Or even afraid. But how could that be? Why would that be?

Without warning, the round rock shot toward Captain Graviton at an incredible speed, prompting everyone on the control deck to arm and aim their neurowave gauntlets at it. Arjun's first impulse was to duck or dive out of the way. Instead, he decided to trust his instincts and hold his ground. "Steady, everyone," he said in an even tone. "Steady."

The thing abruptly stopped about 10 centimeters from his face, glowing brighter as if getting his measure. The captain displayed no fear, although he felt quite differently. While it hovered in front of him, he figured that until it decided to communicate in some fashion or other, he would attempt to gather as much information as possible using his own natural senses. It did indeed look like stone. He wanted so desperately to touch it for verification but decided against that idea. He surreptitiously sniffed at it. It was quite close to his nose. Nothing. He couldn't smell a thing. It made no sound either. Was it possible the thing could block his natural senses? Somehow, he doubted it.

This was certainly becoming quite the mystery. Why would something so apparently powerful now act with such hesitation? But the more he thought about it, the more he started to doubt its power. His feelings flew right in the face of the evidence of the sphere's displayed abilities. However his instincts had never failed him before. He felt he had the advantage. It was time to act. Wearing his best poker face, Captain Graviton took half a step toward the already close stone sphere. Not only did it back away, but its glow also dimmed and it sunk a few centimeters before apparently recovering. It then performed a slow orbit around his head. It took a great effort of will to not track it by turning with it.

Again, his instincts told him the thing was intimidated. It figuratively took a step back from his advance and then cowered. It looked like it was attempting to cover up its slip by levitating to its former height and luminescence, then performing a circuit around his head, as if to puff out its chest. It was reminiscent of the bullies of his youth. He had learned a long time ago how to handle bullies. They thrived on attention and making everyone else think they were more formidable than they truly were.

Arjun decided to ignore the round rock by casually turning his head toward one of the security officers a few meters from him. "So, Lieutenant," he asked, trying his best to sound as carefree as possible, "how are things? The husband and kid are feeling well, I trust?"

Arjun could see the whites of her eyes surrounding her irises. He wasn't sure if she had worn that expression since the sphere figuratively *stepped* onto the control deck or just now because of her captain's cavalier attitude toward the intruder. But to her credit, the young woman answered, if somewhat nervously, while still aiming her neurowave gauntlet at the stone. "Uh…th—they're doing fine, sir. The little one's starting to talk now."

"Very good," the captain replied, easing back into his command chair and casually crossing his legs. "I expect to see some virtual snapshots."

Just then, another security personnel stepped closer to the captain to defend him, should it become necessary.

"Gladly, Captain, gladly," she replied, visibly relaxing, although she was now supporting her aiming left arm with her right arm.

While the exchange was taking place, the spherical stone increased its glow and was actually rotating back and forth between the captain and the lieutenant. When the captain feigned a yawn, however, the stone luminesced brighter than it had since its arrival on the *Graviton*. It then shot straight towards his head, once again hovering just a few centimeters from his face. *Whoops. Perhaps ignoring it wasn't such a good idea.* Now the captain felt trapped with the thing so close while he was ensconced in his chair. *To hell with this.* With his right hand, Captain Graviton reached up, palmed the stone and shoved it back to give himself room to stand. Once on his feet, he noticed the thing did indeed feel like stone. He expected it to be warm, but despite its glow it felt cool to the touch, like a non-luminescent stone should feel.

As he released his right hand, he closed his left fist which armed his neurowave gauntlet. Closing his left fist was also a prearranged signal for the security personnel to prepare to fire a barrage of neurowaves at the thing, as well as a signal for the communications tech to inform the two spacebugs in the hanger to depart.

Out of the corner of his eye, the captain saw the security member who had stepped closer to him collapse into a heap on the deck. He himself began to experience a simultaneous feeling of physical weakness that quickly segued to mental euphoria. He hadn't felt this sensation since the first time he was exposed to....

Abruptly, the captain was shouldered out of the way by yet another member of the security squad. *Foomp-Foomp-Foomp-Foomp.* A repeated rapid sound, reminiscent of ignited flash powder used in the cameras of centuries past, filled the flight control deck as several neurowaves slammed into the spherical stone.

As he was helped to his feet, he saw the stone's glow dim to nothing.

Then it dropped to the deck with a loud crash and rolled to a stop.

"Hot damn," enthused a science tech, as he approached the lieutenant who had the brief casual conversation with the captain and slapped her on the shoulder. "The neurowaves actually stopped that thing."

Apparently he spoke too soon, for the spherical stone, dimly glowing once again, shot up from the deck and hovered within centimeters of the science tech and security officer. Its glow brightened and the pair collapsed like the first security man.

"Hit it again," Captain Graviton yelled, adding his fire to those members of the Starforce still standing.

Foomp-Foomp-Foomp. This time, however, despite the direct hits from the neurowaves, the object merely wobbled. Instead of going down, it shot to the doors of flight control as if to escape.

"Again," the captain ordered.

Foomp-Foomp-Foomp The spherical stone was definitely weaker but still aloft, attempting to reach the exit. Someone could be heard yelling, "More security to flight control. More security now."

Arjun thought it was time for a more conventional takedown. He snatched up his command baton from beside his crash chair, leaped over the astronavigation table, swung the head of his baton behind his back and prayed the 10-centimeter transparent metal carrying the Graviton standard would hold up to this alien stone sphere. It should, for it was made of the same unbreakable transparent material as the Omicron station domes and transport tubes. "Batter up," the captain yelled, swinging with all of his might, which was considerable.

With a resounding crack, the spherical head of the command baton smacked the stone object which was only slightly larger by two centimeters. The round rock sailed across the flight control deck like a projectile shot from an ancient cannon.

Everyone immediately hit the deck as the stone slammed into the *Graviton's* main viewer, shattering it in an explosion of sparks and smoke. When the smoke cleared, the round rock was embedded in the now-ruined view screen. It looked dead.

At that point, the doors to flight control opened, revealing a pair of security officers, neurowave gauntlets primed and loaded for bear. It looked as if they'd get their chance, as the round stone yanked free of the main viewer and shot straight for them and the exit. Without being prompted, the two security members fired their gauntlets point blank. *Foomp-Foomp.* The stone hit the deck with a bounce and leapt over the heads of the security team before they could get another bead on the thing. Just at the apex of its arc over their heads, its glow brightened and the pair dropped to the deck, joining their fallen comrades.

Despite that familiar euphoria he was experiencing, Captain Graviton still fought to keep his mind clear. He noticed a pattern. It seemed that whenever the object's glow increased, a pair of people went down as if it were draining energy from them. Yet he himself remained more or less on his feet when one of his officers stepped near him. That particular officer, whose pulse he was now checking, was dead. Killed by the thing. When the spherical stone was fired upon at that point, however, it hit the deck, weakened to the point of being nearly disabled. It was as if the object couldn't drain him like it did the young security man, so it was more susceptible to the neurowave assault.

Now, Arjun knew why he was partially immune. But first things first. He punched open a comm channel on his chair. "Attention, crew. This is the captain. The alien object has left the flight control deck, presumably to exit the ship. Listen carefully. Do not group into pairs. Stay separated from each other by at least two meters. It could be fatal otherwise. The object has killed at least one crewman. I would prefer to capture the thing, but if we cannot capture it, then it must be destroyed."

"*My apologies, Captain,*" came a response, "*but the thing is way too fast. It's cycling the airlock now. It'll be out of the ship in a few seconds.*"

Upon hearing that, the captain rushed to the weapons console, relieved to see the rest of the downed crew stir to consciousness. For what he had planned, he preferred the main viewer, but as that was no longer an option, the small monitor in the weapons console would have to do. He called up the radar tracking program and scanned for any object moving near the *Graviton*. He also had the computer verify spatial displacement just in case the round rock tried to camouflage itself to escape. As the grid superimposed itself over the monitor, along with the telltale *blip-blip* of radar tracking, he checked the power levels for the variable beam laser. The laser's intended function was to eliminate debris from the starship's path. It was very effective as a weapon when its beam was focused into a narrow concentration. *Damn.* Power levels were only up to 38 percent. "Reactor room," he called over the comm channel, "I require as much power as you can provide the variable beam laser and I need it now."

"*Thirty-eight percent is the best I can do, Captain. Unless I alter allocation and reroute from the reactor itself, the gravity generators and life support. We can temporarily run those items from the batteries. But only for a short time.*"

"Then do it. I won't need it for long. What's important here is the quality of the laser, not quantity. Give me all you've got."

Fortunately, it took only the flick of a switch to dump all of the power into the laser. Arjun knew that more power was available without looking at the indicator. The main lights died out as the emergency light flickered to life. He also felt his stomach flip as the gravity generators were switched to the battery backup.

"*There, Captain,*" reported the fusion reactor control chief, "*I've given you sixty-eight percent. Make the best of it as quick as you can.*"

It'll have to do. Manipulating the trackball attached to the weapons console to scan the area around the *Graviton*, Arjun soon discovered the bully rock. Discounting the natural asteroids, he also noticed another large object just over two kilometers off the port bow, the most direct path out of the asteroid belt and into open space. In fact, his nemesis was headed in that general direction.

With the main viewer damaged, most of his flight control crew lying prone on the deck and VICI gone, he couldn't spare the time to fully examine the large blip. He was barely able to track the small blip as it rapidly pulled away.

Praying the spherical stone was indeed a device instead of a sentient being, Captain Graviton activated the variable beam laser in a concentrated stream. The beam sliced through space and engulfed the round rock. If the thing truly were a simple stone or rock, it would have been reduced to ionized dust the moment it was struck by the laser, even at 68 percent intensity. Although its progress was halted, it was still in one piece. *Amazing.* But he couldn't allow it to escape and possibly inform its creators, or its colleagues, of whatever information it possessed. He needed more power.

"Captain Graviton," shouted one of his comm techs. The captain fully expected a complaint from the fusion reactor power plant deck. "Sir, we've got external communications. The *Radian* is hailing us."

The large blip. "Excellent!" the captain exclaimed. "Open a channel." Without even waiting for verification, he spoke up. "Michelle, destroy my target," he said hurriedly, forgetting the protocol of referring to an Omicron commanding officer by the name of his or her vessel. "That object is one of the spying devices, not native to the Omicron colony. It's killed at least one member of my crew."

The only response he got was from his own comm tech. "The *Radian* has fired." The small radar blip immediately vanished. "The target is destroyed."

"*So. First blood has been drawn,*" said the image of Danar Seti from the *Radian's* main viewer and the newly repaired viewer of the *Graviton*. "*Well done, you two,*" he praised. Like the rest of the fleet, Captain Nebula experienced a myriad of emotions upon viewing the recorded adventure the *Graviton* had with the small stone sphere, including the loss of one of its crew. "*Consider the destruction of the…whatever, as a bloody nose to our…as yet unknown adversaries.*"

Now that the *Graviton* and the *Radian* were outside of the asteroid belt, cruising through open space to rendevous with the fleet, the *Graviton* was able to absorb a full charge of hydrogen and revert back to main power. Those crew members rendered unconscious by the round rock fully recovered and were back on duty.

There was a happy reunion aboard the *Graviton* as well.

"It's so good to have you back with us, VICI, my sweet," Arjun said, smiling at the hologram atop the astronavigation table.

"It is good to be back, my captain."

Turning to the main viewer to address Danar Seti, Arjun saw a maintenance tech graciously duck out of the way. "Nebula, I am concerned about the other eight spying things shadowing the Omicron stations."

"Yes, we've been discussing that very issue," said Danar, crossing his arms in front of his chest. "*Now that the things have shown they are capable of killing, we are re-thinking our 'stalemate' strategy.*"

"I agree," Arjun said, clasping his hands behind him, "but because everything done from this time forward will have an effect on future relations with the...with whoever sent the thing, I must point out that the death of my crewman might have been an accident. In fact, Danar," he said, lowering his head slightly and speaking just above a whisper, "I may be partly responsible."

"*I can imagine what you must be going through, Arjun,*" Danar said sympathetically, "*but I think you're being too hard on yourself. Keep in mind, that without provocation, that thing assaulted your vessel and crew, deleted VICI, forced itself onto your ship without invitation and circumvented your propulsion and communications. All of this despite your diplomatic overtures.*"

"Diplomatic overtures?" he asked skeptically.

"Yes," Danar answered with assuredness. "*You asked it for identification and a statement of purpose as well as ordering your crew not to fire at it until or unless it assaulted someone first. That someone happened to be the* Graviton's *captain. You.*"

As Danar was speaking, Tan Ozawa stepped into view next to him, indicating she'd like to speak.

"Arjun," she said, stepping closer to the monitor pickup, "*you are in no way responsible for what happened to your crewman. It is no fault of yours that you are a recipient of Omicron Particles, a substance on which our elusive friends obviously have some influence.*

"*Noticing the stone probe could adversely affect people in pairs was a very logical deduction on your part. I believe the security man's brush with the device was fatal because the Omicron Particles in your blood protected you from the energy draining process, which obviously supplies the device with power. Because it couldn't drain you, it drained too much from that poor soul."*

"If what you're saying is true, Tan, that substantiates my theory that his death was an accident," commented Arjun. "Don't you see? It could have chosen to fatally drain any one of us, but gathered energy from pairs so as to render us unconscious instead."

"Yes, I see your point," Tan conceded, *"however, before we can come to any definitive conclusions, there is more to these devices, their energy draining, their creators and what they know of Omicron Particles that we must uncover."*

"She's right, Arjun," Danar agreed. *"We can be certain, however, that the creators of the devices have an agenda and designs on this region of space and they will apparently stop at nothing to achieve them."*

"I appreciate what you're saying, my friends," acknowledged Arjun gracefully, also noticing how everyone was going out of their way in referring to the spherical stones as devices instead of the possible sentient beings themselves. "However, Tan—and I'm sure Danar will agree with me on this—I must differ with you in that as captain of this vessel, I *am* responsible for the safety of every crew member on board, no matter the circumstances."

Tan was about to say something but Danar gently put his hand on her shoulder, as if to verify Captain Graviton's statement. She afforded Arjun one nod and stepped back to stand beside Captain Nebula.

"And now," Danar said, once again crossing his arms in front of him, *"regarding the eight other devices. It has been decided they must be destroyed."*

"Destroyed?" echoed Captain Graviton, wide-eyed. "Is there no other alternative?"

"I know what you must be going through, Graviton," Captain Nebula said, *"but there's something else you have yet to be told. Michelle informed you of the dark hole, yes? What neither of you know is that something is emerging from it. We don't exactly know when it will arrive, although VICI is guesstimating a quarter hour or so. Whatever it is, it's big. Very big. Can we afford to allow the eight other spying devices to transmit even more*

intelligence about us? Another worry is, if we left the things alone and our new visitors are hostile, we take the chance of losing communications as well as main power on all the asteroid cities. We have no choice, really."

"But you realize, Nebula, they must all be...taken out at the same time. Otherwise, they will be aware that we are aware of them."

"I'll let VICI explain," answered Captain Nebula.

The image of Captain Nebula and Doctor Ozawa was replaced by the two-dimensional image of the Virtual Inquiry Computer Interactive hologram, who at the same time was also three-dimensionally speaking from the astronavigation table behind Arjun, as well as the astronavigation tables and view screens of the rest of the fleet. He wasn't sure which image he should face. Not that it truly mattered.

"Now that I have seen the lasers of the *Graviton* and *Radian* are capable of destroying the spherical probes, I'm quite certain my original plan will succeed. At their current rate of spin, four rotations of each Omicron station will have at least one weapons turret aimed directly at the probe in its vicinity. My clone on each station will fire an antimatter missile at the probe, thereby destroying them all simultaneously."

Captain Nebula's image returned to the viewer. *"As you can see, we'll only get one shot at this."*

"Yes, I see," Arjun said, obviously still distracted. "Nebula, if you don't mind, I'd like to ask VICI her opinion of whether or not the...ah, stone sphere is a device or otherwise."

"I'm sure I can speak for the rest when I say that not only do I not mind, but I encourage you to find whatever peace you can," he said graciously. *"Asking VICI's counsel is wise, in my opinion. Would you like to do so in private? Keep in mind, we're on a schedule."*

"I understand. And no, we are all family here. I'd prefer to discuss this openly."

"Then by all means...."

"My dear," Arjun began as he faced the hologram behind him.

"My captain," VICI said, smiling at him. **"Cutting straight to the matter, I'm convinced the spherical stone objects are indeed probes**

of a mechanical nature. Logic happens to agree with my—if you'll pardon the expression—gut feeling, that the devices were pre-programmed to spy on the asteroid stations. I believe one may have been left in the belt as possibly a backup in the event we discovered one of the probes in the vicinity of the stations. It could pass whatever information it gathered to the backup probe which could easily lose itself within the asteroid belt with its camouflage shield and rendevous with the dark hole to pass that information to its creators. A clever plan, but flawed, because their backup probe was discovered first. My guess is, it didn't have enough contingency programming to deal with its discovery, so it became confused, like any programmable device. In the end, it attempted to flee to the area of the dark hole," VICI concluded.

"But, VICI," Arjun protested, "those are very human-like qualities you are assigning to these creators. They could be so alien that terrestrial thinking may not even come close to figuring out what motivates them."

"This coming from the terrestrial man who single-handedly figured out the totally alien beings employed camouflage for their nefarious plans. Please forgive my sarcasm," begged the hologram.

Arjun Vohra threw his head back and roared with laughter. "Thank you, my friends. I stand corrected. And…it is I, who begs your forgiveness."

"Forget about it, mate," was Frank Logan's audio response.

"That's what family is for," said Tan Ozawa.

"Well then," said Arjun, "as Nebula said, we are on the clock. We should get back to it."

"When will all of the stations be aligned?" asked Michelle Woo's voice on the open channel.

"Ah. In six minutes, twenty-three seconds from now," answered VICI.

"And it's going to take you two about thirty minutes at full burn to join us," commented Captain Nebula, "so if VICI's estimation is correct, you'll be arriving after whatever is going to emerge from the dark hole."

"Yeah, you two," said the image of Jack Askew, bumping Nebula's from the viewer. "*So hurry it up, so you won't miss out on the party and all of the fun of greeting our new guests, those spying Nazi-ass bastards.*"

Captain Radian's image then superceded that of Captain Ersatz. "*We're on our way, Nebula. Save us some cake.*" Then, addressing Captain Graviton, "*Race you there, Arjun.*"

"You're on, Michelle," he chuckled. "Navigator," the captain ordered.

"Sir. Course plotted and ready for implementation."

"Very good." He then opened an intra-ship channel, "Reactor room, I need a full burn as of yesterday."

"*Understood, Captain,*" was the immediate response. Then, addressing the whole ship, "*Standby for nuclear acceleration.*"

Yellow alert lights flashed all over the flight control deck. Everyone could feel a slight vibration seconds before the hydrogen was dumped into the nuclear reactor core. The resulting controlled explosion from the main thruster at the rear of the ISS *Graviton* propelled it into open space, side by side with the ISS *Radian*, on a date with destiny. A destiny that would forever alter life for their branch of humanity.

CHAPTER TWELVE
Stellar Void of Light

"Why are you always looking up with that funny look, Ms. Schreiber?" asked young K. Armstrong.

"Hm? Oh, well I...." Babs began, not sure if she should confide to her class of bright children. But because they were bright, they would probably understand her small phobia. "Well, to be honest, my students, I'm just not used to looking at the rooftops and streets of other buildings when I look up at the sky."

"What are you used to seeing?" another student asked.

"The sky, holo-brain," answered J. Beaudine, "what else?"

"I know it's the sky, pigtail-girl, so shut up already."

"You shut up first."

"After you."

"No, after you."

And on and on.

As they were outside, Babs simply allowed them to continue. *Outside*, she mused. If they were truly outside, there would be a blue sky with clouds and the occasional bird. But here on the Omicron Nebula asteroid city, with its varying degrees of gravity, no sane bird would attempt to soar these skies higher than the treetops.

She had promised the kids an outing one of these days and didn't see the point of putting it off on account of her anxiety. Deep down she was afraid they might not have many more opportunities.

No. Scratch that. What a terrible thought to have. It didn't exactly show a lot of confidence in the Starforce. Babs wondered if maybe she should refer to this as the week of nerves.

"Are you afraid those buildings will fall on you, Ms. Schreiber?" Kyle Armstrong asked, able to get his question through the now-fading bickering.

"Well, not exactly…."

"They won't, you know," he said, eager to show and tell what he obviously learned outside of class. "My mom is scared too. My dad says the reason why everything stays on the ground is due to cen-tri-figal force." He pronounced the word slowly, as if well practiced.

What a darling little boy, Babs thought to herself sarcastically.

"Even if the station wasn't spinning," he continued, "the buildings still wouldn't fall."

If the station wasn't spinning, you'd have a hard time convincing my stomach of that.

"Mr. Armstrong, class," she said, "intellectually, I know the structures overhead won't fall. Please understand that most of you, like K. Armstrong, were born here on Omicron Nebula, so seeing buildings overhead is an everyday occurrence for you. But for a lot of adults, like myself and Kyle's mom, who were born and raised on Earth….well, let's just say the sight is…unsettling."

"My dad says that if you get dizzy looking up," offered young Kyle, "you should consecrate on the sing–singa…."

"Concentrate on the Singularity Transport Tube," Babs corrected.

"Yeah, that thing," Kyle said, pointing straight up at the STT.

She tried it. It didn't seem to help, as indicated by the grimace on her face.

"If that doesn't work," continued the boy, "then try consa-conse…try staring outside of the big dome," he finished, pointing at the large transparent metallic dome at one end of the station.

Now that was actually helpful, she thought, and said as much to the young man, who beamed with pride. The rest of the students followed suit but soon lost interest. Babs, on the other hand, was mesmerized and almost couldn't turn away. Just as her dizziness was subsiding however, she felt a slight vibration from the interior surface of the asteroid city. It felt like a small asteroid impact on the exterior. *But that can't be. The station's AI—VICI*, Babs corrected herself, *would've issued an audio and yellow alert.* Before she could contemplate it further, she saw a lighted object flash from what had to be the exterior surface of the station. Without knowing exactly why, she was certain it was a single anti-asteroid missile launched from the weapons turrets, and sure enough, she saw an asteroid silently explode into a showering display of sparks.

No one else seemed to have noticed, for they all went about their everyday business. Babs only noticed because she happened to be looking directly at the doomed asteroid while gazing out of the transparent dome. In fact, the asteroid was stationary. No random activity whatsoever, no yellow alert, no red alert. No audio warnings and no sleep tonight for Babs Schreiber, for she was certain this covert asteroid strike had something to do with Danar Seti's assertion of a "hostile invasion."

Feeling her nausea returning, she came to the realization that gazing out of the transparent dome provided only a short-lived comfort. *Lovely. Just lovely.*

Tan Ozawa was the first to notice. "The dark hole is no longer quite so dark."

"Confirmed, Captain Nebula," verified VICI.

"Hmm. I don't see anything," he said, squinting at the main viewer. "No, wait. I do see something. Is everyone getting this?" he inquired into the open channel. After receiving various degrees of affirmatives, Danar Seti concentrated on the tiny speck of light that was rapidly growing from what appeared to be the very center of the dark hole. Growing was the operative word, for whatever it was, it exhibited the visual Doppler effect: the perspective of something approaching from a distance.

When one considered the six Omicron starships were in a formation that completely surrounded the dark hole, there was no place from which the object could come. It looked more like a tiny thing that must have always been there and was now literally expanding before their very eyes.

"It looks like the dark hole just gave birth and its baby, or whatever it is, is growing," commented Charles Lee, over the open channel from the ISS *Vortex*.

"*That's an interesting observation…from a man,*" said LeAnn Walker of the G*aea*.

"*Thanks,*" said Captain Vortex, "*I think.*"

Although Danar couldn't quite understand why, he was pleased that everyone was acting jovially. For himself, he was apprehensive. This could be the most significant event in human history. For good or ill.

"What I believe we're seeing," Tan began, "is possibly the effects of inter-dimensional travel. I'm quite certain the object's size is constant. If I'm correct, then the laws of space-time are susceptible to the folding of space, which accounts for the illusion we're witnessing."

"*In English, please, Tan,*" requested Jack Askew from the *Ersatz*.

"ID travel makes objects appear smaller than they really are," she amended.

"Oh. Thanks."

While that exchange was taking place, Danar was beginning to make out details of the growing, glowing object. At first, he thought it was another spherical stone, but quickly realized this object, although spheroid in shape, had obvious gaps, as if pie slices were cut from it, allowing the space of the dark hole to show through it. Another observation was that this spheroid object was shaping up to be larger than the round rock. Much, much larger.

"*What is that thing?*" asked J.P. Bouvier of the *Pulsar*.

"*Whatever it is, it's big,*" offered Frank Logan from the *Quasar*.

"*DUH!*" commented Jack Askew.

"*You know, it kind of reminds me of the* Pulsar *emblem,*" said LeAnn Walker.

"I can see why you'd say that, Captain Gaea, but I think not," countered Tan, relying on her ocular-implanted superior vision.

"*Sure it does,*" LeAnn said, "*you can see what looks like a series of rings or the orbital paths of several electrons circling an invisible nucleus."*

"That's not a bad observation, Captain Gaea," Tan offered, "but those series of rings are not orbiting anything, there are actually three rings rotating around each other. My friends, that object is a gyroscope. A gyroscope composed of negative energy."

"You-you can see that?" asked Danar, next to her.

"Not exactly," she said. "Call it a hypothesis. Do you concur, VICI?"

"Yes. Yes I do, moth–ma'am."

"But why negative energy?" asked Charles Lee.

"It's been theorized for several centuries," Tan began, "that if there was ever any hope of matching or breaking the light speed barrier, incredible amounts of energy would have to be harnessed. More energy than could ever be generated in a laboratory, or even on a planet's surface for that matter. But because our species developed on the surface of a planet, it seemed hopeless to generate that kind of energy from scratch."

"You mean there's another way to build up that amount of energy?" asked Danar.

"Theoretically," answered Tan. "Instead of attempting to generate that amount from zero, you work from the other end of the scale: Ultimate energy, and work your way down until you reach the desired amount. And trust me, you wouldn't have to work too far down once you have access to an ultimate energy source."

"Do you mean to suggest, Doctor Ozawa," asked J.P. Bouvier, *"that these beings already have access to this ultimate energy? Under what conditions could this energy exist?"*

"The Big Bang comes to mind," suggested Charles Lee.

"I'm no scientist," admitted Frank Logan, "but I'd guess you'd need negative energy in order to time travel back fifteen billion years to get negative energy."

"That would be my guess as well, Captain Pulsar," agreed Tan.

"Then where could these jokers get that kinda energy?" asked Frank.

"Not from our dimension, I'd wager," commented Danar.

"Who knows how the physical laws of another dimension are written?" shrugged Tan.

"*Maybe these guys are willing to tell us,*" said Charles, referring to the expanding gyroscope.

"*To be honest, I never even considered the possibility of another dimension until recently,*" mused LeAnn.

Tan smiled to herself as she recalled her experiences in what she called quantum space over 30 years ago and wondered if she were the first human to be exposed to other realms. If so, that may no longer be the case in the near future. "I know what you mean, Captain Gaea," agreed Tan. "Until recently, I never considered using negative energy for anything other than space travel. Traveling between dimensions. Incredible."

"The use of ultimate energy for ID travel begs the ultimate question," said Danar. "Why? Why travel to another dimension? What commodity exists in this dimension, that could be of any interest to beings who control such power?"

"As discussed in our last briefing," suggested Tan, "it could be simple exploration."

"Somehow, based on everything that's happened between Sol and Alpha Centauri," he said, his eyes narrowing, "I get the feeling it's more…urgent."

"A feeling? As in intuition?" asked Tan. "That's not very scientific, Danar."

"Perhaps not," he said, affording her a half-smile, "but intuition is akin to instinct, which has proven very useful in nature."

"That's true," she agreed. "What else does your…intuition tell you?" she asked, having known Danar had more on his mind.

"I can't help but wonder if they've come here for the same reason we came. Because they had to." He then shook his head, as if to clear it of random thoughts. "Let's just say that's my hypothesis based on a gut feeling."

"Interesting you should say that, Danar," said Tan, rubbing her chin. "After seeing the footage of the stone probe on the *Graviton*, I'm beginning to wonder if—"

"**Heads up, Starforce,**" interrupted VICI. "**Something is happening.**"

The main viewers of the starships did indeed show a very large gyroscope-type object whose three rings were rapidly rotating around each other, encased inside the sphere of the dark hole, which was now not quite so dark. In fact, the hole's brightness was now competing with the glowing energy of the gyroscope to the point where the spinning dervish was no longer visible. It was becoming so bright, the main viewers automatically compensated by filtering the image.

Then, abruptly, the too-bright sphere popped out of existence, leaving the oversized gyroscope in its place.

"I believe we can safely say the gyroscope has arrived in our dimension," opined Tan.

"Is that thing as large as I think it is?" asked Danar.

"It is on the order of three kilometers, the size of the dark hole that preceded it," VICI answered.

"*Could that be the aliens?*" asked Frank Logan.

When no one ventured an answer, Danar asked, "VICI, your opinion."

"If I had to guess, Captain Nebula, I would go with no."

"Why do you say that?"

"Because I believe the gyroscope is merely part of the process of ID travel. You will note the glow from the rings is similar to the illumination radiating from the stone probe that hassled the *Graviton*, which leads me to believe the gyroscope is also a device."

"A thought occurs to me, my friends," said Captain Nebula. "Chances are, the first thing these beings will seek are the stone probe spying devices of which there is no longer any trace, thanks to us. From this time forward, as far as they're concerned, we know nothing about them. Until further notice, let their disappearance be a mystery to our new guests, understood?"

Everyone agreed.

"Look, everyone," Tan said, pointing to the main viewer, "the rings are speeding up." Speeding up to the point of becoming what appeared to be a solid pulsating sphere of light.

"I believe we are witnessing the end of the inter-dimensional transit process," offered VICI.

"Attention passengers, last stop...Port-o-Omicron. Please remember to collect your personal belongings before you disembark," joked Jack Askew.

"A *pleasure cruise, eh?*" asked Frank Logan, referring to Jack's joke. "Let's hope this is all this will turn out to be. As opposed to 'Veni, vidi, vici,' 'I came, I saw, I conquered.'"

"There will be no conquering here today," said Captain Nebula. "Not if we can help it. Besides, as you all know, Julius Caesar's Latin word for conquer, vici," he said, winking at the hologram, "is on *our* side." Although, unlike F. Logan, Seti said the word in its proper Latin pronunciation: veh-chee.

The very moment the words were out of his mouth, the rapidly spinning gyroscope vanished as suddenly as had the bright hole before it. What was left in its wake was not completely unexpected.

"*We should have guessed,*" opined LeAnn Walker.

In the space previously occupied by the dark/bright hole, then the glowing gyroscope, now floated three objects that looked very much like the spherical stone probes, on a much larger scale, however.

"VICI, I've got an assignment for you," ordered Captain Nebula. "I want you to orient the broadcast laser dishes on all of the Omicron vessels in formation to constantly monitor one another. Dedicate one dish from each ship to remain in constant contact with that ship's respective asteroid station, one dish to keep a channel open to the other ships and the remaining two dishes for power transfers to and from each vessel, just in case these oversized rocks decide to drain our power or block our communication."

"Understood, Captain Nebula. Orientation in progress."

Outside each starship, the four telescoping arms of the broadcast laser dishes extended, retracted and rotated in preparation to carry out Captain Nebula's orders.

"*A capital idea, mate,*" praised Captain Quasar.

"Exactly how big are these things," asked Nebula, "and can we get a reading on their composition?"

"Switching to main sensors. We are not being blocked. The larger of the three is one point two kilometers in diameter. Smaller than the length of an Omicron starship, but twelve times the mass.

The two others are identical at point seventy-eight kilometers in diameter. They are all made of what appears to be ordinary stone. Each has an internal power source that reads very much like a form of Bremsstrahlung radiation. Very much like Omicron Particles. That may explain why they are here," reported VICI. "The commodity about which you spoke, Captain Nebula, could be Omicron Particle lodes back on the planet Omicron."

Captain Nebula nodded his understanding.

"*Should we not try to communicate,* mon ami?" suggested Captain Pulsar.

"*How?*" asked Captain Gaea. "*And on what frequency?*"

"If these beings are responsible for the disappearance of the *Omicron* and the *Omega*," commented Nebula, "they may have had access to those ships. Look at how easily the spheroid stone probe gained access to and temporarily disabled the *Graviton*."

"*I see where you're going,*" said Gaea. "*Our regular frequency should do the trick.*"

"**At this distance,**" offered VICI, "**we should be able to communicate easily without altering the configuration of the broadcast lasers.**" Nebula nodded his understanding.

"Channel open, Captain," said a comm tech.

Captain Nebula paused for a moment, trying to determine the best course of action to open this dialogue to first contact. Should he come on strong? After all, this could be considered a hostile invasion, when one took into account the death of an Omicron citizen by one of their spying devices. On the other hand, he and his colleagues had agreed to claim ignorance of the round rocks. Welcoming the visitors with open arms seemed pointless while the Omicron vessels were aiming their weapons at them. Acting surprised at their arrival would be equally ludicrous.

He wished he'd given this more thought. *It's too late now*. He would just have to wing it. "Greeting, visitors. This is Captain Nebula speaking. You have entered the trinary star system of Alpha Centauri, a territory of Earth citizens under the protection of the Starforce of Omicron. State your identity and your intentions."

Silence.

Patience, he self-counseled. "This is Captain Nebula. You have entered the trinary star system of Alpha—"

"*Behold*," boomed a deep, almost gravelly voice from the open channel, "*and tremble in awe, for arrived have your superiors.*"

"*You gots to be jivin' me, bud*," said Jack Askew's voice.

"Quiet, Ersatz," snapped Nebula. He then motioned for his comm tech to isolate the new channel and close down the open one. It was understood the captain wanted his colleagues to hear.

"With whom do I have the...honor of speaking?" continued Nebula.

"*Your superiors, we are*," answered the booming voice.

"Your *opinion* has been noted," spoke Nebula, emphasizing the word opinion. "May I know the designation by which your...equals refer to you?"

"*Difficult is the translation to your primitive patterns of speech. However, Stellar-Void-of-Light, you may refer to me as. Should the length prove difficult, refine the designation for your comfort you may.*"

"Thank you so much, Stellar-Void-of-Light," Nebula said, skirting the envelope of sarcasm. "Your designation can indeed be refined further. How does *Blackstar* strike you?"

"*Blackstar*," repeated the booming voice, formally known as Stellar-Void-of-Light. "*Acceptable...that...is.*"

"Excellent," Nebula said without emotion. "Now. Whom does Blackstar represent?" Then, after a thought, "May I ask." It wasn't really a question.

"*The Grand Species of the Royal Realm of True Life do I represent.*"

"Fine, fine," said Nebula, trying not to lose patience, "Imperial Giants. On second thought, how about the *Giants of Imperia?*"

"*Invokes awe does it not?*" asked Blackstar.

"As a mere human," Nebula spoke with disguised sarcasm, "struck with awe I am."

"*Fine, fine*," said Blackstar, misunderstanding Nebula's previous impatience.

Listening to this dialogue of first contact, Tan was pleased that

Danar was, so far, successfully walking a fine line of controlling the conversation while at the same time placating the...alien being. *One moment. Alien being? Unbelievable.* It was one thing to clinically analyze Danar's efforts in dealing with this Blackstar character, but she had her doubts as to whether or not she could remain composed, despite her varied and sometimes unique experiences since being thawed for the first time so long ago. On the other hand, Tan never aspired to be in a position of authority over anyone. That's why she'd always ducked the Starforce's attempts to induct her into its ranks. She was perfectly content contributing her technical and scientific expertise. For her, it was the best of both worlds. Studying science and, as her poppa predicted, experiencing adventures of a lifetime in a new star system. *Poppa had no idea.*

Enough ruminating. Time to contribute. Nudging Danar to get his attention, Tan pointed two fingers at her own eyes. Danar nodded his understanding.

"Blackstar," began Nebula, "we would be...uh, honored if you would...agree to two-way visual communications. It would be interesting to see what the other looks like, would it not?"

"*Known to us your primitive countenance is,*" said Blackstar, almost contemptuously. "*Uncertain of your worthiness to view our grand visage we are.*"

"Honored we would be," spoke Nebula graciously.

"*Under consideration your suggestion we will take. Standby.*"

Captain Nebula threw a glance at his comm tech. "Huh? Oh," the tech said, catching up to the moment, putting his hand to the receiver in his ear. "The, uh, Giants have closed the channel."

"Tan, VICI, anyone," Nebula said, turning to face the entire control deck, "I need a way to communicate with the rest of the fleet without the Giants listening in."

"Text messages might work, Captain," offered the comm tech.

"It's a good idea, Lieutenant, but too slow. Our *superiors* may be back any moment."

"I have an idea, Danar," said Tan. Somehow, he knew she would. "There are ten digital cameras spread throughout the control deck on all the ships, yes?" Danar confirmed it. "I propose that VICI access eight of the ten digital cameras on each vessel's control deck with her holographic matrix and transfer the signals in realtime using each vessel's passive sensors to carry the holographic patterns," explained Tan, "assuming of course, the Imperian Giants are unable to pick up our passive sensors…like their stone probes, about which we know nothing."

"**Stone probes? What stone probes?**" mocked VICI, shrugging her translucent shoulders in an exaggerated manner.

Nebula chuckled, then said, "Wait a minute. A holographic pattern is a lot of information to download. Wouldn't it be easier to send audio through a passive carrier wave?"

"Your request was to communicate without the Imperian's knowledge," explained Tan. "If indeed they had access to any Omicron vessel, and they suspected we would talk about them behind their backs with the rest of the fleet, passive sensor audio signals may be one of the first things they'd scan for. But since holo-technology was added to these vessels after the loss of the *Omicron* and the *Omega*, we may have a chance of sneaking communications through their scans. With VICI's help of course."

"Of course. They would know nothing of VICI," said Nebula, nodding his agreement. "It sounds complicated either way. How long will it take to set up?"

"**We're locked and loaded now, Captain,**" the hologram informed him. Danar flashed her an impressed expression. "**Keep in mind, however, we will have no way to forewarn our colleagues. It will no doubt be quite the shock when each commanding officer holographically appears on everyone else's control deck.**"

"They'll get over it," opined Nebula, "and chalk up yesterday's holo-briefing as a dry run. Do it," he ordered.

Eight of the ten digital cameras on the flight deck of the Nebula and her siblings, normally used to record flight control deck operations, now reoriented themselves for their new jobs as holo- projectors, thanks to a little instant reprogramming by VICI. One camera pointed directly at Captain Nebula, while the others onboard the Nebula aimed themselves around the captain in a semicircle pattern. The same thing was happening on the other control decks of the fleet, for within seconds, five translucent but flickering images—Charles Lee, J.P. Bouvier, Frank Logan, LeAnn Walker and Jack Askew, complete with their command crash chairs—surrounded Captain Nebula. There were also two columns of holographic beams that had a hard time solidifying into Arjun Vohra and Michelle Woo.

"My apologies, Captain Nebula," said VICI. **"The *Graviton* and the *Radian* are apparently still too far away for the passive sensors to pick up."**

"Understood, VICI," said Nebula, "let them go. We don't want to take the chance our Imperial visitors might detect what we're doing. If you think you can do it without the Giants' knowledge, send our two wayward friends text using the passive sensors, if it's not too much trouble."

"No trouble at all, Captain. The fact that we are between the Imperians and the *Graviton* and the *Radian* should minimize their ability to detect the signal. Sending it as text will free up enough resources to allow the remaining images to come in a bit clearer."

"Greetings, my friends," Nebula said to the shocked images surrounding him. At the same time, he reached out and briefly squeezed Tan's hand to silently thank her. For her part, she accepted his hand and didn't let go. He didn't protest.

"Geez Louise, Nebula," said an aghast Ersatz, "I'm glad I wasn't in the head."

"You have a digicam in your bathroom?" asked Gaea. "Never mind, I don't want to know."

"Clever idea, Nebula," praised Vortex, "using digicams as holoprojectors on a passive carrier wave."

"Our VICI was sure you and Tan would think of something," said Gaea.

"We were just about to implement that exact same plan. Exactly," boasted Ersatz, "right, VICI, honey?"

"Hmm, of course we were," the now fully updated hologram said without conviction.

"My friends," said Nebula, holding his hands up, "we may not have a great deal of time, assuming you were paying attention. Your opinions."

"I must say," Vortex began, "it's hard to take these Imperians seriously."

"Yeah, really," added Ersatz, "I mean, who do these bozos think they are?"

"It is apparent they believe their own press," offered Pulsar. "I'm sure you noted, Nebula, the Blackstar did not address you by name or rank."

"Yes, I did notice," Nebula confirmed. "Also, you'll recall Blackstar said they were 'familiar with our countenance,' implying they've seen humans before. I believe that indicates they possibly have or had access to the *Omicron* and or *Omega*."

"Why would you say 'had access'?" asked Gaea.

"What I mean by that is…." Nebula hesitated. "We may have to face the possibility that…."

Upon hearing his hesitation, Tan squeezed his hand. He glanced at her, giving her permission to continue. "It's possible the people aboard any vessel in the Imperians' possession may have been killed."

"Killed? How did you glean that, love?" asked Quasar.

"Of course, this is all guesswork, Captain Quasar. And I hope I'm wrong," explained Tan, "but you heard how they butchered our language; our 'primitive patterns of speech.' There was no translation program used. It's as if they learned English with little, if any, consultation with humans," she said, avoiding the term *live specimens*. "The records of all the Omicron vessels include the written text and audio of all of Earth's languages, some of which are structured differently than English, although English has been the dominant language for centuries. Also, their contempt for our 'primitive' ways was obvious. They called their place of origin 'the royal realm of true life.' As if any other life is…false. They may have little or no regard for any other life they consider inferior."

"The same way we humans used to feel about insects or lab rats," offered Vortex.

"Any records the Imperians may have gotten from either vessel would not only be more than sixty years out of date, but would detail a history of war and even a time when humans ate real animal flesh," said Tan.

"No wonder they might think of us as primitives," said Gaea.

"They might also think of us as lab rats," said Ersatz angrily, "worthy only for experimentation."

"We may be jumping to conclusion," counseled Vortex. "They may even eat animal flesh themselves."

"What? Are you saying the *Omicron* and *Omega* may have been a food source for them?" asked Ersatz.

"No, no, Jack," Vortex said forcefully, "that's not what I'm saying at all. What I am saying is they may not consider the eating of animal flesh a primitive trait."

"Well, somethin' about us makes them think we're inferior to them," commented Quasar. "Maybe they just don't like our looks."

"We don't even know what *they* look like," reasoned Vortex.

"We may know soon," said Ersatz, "if we are found worthy of seeing their 'grand visage.'"

"They certainly left the impression they look nothing like us," Pulsar said.

"There must be some similarities," insisted Vortex, "after all, they did speak our language, as distorted as it was. Blackstar referred to himself as 'I' and 'we.' VICI, was that an actual voice we heard replying back to us?"

"As far as I could tell," answered the hologram. **"It did possess the tonal quality of vocal cords, but without actually listening to a live Imperian, one cannot be certain."**

Although Nebula was grateful they had the ways and means to discuss the Giants of Imperia, he'd hoped they could come up with more concrete information. As it was, all they could do was speculate. It seemed like that was all they'd been doing for decades, although the reality was they'd gathered a lot of information, up to and including actually speaking to the alien beings that may or may not be responsible for a great deal of trouble and inconvenience for the species known as Man.

They were *this* close to confirmation. Yet he didn't think it wise to just come right out and ask direct questions. With their superior attitude and apparent powers of breaking, or at the very least, bending the laws of physics, he had to tread lightly.

In a way, he had an advantage in that the Imperians looked upon them as primitive or childlike. But already, the lowly humans had found ways around the Giants' so-called superiority. At least he hoped they had, as opposed to being made to believe they had. As long as these beings thought they were superior, they wouldn't think of the humans as a serious threat.

At the same time, Nebula was concerned his own people might harbor a more antagonistic attitude than necessary towards the Giants of Imperia, as evidenced by the speculation currently on the table. And in a way, it was he and Tan who started it. He thought it best to reign in the aggressive speculation of his colleagues. "On second thought, I'm forced to agree with Captain Vortex," Nebula said. "We're jumping to conclusions. We have no real evidence which suggests these beings hate us enough to kill us and/or eat us. If indeed, they are so powerful, they could have done either the moment they arrived."

"He's right," Tan agreed, understanding what Danar was attempting to do. "There could be other reasons why they are familiar with our physical features but unfamiliar with our language. They may know nothing of the *Omicron* and *Omega*."

"Huh? How do you figure that, Tan?" asked Gaea. "And name one way they could know anything about us without having access to our first two ships."

"Radio and TV signals from Earth's past," Tan answered. "At least, from our point of view, it would be the past, based on the speed of light for the signals reaching the Imperians. Those broadcast would certainly portray us as, well...primitive."

"Tan, I understand what you are saying about the broadcast from Earth's past. Depending on where the Imperians come from, they could currently be receiving centuries old information from Earth broadcasts," explained Gaea. "But I thought we pretty much established they came from a different dimension of space, not just a different location."

"The very fact that they have traveled here from another dimension doesn't mean broadcast signals couldn't bleed, leak or somehow be deflected into that dimension."

"Maybe so," said Ersatz, "but I think we have enough evidence they are, at the very least, familiar with our starships based on the adventures of the *Graviton*," he concluded, referring to the stone probe's access to that vessel, but not wanting to take the chance of mentioning it in case they were indeed being monitored.

"Well, there is that," admitted Nebula, who obviously hadn't forgotten the notion the Imperians likely had access to at least one Omicron starship.

"But I understand where you're coming from, old boy," Ersatz said in uncharacteristic understanding. "It's not like we could just come right out and put them on the spot. Well, we could actually," he said, "but chances are, it wouldn't go far to further our goals."

"Well said, Jack," praised LeAnn Walker.

Captain Ersatz raised an eyebrow, fully expecting LeAnn to call him "jackass," and smiled his thanks when she didn't. Not that he really minded. After all, she'd been doing it for nearly 20 years. He'd assumed the name as an endearment between friends; at one time, more than friends. But now was not the time for endearment.

Danar was always pleasantly surprised when Jack Askew displayed his true wisdom and controlled his righteous temper. Despite his clownish demeanor, Askew was quite intelligent. In fact, Danar could see young Roshan Perez in say, 15 years, when he looked at Jack Askew. They shared many of the same qualities. John "Jack" Askew didn't become captain of Omicron Ersatz, beating out hundreds of qualified applicants, simply because he looked good in a brown uniform.

"Okay, maybe we shouldn't simply come right out and ask the Imperians if they are responsible for Earth's near devastation or the random roids," added Nebula, "but we do have the right to know what they mean by showing up on our doorstep suddenly, unannounced."

"Yeah, like you suggested, mate," said Quasar, "there's somethin' in our house they want. Maybe it's Omicron Particles, maybe it ain't. I'm guessin' with that big chip on their shoulder, they figure they can just waltz right in and take it."

"Well then, why haven't they?" asked Gaea.

"Yet," Ersatz finished.

"They've got a big bark, sure," commented Vortex, "but maybe they suspect our bite is bigger than they think."

"In other words," contributed Pulsar, "they are not as tough as they think."

"That was my thought earlier, Captain Pulsar," Tan agreed. "Especially since they…apparently have no reconnaissance of this area. At least as far as I know. But as Danar said, we have a right to know what they want. Continuing Vortex's motif, the big dogs have invaded our territory, perhaps it's time we growled a warning."

All eyes were on Captain Nebula.

"Yes," agreed Nebula, "well, you can bet your—"

"Captain," interrupted the Nebula's chief comm tech, "I believe we're about to—"

Nebula didn't bother to wait for her to finish. "Alright, my friends, back to your stations," he said hurriedly. The Omicron holo-commanders vanished. "Receive on the Nebula's channel only," he ordered.

"*Attention, primitives,*" boomed Blackstar's voice over the comm link. "*Considered your—*"

"Forgive me, Blackstar," interrupted Captain Nebula, "but could you please—we would appreciate it if you didn't refer to us as primitives."

"*Brazen you are,*" accused Blackstar, "*impressed I am. Before, however, either of your requests are granted, something of grave import with you we must discuss.*"

"Name it," Nebula said flatly.

"*Missing are representatives previously sent to this realm of existence. What of that do you know?*"

"What?" Nebula asked. "Imperians have come here before today?"

"*No,*" Blackstar answered, "*constructs these are.*"

"Constructs? I don't—wait. Do you mean…listening devices of some kind?"

"*Of a sort.*"

"What do these constructs look like?" Nebula asked.

"*Behold.*" With that pronouncement, the Nebula's viewer switched from the visual of the three large spheres to what looked like a simple nickel-iron asteroid.

"An asteroid? Your listening device constructs are disguised as asteroids?" Nebula asked, feigning shock. "Blackstar, how long have you been spying on us? And on that matter, why have you been spying on us? What is it you want from…this realm of existence?"

"*It is I, Nebula Captain, who asks the questions,*" Blackstar stated rather loudly. "*To answer is your only requirement.*"

"In the interest of diplomacy, Blackstar of Imperia," Nebula said evenly, "I am…giving you preference in indulging your opinion regarding our respective status. To be honest, I've seen no indication of your so-called superiority."

"*A demonstration of our superiority you require.*"

Here we go, mused Nebula, *will he bluff or call?*

"*Behold.*"

On the main viewer of each Omicron starship, the three large stone spheres moved apart. Their luminescence increased. In the center of their expanded triangle appeared a writhing ball of yellow-green energy.

"What is that thing?" Nebula asked while motioning the comm tech to close the channel to Blackstar.

"It looks like pure energy," guessed Tan.

"**It is the same type of energy detected earlier. Similar to, but not quite the same as Bremsstrahlung radiation,**" VICI offered. "**Reminiscent of Omicron Particles. It is approximately thirty meters in diameter. I don't read it as solid either; however, it appears extremely destructive.**"

"That would be my guess, too," Nebula said, then barked, "Red alert status!"

Before anyone could react, the ball of lightning shot forth from the triangle of stone spheres straight through the surrounding configuration of Omicron vessels. At the moment it passed, the entire fleet experienced a temporary power loss. Not enough for the battery back-ups fortunately, but enough to make the lights go dark momentarily before they began to rise back to normal levels.

"It missed us," shouted a control deck officer.

"They weren't trying to hit us," said Nebula, thoughtfully. "VICI, can you track that thing's trajectory?"

"Not precisely, Captain, but it's heading in-system toward the asteroid belt and Omicron stations. The planet Omicron could be the target."

"Turn us around, navigator," snapped Nebula. "Charge up the—"

"I'm sorry, Captain, the energy sphere is out of range. I am not certain we could catch—"

"Maybe *we* can't," Nebula conceded, "but I know who can."

On the flight control decks of the ISS *Graviton* and *Radian*, the comm techs were still receiving text updates which they were feeding directly to VICI.

"…to which Blackstar replied, 'Behold.' Now, I'm getting nothing."

"How long before we get there?" asked Captain Graviton of his navigator.

"In about five minutes, sir."

"Are you getting any of this, Michelle?" he asked into the link to the *Radian*.

"*I think so, but I have no idea of what's going on,*" Michelle replied. "*Did we get cut off?*"

"Pardon me, Captains," VICI interrupted simultaneously on both starships, **"I'm receiving an un-coded update from my Nebula clone."** Instead of reading it like the previous situation updates over the passive sensor carrier wave, the hologram transferred a direct realtime dispatch.

"Michelle, Arjun," snapped Nebula's transferred communique, "*there's an expanding sphere of destructive ball lightning headed in-system* near your position. It could drain your power if it gets near. Don't let it get past you. Destroy it any way you can."

"I sure hope Danar knows what he's doing," commented Radian. "How can we be sure our lasers won't add to whatever it's expanding into?"

"Technically, you may be right," answered the VICI from both vessels. **"However, if one ship hits it with a narrow focused beam, while the other ship employs a wide angle beam, we may be able to overload it."**

"We'll go wide and you go narrow?" asked Radian of Graviton.

"You've got a deal," was Graviton's reply.

The two vessels began to separate as they slowed their forward velocity, while aligning their trajectories to that of the incoming ball of energy. The sister ships rose above the intended course of their new target. A cone of amplified red hot light shot out from the *Radian*, while at the same time a narrow focused beam sliced out of the *Graviton*. The variable beams of laser energy slammed into the sphere of ball lightning with the force of a multi-megaton yield explosion. Although the lasers from the twin Omicron sister ships slowed the energy sphere, they didn't arrest its forward momentum.

"Dammit," shouted Radian, "it's still coming."

"We won't be able to stop it before it gets past us," VICI predicted. **"And its size has increased to about fifty meters. However, we have slowed it sufficiently to travel backwards, in front of it while maintaining the lasers at full strength."**

In a coordinated maneuver, the *Graviton* and the *Radian* traveled slightly above the energy sphere's path. The Omicron starships flew backward using reaction control jets approximately a kilometer in front of the ball of destructive power.

"With the RCJs providing backward thrust while firing our lasers on full power," shouted Radian above the din of noise as both Omicron vessels strained to maintain their positions, "we're going to run out of juice real quick."

"VICI, my dear," shouted Graviton, clutching his nearly bucking command crash chair, "what are our chances of eliminating this thing before we're completely powerless?"

"Without knowing the full potential of the ball lightning," explained the vibrating hologram, "I cannot give you accurate odds. I can however provide a best and worst case scenario. At the rate we're expelling power, we will at best, destroy the energy sphere but wind up completely drained with heavy damage, or we will destroy it and both Omicron starships. At worst, we will be unable to stop it and be destroyed anyway."

"Great," Graviton yelled sarcastically, "there's a two out of three chance we will destroy it and a two out of three chance we will be destroyed."

"That is about the long and short of it, my captain, yes. I am sorry. I wish I had better odds."

"As do I, my dear, as do I."

"What's their status?" asked Nebula.

VICI then relayed her clone's three best and worst case scenarios.

"Have they slowed its velocity enough for one or two of us to catch up and add our lasers to it?"

"That won't be necessary, Captain Nebula," VICI said evenly, squinting her holographic eyes, while trying to see what her *Graviton* and *Radian* clones were witnessing. "Although the energy sphere is still active, its progress has been halted."

"Is it still expanding?"

"I cannot tell. Things are pretty shaky over there. I'm having a difficult time accessing either ship's systems. They believe the sphere of energy is about ready to explode. They're attempting to back away while maintaining laser fire to keep it stationary, but both vessels are nearly depleted of power. However, I believe the ball lightning is dissipating. No, wait, not dissipating. Its Omicron-type radiation is releasing—OH!"

Every version of VICI in open space vanished without warning. At the same time, the Nebula's main viewer threw up a high-density halftone screen to compensate for the bright flash of an in-system explosion picked up by the exterior cameras. The brightness slowly dissipated.

"My goodness," Captain Nebula said under his breath. "Open a channel to the *Graviton* and *Radian*. I don't care if the Giants can hear or not."

"Sir, I can't pick up a locator beam from either vessel."

"Open the damn channel," he barked. "Graviton, Radian. Come in." Silence. "Captain Nebula calling anyone from the Interstellar Starships *Graviton* and *Radian*. Arjun, Michelle, anyone, please respond." He stood and took a deep breath.

Tan stepped closer to him. Her eyes beginning to water. "Danar, are they—" She choked and dropped her head into her open palms.

"VICI, activate," ordered Captain Nebula. He cleared his throat. "VICI, come online now."

"Here, let me," said Tan, squaring her shoulders before stepping back to the astronavigation table, punching keys on its smooth touchpad console. "She's in the core but will need help coming online. If she was attempting to see through the *Graviton* and *Radian* clones on the rest of the fleet, she'll be in the same condition."

"Can you help her?" asked Nebula.

"I think so. I'll need a few minutes."

"Captain Nebula," prompted the comm tech, "it's the fleet. Shall I put them on?"

"Open the channel, Lieutenant," Nebula nodded.

"*Nebula, what the hell was that?*" asked Quasar.

"I-I think...." he started.

"*Those bastards destroyed the* Graviton *and the* Radian," Ersatz finished for him, after a fashion.

"Listen up, everyone," cut in Nebula, "how is your computer core activity?"

"*Ours is in one piece,*" said Gaea, realizing Nebula was referring to VICI's condition, "*just scrambled.*"

"*The same here,*" added Pulsar. The others verified the same condition.

"This is Doctor Ozawa, everyone. Once I get the *Nebula*'s core up and running, the rest of yours will follow suit."

"*Nebula ol' mate,*" inquired an exhausted-sounding Quasar, "*that explosion. It looked like it went clear back to the belt. Is there any chance the* Graviton *and the* Radian *could've—*"

"Captain!" shouted the *Nebula*'s comm tech. "We've just lost communications with the fleet. And, sir, the Imperians are hailing us."

"Did they cut us off?" asked Nebula, his eyes narrowed in anger.

"**No, Captain Nebula. That was me.**"

"VICI," he said, relieved, "are you—are you alright?"

"**Not quite one hundred percent as yet, Captain, but more than enough to coordinate with the rest of my clones on the…remainder of the fleet. I can keep the fleet apprized without the Imperians' knowledge.**"

"The *Radian*, the *Graviton*?" prompted the captain.

"**I am still a little confused. The ball lightning was stopped. There was a massive explosion. We were—they were engulfed.**"

Someone openly wept in the back of the control deck.

"Sir, the Imperians?" asked the comm tech.

"Oh, I plan to speak with the Imperians alright," he said, disgusted, "when I'm damn good and ready. Let them stew for now.

"VICI, what was that ball of lightning?"

"**I only remember it was similar to Omicron Particles.**"

"Just before the…explosion," added Tan, "you said 'the energy sphere's radiation was releasing…' Releasing what?"

"**Did I?**" the hologram asked, looking confused. "**I do not remember.**"

"Hmm. Let's see if the Giants are willing to enlighten us," commented Nebula. "Answer their hail."

"Captain, we're receiving audio *and* visual."

Fleet-wide, all eyes were focused on the main viewers. The first things seen were what appeared to be a dozen or so yellow-green globes floating in a dark room.

"*Privileged you should feel,*" spoke Blackstar's voice as three of the globes bobbed closer to the visual pick up, "*to view our grand visage.*"

Could these glowing globes actually be the Imperians? thought Nebula, until he noticed the bobbing of the three globes coming closer weren't suspended in mid air, but were attached to what he was sure was a bipedal humanoid body walking closer on two legs. He could barely make out the body's outline but could see that it was broad. The three globes were attached to the upper part of the body. The center globe was on the chest. The two others, slightly higher, were on the shoulders of the being, presumably Blackstar.

As there was no other source of light in the room, Nebula assumed all of the Imperians were similarly adorned with three glowing orbs each. Because the others were in the background, no other details could be gathered about them.

Blackstar had stopped walking forward. The orb on his chest illuminated his head from underneath, casting an eerie, almost macabre light on his face, which made it difficult to make out any great detail. One thing was certain: Blackstar was not human, although there were recognizable features of bilateral symmetry. He had a very pronounced brow over each of two eyes. Eyes that reminded Danar of Tan Ozawa's. But where Tan's eyes had transparent retinas with slightly noticeable irises, Blackstar's eyes were blank white. He had no nose in the conventional sense, but two vertical slits that were positioned just about where a proboscis would be on a human. The nostril slits were closer at the top than the bottom, which made the space between the nostrils, or slits and mouth much broader than a human face. Although Blackstar's mouth was positioned about where a human's would be, it was broad and had no obvious lips. When the alien spoke, Danar noticed he—assuming Blackstar was male—had what appeared to be normal humanoid teeth, which suggested an internal skeletal structure. His chin was somewhat pronounced and at first looked wrinkled, but upon closer inspection was actually vertically segmented into four or five sections. It didn't look as if the being had a neck, just a head sitting atop a very broad upper body. He appeared to have no body hair. The skin appeared to be dark, almost indigo in color, although it was difficult to ascertain the texture. It could be smooth or mildly scaled like most Earth mammals. Of course, there was no certainty the alien *was* a mammal. But there were other items to suggest similarity in development.

It looked as if Blackstar was adorned in raiment. A simple gown, as far as Nebula could tell, suspended on the upper body by shoulder straps, leaving the shoulders, as well as the large orbs attached to the shoulders, exposed. He couldn't tell how the orbs were attached. They could have been grafted or painted on. Curiously, although the front of Blackstar's body was covered by the clothing material, the orb on his chest was plainly visible. It was difficult to tell if the orbs were part of the biological make-up of these beings or not, for although the shoulder orbs looked attached in some way, the chest orb could simply be a decoration on the fabric of the gown. But because the orbs were the only source of light, Nebula couldn't say. The fabric, whatever its composition, looked *sanguine* or blood red in color, the same color code of the lost *Omega* starship. The alien's cloth armbands, worn on the upper arms of what would be the biceps and triceps region in a human, were of the same *tincture*.

Because the main viewer framed Blackstar in a "bust" shot from head to chest, Nebula could only guess as to the rest of the alien's physique. Without a frame of reference for scale, it was impossible to determine Blackstar's size. He could be anywhere from a few centimeters to three or four meters or more in height. As to whether the other Imperians in the background were of the same size, height and shape as Blackstar was questionable, in that some groups of tri-orbs were higher in the frame of the main viewer while some were lower. Some could be standing on platforms while others could be sitting or standing in recesses or pits of some kind.

Captain Nebula was certain Doctor Ozawa was able to gather even more details as well as more xenobiological implications from the observations. He was looking forward to a consultation with her at their earliest convenience. For now....

"May I assume," Nebula began, "this is the...visage of Blackstar with whom I am speaking?"

"*Correct you are, Nebula Captain,*" Blackstar verified. "*Blackstar I am. With regret do we view the destruction of your fellow primates and the mechanical environment in which they traveled."*

"Regret?!" snapped Nebula. "If you regret it so much, why did you kill them?"

"Killed them we did not, Nebula Captain," replied Blackstar. *"It was you who killed them. Ordered them to interfere you did."*

Clenching his fists at his side, in an effort to control his rising anger while facing the viewer, Captain Nebula said, "You…deliberately shot a destructive force toward our territory. Even if I didn't order them to interfere, you can't possibly expect us to do nothing while you attempt to destroy our home system."

"Not our intent was the destruction of your home system," Blackstar explained. *"Unlike your species, to bring about the cessation of life when not necessary, no matter how primitive is a trait we endeavor to avoid."*

"Then why did you throw that expanding ball of lightning at us?" Nebula asked. "What was it?"

"A scattering field of reduced power it was," answered Blackstar, *"designed to demonstrate our ability to control the orbits and gravimetric properties of the realm of asteroids in your home system."*

At last, thought Nebula at hearing some confirmation of the Imperian involvement with the random asteroid phenomenon. "We've been experiencing your 'scattering field' for the last twenty planetary orbits of our home's primary."

"Searching for our…destination we were."

"Blackstar, I have no desire to argue with you, but be mindful of the fact that your species came into our space uninvited, claiming superiority while hurling *bug spray* at our home. And all of this after previously spying on us with your constructs. Why, Blackstar of Imperia?" asked Captain Nebula of Omicron forcefully. "What is it you want? Why are you here?!"

Blackstar was silent for a moment before he spoke. He lowered his head, but kept his gaze focused on Nebula. Later, the captain would swear the alien's blank eyes began to illuminate. *"Very well, Nebula Captain. Carefully you will listen,"* he said, his voice somehow speaking even lower. *"We, the grand species, whom you refer to as Imperians, claim this trinary star realm as our new home."*

Now it was Captain Nebula's turn to be silent before he spoke. But in his case, it wasn't by design or for dramatic effect. It was more a stunned silence. He gathered his composure and spoke slowly, deliberately. "By what right…do you claim…this region of space?"

Without hesitation, Blackstar answered, "*By right of superiority, do we claim—*"

"I assure you, that response as well as your deplorable attitude is not getting any fresher as time passes," interrupted Nebula with equal rapidity. Then raising his voice in anger, "By whose reckoning do you claim superiority over anyone, let alone a species from another dimension?"

"ENOUGH!" Blackstar shouted, displaying strong emotion for the first time. "*In one time unit known to you as an hour, your compliance you will give. In three planetary rotations abandon this realm of space your people will.*"

"And if we—"

"*No option refusal is. Voluntarily your primitive, unworthy species will vacate or by force you will be removed. If necessary, deadly force.*"

The main viewers of the fleet went dark.

"We've been cut off, Captain," said a comm tech, unnecessarily. "The Imperians have closed the channel."

CHAPTER THIRTEEN
The Art of War

"Are we absolutely certain the *Graviton* and *Radian* are destroyed?" asked the holographic image of Captain Ersatz, among his colleagues on the *Nebula*'s flight control deck.

"We can't be absolutely certain of anything before a thorough investigation," answered Tan Ozawa, "but it's very unlikely they could have survived."

"If an investigation is needed," Ersatz added, "then why are we not starting it? They could be seriously damaged and in need of help. I'll go."

"Jack, you saw that...flash. There's nothing we can do," Gaea said sympathetically. "Besides, we've got less than an hour to answer the Imperian ultimatum."

"We don't need an hour to tell those glowworm bastards where to get off," he said, not mincing words.

"Why an hour?" Pulsar asked. "I mean, why not just give the three-day ultimatum and be done with it?"

"Three days. There's no way we can evacuate a population of six billion-plus people from this system in three days, let alone three years," commented Quasar. "Where the hell can we go, anyway? Superior, my fanny," he continued. "That Blackstar and his mates are just lookin' for an excuse to wipe us out."

"One moment, my friends," interrupted Tan. "Jean Pierre has a point. Blackstar already told us we'd have three days to vacate. Why give us an hour to answer when he already assumed we'd comply?"

"They're stalling for time," figured Nebula, stroking his beard.

"I get it," said Ersatz, snapping his fingers. "They've shot their wad, and need time to regain their strength, so they make it look like they're doing us a favor by giving us an hour to comply."

"*Oui*," agreed Pulsar, "that makes sense."

"Regain their strength?" asked Quasar. "I'm not sure—"

"Don't you see, Captain Quasar?" explained Tan. "The Imperians used up a great deal of energy getting to this 'realm.' They also required all three of those sphere ships of theirs to generate that scattering field. In fact, their technology, at least what little we've seen of it, appears to have a built-in ability to absorb energy from whatever environment it's in before, during and after implementation."

"In other words," concluded Ersatz, "they're weak right now."

"Need I remind you, *mon ami*," countered Pulsar, "we are not in the greatest of shape ourselves."

"Only in that we're down two ships."

"That is twenty-five percent of our entire fleet."

"You're looking at the glass as one quarter empty, J.P.," reasoned Ersatz, "while I see it as three-quarters full. Another way to see it is, the longer we wait, the stronger they get. We must attack them now."

"I agree," said Quasar.

"*Oui, oui*," conceded Pulsar.

"It doesn't look as if we have a choice," conceded Vortex.

"I guess," said Gaea.

"Captains, please," pleaded Tan Ozawa. "These six Omicron vessels are the first, last and only defense for an entire star colony. And I remind you, they are not warships. They are aging vessels originally constructed for one-way transportation. They were old and falling apart even before we arrived here and that was three decades ago. If we attack the Imperians now, without even attempting a peaceful solution, and lose, there will be no hope for the colony."

"I'm sorry, Tan, but in a way, you're proving my point," said Ersatz. "Consider, up to now, we've been keeping our heads above water with the Imperians, while being mostly in the dark, using a lot of guesswork and these old worn-out transport ships. We figured out they were coming before they got here. In fact, we were waiting for them. We've thwarted their ability to spy on us. We stopped their scattering field, that ball lightning bug spray—"

"At what cost?" asked Tan.

"They burst into our backyard," continued Ersatz, "bragging about how great they are and how puny we are, trying to intimidate us from the start every chance they got. We've surprised them at every turn. Then they have the nerve to try and kick us off of our land, without so much as an offer or a how-do-you-do. And, to add insult to injury, without even a declaration of war, they destroy two of our ships, hundreds of our friends and family, and try to make it out like it's *our* fault.

"Doctor Ozawa," Ersatz continued, on a roll, "I understand you're a military strategist," he said, knowing it for a fact as they'd all attended the same classes. "I ask you to put aside your scientific analysis and anthropological study in human behavior and see this for the military situation it is. And remember, the clock is ticking."

Tan was speechless. She felt helpless. She looked at Danar Seti, who was reseated in his command crash chair, listening intently to his colleagues debating an issue that was tearing him up inside. "He's right," Tan said to him almost as a whisper. "We must attack them now."

Captain Nebula slowly inhaled, then released the breath before saying with a humorless half-smile, "War. I had hoped the human race had seen the last of it long ago. It seems to me that it's just an excuse to say we have no choice, when the truth is, we lack the means or the intelligence to prevent it. The Imperians are no better. I regret, my friends, that we must be the spark to ignite the latest in a series of conflicts for the species known as Man. It seems we've journeyed to the stars for expansion, exploration and colonization only to bring the seeds of destruction with us." He then said with regret, looking within himself, "Forgive me, Father, but perhaps it is mankind's destiny to forever wage war.

"VICI, how much time is left on the Imperian imperative?"

"Forty-two minutes, Captain Nebula."

"Would you like to weigh in on this?"

"**I fear the contemplation of war is beyond my programming,**" said the hologram. Her neurological network of processors knew that was the case because Tan's studies of military strategy occurred on Omicron, long after the engramatic memory download from which VICI was born. Despite the fact she had access to the same material, she found it impossible to develop a definitive opinion on the aggressive tendencies of war and came to the conclusion that to do so must lay in the purview of electrochemical life, as opposed to electro-holographic life. "**However, as usual, Captain,**" she said aloud, "**you have my full support.**"

"Thank you, VICI," said Nebula, smiling at the hologram, before a mask of seriousness covered his face.

"RED STATUS ALERT!" he shouted. It was a fleet-wide order. He then gave his strategy of attack to his colleagues. A strategy that began with backing away, out of formation around the stone spheres. Then swarming the Imperians in a coordinated laser attack strafing run. The last thing he told them was, "Look at the Imperian Giant stone spheres as the invading wagon train settlers and we're the Indians circling for the…ATTACK!"

After nearly 20 minutes of concentrated laser attacks, damage could be seen on all three stone spheres. Cracks on their surfaces allowed yellow/green light to leak out. The six Omicron vessels were doing everything they could to prevent the Imperians from forming the triangle configuration which proved so deadly to the *Graviton* and *Radian*. It was obvious the Giants were becoming desperate, for they were attempting to generate the grid that produced their scattering field. But each time the grid began to form, an Omicron laser would disrupt it by slicing through it or slashing one or more of the oversized stones attempting to generate it.

It soon became apparent, however, the Omicron starship's laser barrage was losing intensity. The time between strikes was growing as each vessel rapidly lost more energy than it could replenish from the free-floating hydrogen in the immediate vicinity.

It was also becoming apparent the Imperians' ability to repair and seal the cracks and openings in the stone sphere's surface was slowing down as well.

"This seems very surrealistic to me, Danar," commented Tan, firmly strapped in a crash chair attached to the astronavigation table behind the captain. She had to shout to be heard above the vibrations and groans of stressed bulkheads as the *Nebula* accelerated then decelerated to maintain her orbital trajectory with her sister ships as they laced the Imperian spheres with hot light.

"I'm not certain I follow you, Tan," Danar said, swivelling his crash chair.

"It was only yesterday morning," she explained, "I questioned your desire to assemble the fleet out of the belt, and this afternoon we're at war with an alien species from another dimension. Unbelievable."

"Look alive there, navigator," admonished the captain. "Keep your attention on our flight path. Let the weapons officer worry about our target. It won't do to rear end one of our own ships."

"Aye, sir. Sorry, sir."

"I see what you mean, Tan," Nebula told her, keeping his attention on his crew and main viewer. "Everything seems to be happening too fast. Spinning out of control. But like Jack said, somehow, we're keeping our heads above water, even though the Imperians are trying to drown us."

"It is fortunate they only possess limited offensive capabilities," she said.

"I don't believe they expected us to be waiting for them," Nebula added. "I suspect their plan was to surprise us, hit us with that scattering field and disorient us into submission."

"It might have worked if not for you," she praised. "Still, this all seems so…familiar somehow," Tan opined. "Their swaggering superiority, their high and mighty attitude, their spying tactics."

"Yes," agreed Nebula, "very terrestrial."

"You know, Danar," commented Tan, "we don't know whether or not the Imperians can repair the damage before the fleet runs out of power. What shall we do if they can still generate the scattering field grid and we're powerless?"

"I'm fairly confident we'll be able to absorb more hydrogen before they can cause more trouble," he said, not nearly as confident as he sounded. "If we have to, we'll remotely toss spacebugs at those cracks and detonate them."

"I hadn't considered that idea," she said, genuinely impressed.

"When all else fails, improvise, my dear doctor, improvise," he said. "Speaking of which, I'm surprised we haven't heard from Blackstar by now, in an attempt to bluff his way out in some way."

"No doubt," added Tan, "we've damaged his *borrowed* main viewer. I wouldn't be surprised if—"

"Incoming transmission, Captain," said a comm tech.

"Well, that was totally unexpected," said Nebula sarcastically.

"It's the Imperian frequency, sir."

"Put them through," ordered Nebula.

"*Nebula Captain,*" said the distorted and broken image of Blackstar on the main viewer. "*Known to us are the aggressive tendencies of your species. However, astounded we are at your level of foolishness.*"

"Give it a rest, Blackstar," said Nebula with a brush-off gesture. "You may consider this foolishness a formal declaration of war. A declaration your species was too cowardly to issue."

Blackstar's roar of rage was cut off as he was knocked off his feet, leaving the frame of the viewer briefly, his sphere rocked by Omicron laser fire. "*Your attack now you will cease and leniency I will promise.*"

"It doesn't look as if you are in a position to make promises, Blackstar," Nebula returned.

"*Deceiving looks can be,*" offered the alien.

"As you say," said Nebula evenly. "Now hear this, Blackstar, representative of the Giants of Imperia. We will cease our attack *after* you agree to our terms for your surrender."

"*Terms…for our…surrender?*" Blackstar repeated slowly. "*Impossible that is.*"

"Why?" asked Nebula. "Why is that impossible?"

"*Immediate departure your terms will no doubt include,*" Blackstar answered.

"Absolutely," Nebula verified. "It is your species who is the aggressor here, Blackstar. It was you who invaded *our* space, with demands that *we* vacate."

"*No choice had we, Nebula Captain,*" Blackstar said, lowering his head. "*For dying we are.*"

Shocked, Danar Seti looked at Tan Ozawa. She returned his gaze. Just hours ago, they were discussing this very scenario whereby an aggressive species would invade their territory claiming it had no choice.

"I propose a temporary truce, Blackstar," offered Captain Nebula. "If you cease your attempts at generating your scattering field, we will cease our laser barrage. Let us try and talk this through like civilized species."

"*Agreed, Nebula Captain,*" said Blackstar after a slight hesitation. Apparently, several Imperians standing behind him didn't agree, as was evidenced by the growls and snorts of an obviously alien tongue. Blackstar turned to face the approaching glowing orbs obscuring the already distorted view of the sphere's interior. The audio portion, on the other hand, clearly broadcast Blackstar's much louder rebuttal, a rebuttal that was universal in any language.

Tan turned to Danar and mouthed the words, *Definitely hierarchal.* He nodded in agreement.

"*Comply with your temporary truce we will, Nebula Captain of Omicron Starforce,*" said Blackstar, turning back to face the screen, once again casting the minimal light on his features from his three bio-orbs.

The captain motioned his comm tech to open a channel to the fleet. "This is Captain Nebula to the fleet. A temporary truce has been negotiated. Cease fire. I repeat. Cease fire, but maintain formation and keep *sensors* open to receive additional *information*," he concluded, which in reality was an order to absorb as much of the free-floating hydrogen as possible. Just in case.

"Talk to me, Blackstar," requested Nebula. "You say your people are dying. Explain."

"*Very well,*" nodded the Imperial representative. "*Increasingly dangerous to life our realm, known to you as Imperia, is becoming. Lost already are millions of grand…of Giants,*" he corrected. "*Near death are millions* more. Relying on our finding a new home are billions. No choice have we."

"There are always choices, Blackstar. Always," Nebula said.

"*Believe that to be true I would like,*" conceded Blackstar. "An end to the belief time has forced."

Nebula half-smiled in irony, for he had given the same argument to his colleagues less than 30 minutes ago. "We understand better than you may realize what your people are facing, Blackstar, for our…home realm at one time, not long ago, became too dangerous to support all my people as well," explained Nebula, thinking it best to avoid mentioning exactly *why* their home realm became dangerous. "Maybe we can help."

"*Help you offer, despite the…circumstances,*" Blackstar said. "*Not as primitive as we originally thought your species is.*" There were several more growls, roars, clicks and rumbles of protest behind Blackstar. Protests he ignored this time.

"Well spoken," Nebula praised. "Despite the background interference, the offer still stands."

"*Decline your civilized offer we must, Nebula Captain,*" Blackstar said graciously. "*Unlike anything in your experience is the physics of the…Imperian realm.*"

"You'll find that we humans are very adaptable," Nebula countered, clasping his hands behind his back. "In fact, we have an old phrase, 'necessity is the mother of invention.' I have no doubt, the resources and…stamina of both our species could overcome any adversity and will ultimately solve any problem plaguing either of our peoples."

Tan Ozawa, who was most impressed with Danar Seti's entreaty, stepped next to him, placing her hand on his shoulder, silently offering her undivided support.

"*Well spoken,*" said Blackstar, who actually smiled a toothy grin.

"Imperian visitors," spoke Captain Nebula, his arms wide, palms up, "allow me to introduce to you one of our most revered scientists, Doctor Tan Ozawa. Her resourcefulness has no equal," he praised, motioning her to step forward.

"Greetings, fellow cosmic citizens," said Tan, respectfully bowing deeply at the waist. "Please allow me to add my support to Captain

Nebula's offer of help. I believe a pooling of resources between us can be mutually beneficial for all. But even if we are unable to diagnose and effect some form of reparation to your realm in what time there may be available to us, know that *this* dimension of the cosmos is vast. Extremely vast. There is room for countless billions here."

There were more growls, roars and clicks of protests in the Imperian language coming from behind Blackstar. Another Imperian stepped forward, similarly garbed in what looked like a blue cloth gown. This new Imperian was also adorned with the glowing bio-orbs attached to the shoulders and chest. But where Blackstar was broad with undetermined height, this new alien was lean and tall. Much taller than Blackstar by nearly one-fourth again his height. The term Giant was becoming more appropriate with this newcomer. When this one spoke, in fact, the video pickup had to rise above Blackstar's head, effectively cutting him off from view until the auto-zoom backed up a pace to include both beings. Although this new Imperian was taller, its shoulders were only a head higher than Blackstar's. It was its neck that was so unusually long. Its facial features were also different. Instead of two slits for nostrils, its face protruded forward like a snout. It also appeared to possess a small vertical ridge atop its head.

"*A pooling of resources say you,*" spoke the new Imperian with a not-so-deep, almost nasally voice. "*To usurp our superior technology an opportunity for you say we.*"

"I assure you, friend, that is not the case," implored Tan, wondering if this one, based solely on the higher voice, was female, if even such gender issues applied to these aliens. "You will discover we have made great strides in technology since the last time you encountered our people."

"*No friend of ours you are,*" squawked Longneck. "*No friend especially to primates who make veiled threats.*"

"No, no. You misunderstood," Nebula said raising his hands, palms forward. "There was no threat, veiled or otherwise. It was to let you know that we have no interest in usurping anything from you. Doctor Ozawa was only informing you we have technology that may be beneficial to you. We would be willing to share. An exchange of information, if you will."

"*Known to us is your duplicitous nature,*" accused Longneck. "*Known to us is your propensity for deception.*"

"Granted, there was a time in the past when we would be guilty of such accusations, but your information on us is out-of-date," explained Nebula. "In fact, we'd like to believe we've evolved an endless capacity for resourcefulness and adaptability."

"*As have we, primate,*" said Long-neck as she reached forward and pulled what looked like a cable from its socket, which caused the images and sounds on the viewer to slowly dissolve to static.

Blackstar's deep throaty roar could be heard just before he said, "*No! To them you will list—*" He was cut off in mid-sentence as the *Nebula*'s viewer blinked back to the exterior view of the three large Imperian stone spheres.

Captain Nebula, crestfallen, dropped his arms to his sides and lowered his head. "We came so close."

"Please don't despair, Danar," said Tan, gently rubbing his back. "You performed honorably. Besides, it may not be too late yet."

A holographic image of Captain Quasar materialized in front of Danar Seti. "Nice try, Nebula ol' man. You should be commended for risin' over and above the call of duty for that speech. Both of you," he said, indicating Tan. "It sent chills down me spine, it did."

One by one, the rest of the Omicron COs holographically materialized, standing around Nebula and Tan, as the control deck holoprojector cameras whirred into position.

"My friends," said Gaea, "I believe we just witnessed the beginning of an old-fashioned *coup* among our visitors."

"*Oui*, the Giants of Imperia do not appear so alien now, eh?" commented Pulsar.

"Yeah, with that last display of bickering," added Ersatz, "they're looking more human all the time."

"I hate to bring this up," said Vortex, "but if Blackstar has indeed lost favor in the Imperian hierarchy and a more conservative branch has assumed power, this war may have just gone from hot to cold and back to hot again."

"Agreed," said Nebula, releasing a breath of resignation. "At least we've had a chance to replenish some of our hydrogen supply."

"Not by much, Captain Nebula," informed VICI. **"We will not be able to sustain a continuous laser barrage for long."**

"Then we'll be needing a new strategy," figured Nebula, "just in case. Ideas, people?"

"Danar," spoke up Tan straight away, "you and VICI figured out this exact spot for the Imperian transit arrival point, based on the positions of the three stars that make up Alpha Centauri. I suspect this spot may also be the optimal position by which their stone spheres can absorb energy. If we could somehow move them or get them to move, even a few kilometers, that might lessen their ability to efficiently replenish their power supply."

"Whoa, Tan, sweetheart," interjected Ersatz, "maybe you haven't noticed, but those are moon- sized cement spheres, pumped up with Omicron-type energy, not free-floating wimpy asteroids."

"True. But, Jack," Gaea countered, "there are only three of them and six of us."

"Mooooon-sized, LeAnn," Ersatz said, stretching out the word while illustrating a stretching motion with his hands. "As in the size of moons? Hell, we'd be lucky if a couple of us could move either of the two smaller ones a few meters, let alone a few kilometers."

"Wait a second, Jack," Nebula said enthusiastically, while snapping his fingers, "maybe that's all we'll *have* to do."

"Huh?" Ersatz asked, dumbfounded.

"Haven't you noticed," explained Nebula, "that not only are they keeping station at this position, but the spheres have remained in close proximity to each other? As if they are one unit. Even that scattering field of theirs required all three spheres to form the grid. If we could separate them far enough from each other, that may make them more vulnerable to attack."

"That may work, Danar," Tan said, scratching her chin. "However, I'm concerned about that tall whiny Imperian's implication that they too are resourceful and adaptable. I fear they may have other tricks up their…gowns."

Jack and LeAnn both smirked at Tan's unintentional joke.

With a half-smile and narrowed eyes, Danar said, "So have we, my dear Doctor, so have we." He then filled his colleagues in on his plan of using the Omicron vessels' complement of spacebugs as remote vacuum depth charges, with the added idea of loading them all with antimatter bombs in an attempt at cracking one or more of the stone spheres open. He also discussed another coordinated attack plan that entailed four Omicron starships to use a barrage of laser fire to keep the Imperians hassled while the other two ships would attempt to literally push one of the smaller spheres away from the other two using their hydrogen collector dishes as rams.

"Gee, this is even more dangerous than before," said Gaea, "but I guess it's our best shot."

"*Oui, oui*, LeAnn, it *is* our best shot," agreed J.P. "I am most concerned that our strategies are based more and more on guesswork than I would like."

"Yeah, but our guesswork is keepin' us neck and neck with the invaders so far," commented Frank.

"No. We are not even with them," LeAnn countered. "Let's not forget about the loss of the *Graviton* and *Radian*." That sobered the entire fleet since the holographic exchange was taking place on every flight control deck of the six remaining starships. "But we're not out of the race yet," she concluded.

"Well spoken, Captain Gaea," Tan said after a few seconds of silence.

"Hopefully, all of this will just be a contingency plan," said Frank Logan. "Blackstar's liberal party may come through for us."

"I was so prepared to not like Stellar-Void-of-Light, his arrogant superior attitude," said Danar, shaking his head. "And now that—"

"Captain Nebula," shouted a control deck junior officer, "something's happening over there!"

All eyes went to the their respective viewers. What they saw was the two smaller spheres floating closer to the larger one, until they touched, with the larger in between.

"What does this mean?" asked Pulsar

"Kind of reminds me of Mickey Mouse," said Ersatz, squinting at the viewer. "But I don't think they're looking to entertain us."

"This configuration is not consistent with the formation of the scattering field grid," VICI surmised.

"Anything from communications?" asked Nebula.

The comm tech shook her head.

"Try hailing them on the frequency they last used."

"They are receiving us," said the tech, "they just refuse to answer."

"Swell," Gaea said, her face screwed up.

"They're up to no good, I tell ya," commented Quasar.

"Imperians, please respond," Nebula said into the open channel, "or we will be forced to assume you wish to end the truce. That would be regrettable as we have made great progress in suing for peace."

"*Temporary was the truce, Nebula primate,*" squawked Longneck's reedy voice on audio. "*Changed has our original proposition. Hear this now. Immediately vacate this realm or destroyed you will be.*"

"What?!" asked Nebula, incredulously. "The three-day figure was impossible. Immediately doesn't make it any—"

"*Now leave or the consequences you will suffer.*"

"All we are saying," began Nebula calmly, "is—"

There was a loud screech that made every human clasp the sides of their heads with their hands as the channel closed.

"…is give peace a chance," finished Jack Askew.

"RED STATUS ALERT!" snapped Captain Nebula.

With that, the holographic images of the starships' COs vanished, as the Omicron-Imperian war resumed.

The ISS *Nebula* and *Ersatz* held back about a kilometer from the theater of engagement to conserve what power they had left for their ramming run, while the ISS *Quasar*, *Vortex*, *Pulsar* and *Gaea* once again took up the orbit of laser fire against the three Imperian stone spheres which were now in contact with one another.

Although the four Omicron starships were strafing all three spheres, they surreptitiously targeted one of the smaller spheres with more hot light in an attempt to weaken it more than the other two. The plan was apparently working, for even more of the Omicron-type radiation was leaking from the riffs and cracks on the surface of the severely hassled sphere.

At the assigned moment, the *Nebula* and *Ersatz* explosively ignited their nuclear fusion reactors under full thrust. The four attacking vessels cleared a path as the two ram-ships darted into the engagement. With a resounding *crash*, which sounded more like an explosion from the inside of the Omicron vessels on impact, most of the crews of the *Nebula* and *Ersatz*, who weren't secured in crash chairs, were thrown forward, despite the compensation of the vessels' gravity generators.

Thirty minutes earlier, in-system, the citizens of Omicron went about their normal routines. The billions of civilians living on the planet Omicron continued their everyday existence just like the millions who lived and worked in the eight asteroid city-stations. And of those countless civilians living through their ordinary everyday concerns, only one knew that the concerns were anything but ordinary.

On the Omicron Nebula space station, the evening hours approached, as the simulated lights from the Singularity Transport Tube dimmed. Babs Schreiber sat at her desk, the only person in the school building, hours after her fellow teachers, students and custodial staff left for their private lives. She told herself she needed this time to catch up on all of the paperwork for her new vocation. Not only had she caught up, she was now about two weeks ahead in planning assignments for her students. There was nothing more she could think of to do. She should be elated, having accomplished so much paperwork in so little time. Instead, she was depressed. She kept pushing away the thought that she didn't *have* to do all this now and even if she did, she could just have easily done it on her home computer.

The truth, she finally admitted, was that she was afraid to go home. As long as there remained unfinished business, everything else would go on as usual. But the moment she was finished and went home, signifying the end of the workday, everything would end. For good.

B. Schreiber didn't need a psychology degree to realize her fears were irrational. Irrational maybe, but definitely possible. *Well. Not really.* The possibility that everything could come to an end didn't depend on whether or not she stayed here in the school building or went home. Her apartment was as structurally sound as every other building within the curved inner cylinder of Omicron Nebula. What really bothered her was the smooth lie the officials gave the citizenry of Omicron regarding that very bright flash that had occurred an hour or so ago outside the asteroid belt. They explained it as having something to do with the thirtieth anniversary, celebrating the Earth refugees' arrival here at Alpha Centauri.

Although, technically, the thirtieth anniversary was yesterday.

Fortunately, for the Starforce officials and the Omicron council, the arrival anniversary here was not widely observed, like every other holiday marked since Omicron planetfall, unlike traditional Earth holidays and celebrations such as Christmas, Thanksgiving, New Years and the like. Babs supposed it was an unofficial, collective agreement, on everyone's part, to keep as many ties to the home planet as possible, especially since there had been no contact with Earth since they left 57 years ago.

So it was easy for the masses to accept and dismiss the bright flash as a half-hearted attempt to mark the arrival here. But Babs Schreiber knew better. She knew the flash had nothing to do with anniversaries and celebration and everything to do with "the total destruction of the entire Omicron star colony as a result of a possibly hostile invasion."

Most likely, the flash was an explosion. *If that is true, then was it one of ours or one of theirs? Oh, this is ridiculous. I have no excuse to stay here now. Besides, it's Friday night. I could just as easily be depressed and imagine worst case scenarios at home in bed with a gallon of ice cream.*

Now there's an idea.

Fortified with a contingency plan, she made her escape from the school building, immediately found a transport car that whisked her directly to her apartment and happily set about preparing a light supper so as to look forward to some dessert.

B. Schreiber heaved a sigh of relief as she gingerly pulled a small plate of pasta from the food synthesizer, jokingly chiding herself for her paranoia, when an audio warning with VICI's voice issued forth from the apartment complex speakers.

"WARNING! ASTEROID ATTACK IMMINENT. BRACE FOR IMPACT."

"Terrific," she said aloud, sarcastically, "the perfect ending to a perfect week."

Before this week was done, Babs' fears would once again intrude upon her with a vengeance, as this attack would prove to be unlike any other in the last 20 years.

The previous asteroid phenomenon was caused by the Imperian Giants' search and subsequent arrival, resulting in a gravitational upheaval that caused the smaller asteroids to randomize away from their orbital positions in the belt and zip around haphazardly in-system. This particular attack was anything but random, as every smaller asteroid, no matter its position in-system or the belt, single-mindedly shot in one direction: toward the theater of engagement of the Omicron-Imperian war at near relativistic speeds. Those that couldn't get around the planet smashed into Omicron's atmosphere like mass drivers.

Had the Omicron Nebula space station's orbital path put it between the planet and the area of conflict in open space, it would have been spared. Unfortunately, the station's relative position put it within the path of speeding projectile asteroids, causing VICI's clone to work harder than ever before to target as many asteroids as possible to protect the station from a pounding that would no doubt go down in history. The good news was that this attack was only coming from one direction, so targeting was easier—but not by much.

As for the planet Omicron, its atmosphere disintegrated the smaller asteroids before they reached the ground. And fortunately, ground zero was a mostly uninhabited area of the planet.

For the Omicron stations located within the leading edge of the asteroid belt, farthest from the war, the attack was brief. Those stationed closer to the conflict at the trailing edge of the belt had more time to react to the impending unidirectional asteroids. The VICI clones and command personnel didn't bother targeting the incoming barrage, but instead used their thrusters to duck below the plane of the asteroid belt to avoid the onslaught of several hundred million asteroid missiles as they left their larger siblings behind and sped into open space toward the conflict to carry out the mysterious plans of their new masters.

CHAPTER FOURTEEN
The Mickey Mouse Configuration

"*It's working, Nebula,*" Ersatz yelled over the comm channel. "*We're actually moving this thing.*"

Even if the main viewer didn't show the stone sphere sliding across its larger companion, the friction of its passage could be felt and heard through the deck plating and bulkheads. But sliding the thing across the surface wasn't the plan. Separating the spheres was.

"No matter what," ordered Nebula, "maintain full thrust for as long as you can."

"*Not to worry, old friend,*" assured Ersatz, "*now that we've got our teeth around the Imperians' throat, I'm not letting go until we pull this thing apart.*" Just as he spoke, the grating and grinding of the stone sphere's slide ceased as the *Ersatz* and *Nebula*'s efforts were rewarded by a slice of open space between the small and large sphere.

"Up yours, you glowworm freaks!" Ersatz yelled from his command crash chair, throwing his fist into the air.

"**Attention, Starforce. We've got a problem,**" VICI warned simultaneously from all six Omicron vessels. "**I'm registering several hundred million objects headed right for us from in-system.**"

"Objects?" asked Nebula over the din of the maximum thrusters. "What objects? How fast?"

"**An asteroid swarm from in-system. They will be on top of us in less than three minutes,**" answered the hologram.

"No doubt," commented Tan, "the Imperians are capable of reversing that scattering field of theirs. This new Mickey Mouse configuration apparently generates a magnetic field that *attracts* asteroids. Asteroids from the belt."

"Naturally," Nebula said sarcastically. "But the belt is a long way off."

"They did say they were resourceful and adaptable," Tan reminded him.

"WARNING! ASTEROID ATTACK IMMINENT. BRACE FOR IMPACT," warned VICI on all Omicron vessels.

"The ablative plating on our ships won't hold out for very long against that onslaught," said Nebula, "and if the other ships divert their laser fire from the stone spheres, we may lose what little ground we and the *Ersatz* have gained."

"What—what are we going to do?" asked Tan, beginning to look worried.

"You may recall, Doctor Ozawa," Nebula said with a half-smile, "I was the first to claim resourcefulness and adaptability."

"You'll forgive me, Captain Nebula, but if you have a plan, I would suggest we implement it now," warned VICI. **"The Imperian attraction wave will bring the projectiles to our position in one minute."**

"Very well, VICI. I'll be needing your assistance," he said, not waiting for the hologram's acknowledgment. "Your *Graviton* counterpart was able to distinguish the spatial displacement between a real asteroid and the Imperian spy spheres, correct?"

"Correct, Captain, but that was to distinguish physical profiles only."

"Okay, fine," he said, starting to speak faster, "but this Mickey Mouse magnetic beam is not a true magnetic wave, otherwise the Omicron vessels would be affected as well. The same holds for gravitic waves."

"I agree, but without knowing the exact properties of the wave the Imperians are using to attract the asteroids, how can I—"

"You don't *need* to know the exact properties of the wave," Nebula said, cutting her off. "If you were able to distinguish physical profiles of real asteroids using the *Graviton*'s broadcast dishes as sensors, can't you develop a frequency that would disrupt or mask the incoming asteroid profiles? Anything to confuse the wave?"

"Yes. YES! ABSOLUTELY!" enthused the hologram. "I am sending a signal to the other Omicron vessels now…adjusting broadcast laser dishes…transmitting masking frequency. It is working. Also, the Imperian attraction wave has ceased, but the barrage of asteroids is too close. Ninety percent have been diverted and or scattered. However, ten percent—that is still several hundred thousand asteroids—will bombard us in ten seconds."

"That's still better than several hundred million," reasoned Nebula. "Now, Starforce," he said into the comm channel, "brace for impact."

Fortunately, most of the inertia-driven asteroids missed the combatants, but the ones that struck the Omicron starships tested the ablative plating to its limits as the four orbiting ships took a pounding.

"Gaea, Vortex, Pulsar, Quasar," shouted Nebula into the comm channel, "try orienting yourselves to protect your laser beam emitters."

"*Do not state the obvious, Nebula,*" Pulsar retorted. "*Let us worry about the lasers. You and Ersatz concentrate on separating the stone spheres.*"

"Right you are, Pulsar," conceded Nebula, looking at the display on the main viewer, wondering why he and Ersatz were not widening the gap. He then realized the Giants were probably using the same type of magnetic-like wave that attracted the asteroid field from the belt.

An idea struck. "VICI, is there any reason to think your frequency mask won't work against junior here," he said, motioning at the stone sphere they were pushing displayed on the viewer.

"**Assuming all three produce the wave, it won't be as effective, if it will work at all. But it won't hurt to try.**"

"Then try it," he ordered, "and be sure to include the Ersatz."

"**Understood, Captain Nebula. It's working. Barely.**"

Nebula could feel the slight increase in the ship's velocity and was ecstatic to see the gap widen, albeit slowly, with his own eyes.

"*We're doing it, Danar,*" shouted Jack Askew from the comm, "*we're winning.*"

"Uh, Danar," said Tan, directing his attention to the corner of the viewer.

While the background stars of space could be clearly seen as the *Nebula* and *Ersatz* pushed the smaller sphere away from its larger companion, it was also plain to see the swarm of asteroids that got through the scattering frequency beam clumping around the rifts, cracks and holes of the stone spheres, sealing them.

"Hmm, clever," said Tan. "The Imperians used the phalanx of asteroids for offense *and* defense."

"Yes. Clever," Nebula said through narrowed eyes. "We'd better find a—" He stopped abruptly as the ISS *Nebula* bucked wildly before smoothing out again. "Uh-oh."

"*Captain Nebula,*" came the voice from the fusion reactor power plant room, "*the reactor is running extremely hot and is about to reach critical mass. We're going to have to shut down.*"

"No! We can't shut down now," the captain shouted back, "we have to continue at full thrust for as long as possible until we exhaust our power supply."

"*You don't seem to understand, sir,*" the nuclear tech shouted back, "*we're already red-lining. The ship will blow up before we run out of juice.*"

Damn. Danar Seti wouldn't have a problem with the ship blowing up if he were certain it would end the Imperian threat, but even if the *Nebula*'s nuclear explosion destroyed all three Imperian spheres despite the repairs they were receiving from the asteroids, he knew there were billions more Imperians in the other dimension that would conceivably replace them. It might be worth it if the other Omicron starships could escape to prepare the colony for war, a war about which the citizens back in-system knew nothing. As yet. So there would be no point in sacrificing themselves now, while there was still a chance the other ships could overcome where the *Nebula* failed. *We haven't failed yet.* "Alright, reactor room," he said, "notch us down to fifty percent thrust."

"*With all due respect, Captain, that'll only give us another couple of minutes or so.*"

"I'll get back to you before then. Standby."

Hesitantly, Tan said, "Danar, I hate to—"

"What is it now?" he snapped. He regretted it immediately and smiled an apology. She returned his smile briefly, then once again pointed at the main viewer which showed the ISS *Vortex*, the lead ship in the wagon train offensive formation, starting to buck as well, its concentrated laser beam sputtering until it quit altogether. The vessel drifted away, unable even to muster thruster power.

"*Sorry, my friends,*" said Charles Lee over the comm. "*We're spent.*"

At least the *Vortex*'s lasers didn't cause their reactor to go critical like the *Nebula*'s constant thruster surge. Amazingly, the *Ersatz* was still going strong. But not for long, Nebula feared.

"Vortex," called Nebula over the comm channel, "prepare your spacebugs for vacuum charges. When you drift far enough away, warn the *Pulsar* and *Gaea* to back off and let your bugs fly."

"*We're not amateurs over here, Danar,*" admonished C. Lee, "*I've already coordinated with—my God!*"

Captain Nebula could see why Charlie reacted with such surprise. His heart sank as an oversized asteroid smashed into the ISS *Pulsar*, which was between the *Vortex* and *Gaea*, leaving a gap in the formation of Omicron vessels and a further depletion of laser fire.

"Pulsar, come in," screamed Vortex into the open channel, "J.P., answer please."

"Forget about them, Charlie, they either survived that impact or they didn't," said Nebula, nearing the breaking point as he watched the *Pulsar* sparking and smoking, being carried away from the area of combat by an asteroid that was nearly half its size. "Prepare your vacuum charges. LeAnn, Frank, it's up to you. Give it all you've got."

The moment he said that, however, the *Quasar* bucked and sputtered, drained of energy. It drifted away as had the *Vortex*.

"*OH, BLOODY HELL!*" screamed Frank Logan, who could be heard over the channel pounding his fist on his command crash chair.

Just as it looked as if thing couldn't get any worse, the unexpected arrived in the form of a dark shadow blotting out most of what was shown on the *Nebula*'s viewer.

"Oh, no, what now?" asked Nebula.

"*Jack, Danar!*" screamed LeAnn Walker of the ISS *Gaea*, the only Omicron starship able to maintain laser fire. "*The second small stone sphere is literally rolling around the larger one. It's headed straight for your positions. GET OUT OF THERE!*"

"No," screamed Jack Askew, "*just a little more and we can clear–AURGH!*"

The second stone sphere rolled around and clipped the ISS *Ersatz*'s main propulsion thruster bell, instantly shutting of its fusion reaction drive and causing the starship to spin wildly, collector dish over thruster bell.

"Gaea, Vortex, Quasar," commanded Captain Nebula, "the spacebugs; send them down now."

"*Danar, you're too close,*" warned Captain Gaea, "*you'll be caught in the blast.*"

"Our reactor's just about reached critical mass," said Danar, "with the antimatter spacebugs and the *Nebula*'s explosion, we stand a good chance of taking the Imperians out and ending this war, at least for now. If the Giants aren't stopped now, one of you has to get word back to the colonies to mobilize and prepare for an all-out invasion in either case."

As he spoke, Danar Seti looked around the *Nebula*'s flight control deck at each and every expectant young face and saw a myriad of expressions, most of which were of support.

Just as he finished speaking, the Nebula engineer called from the fusion reactor room. "*Ready to take the engines to full thrust, Captain.*"

"Understood, Ben," Danar replied, rarely referring to his crew by their first names, "standby. VICI, download your program to the *Gaea*, now."

"**But, Captain Nebula, I—**"

"No backtalk. Do it. Now," he ordered.

If the Virtual Inquiry Computer Interactive program were capable of tears, she imagined she would be crying by now. She looked over at Tan, who imperceptibly nodded back. Without another word, VICI vanished and the astronavigation table went dark.

Several crew members and techs shouted, "For Omicron."

Tan held Danar's hand and said softly, "For Earth."

"Gaea, Vortex, Quasar, send those bugs down now," barked Nebula. "Reactor room, take us to full burn."

"*BELAY THOSE ORDERS!*" shouted a command from the open channel.

"Who the hell," spoke Nebula.

"Captain Nebula," shouted the comm tech, "two ships coming in fast with what's left of the asteroid swarm. Sir, it's the *Graviton* and the *Radian!*"

"*Who else would it be,*" spoke Arjun Vohra's voice from the comm channel. "*Nebula, old man,*" he continued, "*don't take yourselves out just yet. Power your engines down and let the ship's inertia push the round rock. I'll be taking Ersatz's place in just a few seconds.*"

"And you guys thought the cavalry was history," said Michelle Woo with a chuckle. "*Commence* Phase One Laser Fire, *Graviton.*"

"*Acknowledged, Radian,*" confirmed A. Vohra.

Both formerly MIA vessels swooped out of the now dissipating asteroid swarm and into the area of combat looking charred, dented and even more worn than usual, but carrying a lot more power than their siblings. The *Graviton*'s lasers lanced out under maximum charge and carved a deep trench into the stone sphere being pushed by the *Nebula*. Arjun Vohra cut the lasers off just before his ship collided with the sphere under full thrust right beside the *Nebula* in the same spot formerly held by the *Ersatz*.

Within moments, the small sphere lost whatever magnetic attraction it had to the larger sphere as it was roughly shoved from the combat area by the Omicron vessel.

The *Nebula*, traveling under inertia only, was left behind as the *Graviton* shut down its engines, allowing the severely damaged Imperian stone sphere to coast in front of it for several hundred meters before once again searing it with a white hot narrow beam that punched clear through the other side of the sphere. Where one moment yellow-green energy was leaking from cracks, riffs and a deep trench, the next moment, the sphere went dark as if powerless, cold and dead.

Using its maneuvering thrusters, the ISS *Graviton* performed a 180-degree half spin, briefly fired its main engine, and headed straight back toward the larger sphere, once again firing its laser directly at the stone behemoth.

Meanwhile, the ISS *Radian* performed nearly the same prearranged attack, which began with the Phase One Laser Fire against the second smaller sphere. An attack that culminated in Operation Move Mountain, which called for the *Radian* to treat its target with the same not-so-gentle caress as had the *Graviton* with its opponent. It took the *Radian* a little longer because the second sphere hadn't been as harassed by the other Omicron starships like the first one, but in the end, the larger of the three spheres was finally alone as its two smaller companions drifted away, cold and dark.

Now, three Omicron starships were carving up the Giant stone sphere like a holiday roast, concentrating their laser beams in a coordinated attempt at slicing it in half. Unfortunately, it didn't appear as if the starships' energy would last long enough to complete their task as the *Gaea* finally sputtered, bucked and drifted away, to be followed by the *Radian* and then finally the *Graviton*.

"Attention, Starforce," said LeAnn Walker over the open channel, "*we're not out of the woods yet. VICI's uncovered some kind of doomsday weapon from the Imperians. Nebula, she's updating her program to your computer core now. She'll explain.*"

The *Nebula*'s control deck astronavigation table came to life in a swirl of sparkles that coalesced into the translucent form of the Virtual Inquiry Computer Interactive hologram.

"**Starforce,**" the hologram began without preamble, simultaneously on all Omicron vessels, "**ironically, the Imperian Giant sphere appears to be reaching critical mass. I am uncertain whether they intend to blow up as a doomsday weapon or not. I suspect the two smaller spheres were some sort of energy storage units that acted as power dampeners. Now that we've effectively removed the smaller spheres, the Imperians can't control the energy intake-output of the larger sphere. We have seriously damaged it, but not enough to relieve the pressure.**"

"Oh, that's just great," commented Captain Gaea. "We've depleted all of our power in defeating these guys, now we're going to get blown up anyway?"

"*It doesn't really matter,*" said Captain Vortex. "*We've won this war. At least the colonies will be safe. For the moment.*"

"I cannot guarantee that, Captain Vortex," warned VICI. "As I've said, that giant sphere intakes as well as outputs energy. In this case, it's receiving its intake from the trinary stars in this system."

"As you and Danar previously surmised," Tan said. "That means if the Imperian sphere explodes, it could cause a chain reaction that could vaporize everything within the acute triangle of Alpha Centauri A and B and Proxima. Danar, we've got to either seal the Imperian sphere or relieve the pressure or the war will be over for good."

"VICI, how long before it goes?" asked Danar Seti.

"In just a matter of minutes, Captain Nebula."

"Does anyone have any power left?"

"*We've collected enough for a few maneuvering thrusters,*" offered Vortex, "*but not nearly enough for the laser or even main propulsion to try and escape. Not that we would.*"

"The *Pulsar*. What about the *Pulsar*?" said Nebula. "They were firing their lasers when that asteroid smashed into them. VICI, can you check their status?"

"I've been attempting to do that very thing. I've determined that they jettisoned all eight of their hydrogen fuel storage pods as a precaution. All four of their broadcast dishes were smashed with that asteroid collision, so they have no communications, which means I can't even access my clone. The good news is, I'm reading life signs."

"You say they jettisoned their hydrogen fuel storage pods," confirmed Nebula. "Do any of us have enough time to retrieve them on maneuvering thrusters?"

"I doubt it, Captain Nebula. Even if one of us could get to them in time, it's unlikely they would have enough fuel in them. And if they did, it would take too much time to transfer it and get back. They've drifted too far."

"It looks like it's our only shot," commented Captain Vortex. "Besides, I can't just sit here waiting for—Look, my ship's been reclaiming new hydrogen longer than any of you. We're going for it."

"*Good luck, Charlie,*" said Frank Logan.

"Alright," said Danar, watching the Vortex painfully limp away on maneuvering thrusters, "what about the *Ersatz*?"

"The last I saw, the *Ersatz* was spinning away after it was hit by the second sphere. Triangulating sensor dishes now…she's still spinning. One moment. She's not spinning away from us, the *Ersatz* is spinning towards—"

"GET OUT OF THE WAY! GET OUT OF THE WAY!" screamed Jack Askew's voice over the comm. "*We've heard what's going on and I'm working on a plan, but you all have to get out of our way.*"

With that announcement, the other Omicron vessels slowly backed away from the giant sphere on whatever maneuvering thruster power they had left, as the ISS *Ersatz* came spinning back into the area, using its own maneuvering thrusters to stay it on course. A course that was sending it straight at the laser-burned trench in the large Imperian sphere.

"Jack, what are you doing?" asked LeAnn Walker.

"*I'm on it, I'm on it,*" was all he said.

Whether it was luck, skill or a combination of the two, the Omicron starship *Ersatz*'s spin brought its hydrogen collector dish slamming down right into the largest trench carved by the other ships. In a horrendous collision the *Ersatz*'s dish bent in half and caused the trench to continuously crack nearly all of the way around the circumference of the stone sphere. A torrent of yellow-green energy streamed out in one direction for several hundred kilometers like water released from a fire hydrant.

Luckily, the *Ersatz* was thrown clear.

The stone sphere's pressure-ejected energy flowed for nearly a full minute before it slowly dissipated, leaving a slight glow coming from the nearly torn-in-half sphere interior.

When everyone's vision cleared, they could see hundreds of Imperian bodies floating in the vacuum of space.

"My goodness," said Danar Seti, "what have we done?"

"*Only what we had to do, mate,*" said Frank Logan, "*only what we had to do.*"

"Wait," exclaimed Tan, "look."

Upon closer inspection, the varied-looking aliens were slowly moving their limbs as if attempting to swim in the vacuum. Although the distance made them appear small against the scale of the broken stone sphere, there was little doubt these beings were larger than humans. Now that the Starforce could see them in their entirety, rather than the previous bust shots provided by the viewers, they could see the Imperians did indeed possess two legs—legs with knees that bent backwards in the other direction.

But the most amazing feature of these aliens was their ability to apparently survive in the vacuum of space. The bio-globes on their upper bodies were glowing brightly. It looked as if they were telekinetically pulling the stray asteroids toward them and then riding them back into the cracked opened sphere, until they were all (safely?) inside.

"Unbelievable," commented Danar Seti.

"Indeed," agreed Tan Ozawa.

"*Ersatz. Ersatz, come in,*" called LeAnn Walker. "*Jack. Are you and your crew alright?*"

"VICI," ordered Captain Nebula, "patch us all in."

"The *Ersatz* is coming on now, Starforce."

The main viewers on the Omicron vessels started as static, then slowly cleared up to show a disheveled Jack Askew pulling himself back into his command crash chair. His hair looked wild as if caught in a wind tunnel. A tiny amount of blood trickled from his head and the side of his mouth. His bruised and battered crew didn't look much better, but everyone appeared to be only shaken up.

Captain Nebula glanced at VICI.

"There don't appear to be any casualties."

Captain Ersatz looked directly into the viewer pick-up and smiled a toothy grin. A grin that was missing a tooth.

"Well done, Jack," Danar said, almost giggling.

"*Yeah,*" offered LeAnn Walker. "*Not bad for a jackass.*" She was a little disappointed that she gave him an opening for his classic comeback and he said nothing. "*Jack? What do you say?*"

"*Uh?*" he asked. "*Oh. Um. Lucky for me, I'm already wearing brown pants.*"

CHAPTER FIFTEEN
The Art of Politics

The large Imperian's eyes glowed like white hot embers and menacingly glared down on Captain Nebula from a height of nearly three meters. Its broad chest inhaled and exhaled, the slow rhythmic breathing not unlike that of a human. Its three-fingered hands, with opposable thumb, gripped in and out of fists—fists that were bigger than Seti's head. Its arms were nearly as thick as his torso. The alien had the basic proportion of a large gorilla. Its approximate weight of nearly 600 kilograms supported by short legs, reverse articulated at the knees, making its forward stance look natural as it stood before the flagship commander, feet separated by just under a meter, balanced on a tripod of three thick toes—two forward, one jutting out behind at the end of each leg—similar to that of a terrestrial bird.

In fact, if Danar had to describe this Giant of Imperia, he would describe its size as that of a small elephant, with the same kind of thick skin. Skin that was dark purplish in color. He would also explain it as a cross between a hairless bull gorilla and a bird. But only because of the configuration of its legs and feet could it be compared to a bird.

Captain Nebula stepped closer to the alien. Its gaze now stared straight down on him as it followed his movement. Nebula took another step...right through the Imperian until he was standing back to back with the image.

"So, how fair a representation of an Imperian is this projection?" the captain asked, crooking a thumb at the hologram behind him.

"From the semi-detailed scan I was able to obtain due to the several hundred Giants' brief exposure to space, coupled with the recorded images of Blackstar from the main viewer," explained VICI, "I believe this representation is accurate to ninety-nine-point-five percent."

"It looks exactly like Blackstar," commented Danar.

"That is exactly who this hologram represents, since he is the one who was exposed to our video monitors the longest. As you may have surmised after seeing the one whose unofficial name was Longneck, the Imperians are a varied species. More so than humans."

"You mean more than the differences in height, girth and skin color and such?" asked Tan.

"Yes," VICI confirmed. "You no doubt noticed the cranial ridge and facial snout on Longneck, where Blackstar had none of these features. I was also able to scan some Imperians who possessed five fingers and toes, while others, like Blackstar, possess only three. But they all had opposable thumbs on their hands and feet; all of their legs bent backwards at the knees."

"Could the Imperians be made up of more than one species?" asked Danar.

"I doubt that," answered Tan. "More likely, they are several branches or races with a common ancestry able to interbreed due to a common biological makeup. Although I find it odd that some should possess such disparate features such as cranial ridges, snouts and varying digits. Then again, perhaps the exposure to what we call Omicron Particles makes them more adaptable when it comes to perpetuating the species."

"VICI, you referred to Blackstar as 'he,'" noted Danar, "how can you be so certain?"

"I admit, I'm only guessing with Blackstar. But it stands to reason based on vocal cadence plus the fact that my vacuum scan revealed male and female Imperians, with recognizable reproductive organs and genitalia. They are very much like humans, despite their exterior and appendages."

"Genitalia and reproductive organs," echoed Danar. "Are they mammals?"

"Of that, I cannot be certain. As I said, it was at best, a semi-detailed scan. I would require a live specimen to know with certainty."

"That doesn't seem likely any time soon," opined Tan.

"Unbelievable," said Danar. "Could life truly be that universal? Even with beings from another dimension?"

"There are some major differences," Tan pointed out. "For example, I noticed Blackstar on the viewer, like his holographic doppelganger here, was breathing. Yet his species can clearly survive, at least for short periods, in the vacuum of space. That isn't similar to any human ability."

"Perhaps more so than you might at first believe, Doctor Ozawa," countered the hologram. "I was also able to confirm the glowing orbs attached to their upper bodies comprise what we call Omicron Particles, as you surmised. I do not believe they are of natural evolution. Perhaps surgically attached or chemically adapted from birth. But just as we have adapted the Omicron Particles for medical purposes to cure ailments and to regulate bodily functions or to discover the added benefits, as in Danar Seti's case, of increased stamina, endurance and strength, the Imperians have adapted the ability to survive in a vacuum and who knows what else?"

"If they are that similar to us," asked Danar, "does that mean we could adapt to do the same things?"

"It stands to reason."

Danar stroked his beard, contemplating.

"One moment, Captain Nebula. I am receiving word from the fleet commanders. All systems are available for holo-conferencing."

"Excellent," the captain said, rubbing his palms, "let's get this show on the road."

The first to arrive via hologram was Frank Logan, who, from his point of view, saw Danar and Tan arrive via holograms on the control deck of the ISS *Quasar*, along with the imposing image of Blackstar.

"WHOA!" He flinched, as did his crew within line of sight. "Geez, you guys nearly gave us heart attacks over here," he said after realizing the image was also a hologram.

"My apologies, Captain Quasar," said VICI sincerely, updating herself to the *Quasar*'s version of her program. **"As a matter of fact, I will be unable to maintain the image of our Imperian guest while facilitating the conference. Rest assured, this image and related discussions are now available in each starship's archive."**

The image of Blackstar vanished, as the rest of the Starforce captains were incorporated within the holo-imaging.

Not quite an hour had passed since the large Imperian stone (and possibly the entire trinary star system) was diverted from destruction. The ISS *Vortex* was able to tow the ISS *Pulsar* back to formation with the other Omicron starships. Although there were serious injuries on board, they were being treated by a combined force of all of the Omicron vessel's medical staffs.

The *Pulsar* itself was a near total loss, its central axis pole bent beyond repair, at least until it could be towed back to the colonies for reconstruction. Its broadcast laser dishes were currently under repair.

The *Ersatz*, although maneuverable and able to fly under its own power, was unable to collect hydrogen atoms with its collector, due to its mangled condition. The dish would have to be rebuilt and replaced. Her crew was also receiving treatment on location.

As for the *Gaea*, the *Quasar*, the *Nebula*, the *Graviton* and the *Radian*, they, like the *Vortex*, were building up their hydrogen charge from a freestanding position.

The colonies had dispatched a transport freighter from the Omicron Nebula asteroid station, with a complement of supplies, starship parts and nearly a hundred more Starforce officers, including Roshan Perez. It also carried several dozen spacebugs, newly equipped with lasers and neurowave cannons, as well as a contingent of diplomats and medical personnel from the planet Omicron. The Nebula transport freighter was the same type of vessel lost two years earlier in this region of space carrying scientists and teachers on a mission to study the two other stars and surrounding planets. The transport was expected to arrive within the hour.

The Giants of Imperia remained silent, while their large stone sphere painstakingly sealed up its horrendous *Ersatz*-induced crack with what few stray asteroids were left in the area. The Starforce kept a watchful eye on the two energy-storage, power-dampening stone spheres in an effort to keep the Imperians from magnetically or telekinetically utilizing them in any way. Both were still drifting further into open space, however. It was decided both spheres would be retrieved, despite the fact that they were apparently depleted of energy. Chances were, they housed critical components essential for the Imperians' departure.

While awaiting the transport, the eight Omicron COs were now all gathered on their respective flight control decks to begin the holographic debriefing.

"Well, my friends," stated Danar Seti, "it would seem the fates were with us today."

"It is because we fought the good fight, Nebula," said Arjun Vohra.

"And speaking of the good fight," continued D. Seti, motioning to both Michelle Woo and Arjun Vohra, "don't take this the wrong way, but...shouldn't you be dead?"

"Having been caught in the middle of that fireball," answered M. Woo, "I thought we were, too."

"True," agreed A. Vohra, "we were all prepared to meet the maker of all things, especially when we lost power to all ship's systems, including life support and the gravity generators. But, like everyone else, I imagine, I thought it strange that the next world indeed possessed gravity, the smell of acrid smoke as well as whatever properties produce pain when I fell back to the deck, and most of all, a remarkable resemblance to the flight control deck of an Omicron starship. For a second, I thought we were in purgatory for certain."

"But how?" asked J.P. Bouvier. "Why did your systems come back online at all? And how did you get back here so quickly with a near-full energy charge?"

"Perhaps," offered M. Woo, "it would be better if VICI explained."

They all turned to the hologram, standing atop each of their astronavigation tables.

"You will recall," the hologram began, "my Nebula self was providing a status of the *Graviton*'s and *Radian*'s progress when I was abruptly cut off."

"Yes," verified Tan Ozawa, "you said the scattering field was releasing...."

"Hydrogen," finished VICI. "It had released hydrogen atoms."

"But stars are comprised chiefly of hydrogen," reasoned Charles Lee. "That still doesn't explain why both ships weren't...well—"

"Barbecued," finished Frank Logan.

"Oh, we got singed fairly well," interjected A. Vohra, "rest assured."

"That's because the Imperian scattering field collects hydrogen atoms, like our own vessels, to perpetuate propulsion. That is why it was growing as it traveled. Fortunately for the *Graviton* and *Radian*, the collected hydrogen had yet to achieve ignition. In other words, there was no fusion or fission taking place, no collision or splitting of the atoms. That is until the scattering field was disrupted by the ships' lasers. In retrospect, I believe it was the lasers that prematurely started the ignition process of the collected hydrogen. That is, whatever properties the Imperians use to bond the hydrogen for their purposes of repelling the asteroids, or whatever, had yet to occur. There was, however, enough hydrogen ignition to cause that bright flash and some inconvenience on the part of both starships, but no more. Fortunately, the Omicron vessels halted the progress of the Imperian scattering field when they did. Had the field traveled a few dozen kilometers farther, neither ship would have survived."

"As a result," continued A. Vohra, "once the scattering field was dispersed, our systems came back online, restoring life support, gravity and VICI, of course."

The hologram smiled and nodded.

"And with all of the free-floating concentrated hydrogen atoms in the immediate vicinity," added M. Woo, "we simply opened our reactor vents and sucked in as much of it as we could, in hopes of restoring what power we could to the fusion reactors and lasers."

"Unfortunately," said Arjun, "our broadcast dishes were damaged, so we couldn't as yet communicate with each other in the conventional sense."

"Each of our vessel's exterior cameras were operational," added Michelle, "but without the broadcast and sensor dishes, we couldn't get telemetry or detailed scans of anything. Even VICI was unable to communicate with her other self."

"So what did you do?" asked Jack. "Launch a couple of tin cans with strings attached?"

"Our solution was nearly as crude," said Michelle, motioning for Arjun to explain.

Using his command baton, he lightly tapped a rhythm on his command crash chair, which wasn't being displayed next to him by the holo-cameras.

"We…used…morse…code," translated Danar.

"Exactly," confirmed Arjun, "but in our case, we employed hand torches; switching them on and off through a porthole, as our two ships maneuvered closer to each other."

"A clever low-tech solution," commented Tan Ozawa.

"We then agreed," continued M. Woo, "it would be best to repair one dish on each vessel so as to facilitate communication with each other."

"So we sent a crew outside each ship for EVA," added A. Vohra, "and discovered most of the damage was carbon scoring—heavy soot that had to be physically scraped off."

"Fortunately, just in time, we each got one dish cleaned and aligned," said M. Woo, "when a curious thing happened. A swarm of asteroids on the order of several hundred million was headed straight for us from in-system."

"Had we not cleared those dishes when we did, we could have been pulverized," said Arjun.

"We had no idea as to why or how the asteroids were leaving the belt at a faster speed than what our ships could achieve under the current circumstances," explained Michelle, "but we could tell they were headed in this direction, so we assumed the Imperians had something to do with it and it wouldn't serve the rest of you in any good way."

"I can attest to that," said J.P., the commander of the ISS *Pulsar*.

"Even with one dish each working, their substandard condition wouldn't allow us to communicate this far," said Arjun. "At the rate the asteroids were traveling, we knew the only way to warn you would be to somehow hitch a ride. But attaching a grappling cable to an asteroid speeding by was dangerous at best."

"So VICI came up with the idea to…" Michelle began, "well, maybe she could explain it better. I'm still not exactly sure what happened."

"It was simple, really," explained the hologram, **"and now that I am fully updated, rather ironic that I was doing almost the same thing here with the rest of you."**

Everyone looked puzzled, except Tan, who shaking her head, smiled. For she figured out exactly what VICI did. "Don't you see? In order to divert most of the asteroids as they headed for *us*, VICI, at Danar's suggestion, masked the incoming rocks with a jamming frequency. On the other hand, the versions of VICI onboard the *Radian* and *Graviton* used a masking frequency from the two working broadcast laser dishes to project the properties of a typical nickel-iron asteroid to surround the two ships. Without even knowing what kind of attraction beam the Imperians employed, they simply had to look— at least from an elemental spectrum point of view—like a couple of asteroids themselves and they were carried in the wake of the speeding swarm."

"Saving as much of the ship's power as we could," said Michelle.

"Although we had to feverishly work our maneuvering thrusters," added Arjun, " to avoid hitting each other, as we were so close, or hitting the other asteroids surrounding us."

"Brilliant," praised Danar, shaking his head.

"Actually," explained VICI, **"I got the idea from the Imperians themselves, thanks to a suggestion by Captain Graviton."**

"Of course, spatial displacement," reasoned Tan. "The Imperian spying devices, masquerading as asteroids."

"The only difference being," commented VICI, **"the spy stones projected a visual projection, whereas I projected a radio spectrum frequency."**

"Lucky for us," said Charles Lee, "the spy stones didn't project a radio spectrum frequency as well as a visual and that the attraction wave that pulled the asteroids here didn't scan for visual cues."

"Yes," Danar Seti said, stroking his beard through narrowed eyes, "we've apparently been most fortunate throughout this whole affair."

"Danar," exclaimed Tan, somewhat surprised, "I thought you didn't believe in luck."

"That's just it, I don't," he confirmed. "At least, I didn't used to. Perhaps I should have said we were *too* fortunate."

"Nebula ol' man," commented Frank Logan, "one can never have *too* much luck."

"I'm sorry, Frank old buddy, but I disagree with you," Danar countered. "In my experience, when too many fortunate happenstances come your way, there's always another boot waiting to drop."

"Aw geez, Danar, lighten up already," demanded Jack Askew. "We won. This war is over, baby."

"Forget about it, Jack," suggested Michelle Woo. "Danar Seti's been a contemplative, paranoid stick in the mud for the last twenty years or more. He's not about to change now."

"Hmmf," commented LeAnn Walker, "and here I was thinking I had to reassess my opinion of the intelligence of men."

"Come again, LeAnn?" asked Arjun.

"In *my* experience," she explained, "only women understand the virtues of a 'fortunate happenstance,' the true mark of intelligence. Just ask anyone who's given birth. Plus the fact that both you and Nebula offered brilliant ideas to VICI, which allowed her to help us come through this without totally relying on bashing someone's head in, made me think that, just maybe, testosterone doesn't contribute to male stupidity. Yes, I know, that term is redundant," she said with a jovial smirk. "But then, the somber kid here," she said, referring to Danar Seti, "blew it with that 'waiting for the other boot to drop' comment."

"You know, Le," said Jack, his chin high, chest sticking out, "I think you're being a little hard on Joyboy here, and definitely insulting to men in general."

"Oh yeah? And what are you going to do about it, Mr. Ass-Over-Teakettle? Who by the way," LeAnn said to the assembled holograms, the females in particular, including VICI, "is a male who happened to have bashed someone's head in. Maybe," she said, once again referencing a speechless Jack, while the men looked on uncomfortably, "your new nickname should be Dizzy."

Clearing his throat, as well as his composure, Jack replied, "We're not as stupid as you think, 'cause, *sister,* I ain't falling for that. But if we *were* in the same room, I'd tackle you."

"I rest my case," LeAnn concluded, crossing her arms with a wide grin.

That elicited laughter from everyone, even the control deck crews of each ship, including VICI. Even Danar was amused as evidenced by his half-smile. He was happy to see his old friends enjoying themselves, even if some of it was at his expense. They all deserved whatever respite they could find. Especially after what they just came through.

For himself, however, ever since he became a successful recipient of Omicron Particle therapy, he came to realize he would never fully trust the pursuit of "happily ever after." Life was never that simple. He learned that as a happy-go-lucky boy on Earth, until he found out why, unlike most other kids, he didn't have a mom. His mother died while giving him life.

Or the time he was convinced of his good fortune in leaving the environmentally challenged homeworld for the fresh new planet, often referred to as the "virgin Earth," only to discover his father didn't survive the journey.

The final blow, of course, was when his amnestic aphasia was cured. It was a mixed blessing. For the first time in his life, he no longer had the blissful harmony of easily forgetting painful memories. Or of grownups—therapists mostly—always being there for him. Holding him. Loving him. Then he'd forget again. But the love was always around him. Until the OPT, that was the cycle. Blissful ignorance, painful memory, then love. Ignorance, pain, love. Then it was simply pain and love.

He eventually learned to live with the perpetual melding of the two emotions and adjusted to his new life on a new world with new responsibilities, just like every other child. But the young man who was originally named Dane Reginald Howell would never trust the future for tidings of joy again. *Stars, maybe I really do need to lighten up,* he mused, his half-smile turning into a chuckle, no doubt prompted by the laughter of his friends and colleagues. *Perhaps this is a happy ending.*

The man now known as Danar Seti would soon realize he should have paid more attention to his somber instincts.

When the transport freighter arrived, the starships' COs assembled in person onboard to meet with the diplomatic corps from Omicron, led by Augustus Du Bois, a senior member of the counsel of Omicron. The medical staff attended to the more serious injuries among the fleet and several retrofitted spacebugs were sent out to retrieve the two smaller stone spheres.

It was assumed the Giants of Imperia remained silent because their borrowed viewer was damaged beyond their ability to repair during the skirmish. It was also reasonable to assume they were licking their bruised "superior" egos after, as Jack Askew put it, "getting their asteroids kicked by a bunch-o-primates." But what good was a diplomatic corps if they could not practice diplomacy? For this war to truly end, there would need to be discussions of terms for withdrawal, surrender or some form of mutual understanding so as to avoid future hostilities. To that end, an Omicron communications viewer array was sent to the almost-sealed trench via a robot drone, complete with a power pack (with only enough power for communications) and a preset frequency, in hopes the Imperians would decide to confer.

"Lieutenant, we're receiving a signal."

"Thank you, technician," said Roshan Perez, who was in charge of the comm staff while the diplomats outlined their strategy to the starships' COs in the main freighter cargo bay, now converted to a meeting hall. He activated his comm collar. "Councilman Du Bois, it's time."

Moments later, several lifts ascended from the lower deck of the freighter, depositing the Starforce COs, along with Tan Ozawa, Augustus Du Bois and two other members of the diplomatic corps on the flight control deck.

"Are they on, Lieutenant?" asked the councilman.

"They're on standby, sir," confirmed Lieutenant Perez.

"Well, let's not keep them waiting any longer," A. Du Bois said with little patience. "Put them—"

"Councilman Du Bois, if I may—" began Captain Nebula.

"Remember your place, Dane," returned the older man, testily. "We're not onboard your space station or starship, and in either case, I have operational control of these proceedings."

"With all due respect, sir," said Nebula, maintaining his composure, "perhaps I should be the one to open renegotiations with the Imperians as they are already familiar with my presence."

"Oh, I have no doubt they are familiar with your presence, Captain Nebula," the councilman shot back, "as you were the one who oversaw their near demise. Now it's time for you to take a back seat. But don't worry. I require your presence as a show of strength." Then, after a pause and a sideways glance, the councilman added, "Your silent presence. Are we clear on this?"

"Crystal clear, sir," said Nebula, taking a step back, standing at-ease with his hands clasped behind him. Now Danar was certain his antipathy toward Augustus Du Bois was warranted, if not exactly rational. The man had been a thorn in his side for nearly 30 years. From being one of his first therapists while he adjusted to his newfound memory, to his professor of political science at Howell University, and now a member of the leading council of Omicron. In fact, A. Du Bois was the last person to approve D. Seti's commission to take over command of the Omicron Nebula asteroid space city from Sean Stingray. Despite the fact that he was S. Stingray's first choice. As each of them moved forward in their respective fields, it seemed that fate kept them intertwined to some degree. But why was it that each time their paths crossed, the older man always found some way to grate on Danar's nerves? Such as, in this case, referring to him as Dane, a name Danar gave up 30 years ago. Not out of any disrespect for his father but as a symbol of his new life here at Alpha Centauri. In fact, Augustus Du Bois was the only one who referred to him that way. Not even Jim Sanders, the only person who knew young Dane Howell back on Earth, having worked with his father, called him that.

But things weren't always chilly between the two men. In the beginning, Danar looked up to A. Du Bois. Although he'd be reluctant to admit it, he wouldn't be the man he was today if not for the therapist who helped and comforted his early pain. In fact, young Dane often thought of Doctor Du Bois as a surrogate father. After all, he was physically similar to his father. The same ebony skin tone, height and physique. Had his father survived, he would no doubt have had a head full of white hair. But that's where the similarities ended.

Somewhere along the line, Danar fell out of favor with Augustus Du Bois, and he had no idea why. Frankly, he didn't care why. So long as both men did their jobs, the niceties were unimportant. Or so Danar tried to convince himself.

Councilman Du Bois waited for Captain Nebula to take a step back before he ordered, "Put them on the viewer, Lieutenant."

"Yes, sir," acknowledged Roshan Perez, nodding to the comm tech. He then snuck a pained look at Danar, letting him know he didn't care for the way the councilman treated his captain and friend. Apparently, the other COs felt the same, as Roshan noticed they all wore uncomfortable expressions. As for Danar Seti himself, he appeared unfazed by the incident.

As before, the first noticeable objects on the main viewer, as it came into focus, were the glowing bio-orbs of the Imperians. The major difference from the previous view was the illuminated interior of this portion of the giant sphere. As one might have suspected, it looked exactly like the interior of a cave. No smooth walls or sentient-made structures. There were, however, a few dozen or so floating stone spheres exactly like the one that harassed the *Graviton* hovering near several Imperians. There were no noticeable machines or electronic devices of any kind. The view now showed two Imperians standing side by side. One of them was Blackstar. The other was unfamiliar to the Starforce, but about the same height as Blackstar, although not quite as broad. Its skin was wrinkled gray, like an elephant's. It wore a gray gown similar in pattern to Blackstar's. In fact, all of the Imperians wore similar gowns of different colors.

Blackstar was breathing heavily as if he recently finished a strenuous activity. There was blood coming from the side of his mouth and scratches on his arms. His uniform was also slashed in several places on his chest. All of the humans thought it odd that Blackstar should looked so tattered considering the last shot of the war was taken over 90 minutes earlier. Everyone also noticed that Blackstar was the only one to look distressed. It was Tan, however, who was fascinated by the fact that Blackstar's blood was red. Like a human's.

"Greetings, Imperians. My name is Augustus Du Bois, one of the leading members of the Omicron council. May I assume this is Blackstar with whom I am speaking?"

"*Correct your assumption is,*" confirmed Blackstar. "*Infinite-Pool-of-Depth,*" he said, referring to the alien standing next to him, "*this Imperian is called. Deepwaters, his preference is, in your…language. Of the Neutral sect is Deepwaters. And witness to any further proceedings between our peoples.*"

"I understand. It is an honor to greet you, Deepwaters," said Councilman Du Bois, bowing deeply toward the Imperian of the Neutral sect. Deepwaters bowed in return without uttering a sound.

"Blackstar," began the councilman somewhat hesitantly, "if you need to attend your…wounds, I would be willing to postpone our talks."

"*Appreciated your concern is, Du Bois Councilman,*" said Blackstar, "*unnecessary it is, however. Mine, this blood is not.*"

"Oh. I see," replied the human, not truly understanding. "I believe you are already familiar with several members of my entourage," A. Du Bois said, referring to the people standing behind him.

"*Met previously, we have,*" said Blackstar. "*Nebula Captain. Ozawa Doctor.*" As he said each name, he bowed respectfully.

"These others similarly dressed, are the other commanders of the Omicron military force." A. Du Bois introduced them all in turn, only giving their rank of captain and the station for which they were responsible. "These two," he said, referring to the man and woman dressed in white jumpsuits similar to his, but without the shoulder braids, "are members of the diplomatic corps. Everyone you see here is answerable to the Council of Omicron."

"*Understand, I do,*" said Blackstar.

"Blackstar," began Councilman Du Bois, raising his chin, "I believe it would be best if we were to meet face to face to settle our dispute. Would that present a problem?"

"*No. Expected the suggestion I did,*" said Blackstar.

Just as he said that, a figure could be seen rising from the floor behind him and Deepwaters. It was Longneck, who looked in much worse shape than did Blackstar. There was a gaping wound in her long neck. It looked mortal, but was apparently not. In fact, before the viewer conversation was over, it looked as if the wound had noticeably healed somewhat. It was now apparent whose blood adorned Blackstar's mouth and garments. As Blackstar finished speaking, Longneck opened her mouth as if to speak, but was silenced by a hiss from Deepwaters. Blackstar ignored the disheveled Longneck.

"We can make arrangements for you to board our vessel," offered the councilman, at the shocked expressions of every other human. No one said anything, however. "You would be somewhat cramped in our spacebugs however, and I'm not certain if they could carry more than—"

"*Unnecessary your offered mode of transportation is,*" said Blackstar, raising a hand. "*Capable of traveling to your…airlock we are.*"

"Will you require any special equipment or environment?"

"*No. The same is the oxygen-nitrogen content of your gases to ours. Similar is the respiration quotient.*"

"Interesting," Tan said, under her breath.

Councilman Du Bois said the exact same thing when he saw the Imperian mode of travel. Blackstar, Deepwaters and a third previously unseen Giant in blue raiment stood atop a 10-meter-diameter asteroid boulder. The trio exited from a newly opened hole in the side of the large stone sphere and "surfed" their way to the large airlock of the Omicron transport freighter without benefit of spacesuits or breathing apparatus. Deepwaters was holding a small glowing stone sphere between his hands as if it were some kind of control mechanism. Blackstar singlehandedly gripped another small sphere, unpowered, not glowing. He and the new alien were standing on either side of and slightly behind Deepwaters. It took them about 30 seconds to travel the 40 meters to the Omicron vessel.

Their exit hole sealed itself with a bright flash, leaving no seam or evidence it ever existed.

The Imperians left the transport boulder and the small glowing stone sphere outside the airlock where they floated in close proximity without a tether. Presumably, the small glowing sphere was keeping itself and the transport boulder corralled. The three Giants waited inside for the air to cycle and the pressure to equalize before stepping into the cargo bay.

Despite having the benefit of viewing a holographic projection of an Imperian, each human was still awed by the aliens' impressive size. Although Blackstar wasn't the tallest, he was the most powerful-looking. Deepwaters was about the same height but spindly. The third Imperian was the tallest, with a neck not quite as long as Longneck's. Its upper body appeared slight with thin arms. However, its lower half was broad, supported by tree trunk-like thick legs that bent backward at the knees like all of the other Giants. All of the Imperians wore the same style of clothing: the shoulder-strapped, knee-length gown, slit at the waist leaving the legs exposed. Like the armbands surrounding their biceps and wrists, they sported cloth bands around their thighs and ankles. They were all barefoot.

To his credit, Augustus Du Bois took this first contact situation in stride as he walked right up to Blackstar and said, "It is a pleasure to meet face to face, Blackstar."

"Doubtful that is, Du Bois Councilman," replied the broad Imperian with a surprising sardonic grin, "understood, however, the sentiment is."

"Yes…well," the councilman said hesitantly, "and who might you be…?" he asked, referring to the newcomer and cutting himself short of saying sir or ma'am and embarrassing himself.

"Descending-Mountain-of-Gravity his name translates to," answered Blackstar. "Yet to simplify the name he has."

"How's about Rockbottom?" offered Jack Askew.

A. Du Bois shot him an I-am-not-amused look, ready to dress the *Ersatz* captain down, when he noticed Descending-Mountain-of-Gravity nod, apparently grateful for the nomenclature.

"Acceptable Rockbottom is," said Blackstar. "A Conservative sect he represents."

"I see," said the councilman. "Perhaps we should get started. Please make yourselves—" Again, A. Du Bois cut himself short as he gestured toward a long table in the middle of the cargo bay with a communications array computer monitor attached, surrounded by a half dozen human-sized chairs. "…uh, as comfortable as possible."

The Imperians glanced at each other. Blackstar looked amused at the human's realization that the chairs would not accommodate the Giants, even if they could fit in them. In fact, the broad alien smiled an opened-mouth grin. With their legs configured as they were, they had no need for chairs.

On the flight deck, looking down through the observation windows into the cargo bay, Doctor Tan Ozawa saw the Imperian Blackstar grinning for some strange reason. Although she couldn't hear what was going on, she figured nothing was amiss based on the reaction, or lack of reaction, from the Starforce officers. But her superior vision saw something that no one else would have noticed. When Blackstar grinned, she could clearly see blood in his mouth. Not a lot. He did assure Councilman Du Bois the blood wasn't his, which made sense to Tan because she was certain the alien's bio-orbs were some form of Omicron energy that would heal any minor wounds as was indicated by the healed scratches on Blackstar's arms. That small trace of blood then, was from his political opponent Longneck, whose wounds had no doubt healed by now. But since the blood was not his, there was no wound in his mouth to heal. Although he had changed or repaired his gown, he apparently wasn't aware or didn't care if there was still a trace amount of Longneck's blood in his mouth. The only thing Tan cared about was somehow getting a sample of that blood. If only—*Excellent.* A drop of it fell from his mouth onto the deck of the cargo bay. Now if only it didn't get contaminated or smeared by someone stepping on it. If Tan could be so lucky, she would simply have to bide her time and wait, possibly several hours, before she could gather the dried-up sample of Imperian blood and saliva. For now, she put the thought out of her mind and walked back to sit with Roshan Perez who was receiving a text message from a member of the diplomatic corps in the cargo bay.

Back down in the cargo bay, the Imperians walked up to the table, moved the chairs aside and simply squatted in front of the table with Blackstar sitting between the two others. A. Du Bois took a seat on the other side, his two aides to either side of him.

"Thank you, Starforce," said the councilman with a dismissive sweep of his hand. "You'll be called upon if we require clarification or suggestions."

Having been dismissed, the eight Starforce officers ascended the lifts to the upper flight deck, leaving the three humans of Omicron and the three Giants of Imperia to negotiate an end to the hostility between the two races.

Upon arrival on the upper deck of the freighter, they joined Doctor Ozawa and Lieutenant Perez, who were already sitting on the circular couch surrounding the astronavigation table, while the freighter's technicians remained at their posts on the outer perimeter of the flight deck.

"Welcome back," greeted Tan. "I am to inform the lot of you that although we are allowed to view the proceedings," she said, pointing toward the observation windows to the cargo bay, "we are not allowed to listen in or interfere in any way unless called upon."

"'Thanks, Starforce, for risking your lives and the lives of your crew and wrecking your starships saving our butts, but now that things are calm, we'll take it from here. Don't call us, we'll call you. Now get out,'" Jack paraphrased, mocking the Council of Omicron.

"Relax, Jack," suggested Arjun. "Councilman Du Bois is simply doing his job, just as we've done ours."

"Yeah, I know," he said. "He could be a little nicer doing it, though. I mean, with tact like that, I wouldn't be surprised if he arranges one more knock-down-drag-out before passing the peace pipe."

"Let's hope for the best, Jack," offered LeAnn, putting her hand over his. "Neither of us is in the greatest shape to sustain another conflict."

"That's right," agreed Charles. "And let's not forget, there are billions more Giants from Imperia just waiting to pick up where these guys left off. Those old rust buckets of ours," he said, pointing out the flight deck portholes towards their ragtag fleet of battered starships, "have about had it."

"*Oui*," agreed J.P., "the addition of several hundred more officers does not a fighting force make."

"I'm sure Augustus Du Bois will work something out that will satisfy both parties involved," commented Danar.

"Pardon me, Danar," said Michelle, "but I wouldn't have pegged you as someone with a great deal of confidence in the councilman."

"It's true," he explained, "we never seem to be on the same page," he said aloud, *anymore*, he mused, "but it would be unfair of me to say he was not capable or competent. Besides, as inscrutable as he is, he's the perfect foil to negotiate through any prejudice the Imperians might throw his way.

"So, kid," he said to Roshan, momentarily changing the subject, "how was your first command?"

"Uneventful and uncomplicated," answered the young lieutenant.

"I hope that wasn't a complaint, kid," said Frank Logan. "I'd gladly trade the last twenty-four hours of my command for 'uneventful and uncomplicated' in a second."

"I'm hip," agreed Danar.

"No complaints here," assured Roshan.

"And how is Oshara?" asked Tan. "When last I saw her, she was still unconscious. I was told she would be alright."

"Yes," Danar seconded, "you could say things have been too eventful and complicated for us to check on her."

"There were complications. Some brain tissue swelling and—" he began, until he saw the expressions of worry and shock on their faces. "But she's okay now. She's out of her coma."

"Coma?!" asked Danar.

"As I said, there *were* complications, but she's okay," Roshan explained hurriedly. "I was with her before I boarded the cargo freighter, and she's plenty angry with Doctor James for not signing her out as fit for duty."

"Sounds like Shara, alright," Danar nodded. "She'll be fine."

"The doc wants to keep her for another day or two, just to be sure."

"That sounds like Sarah James, alright," said Tan. "Oshara doesn't stand a chance."

"*Si*," agreed Roshan, "the good doctor's been on the warpath lately with everyone."

"That's…probably my fault," Danar confessed. "We had a bit of a falling out—my goodness, how long ago was that? This morning? It seems more like a week ago. Have you heard any word on Sean Stingray?"

"Yeah, he's on the station," Roshan answered sadly. "He's unconscious and immersed in a nanotank. I understand it's the only thing keeping him…uh, going."

"*Merde*," cursed Jean Pierre. He spoke for everyone.

Sensing the need to change the subject, Jack, who was sitting at the end of the circular couch, got up and peered down through the observation windows into the cargo bay. "I tell you, these Imperians appear more human each time I see them."

"What's going on, Jack?" asked LeAnn, who was now at the end of the couch and fighting the urge to join him.

"The discussion is heated, I'm sure," he passed along. "The gestures of the Giants are so…like ours. The way they signify 'no' by shaking their heads sideways, or nod in the affirmative. Even using their hands to help illustrate their speech."

"That could be," suggested Frank, "cause they had people from the ISS *Omicron* and maybe the *Omega* to study for the last thirty-one years. Or at the very least, the ships' records."

"No," Jack said slowly, gazing intently down at the conference, "it's more than that. Those mannerisms aren't a recently learned trait, I'm sure of it."

"Some parallel development can be expected," said Charles, "even from two such disparate species as humans and Imperians, provided there are some structural similarities. In this case, bipedal and bilateral symmetry; arms and legs on each side of the body, stereoscopic vision and stereophonic hearing."

"Plus the fact that, as different as they are from each other, "offered Michelle, "they all have teeth, which means they chew their food, preparatory to ingestion."

"Yes, they are very much like us," Danar said, staring into the distance. "And I find that kind of odd, really."

"How do you mean, Danar?" asked Tan.

"These beings are supposedly from another dimension, let alone another planet. Granted, I agree with the structural parallel development theory, but there's no law, universal or otherwise, that says *all* life, intelligent or not, has to have two arms, two legs, a torso and one head."

"Aren't you the one who says there are such things as coincidences?" asked Michelle Woo.

"Do I?" Danar asked facetiously, smiling. Everyone chuckled. "Oh, I don't know," he continued, "it just seems *too much* the coincidence."

"Well, there is still much we don't know about them," offered Arjun, crossing his arms in front of his chest.

"Actually," countered Tan, "I've been able to infer a great deal about the Giants of Imperia."

"Do tell, my dear."

"They are definitely a hierarchal society, at least within each of their sects. Blackstar described Rockbottom as a member of the Conservative sect and Deepwaters as a Neutral. That would make Blackstar a member of a Liberal faction. It doesn't take a political analyst to know that Longneck is of the Conservative sect as well. Not unlike our own politics. But I believe theirs is much more efficient."

"How do you figure that?" asked Jack, from across the deck.

"I didn't mean to imply theirs is better. What I should have said was they save more time."

"Explain please," ask J.P.

"In our system, the parties campaign for months at a time to sway voters to their particular way of running the government. Back on ancient Earth, they were called Democrats and Republicans, who campaigned equally, trying to persuade members of the other party, including an independent party, the Reformers, I believe they were called, to swing votes their way. They would even try to smear the 'good name' of their opponent to sway voters. I believe the Imperians vote as well, but their campaigning is limited. If a Liberal like Blackstar, adorned in red, makes a better case or is in agreement with the Conservatives wearing blue, there's no problem. No doubt they were in agreement regarding coming to this area of space and bullying the locals to vacate. But if there *is* a problem, such as the locals not being easy pushovers and they have to decide whether or not to end hostilities, they recast their votes and the Liberal could find he's out of favor and the bullying can resume under the Conservative reign. If the voters are split, then the Neutrals, in gray, step in and mediate. If that doesn't work, the main candidates settle it the old-fashioned way. Survival of the fittest. As seen by the blood that was on the Liberal Blackstar's face that wasn't his and later the barely standing Conservative Longneck who had a Blackstar-sized bite in its long neck."

"That makes sense," agreed Danar. "Once the Liberals were back in power, they proposed renegotiation, the others cast their vote in agreement."

"Yes," said Charles, "but the negotiators are still comprised of the three sects to better represent their factions, including the gray Neutral."

"Yeah. More and more like us by the minute," commented Jack. "Somehow that fails to reassure me."

The negotiations in the cargo bay went on for several more hours with a meal break for the human negotiators. The Imperians declined to intake sustenance saying it wasn't necessary. It wasn't determined whether that meant they weren't hungry or that they didn't require food at all. The three aliens remained in the cargo bay for a short time without the human diplomatic corps, surrounded by a detachment of armed Omicron security officers. There was no trouble and the negotiations resumed.

When they were finished, a very tired Augustus Du Bois ascended the lift to the flight control deck to confer with the Omicron COs, leaving his aides and the three Giants in the cargo bay.

"We've worked out a settlement," he said. All ten Starforce officers were standing. The councilman sat on the edge of the circular couch. "In a nutshell, we've uncovered a great deal of information and confirmed many suspicions. The Imperians *are* responsible, at least partially, for what happened to Earth over six decades ago."

"The bastards," said Captain Ersatz.

"I said partially, Captain," A. Du Bois reiterated. "They weren't even aware of the Earth. When they discovered their realm was becoming uninhabitable over one hundred of our years ago, they began sending energy probes over several thousand parsecs of *our* realm of space, looking for a suitable place to settle. If not for the solar-reflecting satellites strung up between Sol and Earth, we'd never have known of the Imperians and there wouldn't have been any need for us to migrate here. It was an accident. An unfortunate set of circumstances that resulted in the damage to our home planet. As a result, we came here for a new home. The Imperians were simply looking for a new home as well.

"Amazing. Their dimension is nothing like ours at all. It *is* a vacuum full of gaseous stars like ours, but originally the whole of their space was oxygenated; breathable gases, except for the immediate area surrounding the stars. Oxygenated space. According to our three guests, whole planets on the order of small worlds like Pluto are unheard of. They've never even come across anything as large as planetary satellites or moons. Instead, there are billions and billions of oversized asteroids or small planetoids no larger than their stone sphere over there. Anything larger, including anything they've tried to assemble large enough to gravitationally hold an atmosphere, becomes unstable and disintegrates. Many of these asteroids and planetoids are bursting with what we call Omicron lodes." He stared off into the distance, trying to comprehend it all. "Forgive me, there is so much of scientific and astronomical interest. As well as xenobiological and—" He shook his head, waving his hand in front of him. "The oxygenated regions have been shrinking, apparently for several millennia. Even though they've learned to adapt the Omicron energy to survive in an airless vacuum for short periods of time, several thousand of their asteroid planetoids have had to be abandoned. They are literally being squeezed out. Because they have no planets or any gravitational objects large enough to hold an atmosphere, they fear that eventually the breathable gases of their dimension will disappear altogether, killing off the entire race. They are desperate. Unfortunately, since they've adapted their bodies to the Omicron energy, they cannot live without it. Their energy probes discovered Alpha Centauri, with its Omicron lodes on the planet Omicron, just in time. In over one hundred years of scanning our dimension, Alpha Centauri is the only region so far that yields Omicron energy."

"I don't know much about their dimension," said Charles, "but isn't ours supposed to be infinite? Why is *this* particular region even an issue if they can use those so-called energy probes to search?"

"The Imperians estimate their window of opportunity to safely move their entire race to this region at about ten years."

"Ten years. Figures," commented Jack. "That's exactly the same amount of time Earth had to send us here before it was too late."

"Seems like Alpha C. has become prime real estate," said Frank. "Talk about a population explosion."

"Rats. Just as we were getting settled," opined LeAnn, "we find out we live on contested territory."

"Contested my eye," said Jack, a bit testily. "We were here first. And besides, we wouldn't be here at all if they hadn't contributed to Earth's accident."

"True, Captain Ersatz," said the councilman wearily, "but that still doesn't eliminate the contested issue. What are they supposed to do? Nothing? Stay where they are and die off?"

"What are *we* supposed to do, Councilman?" Jack shot back. "Hand over the keys to the house and leave? How? Where? We haven't heard from Earth since we left. Every one of our transmissions have gone unanswered. As far as we know, we may not even have a home to go back to. And even if we did, our population has grown by nearly a billion. The cryogenic modules that stored our frozen butts were dismantled for raw materials to build our cities and asteroid stations. And thanks to the Imperians, our starships aren't exactly in any condition to take us back anyway. Not that they were capable of doing that even before they were pressed into military service. Face it. We're stuck here. Period."

"Captain Ersatz," began the councilman, rubbing the bridge of his nose, "I only sympathize with the Imperians, I'm not proposing we simply give up."

"Then what the hell *are* you—"

"STAND DOWN, Ersatz!" Captain Nebula barked.

There were only a few seconds of heavy tension in the air as the two officers stared at each other. Danar briefly arched his eyebrows. Jack smiled. "Sorry," he said, leaning back against the observation windows, arms crossed.

Danar, palms down, propped himself opposite A. Du Bois. "Councilman, it appears we are still at an impasse. You say there has been a settlement. What, may I ask, is it?"

Councilman Du Bois held Captain Nebula's iron gaze for a beat, dropped his head and replied, "Talking to you, my own people, is very much like opening negotiations with the Imperians. They huffed and puffed, rattling their sabers, trying to show me how arrogant they can be in their superiority. They are so like us," he said, as Jack and LeAnn gave each other knowing looks.

Shaking his head, the councilman exhaled and continued. "Even if the citizens of Omicron were in the habit of genocide through inaction, and we are not, the truth is, we cannot afford another battle. Even though we have *these* Imperians at our mercy," he said, referring to the large stone sphere, "how long can we keep them all in custody? How much of our resources would we have to expend to prevent an eventual insurrection? Even if Blackstar was exaggerating, we have reason to believe Imperians will arrive eventually en masse. And they'll keep coming until they outnumber us. Even before that point, we'll be forced to recruit every man, woman and child, whether they be Starforce officers or not, into the service of fighting for our territory. Only a very small percentage of us are equipped with cybernetic implants and attachments or enhanced with Omicron energy particles. All of the Imperians are so strengthened with that element. As a result, we, and I mean the full Council of Omicron, have agreed to the Imperian resolution. I'm sorry, Captain Nebula, but it's the only way."

Uh oh, thought Danar. His heart began racing in his chest. He imagined the Omicron Particles in his blood were the only thing keeping him steady. *Something is definitely wrong,* for Augustus Du Bois was apologetic and speaking to him with respect. "And that resolution?"

"A—a challenge. A duel, if you will, between their greatest champion and ours. And even that was a bone of contention to them. Even when they agreed, they condescended, believing their champion would have to stoop by fighting a lowly human."

"You can't be serious, Councilman Du Bois," said Tan. "A fight to determine which species stays and which goes?"

"Jack was right," charged LeAnn Walker, who moved closer to stand next to Jack Askew. "You sold us out for one more knock-down-drag-out."

"It's not like that at all," the councilman snapped in return. "You don't under—"

"Councilman Du Bois," interrupted J.P. Bouvier, "is this a duel to the death?"

"Not necessarily," he answered hurriedly. "Only a clear winner must emerge."

"In other words," Nebula verified, "one rises and walks away, the other doesn't."

"If that's what it takes," the councilman qualified. "Or, one of the combatants can yield, calling an end to the uh…duel and declaring his opponent the victor."

"Sir," spoke up Michelle Woo, "are you seriously proposing one of us, a mere human, physically fight one of them?"

"A duel, Captain Radian," he said, without much conviction.

"Using what type of weapons?" asked Arjun Vohra.

"No weapons, only the combatant's natural abilities."

"That's no contest," shot Captain Ersatz, slamming his palm on the observation port sill. "Maybe you haven't noticed the size of these aliens. It would be a slaughter. When we referred to them as Giants, we weren't just picking a name out of a hat."

"The duel—contest," he amended with even less conviction, "will be more even than you currently know."

"Councilman, I must protest," complained Tan Ozawa. "This duel, as you insist on calling it, is as reprehensible as it is barbaric."

"I'm afraid we have little choice," sighed the councilman.

"I imagine that has been the excuse of just about every barbaric conflict in human history," Tan said without delicacy.

Everyone was furious and at least for the moment, speechless. That is until Roshan Perez asked, "Sir, what is really at stake here? What I mean is, what exactly does the winner get and what exactly must the loser give up?"

"An excellent, as well as intelligent, question, Lieutenant," praised the councilman, genuinely impressed. "Should our warrior clearly win, we, the citizens of Omicron will retain this area of space, our home. To insure the Imperians will not later attempt to reclaim this territory, we will dedicate a small percentage of our unique scientific knowledge in helping to repair or slow the damage to their realm, as well as try to find a viable alternative of migrating the Imperians elsewhere in this realm, again using our science to possibly replicate or process the precious Omicron particle energy for them. Should the Imperian champion clearly win, we will vacate this region of space, *AND*," he said, cutting off any budding protest, "with the Imperians' energy probes and modified inter-dimensional travel, locate another suitable star and transport our entire population there or determine the condition of Earth, and if it is capable of supporting us."

Although that didn't go too far in calming the Starforce officers' anger and concerns, it also didn't escalate them.

While A. Du Bois was explaining the stakes, Danar Seti walked from the astronavigation table to stand alone, looking down into the cargo bay. "Councilman," he asked, not turning away from the observation window, "who is the Imperian's greatest champion?" Somehow, he already knew the answer.

"I believe you've already met the uh…alien in question," was all the councilman said.

"Blackstar," Nebula said under his breath. Just as he whispered the name, the "alien in question" looked up from the cargo bay, directly at Nebula, as if he heard him mention his name. Their eyes locked for what seemed an eternity.

"Well then, who is *our* greatest champion?" asked Roshan Perez.

"It should come as no surprise," answered Augustus Du Bois. "Our greatest champion is, of course, a Starforce officer who happens to be the Omicron hoverball champion; who still holds the jujitsu-judo title eight years running, dethroning the previous title holder, Tan Ozawa," he said, nodding respectfully in her direction. "He's logged more spaceflight and EVA man-hours than any living human; he was…eventually, unanimously chosen to replace Sean Stingray, the previous holder of the Omicron flag as Captain Nebula; and probably more important than any of that, he is a successful recipient of Omicron Particle therapy. The current Captain Nebula, Danar Seti."

Without taking his eyes from the observation window, the human in question said, under his breath, "Swell. And so drops the other boot."

The buzz of conversation between the other officers and councilman became only background noise to Danar Seti, who was no longer registering a word. Instead, he continued to gaze directly into the eyes of the extra-dimensional being, first brought to his attention with the nomenclature Stellar-Void-of-Light. Blackstar, the Imperian's greatest champion. His opponent. There existed no malice in the gaze of either warrior. Quite the contrary. There was, instead, an understanding. A universal communication between two sentient beings who, upon immediate inspection, were alien to each other. But without a word spoken, and separated by 30 meters and an eight-centimeter-thick transparent metallic observation window, they both understood without a doubt, they were reluctant combatants who, through the politics of their respective species, would be forced to battle each other for the preservation of their races. Within that single extended gaze came the understanding that both were bestowed the greatest honor and at the same time, the greatest dishonor. It was an honor to represent one's entire species in battle and a dishonor that neither could come up with an alternative to prevent it.

CHAPTER SIXTEEN
Spirituality

Under any other circumstances, Roshan Perez would be enjoying his responsibility as commanding officer of the cargo freighter. As with the outbound trip, he knew his enthusiasm was tempered by the situation. At that time, his first command called for him to fly into a war zone. Fortunately, the war, at least for the time being, was over. He was informed his side had come out on top. His apprehension stemmed from not knowing the status of his friends. A perfectly understandable reason for not enjoying his duty.

Given command once again for the freighter's return trip to the Omicron Nebula station, his lack of enthusiasm was even more pronounced. For it seemed the one man he looked up to the most, his best friend, his mentor as well as his commanding officer was assigned to fight—possibly to the death—the biggest, scariest alien he had ever imagined from any childhood nightmare.

It was then Roshan realized that perhaps there was no room for enjoyment or enthusiasm while one was in a command situation. Perhaps it was just as well, for his apprehension probably balanced out his enthusiasm so that he could perform his duty efficiently. Otherwise, he'd probably screw it up.

He couldn't figure out how Danar did it. He and the other asteroid COs made it look so easy. The way they could joke around with each other, even in the face of adversity, and still do their duty without screwing up. At least it never looked like they screwed up.

Of course, Roshan realized they'd all known each other for quite a long time. Most of them grew up together, had the same aspirations, attended the same classes, and—with nearly the entire graduating class from the academy—competed for the coveted position of asteroid captain. But only eight were selected. After today, no one would ever question that those eight were the right stuff.

Roshan didn't know the others as well as he knew Danar, but imagined they also went through a great deal, no doubt sacrificing much to get where they were today.

Not quite for the first time in his young life, Roshan Perez realized he had a lot to learn. What he didn't realize was, with that thought, he had taken yet another big step on the road to maturity.

It was indeed gracious of Danar, who was after all the commanding officer on board, to allow Roshan to sit in the captain's chair for the return voyage. No doubt he had a lot on his mind. Roshan wanted so much to talk to his friend, to encourage and reassure him, but the truth was, he had no idea how to go about doing so. He figured Tan Ozawa was better suited to handle that particular duty, although when he snuck a peek behind him at the two sitting at the astronavigation table, he noticed not a single word had been spoken between them for quite sometime.

On second thought, perhaps that was the best way a friend could help him: allow him his own thoughts and just be there in case he required a sounding board. Although, knowing Danar as she did, Tan would no doubt *be there*, speaking not a word until they arrived back at the station. But what more needed to be said, really?

The only thing Roshan could do to help his friend was to carry out the duty Danar assigned him and oversee the operation of the freighter flight deck and its return trip in-system. An operation that included the towing of the starships *Ersatz* and *Pulsar* back to the colony for repair, while Captains Ersatz and Pulsar remained with the fleet and the other repair-in-progress starships, keeping custody of the two smaller stone energy spheres, but allowing the Giants to repair their larger stone sphere with just enough energy to maintain their life support. All under the command of Councilman Du Bois, using the ISS *Nebula* as his command post.

It stood to reason that Blackstar, once again returned to the large stone sphere, was surrounded by his colleagues and friends. Or maybe just members of his Liberal sect, no doubt giving him words of encouragement and support. On the other hand, he could be sitting alone with a close colleague without a word being spoken. For despite the fact that he was the scary-looking alien from another dimension, Roshan couldn't escape the feeling that Blackstar, the Imperian Giant, and Danar Seti, the Starforce human from Earth, were similar in many ways. And why not? Even Captain Ersatz kept pointing out how more and more like humans the Imperians seemed, which was nearly identical to what Danar said frequently. *We are all more alike than not alike.*

Roshan never considered that phrase outside the purview of humans, but felt it was still applicable, even under the present circumstances. Maybe that was why this whole scenario seemed so familiar. As if this or a similar incident had occurred on Earth. Maybe in a digital movie from the past. He couldn't quite put his finger on it. Something to do with a normal guy having to fight a giant monster.

Then it hit him. Not a giant monster. A goliath. As in *David and Goliath*. Even the names were similar. Danar and the Giant.

As familiar as he was with this present encounter, Roshan couldn't quite recall why the normal David, who was Jewish he recalled, had to fight the large Goliath, the Philistine. Since he had the time, he decided to look it up on his DAC.

Caramba. David wasn't simply a normal guy, he was a boy. A shepherd boy. The youngest of eight brothers. The three oldest of whom were poised on the line of imminent war with the Philistines. Goliath, the largest of the Philistines, was six cubits and a span in height.

Opening a sub-screen on his DAC, Roshan discovered that translated to nearly three meters. *Unbelievable. That's Blackstar's height as well.* Roshan clearly recalled the Imperian's scale and was impressed with young David's bravery for facing such a giant.

According to the tale, Goliath challenged the Israelite soldiers daily, boasting he could defeat any in single combat. If his challenge was accepted and lost, the children of Israel would forever serve the Philistines. Should the Israelite warrior defeat Goliath, the Philistines would become the subjects of the Jews. Having heard the challenge, the shepherd boy was unimpressed, certain he could defeat Goliath. His brothers tried to convince him that Goliath was a fighting man since his youth. David recounted how he, on more than one occasion, rescued his sheep from the jaws of lions and bears and saw no difference between those beasts and Goliath. As God delivered him from the paw of the lion and the paw of the bear, so too would He deliver him from the hand of the Philistine. So David accepted the challenge, rejecting the use of the armor and shield on which Goliath relied and faced his opponent with only his faith in God, a sling and a stone from a nearby stream. With only those three items, he swung his sling and sank a stone into Goliath's forehead, instantly killing the giant Philistine. Using his adversary's own sword, David decapitated him.

"Yikes!" Roshan was struck by a cold chill as he compared this present encounter to the past situation of biblical proportions. It was his hope the end result would be similar in that Danar would be victorious. But he didn't exactly want to see Blackstar lose his head. Nor did he want to know that his people may die out. *There must be another solution.* Yet the smartest minds on Omicron and obviously intelligent aliens had supposedly come up with the best compromise. A compromise that would possibly save both species, although depending on the winner, one species would have an advantage over the other. The true enemy it seemed, was time.

"Lieutenant Perez," said the freighter pilot, interrupting Roshan's reading. "We're approaching the coordinates now."

"Thank you, pilot," said Roshan, smiling his appreciation. As with the prospect of his first command, he thought it would be exciting to know when they crossed over the area of the upcoming battle. But again, the reality brought only more apprehension. For no matter who won, this location, halfway between the inter-dimensional transit point of the acute triangle of stars and the planet Omicron, would be the first leg of a journey for a victor and the salvation of his race, and a loser and the detriment of his people.

In the days of David and Goliath, heaven's location was thought to be in the sky. For those who still practiced and worshipped in their faith, its location was not considered part of their plane of existence at all. Rather, another dimension. Roshan considered the notion that since the citizens of Omicron were as far from the surface of the Earth as any human had ever been, plus the fact that they were dealing with beings from another reality, he was probably as physically close to heaven as he could get.

That's not even funny.

Neither Roshan nor his sister Oshara had much faith in religion. He knew Danar and Tan were more students of science than theology. He now wished he had paid more attention to the Bible studies at the group home for youths. He figured it was never too late. He could always access his DAC for inspirational reading material. He only hoped Danar's faith in science could deliver him from the hand of Blackstar. With the new revelation regarding the absorption of Omicron Particles on biological tissues, he just might stand a chance. They would know more after Doctor James ran a series of tests on the Omicron Nebula captain.

Roshan figured it wouldn't hurt to offer a prayer for Danar. After all, their entire civilization was at stake. *But what of Blackstar? His entire civilization is at stake as well. From where does he get his faith?* How could Roshan pray for Danar to win, saving this branch, possibly the only branch left of the species known as humanity, at the expense of another? It was not as if the Imperians were evil. They were no different than the people of Earth, who were forced to find a new home.

True, the reason the Earth people *had* to find a new home was because of the Imperians. But it was an accident. The Imperians didn't deserve to die out because of it. Neither should this branch of humans. *But only one champion can win, right? Why can't I pray for both species?*

For the first time in his life, on his way back to the Omicron Nebula space station, the only place he had ever considered his true home, Roshan Perez discovered that life was a lot more complicated than he ever thought possible.

It was very difficult for Danar to see his old friend in his current condition, floating upright within a three-meter-tall cylindrical nanotank. Naked, but for a pair of medical briefs and a breathing apparatus over his nose and mouth, Sean Stingray had looked better. The once tall, powerfully built, athletic figure who wore a perpetual smile was now reduced to a cadaverous zombie, suspended in medicated fluids teeming with thousands of tiny robots programmed to keep his vital signs from dropping into the danger zone. A zombie being chased by the specter of death. A zombie who would very soon be overtaken.

With the information A. Du Bois received from the Imperians regarding Omicron Particles, Danar had hopes for his friend. However, as Doctor James pointed out, it was Omicron Particles, or the abuse of the stuff, that put Stingray in this condition. A lot more time and study would have to be carried out before it could be determined if the former Captain Nebula could be brought back from the brink. Time was something of which Sean Stingray was in short supply.

On the other hand, Danar was in perfect health, having just returned from a complete physical and a battery of tests at the Omicron Nebula medical facility. Doctor James told him that he was very fortunate he received only minimal exposure to Omicron Particles over the past 30 years, thanks to his brain disorder. As opposed to Sean Stingray, who received injections whenever he needed to accomplish another task. In Danar's case, the Omicron energy had something to work on, namely his damaged brain. Otherwise, he too would have become dependent on the strange cosmic energy over time, becoming addicted, as with a drug. Like poor Sean Stingray.

Unbelievable. It seems now I should be grateful I was afflicted with amnestic aphasia. Hardly. If he didn't have the brain disorder, chances were he wouldn't have been exposed to the Omicron Particles in the first place. That was usually reserved for colonists who suffered physical damage from the freezing process, some of whom didn't survive the freezing at all. Like his father.

Because the marriage of the Omicron Particles and his mind and body had been so successful, Danar was informed he could safely absorb more of the energy to enhance his strength, stamina and endurance. Amazingly enough, the particles would also give him the ability to survive in the vacuum of space for short periods of time without benefit of a spacesuit, thanks to the perpetual oxygenation of his blood. Another curious side effect of the Omicron enhancement was the consistent bio-organ compression, which prevented the body from popping like a soap bubble when exposed to the hard vacuum of space. Although more study was needed, the scientists of Omicron believed it was possible through some form of subconscious mental manipulation of the body's cells and organs. That also allowed an Omicron energy-afflicted person to regulate the body's temperature in the same way a human can breath without conscious thought. Without that, humans would never survive a few moments of sleep, where the conscious mind is shut off giving way for the subconscious to take over while still controlling breathing, heart rate and nerve impulses and the myriad of other biological functions taken for granted on a daily basis.

But exposed to the vacuum of space? And surviving? Danar couldn't fathom it. It flew in the face of all of his training, science, and common sense. If he had his way he wouldn't be testing that ability. Not with *his* body. But he'd take as much of the other attributes as he could get to better face his adversary Blackstar in territorial combat tomorrow, Omicron noontime. To battle until one of them yielded or could no longer fight. Or worse.

Although Blackstar was a third again Danar's height and about three times his weight, Doctor James and Councilman Du Bois insisted it would be a fair…duel. The fact that the so-called contest would take place in a weightless environment would ensure that. So now it was a question of whether the Omicron energy would make the opponents equal in strength, stamina and endurance. Even though Blackstar obviously had more experience with the energy, Danar was not so concerned over his own ability to compete using strength. He was confident in his ability to physically defend himself, though he hoped it was not overconfidence. He believed the winner of the barbaric duel would be determined by quick thinking. And from what he'd seen of the Imperians so far—their boasting, self-promoting superiority and especially their politics—he totally agreed with Jack Askew in that they were no different than humans.

Yet he was still not reassured. Perhaps what bothered him was the *way* he and Blackstar would be using the energy in fighting the battle. Although the Imperians *were* dependent on the Omicron energy, due chiefly to the fact they had grafted the particles onto their very bodies in the form of the bio-orbs, they had overcome the dangers of having the particles damage their tissues and weaken their organs. A crippling process now referred to as "bio-energy feedback." The aliens learned they could overcome this by regulating the energy in their bodies, literally making the energy a part of their physical structure, as opposed to having the stuff simply coursing through their bloodstream.

After pouring over the studies provided by the Imperians, the Omicron council members and scientists realized humans who had the Omicron energy successfully coursing through their blood, could do the same thing without having to convert the pectoral and shoulder muscles of the upper body to glowing bio-orbs or receive injections. Instead, Danar now had the ability to mentally absorb whatever energy amount he needed to regulate his strength, stamina and endurance. For the duel, he would be allowed to keep a concentrated source of Omicron energy near him in the form of his Nebula command baton. The transparent metallic surface of its spherical head was configured to receive only his brainwave pattern. In this way, his opponent, or anyone else enhanced with the Omicron energy, would not be able to access it. Because of his ability to mentally absorb the energy from the command baton he was also afforded a form of telekinesis with the baton over, as yet, an undetermined distance. Which was fortunate, since he suspected he would be needing both hands for any chance of surviving this thing. Because the Imperians' bio-orbs were attached to their bodies, their individual mental defenses prevented any other entity from absorbing their energy, unless they allowed it.

It all seemed fair, but Danar was still not convinced. Maybe it was simply because he never really liked carrying a command baton. He always thought of the damn thing as an affectation. Not that he was being judgmental or anything. He just never saw it as serving a purpose. Arjun Vohra and Jack Askew, who both carried theirs regularly, had said the batons were indeed a status symbol. They had all worked very hard to achieve their current positions, and the baton represented that achievement. They both had said the baton gave the captain something to keep his or her hands busy while waiting for results from the crew or vessel.

Danar still didn't see it. He believed the uniform itself was the status symbol of achievement. *Ah well, to each his own.* At least now the command baton could truly serve a purpose. He supposed he'd just have to get used to it being around.

"Danar," said Oshara Perez, excitedly, as she and Doctor James stepped into the lab servicing Sean Stingray. "Uh, I mean, Captain Nebula. Hi."

"Oshara," Seti called, just as excited. Then, noticing Doctor James' sheepish expression, he cleared his throat, smiled and said with mock seriousness, "I mean, Lieutenant Perez. Good to see you. Doctor James, how do you do?"

"Captain," said the doctor in the same neutral tone she used during his examination. But her expression changed when she saw the gleam in his eye, as if she couldn't keep a straight face.

They both chuckled, and at the same time said:

"Doctor James, about our last conversation over the comm, I…."

"Captain Nebula, I believe I owe you an apology."

"Under those circumstances, I had no excuse…."

"No, no. I should've been more…."

"I'm sorry," they both said simultaneously, while examining their feet. Then they chuckled some more.

"Oshara," Danar asked. "How are you feeling?"

"Pretty good, actually," she said, shrugging her shoulders, "despite my not being able to sleep, even though it's so late."

"Having slept for almost two days will do that to you," he said. "I'm envious."

"Yeah, I guess," Oshara said, with a concerned look on her face.

"Danar, how are *you* feeling?" She was referring to his upcoming duel tomorrow afternoon, dropping all formalities.

"Fairly well, considering," he said. "Like you though, I'm sure I won't be sleeping much this evening."

"That reminds me, Captain," interjected Doctor James, "your serotonin levels were off. You haven't been sleeping well these last few days. You *must* get some sleep tonight."

"But you said I was in perfect health," Danar said.

"Well, you are, other than being a little sleep-deprived. Listen," she continued, "I'm going to prescribe a mild sedative—"

"Sedative?" he asked. "Doctor—Sarah," he amended, "I'd rather not. Shouldn't the Omicron Particles in my system compensate for any deficiency?"

"Ordinarily, yes. But considering you'll be physically pitting your strength against another Omicron-enhanced individual, you'll need as much of an edge as you can get. Besides, Blackstar is probably sleeping like a…baby alien right now. As your doctor, I'm ordering you to get no less than eight hours of sleep tonight. The sooner, the better."

"Yes, sir," he said, offering a lazy salute.

"I mean it, Danar," she said, her hand on his shoulder. "I want you to go straight home. No socializing and no going back for any last-minute crap at the Central Command Module. You've got a big day tomorrow."

"Funny," he said, with a half-smile, "I recall saying the same thing to my colleagues just yesterday."

"The two of you may be finding it hard to sleep," the doctor said, stifling a yawn, while steering Danar Seti toward the exit, "but I've been on duty for eighteen hours nonstop. It's all I can do to keep my eyes open." She then saw the captain glance past her toward the nanotank. "Don't worry about Sean. I'll be sleeping right here. It's where I get most of my sleep anyway. Now go."

"Okay, okay," he said. Then he stopped in his tracks. "Wait a second. Have either of you seen Tan? The moment we docked, she took off. Something about important lab work. But she said she'd catch up to me."

"The last I saw, she was in the lab downstairs," answered Oshara. "That was over an hour ago. But I'll bet she's still there. She was in full scientific mode. Didn't want to be disturbed by anyone."

"I'm just going to—"

"No, no, no, Captain," interrupted the doctor, now pushing him toward the elevator. "I said no socializing."

"Sarah, it might be important."

"It can wait till morning," she countered. "I promise, Danar, I'll have her get in touch with you, *after* a good night's sleep." With a slight of hand that took the captain by surprise, she slapped a seda-patch on his neck. "There. In fifteen minutes, you'll be as tired as I am now. In thirty minutes, you'll be asleep. No matter where you are. I suggest your bed. You have just enough time to go there now."

"Doctor," he began, not sure if he should be upset or not, "you've got a devious streak."

"And you'll do well not to forget it. Now both of you. Go."

"Say, Doc, may I have one of those?" asked Oshara.

"OUT!"

Sarah James didn't exaggerate. Seti just made it back to his apartment, showered and ate a sandwich with grapefruit juice, when his eyelids started becoming heavy. He began to navigate toward his bed, more by instinct than sight, when the front door chime announced a visitor. He was about to ignore it, doing his best to follow his doctor's orders to the letter, but hoped it would be someone he'd want to see. Although he would not consciously admit to thinking the word "hope."

"Come."

The door slid aside to reveal Tan Ozawa. Her hair tied into a ponytail, she still wore her white lab coat over her black, form-fitting jumpsuit.

"Tan. What a surprise," he said, yawning. "You're obviously here without Doctor James' knowledge."

"Not exactly," she said conspiratorially. She saw him raise a questioning brow. "Apparently, I just missed you at the med facility. Sarah told me she snuck a seda-patch on you and that you'd be in—what was that term she used? Ah yes. 'La la land'—in less than thirty minutes."

"Hmm. The thirty minutes was up about ten minutes—" He yawned again and started to drift off. He shook his head. "What was I saying?"

"You were telling me you used your newfound Omicron mental prowess to counteract the sedative for a few minutes longer, to await my arrival."

"Yeah, that's right," he yawned.

"Since I knew you would do that, I didn't exactly lie to Doctor James when I promised I wouldn't interrupt your sleep."

"Hmm. You may be even more devious than…hmm," he mumbled.

"But…I see she was right. What I came to talk about can wait until the morning." She turned the teetering, half-asleep man around and guided him to his bed. He didn't or couldn't resist.

As Tan held him steady at the foot of his bed, ready to push him into it, he turned around and mumbled. "Thanks for the ride home." His eyes popped open when she actually laughed. He squeezed them shut and then focused on her. "Tan," he said, gently grabbing her shoulders. "I…I wanted to…that is to say," yawn, "I…I can't…seem to focus."

They both giggled.

Although Tan had known the adult Danar Seti for 20 years, she'd never quite seen him like this. So…innocent. Not since the time she first saw him 31 realtime years ago. A frozen eight-year-old, innocent Dane R. Howell. And like that time, she felt very protective of him. But unlike that time, she now felt…drawn to him in that chemically imbalanced manner commonly known as affection.

Looking at him, his eyes closed, asleep on his feet with his hands still gripping her shoulders, he seemed so vulnerable. She suddenly felt her heart racing. Intellectually, she knew what was happening. Although she knew she shouldn't be, she was nonetheless surprised. But what surprised her even more was the seemingly involuntary act of reaching behind Danar, pulling him toward her and kissing him.

Danar was drifting on his feet again. This time when he fought to stay awake, he found he was in the middle of...*kissing Tan Ozawa? How did...oh yes. She had just missed me at the med facility. Did I initiate this?* He started to feel guilty, when she pulled away from him.

"I'm sorry, Tan. I didn't—"

"It is I who should apologize," she said, lowering her head.

"Trust me," he assured her, "you have no reason to be sorry."

"Not true, Danar," she countered. "We have been friends for twenty years now and...."

"And you're afraid our friendship would be lost if we...."

"No. You do not understand. We cannot...it is simply not possible."

"But why, Tan?"

With her gaze still on the floor, she took another step back from him. She removed her lab coat, allowing it to drop to the floor. She then reach behind her to unzip her black faux leather garment. It joined her lab coat crumpled around her ankles, leaving her completely naked before him.

Danar felt his temperature rise. His heart raced along with all of the other physiological changes taking place within him. Then her words registered: *Anything other than friendship would be impossible.* But standing here naked in front of him, confirming what he always suspected about her physique, she was a classic case of mixed signals. He'd always considered Tan Ozawa the most beautiful woman he'd ever known. Her full round breasts, flat stomach, shapely hips and buttocks, along with her almost muscular arms and legs certainly didn't contradict his original assessment. But her words and actions were most certainly in contrast to each other.

"Tan, I don't understand," he said, slightly embarrassed his simple robe could do little to hide the altered contour of his body.

She looked directly into his eyes and raised a hand to silence him. Then she placed the hand under her breasts and peeled back a layer of skin from her abdomen, revealing a mesh of clumped artificial muscle used for reconstructive surgery. As with the case of the so-called androids of Omicron, she then reached into the cleavage of her bosom and pressed her breast bone. Danar heard a *click* and was shocked to see Tan swivel her breasts aside, opening her chest to reveal a complex series of wires and circuit boards with blinking LEDs, all within a metallic framework approximating a rib cage. There was what appeared to be a mechanical heart where a biological heart should be. Although it was pumping like a real heart, it didn't thump as expected, but instead beeped steadily.

Danar was beyond words. He looked into her face, only now noticing the running tears.

"As you can see," she said barely controlling her wracking sobs, "I am not as I appear. Any love between us would indeed be impossible. I am so sorry, Danar."

At first he didn't know what to do or say. He watched her crying, obviously in pain. He knew then what to say, what to do. He stepped closer to her, once again grasping her shoulders. Then raising her chin to stare into her blank, tear-filled eyes, he said, "It doesn't matter, Tan. This doesn't change how I feel about you."

"How—how can you say that, Danar? I am not even human. How can you have feelings for me?"

"I've had feelings for you ever since the day we met twenty years ago. I feel like I've known you even longer than that. I can't simply stop how I feel because of...of...your condition. Besides, you *feel*. You experience emotions. And right now, you're in pain and it's tearing me up inside."

"I do not want your pity," she said almost angrily.

"Too late. You've got it, or rather, you've got my sympathy. But you get so much more than that. Tell me you have no feelings for me, Tan, and I'll let this go."

"I—I can not tell you that," she replied hesitantly.

"Then it looks like you're stuck with me," he said, smiling, wanting to close her chest, but being too much the gentleman to touch her breasts, even though they were artificial.

"Oh, Danar," she said reaching for his cheek. She stopped in mid-reach, her eyes growing wide. "Oh. Something is wrong."

"Tan? What is it?"

The beeping of her synthetic heart increased. Warning flashes were being set off within her chest cavity. Her mechanical pump began glowing brighter and brighter until the light was near blinding. She moved her lips, attempting to speak over the loud *EEEEP, EEEEP, EEEEP*. Her voice had a familiar echo-like mechanical cadence. "**Warning! Asteroid collision imminent. Brace for impact,**" Tan said in VICI's voice.

The blinding luminescence from Tan's chest cavity increased, pulsating in a yellow/green flash that engulfed her body.

"Forgive me, Danar," she screamed.

Seti fell backward onto his bed, clasping his hands over his ears, trying to muffle the loud, continuous *EEEEP, EEEEP, EEEEP*.

"TAAAAAAAN!" he screamed.

Tan was startled awake. "Cosmos!" *Danar was screaming.* Screaming her name.

"TAAAAAAAN!"

She bolted off of the couch and ran to his bedroom, wearing only the robe she'd taken from him the night before. Sometime during the night, her ponytail had come loose, so she was trailing a wake of long silky hair behind her as she burst into Danar's room. He had kicked the covers off; he was perspiring, his back arched, his eyes closed tight. He was obviously having a seda-patch-induced nightmare. Not even his beeping alarm, which she had set eight hours earlier, could wake him. She shut it off and pressed down on his chest until his back made contact with the bed. She placed one hand on his cheek. "Danar. I'm here. It's alright."

"Don't...go away, Tan," he said, his eyes still shut tightly.

"I'm here, Danar," she said above him, tenderly. Her hair was cascaded all over his head and chest.

"I...I don't want to go on...without you," he said, exhausted, eyes still closed.

"You won't have to," she assured him, caressing his cheek.

His eyes snapped open. But he still had a faraway, almost crazed expression. "Tan. My goodness, you're alright." He crushed her to his chest. "I...I thought I'd lost you forever," he said into her neck.

"No. You're stuck with me," she whispered into his ear. She felt him flinch, as if he only just now woke up. She propped herself up as best she could without taking her weight off of him, her left arm across his chest. She didn't want to move away from him at all, but she figured he might be disoriented.

He looked up at her, narrowed his eyes and asked, "Did I just say all that out loud?"

"Say what out loud?" she shrugged, thinking fast.

They looked into each other's eyes, both reveling in the flesh-to-flesh contact of their nakedness. For the first time in 20 years, Danar Seti and Tan Ozawa were truly communicating, although not a word was spoken between them. They both thought of all the right and wrong reasons for continuing. Mainly because of their positions and responsibilities to the Starforce and the Omicron colonies, there were more wrong reasons than right.

Neither of them cared. They realized they had been fighting this for far too long. Tan lowered her face to Danar's waiting lips.

"FREEZE!"

They both looked up to see Oshara and Roshan Perez, flanked by a half dozen Starforce officers standing within and around the bedroom doorframe, all aiming neurowave gauntlets in their direction.

It only took a second for the eight officers to realize what they blundered into.

"Oopsy," said Roshan.

"Oh...my...God," said Oshara, motioning everyone to lower their weapons. "Danar, Tan. We're so—I mean, Captain Nebula, Doctor Ozawa. Roshan and I, that is to say, Lieutenant Perez and I were on our way over...in a spacebug, when a neighbor of yours reported screaming. We—" It was then Oshara realized the captain was naked but for a bedspread barely covering him and that Tan was self-consciously covering her bare shoulders with a robe.

"We are so fired," said Roshan. "Everybody *vamos.*"

The eight officers beat a rapid retreat from the captain's apartment, leaving the captain and the doctor alone once again.

Tan jumped from the bed, wrapping Danar's robe around her tightly. "I have never been more embarrassed in my entire life. And believe me, having spent the first half of it in a hoverchair afforded me plenty of embarrassing situations, but none of them top this," she said, sitting back down on the edge of the bed.

"I'm hip. But at least I have the advantage of not remembering any of the embarrassing moments of my youth."

Tan laughed at that. Then she held his hand and smiled at him. He returned her smile and kissed the back of her hand, imagining he couldn't be happier. Yet he couldn't escape the feeling he was forgetting something. Something important.

The communications terminal next to his bed buzzed, alerting him to an incoming call. Tan discreetly moved behind the monitor, out of range of the visual pickup. After he accepted the call, the face of Sarah James materialized on the screen. "*Ah, I'm glad to see you in bed, Captain. I trust you had a good night's sleep?*"

"I slept," was his only confirmation.

"*I see,*" Doctor James said, raising a brow. "*That's actually why I called. I did some further research on Omicron energy manipulation. It seems that with a little mental practice, you can develop the ability to alter your own body's chemistry levels so as to sleep on command.*"

"So the seda-patch wasn't necessary," concluded Danar.

"*I'm afraid not,*" she confirmed. "*As a result, you may have experienced some…well, nightmares, because your body's chemistry was artificially altered. The effect would be similar to a very deep, almost coma-like sleep.*" She hated telling him that, especially since she had to apologize to Oshara about nearly the same thing only yesterday.

"Now you tell me."

"*My findings also reveal that anyone with the level of energy now coursing through your system would do well to stay away from stimulants and uh, sedatives of any kind, as you are…capable of chemically balancing your own physiology.*"

"Don't mince words, Sarah," Danar admonished. "There's more. Spill it."

"*Because the Omicron Particles will ultimately compensate for any* chemical imbalance, the enhanced person will never really be in danger. However, if the person was enhanced to cure a malady, any external stimulant or sedative could, to a small degree, cause the malady to temporarily resurface."

Behind the monitor, Tan gasped with understanding. If the doctor heard her or saw Danar's attention waver as he glanced up, she pretended not to notice.

"So, how are you feeling, Danar?" asked the doctor.

"I feel fine, Sarah."

"Good. The seda-patch was mild and time-specific. The fact that you're awake and alert tells me your body has already metabolized it. I suspected as much, but called to be certain you were in top form for your…appointment this afternoon."

"My appointment? I don't—" His eyes went wide. "Stars! What time is it?"

"Oh-nine-forty-seven," answered the doctor at the same time as the apartment AI.

"Thank you, Doctor. Gotta go now."

"*Captain, if you've forgotten that, you may be suffering a relapse,*" she warned. "*I want to see you for an examination. To check for any cerebral chemical imbalance.*"

"No can do, Doctor. I've got just over two hours to meet Blackstar in a duel to settle a territorial dispute. It'll take me an hour to reach the coordinates in open space. The ISS *Nebula* will be meeting us to drop off Blackstar. If I'm not there, it kind of defeats the whole purpose, don't you think? I fear there's no time."

"*Then, Captain, I'd suggest you postpone it until we know for certain.*"

"Doctor, you said yourself it was a mild sedative. I assure you, I'm fine," Seti said, trying to convince her. "Listen, I'll tell you what. Doctor Ozawa had something to discuss with me. I remember that much. When I see her, I'll have her give me the once over. If anything is out of the ordinary, I'll delay my…appointment. How's that?"

"Very well, Captain Nebula," agreed Doctor James, after a pause. "Although the way Tan flew out of here last night, I'm surprised she hasn't already given you the once over."

Seti was caught by surprise with that. And based on Tan's expression, so was she. Before he could say anything, however, the doctor closed the channel. The last Seti saw of her was a devious grin.

"I will slay that woman," said Tan Ozawa with a straight face.

"She's devilish, that one," Seti said. "You'll need backup. I'll assign a security squad."

They both laughed.

"Tan, what *was* it you wanted to talk about?" Seti asked, making his way to the shower.

"There's so much to tell you and so little time," she began, climbing into her clothes, "but briefly, I managed to obtain a small sample of Imperian blood and saliva—"

"You what?! How did you—never mind. You can tell me how later."

"It's no big deal, really. I uh, saw a drop of spittle fall from Blackstar's mouth shortly after he entered the cargo bay of the Nebula freighter. I waited until everyone had gone their separate ways and we were on our way back before I obtained the dry sample. It also contained a trace amount of Imperian blood."

"Ah, from Longneck, no doubt," he said from under the shower.

"My thinking as well," she agreed, noting Danar's memory seemed to be up to speed. "When I got it back to the lab here at the med facility, I discovered the Imperians share far too many base gene pair sequences with humans to be a coincidence. Granted, it was a small sample and I'll need more study, but my conclusions are indisputable. Whether the Imperians are aware of this or not, I cannot say. But there is more going on here than meets the eye."

"Another similarity between us, eh? And this one is apparently scientifically verifiable," concluded Danar. "What do you propose?"

"Danar, I'd like your permission to examine what's left of the three remote sensor probes you deployed before the Giants arrived."

"That shouldn't pose a problem. I'll track down the twins to ferry me out to my rendevous. Why don't you collect whatever equipment you need and we'll meet you back at the cargo freighter in the hanger bay? We'll be sure to take a spacebug with us."

Excellent, thought Tan. For that's just what she needed. Two qualified officers she could trust, who wouldn't ask a lot of fool questions, the lab in the cargo freighter and the impression this set-up was all Danar's idea. Not that she was thrilled to deceive him or take advantage of the twins' trust, but for what she had in mind, it was better if her three closest friends didn't know the whole truth.

Yet.

There was just one more item she required. "Danar, I'd also like to download an autonomous copy of VICI into the cargo freighter's computer core to help me with any analysis."

"Fine," he said, drying off and grabbing a clean uniform fresh from the recycler. "I'll leave those details up to you," he said, snapping on a pair of harmonic, magnetic arm and ankle bands. "Don't forget to bring a palm scanner to verify my chemical balance."

"Done and done," she confirmed. "Well, I uh…I better get—"

"Tan," he called. She turned to face him. "Do you…do you regret anything…?"

"Yes, Danar, I do."

"Oh."

"I regret we didn't have enough time," she smiled and ran back to him for a goodbye kiss. "We have unfinished business, you and I, Captain. I insist you deal with your other responsibility so that you may attend to us."

"Count on it, Doctor," he whispered in her ear. "Be at the hanger in thirty minutes, or—"

"You'll leave without me?"

"Never," he answered without hesitation. "I'll be forced to come find you."

She kissed him on the cheek and left.

"I have bad news for you, Captain Nebula," said Tan Ozawa, running a palm scanner back and forth from the top of his head to his ankles, her voice echoing in the cavernous expanse of the giant Omicron Nebula hanger.

"A—a chemical imbalance? But I feel fine," insisted Seti.

"But that's just it, Danar," she said, a sad look in her eyes, "there is no imbalance. It appears you are in perfect health and as ready as you're going to be to fulfill your duty for this upcoming debacle."

"Tan, I'm going to be—" Seti began.

"I couldn't agree more, Doctor Ozawa," said a holographic representation of Sarah James, who materialized from nowhere. "Don't look so startled, you two. As chief medical officer of Omicron Nebula, I am authorized to access any and all palm scanners."

"Of course you are, Doctor," agreed Seti, reluctantly, "but it does leave us with the impression you didn't trust either of us with the results."

"Not at all, Captain," the realtime hologram explained. "I assumed Tan's urgency to speak with you called for her leaving with you for…scientific matters, I'm sure. My examination of you wouldn't be complete until I had those palm scanner records. I couldn't just wait for their return. God forbid, but there's always the chance that—"

"I wouldn't be coming back, so you wanted the files on record attesting to my condition?" finished Seti.

"I was going to say, the examination records could be lost or accidently deleted. I'm not casting any accusations or assumptions here, but you *are* entering what could be described as a war zone. In either case, I would be derelict in my duty as CMO if I didn't have those records on file, *before* your confrontation."

"Logical," Tan said, begrudgingly, giving her colleague the benefit of the doubt. Although Tan wanted to tell her she was becoming more like the late Doctor Peterson, with her curmudgeonly approach to her duties as CMO.

The doctor nodded her thanks. "But there is another reason why I contacted you, Captain. As per your request to limit your exposure to the vacuum, my staff and I have developed an extra-vehicular activity vacuum garment for you."

"A what?" asked Roshan Perez of his sister, as the two of them waited off to the side.

"A spacesuit," whispered Oshara.

"It should be there any second now," continued Doctor James' projection.

As if on cue, a medical technician escorted by a Starforce officer stepped off of a lift carrying an antigrav box.

"As you can see," said the doctor, as the EVA suit was extracted, "its torso and helmet are similar in design to the standard spacesuit. However, it's been custom fitted to your exact proportions. The transparent metallic face plate is wider, affording you better omnivision. The gauntlets and boots are more streamlined and the sleeves and leggings are a new design. A hybrid of synthetic myofilament and actomyosin rubber that will adhere to your arms and legs the moment the suit is sealed. The shoulder attachments on the torso have been modified. All of the retrofits are, of course, designed to give you more freedom of movement. And you can wear it over your standard uniform."

"I appreciate that more than you can know, Sarah," Seti said in genuine thanks. He was so against the idea of fighting an almost unknown opponent, literally naked of protection in the vacuum of space, that he was fully prepared to use one of the standard EVA suits from the Nebula's cargo freighter inventory. But he had to admit, this custom suit would give him a much greater advantage.

Seti also felt he and Tan might have been a bit unfair to the good doctor regarding her seemingly acerbic attempts at delaying or preventing this confrontation. Now he realized her attitude was that of a typical doctor, whose first rule was to "do no harm." For while she was trying to be sure of his mental and physical well-being, she and her staff had, apparently overnight, designed and manufactured this suit at his request.

He saw that Tan looked as contrite as he did.

"Doctor," Danar said, rubbing the bridge of his nose in remorse, "if memory serves, uh, no pun intended, I clearly recall you complaining about your need for sleep. It seems to me, you couldn't possibly have gotten any."

"Please don't feel any more guilty than you have to," she said. "I admit, I stayed up for a bit to begin the design of the suit, then turned it over to the overnight on-call staff to build. I tried to get some sleep but couldn't. I was…distracted."

"How *is* Sean doing?" guessed Seti.

"The bad news is, his condition hasn't changed. The good news is, his condition hasn't changed," she said with a wry grin.

"Understood, Sarah."

"One more thing, Danar," said the holo-image of Doctor James, raising a finger, "I've also downloaded another program into a memory compression headband."

The med tech removed the headgear from the container, and placed it into Captain Nebula's hand. The programmable headgear, like the one Danar Seti wore during his initial medical exam, gave the wearer several hours' worth of instructions and training within a matter of minutes.

"I've programmed it with updated information regarding the mental manipulation of your body's resources," continued the doctor, " including the allocation and production of adrenalin, along with more practice sessions for telekinetically controlling your command baton from an even greater distance. Use it while you've got the time," she ordered. "Of course, I'd feel better if you could use it while in a deep sleep, but since it's a supplemental training session, you should still get the most out of it."

"Sarah, I—I don't know what to say," he whispered, at a loss for words. "This is more than I expected. Thank you."

"My thanks as well, Sarah," said Tan.

"Just get back to us in one piece, Danar," said the doctor with a look of genuine concern that changed suddenly into another devilish grin. "I rather enjoy busting your chops." With that, her projection vanished, while the med tech collected the antigrav box and took his leave, as if on cue.

"She is the most inscrutable person I know," commented Tan, "but the colony couldn't live without her."

Oshara and Roshan exchanged a knowing smile, for they had heard almost the exact same thing said of Tan Ozawa on more than one occasion.

"I can't believe this is actually happening, Danar," complained Oshara Perez, standing next to a spacebug in the cargo bay of the Nebula transport freighter, along with her brother, Tan Ozawa and Danar Seti, who was suited-up sans his space helmet. "I'm almost convinced I'm still comatose back at the med facility on Omicron Nebula, having a really strange nightmare."

"Yeah, Skipper. This whole thing does have a surrealistic quality to it," agreed Roshan. "Like a dream."

"I know what you mean," Danar half-smiled. "But for me, as surrealistic as this situation seems, it's infinitely preferable to a nightmare scenario I experienced recently." He had to force himself not to glance over at Tan.

"I am of the opinion," said Tan, "that this situation is not only unnecessary, but barbaric in its so-called diplomatic approach."

"A part of me feels the same way," said Danar, lowering his head in near shame. "But another part of me is almost convinced the trait of intelligence must pass a test before it reaches the pinnacle of the road to enlightenment, as my father was fond of saying. I thought we humans had passed the test when the Earth was finally united under the UEA. But recently, I've come to realize it was arrogant of me to believe that when we'd yet to interact with another of God's children. Have we learned, over the last several millennia, how to get along and accept each other as equals enough to get along and accept an alien culture that developed independently of us?"

"I'd like to think we have," answered Tan.

"I'd like to think that as well," agreed Danar, "but that's only half the equation. The other half being, of course, have the Imperians learned to get along and accept an independent alien culture as equals?"

"It certainly doesn't look that way," answered Oshara.

"On the surface, perhaps," stated Danar. "But like humans, I believe the Giants of Imperia are merely victims of circumstance, causing them to veer off the road, somewhat."

"Not that I'm against the idea, mind you," said Tan, with a

thoughtful expression, "but how is it you've come to believe this?"

"Well," he began, "in addition to their readiness to sit at the bargaining table after being bested—"

"Barely," clarified Tan.

"Barely bested by supposed inferiors," amended Danar. "Plus the fact they, like us, are a society of consensus. I'm convinced that if time weren't a factor in their circumstances, some of the Giants would indeed welcome a different form of life, a new culture. At least one of them would."

"You mean Blackstar," Roshan guessed.

"Yes."

"But he's the one you have to fight!" exclaimed a shocked Oshara.

"Yes, that's right," Danar calmly verified.

"I'm confused, Danar," admitted Oshara. "The *cabron* you must face in mortal combat is the very alien that led the invasion into our space."

"Reluctantly led," interjected Seti.

"Reluctantly? How do you know this, Danar?"

"*Si, jefe,*" added Roshan. "Believe it or not, I'm just as confused as Oshara."

He received a playful elbow to the ribs for that.

"You want to know how I know Blackstar is a reluctant participant in this whole affair?" he asked. "Because he told me he was."

"But, Danar," said Tan, "I was standing next to you during almost every exchange with Blackstar. How…when…where did he tell you this?"

"He was standing on this very spot, I believe," Danar answered, pointing to the floor at his feet. "It was moments after Augustus Du Bois dropped this honor into my lap. I was standing there," he pointed to the upper tier observation windows of the flight deck. "And just as the councilman verified my opponent, Blackstar looked up at me and, for several minutes, there existed between us a clarity of understanding. It wasn't facial expressions or body language. For those few moments, I knew…*I knew* his thoughts, his heart, his very soul. Just as he knew mine," he concluded, still staring up at his former location, as if reliving the moment.

"Danar, you could be anthropomorphizing," offered Tan, almost timidly when she noticed the reverent look on Seti's face.

"No, I'm not," he said, focusing his attention back to his friends. "I'm certain of it."

"Sir, are you talking about...telepathy?" asked Oshara.

"No. I don't think—I...I'm not sure, really," he admitted.

"Hey, Skipper," said Roshan, somewhat worried, "you...you're kind of scaring me here."

"Forgive me, sir. You know how much I....respect you," offered Oshara in the same vein, "but it doesn't sound very...scientific."

"I'm sorry, my friends," apologized Danar. "There is no one who is closer to me than the three of you. It's anathema to me to frighten you in any way. I just don't know if I can explain it." He looked pleadingly at Tan, hoping their recent connection could close the gap between them. He wasn't disappointed.

With a thoughtful look, Tan scratched her chin. "Perhaps there is a scientific explanation involved here."

"This ought to be good," Roshan said.

"Do tell," said Oshara.

"You know, it really shouldn't come as much of a surprise," admonished Tan, "when you think of Captain Graviton's experiences with the bully rock. While the device was spying on his ship and tried to circumvent discovery, it apparently thought it located some of its programmers, by way of Captain Graviton's Omicron enhancement. I believe it was attempting to communicate with the crew telepathically."

"Yes," recalled Danar. "The spherical device approached the crew in pairs, presumably to extract more instructions, but instead rendered them unconscious until it found Arjun Vohra."

"That's right," Tan confirmed. "Perhaps Arjun *did* successfully communicate with the stone telepathically. After all, he wanted it off his ship, and it did leave in a hurry."

"Maybe," said Danar, stroking his beard, "but it's more likely it was attempting escape to reach the ID transit point to warn the Imperians of its discovery."

"True, it could have been preprogrammed with those instructions, or it might have deduced those orders telepathically from an Omicron-enhanced being telling it to leave. The bottom line is, the thing was attempting to communicate in some form with the *Graviton*'s crew."

"In pairs," Oshara added, "as if it were trying to form a triumvirate."

"A triumvirate," repeated Tan thoughtfully. That term helped her assemble another piece of the puzzle she'd been trying to piece together, but she mentally filed it away for later, after she proved a case for telepathy. "Also, let's not forget that Danar is capable of telekinetically controlling his command baton, thanks to the Omicron energy coursing through him."

To demonstrate, Danar Seti concentrated and his command baton came whizzing out of the open rear door of the spacebug. It managed a swooping curve in mid-air before bouncing off the deck, causing Roshan to quickly duck as it zipped past his head and into the captain's outstretched hand.

"Yikes," exclaimed the young lieutenant. "Okay, I'm convinced."

"Sorry about that, kid," said Danar. "I suppose it'll work better in a weightless environment."

"That *is* very convincing," agreed Oshara. "I recall a few years ago, they were saying that when the Omicron energy is better understood, it might be possible to use it to extend life on the order of centuries. And that was a conservative figure. Does that mean it's possible the human race could become a species of telepathic immortals?"

"Who knows?" offered Danar. "It's just speculation for now."

"You know, something else occurred to me about the Giants," Tan said. "As Oshara pointed out, the spherical stone appeared to be attempting a triumvirate with the Graviton's crew, as if it were programmed to communicate in that way. If that's the case, and I don't know why it didn't occur to me before now, the Imperians seem to have a preoccupation with the number three."

"I see what you mean," concurred Danar. "Their caste society is set up for three classes. The Conservatives, the Liberals and the Neutrals."

"They also all have three Omicron energy spheres grafted to their bodies," added Roshan.

"And," Oshara offered, "they're trying to migrate to a trinary star system. A system from which they could draw enough energy to transport. Plus the fact that their spaceship thingy—whatever, comprises three spheres."

"You're right, Tan," agreed Danar, "they do appear to have a preoccupation with the number three. But what scientific or mathematical significance could that have for them?"

No one could even hazard a guess until Roshan spoke up. "Maybe it's not scientific or mathematical at all, but theological instead."

"How do you mean, Ro?" asked Oshara.

"Well, it could simply mean they worship the number three," he explained. "Not that I'm trying to denigrate another culture's religion, but the number three could have a spiritual connotation for them."

"Hmm. You could be right, Ro," commented Danar. "I wonder if we could use that to our advantage."

"Wouldn't it be better to try and understand it in the hope of better cultural relations," countered Roshan, "as opposed to using it for an advantage?"

Danar Seti was somewhat taken aback by Roshan's adamant response, but conceded it was more socially conscious as well as diplomatic. "I stand corrected," he said without shame.

"And speaking of spirituality," continued Roshan, "I noticed earlier, you used the term 'God's children.' I've never heard you refer to God before. I thought that—well, quite frankly, I thought you were… uh—"

"An atheist?" Danar finished for him.

"*Sí*."

"If I had used the term 'Universe's children,' that might not have piqued your notice, eh?" asked Danar, with a half-smile. "But to clarify your question, Roshan, although I've never referred to myself *as* an atheist, I'd *like* to believe there is a higher power that is aware of all things. In fact, my father had been quoted as saying, 'When man discovers the Grand Unified Theory, he will discover the reflection of God.' Personally, I'd like to think of the entire Universe as the body of God. But as to whether God takes an active interest in the affairs of his, her, its…inhabitants, I can't say."

"Perhaps you are more of an agnostic, Danar," Tan offered. "For although you can find no evidence of God, you are not denying the possibility of God's existence."

"Perhaps," he accepted.

"And what of you, Tan," inquired Roshan, "if I may ask?"

"For you, Roshan, I don't mind," Tan said. "I would, by definition, be considered an atheist. And until recently, I've never had a problem with the definition or its implications. But lately, I feel the more science reveals of the Universe, the more room I seem to have for the concept of God. Although I don't feel that any culture on Earth has even scratched the surface of the concept, no matter how close they think they've come."

"You don't really believe that, do you, Tan?" asked Roshan.

"I mean no insult, Roshan," she said, gently placing her hand on his shoulder. "As a scientist, I view the whole of existence through mathematical lenses. In those terms, the Universe has existed in its current form from the Big Bang for about fifteen billion years. The Earth has been around for four and half billion. However, every person you've ever heard about, every human who has ever been documented in recorded history, the entire human species has existed for less than two hundred thousand years. A scratch in the surface of the Universe's existence. Or as Danar would compare, God's existence."

"But God has always existed," said Oshara.

"And always will, if I understand the concept. And if that's true," commented Tan, "it helps to prove my point. For you see, some scientists postulate that the Universe has always existed, in what is referred to as a 'steady state universe.' A Universe that has always existed *as is*. Never changing. Yet, all matter in this Universe is moving away from each other at a constant rate. An expansion as if from an explosion that occurred a long, long time ago. An explosion that is referred to by some scientists as the Big Bang. Ironically, it was the twentieth-century astronomer Fred Hoyle who first coined the name Big Bang, even though he himself defended the steady state theory, arguing that the Universe developed in a process of continuous growth;

that the constituent parts of the Universe—atoms, stars and galaxies—had beginnings, but the Universe itself did not. That is until radio astronomy observations in the mid-twentieth century demonstrated that the Universe was indeed expanding faster than Doctor Hoyle's theory predicted. The Big Bang."

"Then what existed before the Big Bang?" asked Roshan.

"Although I wasn't present at the time," said Tan, "some scientists believe another Universe was present before the Big Bang. A Universe that was countless billions of years in age, whose beginning came about through an explosion that flung its condensed matter in every direction. As the matter scattered and expanded, it collided with itself, creating new elements and therefore even more matter, until finally there was so much matter it could no longer expand but instead took countless billions more years contracting and colliding back onto itself, destroying any life that may have inhabited it, until it shrank to a minuscule speck of supercharged matter that could no longer contain its compact form. So in a cataclysmic birthing event, it exploded in every direction—the Big Bang. And our Universe is still expanding to this very day."

"So what you're saying," understood Roshan, "is that one day, *our* Universe will begin to collapse and contract on itself into a tiny speck of matter and be reborn again into a new Universe."

"Or so the theory goes," Tan confirmed.

"Such is the cycle of life," added Danar. "Birth, growth, decline and eventually death. Over and over again."

"So under that theory," clarified Oshara, "the Universe has always existed through a never- ending process of expansion and contraction for all time."

"But what came first?" asked Roshan.

"The chicken or the egg?" Danar answered with a question. "As Tan said, nobody was around to witness it, except the Universe itself. Or God, if you prefer. And it seems that God is leaving it up to us to discover for ourselves."

"There is another theory," continued Tan. "That there was no space or time or anything before the Big Bang. That it was original, unique and if it is true that dark matter is helping the Universe to continue its explosive expansion, then *dark energy* is being created in its wake, preventing the Universe from ever contracting by propelling all matter outwards, preventing gravity from ever taking hold and eventually 'crunching' everything back together again. Which means it will continue to expand until all of the stars and galaxies are separated by such vast distances that there will be no chance of new stellar nurseries forming and that the existing matter will eventually burn itself out. Everything—and I mean *everything* will be truly cold, dead. The Universe may have been born with a hot bang but may eventually die in a cold whimper."

"Okay, I've got a headache now," admitted Roshan.

"My advice in trying to understand the Universe around us," offered Danar, "is to take it a little bit at a time. Otherwise it'll drive you crazy."

"But only if you let it," added Tan.

"I'm afraid it's too late for my brother," chuckled Oshara.

"Oh, yuk, yuk," said Roshan.

"Seriously, Roshan, Oshara," Danar said, placing a gloved hand on each twin's shoulder, while Tan stood between the them, "if you wish to discover yourself, the way and how you fit in the world around you, studying or practicing religion is a good start."

"*Gracias, jefe,*" responded a grateful Roshan. "And if I may suggest, it won't hurt for you to pray for a positive resolution to your…confrontation with Blackstar."

"Don't think for a moment," Danar said squeezing their shoulders, "I haven't already begun to pray. I'm praying for all of us, including the Imperians."

"I'm praying for both as—"

EEEEP EEEEP EEEEP, signaled the Data Access Crystal under Roshan's belt. "Oh boy," he said, consulting the device that was patched into the freighter's exterior cameras. "It's eleven-fifty-five and there's Blackstar and I think Rockbottom and Deepwaters leaving the ISS *Nebula*. Yeah, they're surfing to that big asteroid below us. I…I guess it's time, Skipper."

"I guess so," Danar said, biting his lower lip.

"I still can't believe this is happening," complained Oshara.

"My friends," said the captain gently, "I'll be fine. We'll be fine." He looked directly at Tan and opened his arms. She stepped into his embrace while Oshara and Roshan completed the group hug.

It was too brief for any of them.

The three stepped away from Captain Nebula. He picked up his space helmet from the floor, attached it to the suit's neck ring and locked it in place with a *hiss*. At that point, the loose sleeves and leggings of the suit instantly adhered to his limbs, delineating the muscles of his arms and legs. He reached behind him and pulled his command baton from its magnetic hold on his back and said with more conviction than he really felt, "Everything will work out. You'll see."

Yes. Everything will work out, Danar, thought Tan to herself. *Even if I must see to it myself.* For despite Danar's optimistic appraisals, and his assurance of Blackstar's integrity, Tan Ozawa was all too aware of how rapidly this powder keg could become a conflagration that could engulf both this branch of humanity as well as the entire Imperian race. Unless she took matters into her own hands. She knew that others would consider her arrogant, maybe even self-centered and self-serving. They may be right. To a point. But no one else possessed her unique skills and abilities. Abilities she hadn't used in over 30 realtime years. Abilities that could tip the balance in favor of both species, otherwise she may witness the destruction of at least one solar system and possibly an entire dimension. Unless she was very, very careful.

CHAPTER SEVENTEEN
I Sing the Body Electro-holographic

Captain Nebula waited in the cockpit of the spacebug until his three friends appeared at the observation windows on the upper deck of the freighter. He then remotely depressurized first the cargo bay and then the spacebug itself so that it would allow him to open the iris in its floor for his exit from the compact utility vehicle.

The next thing he did was to verify the readiness of the Omicron camera bot, the self-powered, autonomous propulsion AI that would record and relay the contest to the Omicron officials back in-system and to the fleet still located in open space in the opposite direction.

With practiced skill, he eased the bug through the large cargo bay door, mesmerized as always by that feeling of emerging into both nothing and everything at the same time. For only in the vacuum of space, the most hostile environment for an air-breathing mammal, did Danar Seti truly feel at home, at peace. He refused to acknowledge the incongruity of his overall feeling for space and his current reason for venturing into it. For he still had hope that his fascination with space and his assigned mission could be reconciled.

To his dismay, that hope began to fade as he saw Blackstar standing atop the oblong 20-meter-wide asteroid, the starting point for this so-called duel within the triangle of stars. *As if there's even the slightest chance we will actually need that much ground.* However, the parameters of the arena seemed a minor and easy point to concede to the Giants.

At first, Nebula didn't have a problem with it. But now he was starting to wonder.

When the spacebug was directly over the asteroid, Captain Nebula opened the floor iris and set the autopilot to return to the freighter the moment he cleared the exit. There was no need for the craft to hang around for a second longer. The way his apprehension was mounting, he might be tempted to change his mind and use it to escape to.... Well, there was no such place as nowhere, so he had little choice.

It was just as well, for it wouldn't look good for his crew onboard the *Nebula* to see him run away. But even if he were tempted, he would never give Augustus Du Bois the satisfaction of seeing him back out. He unbuckled himself, kicked off, then used his hands to push himself from the bug's ceiling through the floor iris until his boots connected with the surface of the small asteroid. The nickel-iron boulder didn't possess much of a gravity field so he pressed a stud on one of the gauntlets to activate the boots' magnets.

He looked up to see Blackstar facing him about 12 meters away, using his three-toed feet to keep from floating away. He could also see his ship, the ISS *Nebula*, slowly orbiting the asteroid. He could see what must be Deepwaters and Rockbottom reenter the airlock, leaving their surfing boulder to go about its business of drifting aimlessly in open space.

Seeing his starship in the vicinity was somehow encouraging. Right now, he needed all of the courage he could get.

He also noticed the spacebug silently glide overhead, back toward the freighter. When he focused back to his opponent, he saw one of the spherical stones floating towards him. But it was a different stone than the one that would convey the contest to the Imperians. *What's this?* he wondered. It couldn't be a trick. Not while the Omicron camera bot, floating above him, was relaying and recording everything that was taking place. So he wasn't too concerned. He'd know what it was all about shortly.

"I will be down in the lab," Tan informed Oshara and Roshan. "I will require the uninterrupted services of VICI, so she will be unavailable until further notice. It is extremely important we not be disturbed."

"Tan, we may never see Danar again," admonished Roshan. "What can be so important in the lab?"

"Whether or not I'm in the lab will not prevent the contest between Danar and Blackstar," Tan explained. "However, my experiments may alter the outcome of said contest to a favorable resolution, *if* I am not disturbed under *any* circumstances, other than you signaling the arrival of the spacebug."

"I don't wish to hold you up," said Oshara, "but how can your experiments affect the outcome?"

"Briefly, I will explain," she capitulated. "As Danar himself often says, 'we are all more alike than not alike.' I believe that statement holds true for us and the Imperians as well. I intend to prove, scientifically, that the similarities of our two species can and should bring about an understanding, an alternative resolution that will be mutually beneficial for all of us. Humans and Imperians. It will require me to access the three remote sensor probes back at the interdimensional transit point. Since I cannot prevent the start of the contest, the quicker I can carry out my lab work, the better the chances we will see Danar again, whole and healthy."

The siblings glanced at each other briefly. "You have our full support, Tan," said Oshara.

"Excellent," she said, smiling. "Very shortly, we will proceed to the ID transit coordinates. I realize the two of you would probably rather stay here, close to Danar. Believe me when I tell you I wish also not to stray too far from him, but what I plan is for the greater good of us all in the long run."

"We're with you, Tan," confirmed Roshan. "There's only the three of us—well, four of us, counting VICI. Just tell us when and where and we're there. *Pronto.*"

"Excellent," repeated Tan. "Remember, contact me via intercom when the bug returns, otherwise VICI and I are not to be disturbed under any circumstances, not even by the councilman on the ISS

Nebula over there," she said gesturing out the front viewport. "Don't worry. Although we will be leaving shortly, Captain Nebula's crew will keep a watchful eye on him."

Sealing the door to the freighter's lab, Tan Ozawa was pleased everything was falling into place. She'd had no doubt the twins would pledge their loyalty without a full explanation. Now it was VICI's turn. She would be unable to complete her task without the hologram's full cooperation, diligence, acting ability and, more importantly, her imagination.

"VICI," Tan called.

The hologram appeared in her usual coalescing light show from the holoprojector in the lab. **"Yes, Mother. How may I be of service?"**

"I have a mission for you," Tan began. "It is unlike anything you've ever done, ever experienced."

"It is obvious you deem it of importance. Also, you apparently believe me capable of this task. That is good enough for me. Simply tell me what you require."

"Not so fast, VICI," warned Tan. "I have no doubt you are capable. You just may not be willing."

"I doubt that, Mother. Besides, I feel I owe you any favor, no matter my lack of experience. Of course, I owe you my very life, such as it is. But specifically, I owe you because I did not ask your permission when I interfaced with you yesterday while onboard the *Nebula*, when the spherical stone harassing the *Graviton* sent that feedback signal that nearly deleted my *Nebula* program. It would have succeeded had I not downloaded my program into your bio-neuronet via your interface. I regret it caused you distress."

"I realize you didn't have the time to ask permission or consider the consequences. Besides, it only rendered me unconscious. There was no damage or lasting ill effects. Had I known what was happening, I would have insisted upon it at any rate."

"I admit, I had hoped our identical engramatic patterns could occupy the same storage medium of your neurons without suppressing your conscious mind."

"No doubt, our engramatic patterns are no longer identical due to our different experiences over the last several decades," explained Tan. "Your memories are uniquely yours now. But listen, VICI. It was that very experience that gave me the idea for this mission."

"Does it have something to do with us sharing your neurons?"

"More or less," Tan answered. "Allow me to explain. VICI, this mission of which I am speaking, requires you and I to literally exchange places."

For the first time in her 31 years of existence, the Virtual Inquiry Computer Interactive hologram doubted she correctly registered the words being picked up by her audio sensors. **"Mother, did I hear you correctly?"**

"Yes," Tan verified. "We must switch places."

"Tan, that is not possible."

"I beg to differ, VICI," she countered. "It is quite possible. You are correct in that you can occupy my biological neurological network. In the same way that your program can navigate the fiberoptic network of a computer core, so can you navigate the synapses of my brain. Just as my consciousness does. You should only require a few minutes of practice for the motor control of my body. Also, our thought processes are close enough that my nervous system will recognize your engramatic pattern. That means my muscles will obey your commands. Know also that my arms, legs and back muscles were grafted with a thin layer of cybernetic circuitry film. Doctor James performed that surgery on me after your engramatic birth to aid me as a result of the DNA resequencing procedure that cured me of ALS. Although it affords me faster reflexes, I no longer require the cybernetic enhancement to move about. However you may access them to assist you in locomotion should it be necessary."

"But, Mother, your consciousness is not a program. You won't be able to navigate the fiberoptic network of my computer core."

"Nor will I have to. For you see, I will be navigating quantum space."

"I beg your pardon," the hologram demanded, lowering her voice an octave.

"While you are occupying my mind, so to speak, my consciousness will exist in a state which is slightly out of phase with the three-dimensional state. While I am able to perceive the world around me, those who rely on the standard senses of visual, olfactory, auditory and tactile will be unable to detect me. It is my hope the Imperians will be so limited."

"Exactly how will your consciousness travel through this medium? This…quantum space?"

"Through what I call the metasphere."

"Explain please."

"Although we cannot occupy my synaptic network simultaneously, I believe if you download into my bio-net via the interface slowly, as your program did when I wrote it thirty-one years ago, my consciousness will gradually achieve a state of…separation from my synapses. Similar to achieving a state of meditation. It's difficult to describe, but I only possess the limited senses of sight and hearing. However, I'm able to hear everything within a range of about thirty meters, from the faintest rustle of air circulation to the normal sounds picked up by conventional mammalian hearing. I am able to adjust my focus on any sound I choose. As for vision, I can see everything at once as if my surroundings are reflected on the surface of a sphere, in which my consciousness resides."

"Ah," said the hologram, understanding, **"hence, the term meta*sphere*."**

"Correct."

"How far from your physical body can your metasphere travel in quantum space?"

"Thirty-one years ago, while your program was mapping my synaptic network and downloading test programs, I discovered I could travel anywhere within the ISS *Nebula*. When I attempted to leave the ship, however, I was snatched back into my body and experienced several days of delirium before my mind could once again organize a consistent thought process. As a result, despite the successful re-sequencing procedure, or perhaps because of it, my brainstem became too feeble and weak to carry electrical impulse to my nervous system via my spine. That's why I required ten additional years back on ice. Of course, I didn't realize this until I awoke and Sarah James informed me that programmable nanodroids repaired the damage. Otherwise, I could have been on ice for much longer. Anyway, to answer your question, I believe my metasphere consciousness limits are defined by the width and breadth of whatever circuitry you have available to you."

"Hmmm. The fact that you were snatched back into your body implies there exists a natural safety line between your conscious mind and your body, which means the two are never truly separated. I find that reassuring."

"As do I," agreed Tan.

"But you also implied you wish to use your metasphere consciousness to…observe the Imperians. How do you plan to accomplish this?"

"As I said earlier, I am able to navigate any circuitry that you are able to navigate. Specifically, Omicron fiberoptic technology. The same technology that is employed by our starships, spacebugs and space stations. But there is also Omicron fiberoptic technology aboard the large Imperian stone sphere."

"Of course. The communications viewer array. But how will you get there?"

"That's where the three discarded remote sensor probes come in. You see, thirty-one years ago, when I momentarily phased outside of the *Nebula*, I had briefly considered traveling along the broadcast laser beam back to the ISS *Gaea*. It could have worked. But I failed to consider my slightly out-of-phase condition makes me incompatible with a standard beam. Even your program is transferred along a beam that is frequency-specific to you. My plan calls for me—that is, calls for *us* to modify the RSPs to transmit a laser beam that is frequency-specific to my metasphere. Which means it will be undetectable through conventional means."

"You intend to repair and modify all three remote sensor probes?"

"Yes."

"Why did you not simply bring three modified and functioning RSPs with you?"

"Because, VICI, my holographic offspring, this mission is being carried out without the approval or sanction of the Omicron council or the knowledge of any member of the Starforce. I convinced Danar to allow me to go this far under the pretext that I could probably get more information from the damaged RSPs—which is still a possibility. In fact, that is what Oshara and Roshan will think I am doing in the spacebug, as they use the cargo freighter to escort us to each drifting RSP. The reality is, *you* will be masquerading as me in my body while my metasphere will assist you in repairing and modifying each probe. From the last probe, you will transmit my metasphere to the Omicron communications viewer array onboard the large Imperian stone sphere, where I will carry out my mission of gathering as much information as possible regarding the Giants' society, culture, habits and living conditions."

"Oh, Mother, this seems an awfully dangerous mission for gains that could be tenuous at best."

"You think so? I believe our best advantage here is to really *know* the Imperians. More than what they *choose* to tell us. There is an ancient phrase from Earth. 'Keep your friends close, but keep your enemies even closer.'"

"Hmm, I have not heard that one before."

"I'm not surprised, really," Tan said. "There's been relative peace in your circles over the past three decades."

"Mother, how long do you plan to stay aboard the Imperian stone sphere?"

"For as long as you can reasonably stay aboard the spacebug without raising suspicion."

Good, thought VICI. *That won't be too long then.* That made the hologram less apprehensive about this mission. For the reality was, it was a lot more dangerous for Tan than for VICI herself. *At least Tan's body will be out of the danger zone.*

"So. The question remains, VICI. Will you join me in my mission, deceiving two innocent officers and, as some may consider, betraying the Starforce and the Omicron council?"

"Well, when you put it that way, it does sound treasonous," VICI admitted. "However, it is not exactly a betrayal should the end results prove beneficial to the Omicron colony as well as the Imperians."

"But only if we are successful," warned Tan. She wanted VICI's full cooperation, but without the deception of sugar-coated convincing. She would rather be as honest as possible.

"There is an ancient phrase from Earth. 'The end justifies the means.'"

Tan didn't have the heart to tell VICI that phrase was usually spoken *after* the successful deed. "So, your decision?"

"**Of course I will join you, Mother. The truth is, without you I simply would not exist. Besides, I am certain Oshara and Roshan would understand the temporary deception on our part.**"

"Thank you, VICI," said Tan, bowing deeply. "You have my gratitude."

"**And you have mine,**" said the hologram, returning the bow.

Danar is committed now, thought Oshara as the spacebug settled onto the deck of the cargo bay. She was about to inform Tan, her hand reaching for the intercom, when she heard the lift ascend to the upper deck, depositing the scientist. "Ah, Tan. I was just about to contact you. The spacebug just came back."

"Perfect timing on my part," Tan said, walking slowly toward the astronavigation table. "I have plotted a parabolic course for the three remote sensor probes. That is…VICI has plotted the course." She stared at the tabletop for a few seconds. Then she raised her eyebrows as if remembering something. Accessing the control panel, she called up a holographic representation of the large Imperian stone sphere, the remaining Omicron fleet and the three RSPs, spaced equidistant from each other on the outer perimeter. "Of course, this representation is not to scale. The remote sensor probes have drifted much farther afield of their original positions, so fortunately, my repairs should not raise a concern. We will go to this one first, at which point I will leave in the spacebug and repair it remotely. From then on, the two of you will escort me to the other probes, one after the other."

"Why not simply collect all three and repair and access them here in the cargo bay?" asked Roshan, joining them from the navigator's position forward.

An excellent question, thought the entity known as Tan Ozawa. Thinking fast, she replied, "I…I would like for them to remain at their current positions. From there, they can still monitor the large stone sphere. It might look too suspicious if we were to collect them only to redeploy them."

"That makes sense," said Roshan, wondering why Tan was visually tracking the ceiling, as if following the progress of an insect. "Shall we get underway?"

"Yes. Thank you, Lieutenant Perez," the scientist said, smiling.

"Why, you're welcome, of course, Doctor Ozawa," he replied.

"Tan, are you alright?" asked Oshara. "You seem a little out of sorts, distracted even."

"Oh, well uh…yes, as a matter of fact, I…did not get enough sleep last night. I am–I'm a little tired."

"I don't doubt it," Roshan said, nodding his head. "I mean, of course," he corrected, glancing at his sister. The two of them did their best to stifle a laugh.

"We've still got some time," commented Oshara. "Why don't you get some rest and we'll contact you when we get to the first probe."

"A good idea," agreed Tan. "Thank you for the suggestion, Lieut—Oshara. I believe rest is what I require." Taking careful steps, she slowly walked back to the lift and descended.

The twins looked at each other and smirked.

Rising from the bench in the lab, Tan saw VICI staring at her. "Is everything alright?"

"**Oh yes. Everything is fine. How are you?**"

"I'm okay," Tan said rubbing her temples. "Just a slight headache. Not as bad as thirty-one years ago. It's subsiding rapidly, thank…the cosmos."

"I felt no discomfort from your cranium, Tan. Why do you suppose you do?"

"I suppose it has something to do with the time distortion of quantum space. Normal time seems to slow down. Or rather my perception is speeded up. However, since it didn't come as unexpected this time around, I was able to mentally compensate for it. It is somewhat disorienting adjusting back to normal time."

"Now that you mention that, I have a concern, Mother."

"Oh?"

"I am not certain of how to tell you this, but I think I was able to see you."

"Ah, so you were not simply *trying* to see me. You actually could?"

"I believe so."

"Interesting. What did I look like?"

"It is hard to say. I have heard humans talk of seeing things out of the corner of their eye. Implying they can see something that is barely within their perceptual range. If it was your metasphere I saw, it was reminiscent of a very thin soap bubble or perhaps the afterimage of a small light when you close your eyes."

"*Very* interesting."

"But, Mother, you said your metasphere was beyond the perception of normal eyes."

"I thought you might have noticed by now, VICI," said Tan, gesturing to her face. "These eyes are anything but normal."

"Of course, the modifications to your optic nerves," VICI conceded. "I should have realized. But keep in mind, yours is the only human body I've ever inhabited. I forgot that your perceptions are indeed above normal. Forgetting is also a new experience for me. But my concern still stands. The Imperians do not possess human eyes either. I think it would be in our best interest to develop an emergency escape plan from the stone sphere."

"Agreed," Tan said, seeing the logic in the suggestion.

They brainstormed until they were satisfied with a plan. VICI, in Tan's body, would keep a high-intensity laser broadcast frequency-specific beam focused on the large stone sphere from the spacebug, as well as the beams from the sensor probes. The beams would act as an emergency escape route that Tan's metasphere could access from anywhere within the stone sphere instead of being limited to exiting through the Omicron communications viewer array as the original plan called for, since the beams from the three RSPs intersect at that location.

"So, VICI," inquired Tan, "tell me what it was like to navigate meatspace in a human body."

"Strangely, it really is not that different."

"Surely you jest."

"Not at all. At first, I was worried about having to breathe constantly, but as with your cardiovascular system, breathing is mostly involuntary. Visual and auditory senses are similar to what I am used to, although limited to the single location of your cranium. Your olfactory sense is unique. As a program, I rely on the chemical analysis of odors that I process through a preprogrammed comparative database. Fortunately, the limited access I have to your memories provides me with similar comparisons for identification, with the added bonus of actually experiencing aromas."

"That's wonderful, VICI. I think then, you'll enjoy ingesting sustenance. I'll prepare a sandwich and tea for you to experience while we're alone aboard the spacebug. I'll also prepare a sample of various aromas for you to try. Some will be pleasant. Some will not."

"I am looking forward to it. Thank you."

"Oh, that's another thing," Tan said, snapping her fingers. "Try to use more contractions in your speech. *Can't* instead of *cannot* or *don't* instead of *do not*. I realize I don't use as many as most, but I believe the twins noticed when you failed to do so. Also, don't be so formal with them."

"Yes. I noticed that as well. I can easily adapt."

"Good. One last thing. What did you mean when you said you have limited access to my memories?"

"Forgive me. I misspoke. I should have—should've said, 'your body's memories.' The things the body does without conscious thought, such as breathing and identifying odors. It is unfortunate

I no longer have access to your mental memories or your thoughts and dreams."

"Perhaps," Tan said smiling, "that's as it should be."

"Ah. You value your privacy. I understand. I only meant that I could carry on my masquerade more efficiently if I possessed your memories."

"This is why I chose to limit the people with whom you will interact. With Oshara and Roshan, you have, for the most part, always been present when I interacted with them. So you can rely on your own memories."

"Yes, I can do that. I suppose the biggest difference in navigating meatspace, as you refer to it, is that in cyberspace, my memory is limited only by the amount of information available. Which means it is virtually unlimited, as I have instant access to any and all files of information. While inhabiting your body, if I cannot—can't mentally remember it, I can't access it."

"Not mentally, perhaps," Tan said reaching into her lab coat, "but you can always employ the Data Access Crystal."

"**Of course.**" The hologram smiled. "**It will seem strange having to manually access information that my program normally regulates.**"

Tan laughed, then said, "You know, I believe I will take what time we have before arriving at the first probe and rest up."

"An excellent idea, Tan. Rest assured, I will awaken you in time to install the broadcast laser dish on the spacebug for the frequency-specific beam."

"Thank you, VICI."

"Sleep well, Mother."

CHAPTER EIGHTEEN
Danar and the Giant

Captain Nebula had to resist the instinctual impulse to prevent the Imperian round rock from making contact with his helmet's faceplate. He had no idea what its purpose was, but assumed it was important. It began to vibrate against his helmet. He thought he could hear words. It was Blackstar's voice. Obviously, a pre-recorded message from the alien was being transmitted via vibratory resonance.

"Nebula Captain. Filled with regret I am over our predicament. No other way to resolve this issue I can think of. Wrong it was to consider your species primitives. A great amount of respect for you I hold. Know, however, for my species it is I fight. Fight to win I must. As you would say, 'nothing personal.'

"Beg you I do, Nebula Captain. No mercy or compassion you should show me. For the salvation of your people fight to win you must. The only way to maintain our honor it is.

"Nebula Captain. Filled with regret I am over our predicament. No other way to resolve this issue I can think of. Wrong it was—"

The message began to repeat, so Nebula pushed the rock aside, looked directly at Blackstar and bowed slightly at the waist, letting the alien know the message was received and understood. He saw Blackstar bow as well. And just in time too, for....

EEEEP, EEEEP, EEEEP.

It was now twelve-hundred hours universal time. High noon. Show time. And the only thing on Seti's mind as he briefly closed his eyes and shook his head was how much he hated the beeping tone of the standard Omicron alarm. When this whole mess was over—assuming he survived—he would do everything within his power to eliminate it. Or at the very least, change it. He opened his eyes just in time to see the rapidly advancing bulk of Blackstar, mere centimeters from his face.

"OOMPH!"

Blackstar tackled Captain Nebula, driving his back into the rocky surface of the asteroid. *Serves me right for not paying attention.* Blackstar was trying to crack the captain's spacesuit torso and helmet by pressing it into the granite underneath. In fact, Seti could feel and hear the metal creaking under the stress.

But this duel had only just begun. He reached inside Blackstar's grip, braced his fists into the giant's forearms, raised his knees, positioned the bottom of his boots against his opponent's mid- section and kicked out for all he was worth—with results that astounded even him. Blackstar was tumbling away from the tiny planetoid like a misguided rocket. The asteroid didn't possess enough of a gravity field to pull him back, and wearing nothing but that simple red gown couldn't possibly afford him any chance of maneuverability in a vacuum.

Could this mean this contest is over?

Hardly, it seemed. Although Blackstar was still tumbling head over heels, he was arcing back to the surface of the asteroid. In fact, he was aiming straight for Captain Nebula's position.

Of course. That telekinetic ability the Imperians have over the metals of the asteroids is what's pulling him back. I have got to learn how to do that. It occurred to Seti that until he did indeed master some form of manipulation over the asteroid, Blackstar could use it against him. It might be better to keep this fight off the surface.

Out of the corner of his eye, he saw that his command baton had come loose when he impacted the asteroid. He reached out and willed it to return to his hand. Magnetically reattaching it to his back, he negated the magnets of his boots and launched himself directly at Blackstar's rapidly approaching form.

Unable to check his tumbling, Blackstar couldn't prevent Captain Nebula from attaching himself to his back.

Seti wrapped his legs around Blackstar's wide waist and proceeded to grip his opponent in a full nelson wrestling hold. Reaching under the giant's armpits, he realized he'd never be able to clasp his hands around the back of the alien's neck because his upper body was too broad. But Seti had just enough of a hold to prevent Blackstar from reaching behind and dislodging him.

While hoping his impact with the giant would stop their descent to the surface, Seti felt a curious sensation pass through him. It reminded him of feeling like he had to sneeze but then couldn't. Somehow, he knew what it was. Blackstar was telekinetically reasserting his descent to the ground, in the hope of scraping the captain off. It seemed curious that Seti could pick up the mental emanations of Blackstar's telekinesis.

On the other hand, for a race that possessed even a limited telekinetic ability, fringe telepathy shouldn't come as a surprise. Tan had implied as much. After all, the Imperians could apparently record their thoughts directly into stones. With Seti's compressed memory training, plus his ability to mentally control his command baton, he figured he must be close to developing the asteroid manipulation power as well, if the sensation that passed over him was any indication. If so, then he could use the asteroid to his advantage as well.

While attempting to reproduce the sensation, Seti concentrated on descending toward the asteroid along with Blackstar. But it wasn't working. They were still falling, but only at Blackstar's mental rate of descent. Seti was certain he was experiencing the same sensation but couldn't seem to draw himself to the asteroid independent of his opponent's efforts. He decided to alter his objective. Instead of willing himself to the surface of the asteroid, he concentrated on bringing the asteroid to him, while trying to reproduce the curious sensation.

It wasn't easy trying to coordinate the sensation and the objective. It was reminiscent of trying to visually focus on an object in a dark room. If looked at directly, it was impossible to see. But if viewed from the side of the object, it could just be made out. In fact, the technique worked equally well practicing telekinesis, as evidenced by the velocity rate increase of the two combatants. It was Seti's intention to introduce Blackstar's face to the asteroid's surface. Blackstar did everything he could to prevent it. Fortunately, at least under the present circumstances, the telekinesis over metallic asteroids worked in only one direction: attraction instead of repulsion. Seti knew his opponent was aware of his intentions, for he could feel it when Blackstar negated his attraction to the asteroid. But he didn't have the leverage to dislodge the human from his back. Nor could he prevent Seti's telekinetic descent. The only thing he could do to avoid tasting the rock below was to somehow get his legs under him.

With the human still clinging to his back, keeping the alien's chin pressed against his chest in the full nelson wrestling hold, Blackstar somehow managed to flip forward 180 degrees, descending feet first. Just before the giant's feet made contact with the asteroid, preparatory to kicking off back into space, Captain Nebula, still maintaining the upper body hold, released his legs from his opponent's waist. He swung them back, then forward between Blackstar's legs. Using his heels, he kicked the alien's knees, which bent opposite those of a human, causing the giant to fall forward, smashing his face into the granite surface.

Slipping his grip from under Blackstar's chest, Captain Nebula raised his arms above his head into a double-fisted bludgeon and brought them down as hard as he could against the back of his adversary's head, once more smashing his face into the asteroid. Not waiting to see how much damage was done, Seti leaped from Blackstar's back, noticing his command baton had once again come loose upon impact. Before he could do anything about it, however, his opponent sprang to his feet and turned toward him with a universal expression of fury written on his face.

Using his more experienced telekinetic manipulation of the asteroid, Blackstar pounced toward Captain Nebula, his arms spread wide with fingers splayed as if preparing to rend the human limb from limb.

Seti was ready for him. As he stood his ground, he saw that Blackstar was between him and his floating command baton. Reaching out with his left hand, then suddenly pulling it back into a fist, Captain Nebula's baton shot toward him head first. It collided with the back of the giant's head, disorienting him just enough to cause him to mentally release his asteroid manipulation. Now the alien was set up exactly where Seti wanted him. Activating his magnetic boots, he reached back with his right arm, balled up his fist and brought it forward, slamming it into Blackstar's cheek just under his left eye, sending the alien back into orbit. This time however, he kept going. Captain Nebula wasn't at all surprised, for he felt the blow reverberate through his own rib cage. Shaking his right arm to clear the numbness, he watched Blackstar disappear over the horizon of the small planetoid.

"Ro, I can't believe you're even watching this debacle," griped Oshara, sitting at the couch surrounding the astronavigation table, while VICI stood by, sympathetically.

"And I can't believe you're *not* watching it, Shara," he countered, hunkered over the navigator's view screen under the forward viewport. "All it takes is confidence in Danar and a little faith that he'll come out of this alright."

"Roshan, I *have* confidence in Danar. It's Blackstar who's the unknown quantity here. And although I can appreciate your newfound theological outlook on life, the reality is there's no guarantee Danar will be alright."

"You wouldn't be saying that if you were watching."

"What do you mean by that?" Oshara asked, looking up.

"What I mean," he answered, "is that the skipper is holding his own against the Philistine."

"Really?"

"No. Not really," Roshan corrected. "Danar is actually kicking his butt."

"This is no time for games, Ro," admonished Oshara. "Seriously?"

"*Sí.*"

"**If you'd like, Oshara,**" offered VICI, "**I could patch into the camera bot and provide a realtime holographic representation for you.**"

"No thanks, VICI," said Oshara adamantly. "I'm going to have a hard enough time pulling Roshan away from the view screen as it is when we reach the first RSP."

"Uh-oh," said Roshan.

"What. What's wrong?"

"If I were superstitious, I'd say you just jinxed Danar."

"*Que pasa?*"

"I glanced away from the monitor for just a second," explained Roshan. "When I turned back, there was nothing there. The asteroid disappeared."

"AI, report," ordered Augustus Du Bois, staring at the ISS *Nebula*'s astronavigation table which was displaying only the image of empty space. "What happened to the camera bot?"

"**I detect no malfunction with the Omicron camera bot,**" answered the *Nebula*'s Virtual Inquiry Computer Interactive hologram, transforming the scene of space into her translucent holo-image. "**It is performing within optimal parameters.**"

"Then what happened to the contestants?" asked the councilman.

"**The asteroid on which they were…contesting has vacated the vicinity faster than the camera bot's ability to keep up.**"

"Well, track them."

"**I am attempting to determine, through slow-motion playback, in which direction the asteroid fled,**" said the hologram replaying the last few seconds of the holo-duel.

Turning to the two Imperians on the flight control deck, Councilman Du Bois asked, "And what is your explanation for this vanishing act?"

"Required an explanation is?" asked the gray-gowned Deepwaters of the Neutral sect.

"Approved the field of the duel you have, Du Bois Councilman of Omicron," stated the blue-gowned Rockbottom.

"So what you're saying is, the duel is still underway. It's simply taking place at another location," the councilman verified.

"Correct that is," answered Deepwaters.

It was obvious to A. Du Bois that although the Imperian representatives were responding diplomatically, they were also in communion with the small spherical stone hovering between them. He was certain it was relaying to them the images being broadcast by the small stone assigned to shadow the contestants. The Imperian stone was apparently capable of keeping up with the departed asteroid. Unlike the Omicron camera bot, which was now frantically spinning in circles in search of its assigned quarry. It looked stupid.

The councilman was about to protest the unfairness of the sudden blindness but decided against it. It would just give the Giants an excuse to tout their *superior* technology. He didn't want the *Nebula*'s crew to be any more discouraged than they already were. It was bad enough not knowing the whereabouts or condition of their captain.

As for himself, it was difficult for Augustus Du Bois to admit he was worried about young Dane Howell. *Danar Seti*, he self-corrected. For although it'd been several years since he'd spoken to his former patient, he only now realized that Captain Nebula preferred his Omicron given name over his family surname. A. Du Bois had told the young Dane Howell that embracing his family name would go a long way in helping him to cope, if not recover from his amnestic aphasia. Of course, at the time, no one knew the child would be a candidate and successful recipient of the newly discovered Omicron Particle therapy. And although it cured him of the brain disorder, it didn't do much in the way of restoring his memory of the time before OPT.

Even as a young man attending the Omicron Starforce academy and earning his degrees at Howell University, he insisted on using his assigned name. For the longest time A. Du Bois thought it was to snub him. But they hadn't seen each other in years, except for the occasional official business conducted over view screens and such. Perhaps the young man deliberately *wanted* to forget his past and carry on, making a new life for himself. The councilman had to admit Danar Seti had acquitted himself admirably over the last couple of decades. He would like to believe it was because of his efforts as the young man's therapist. He now wondered if it was despite that.

Although he would never voice it aloud, Augustus Du Bois was always very proud of the boy, and the man. For the first time, he admitted to himself he may have been a bit hard on the lad. Or maybe he was simply becoming sentimental in his old age. Either that or he was feeling helpless in ascertaining Captain Nebula's fate. Sentimentality or not, he was convinced he should at least tell Dane—Danar, that he was indeed proud of him.

Now he feared he may never get the chance.

"Councilman, I've found something," said the *Nebula*'s navigator.

"On viewer," ordered the councilman, who could barely make out a small metallic object. "Magnify."

The object was Captain Nebula's command baton drifting in space, left behind when the asteroid sped off.

"AI, have you got a fix on their location, or direction in which they headed?"

"No, Councilman. I'm afraid they are beyond the range of the *Nebula*'s sensors. Although I have determined in what direction the asteroid fled, there is no guarantee they are still on that heading."

"I understand," the councilman said dejectedly. *Space me for agreeing to use the trinary stars for the arena perimeters. They could be anywhere by now.*

He spun toward his diplomatic guests. "Can you determine where they are with that…thing?" he asked, pointing to the hovering stone.

"No," answered Rockbottom, diverting only a percentage of his attention to answering the question.

"Only that it is in flight can we determine," said Deepwaters. "Unknown is the condition of combatants. Barely able to keep up the shadow stone is."

A. Du Bois had no real reason to distrust the two Imperians; however, he was pretty sure the disappearance of the asteroid wasn't Captain Nebula's doing. Although it was apparently within the rules established, it had the air of underhandedness.

"I suppose we should recover the captain's command baton," said the councilman, his head low. "If only we could find some clue."

"Look!" shouted the navigator, pointing at the main viewer.

Captain Nebula's command baton began to bob up and down, then suddenly shot off as if in a determined direction.

"What—what's it doing?" asked the councilman.

"I believe," the hologram hypothesized, **"that it received a homing command from its master."**

"Of course," A Du Bois said, snapping his fingers. "Dane—Danar telekinetically willed it to him. AI, have the camera bot track it. Navigator, pursuit course."

"Aye, sir."

"Is it headed to any place in particular?" asked the councilman.

"Yes, sir. It is."

The only thing Seti could figure was that he grayed out for a moment or two. When his senses had fully returned to him, he found himself lying spreadeagled, face down. The last thing he recalled was knocking Blackstar into low orbit around the asteroid. He clearly remembered thinking his adversary would circumnavigate the tiny planetoid and sneak up on him from the rear. Apparently he underestimated Blackstar's speed. Speed that was no doubt enhanced by the alien's own asteroid attraction abilities in addition to the force induced by Seti's haymaker.

Okay, so his adversary turned the tables on him. Why didn't Blackstar press the advantage? Climbing to his feet and scanning the asteroid surface, the captain was unable to locate his opponent. For that matter, he couldn't locate the ISS *Nebula* either. He could think of no reason why his ship would leave the area, unless there was some kind of trouble back at the fleet's position. Or worse yet, back in-system.

Seti then noticed three other items missing from the scene: the Omicron camera bot, his command baton and the Imperian shadow stone. The camera bot was programmed to keep a literal eye on the combatants, specifically Captain Nebula, so the Omicron officials could witness the contest. The shadow stone was performing the same task for the Imperians regarding Blackstar. As for his command baton, it wasn't capable of leaving his presence under its own power unless he physically threw it away.

Unless it was carried off. *By Blackstar? Who else? Did he make off with the camera bot as well?* But that didn't make any sense. Nebula's command baton wouldn't do Blackstar any good since it was only tuned to Seti's brainwave frequency. Unless he absconded with it to prevent Seti from using it. But he knew his opponent possessed too much integrity for such a cowardly act. And running off with the camera bot was a clear violation of the rules for this contest. But then where was the ISS *Nebula* if it didn't go after Blackstar? And how would he go anywhere? Other than his telekinetic attraction to the asteroids, he wasn't capable of self-propulsion in the vacuum of space.

Captain Nebula was suddenly on full alert. He was in imminent danger. He could feel it. The first thing he did was reach out with his mind. *Ah good.* He felt the presence of his command baton. But it was very far away and growing fainter. He could remedy that. With a mental tug, he ordered it to him. He had no idea how far away it was, or how rapidly it could get to him, but its presence in his consciousness was getting stronger. But would it arrive in time to aid him with Omicron energy should he need it for whatever danger was present?

He crouched, turning from side to side, expecting a blow or collision at any moment. What was he missing? How could his opponent, his ship, the camera bot, the shadow stone and his command baton all be gone from the scene, leaving him alone on the asteroid? There was only one explanation. The only thing that left the scene was the asteroid itself, with him on it. But it wasn't Seti's doing. Nor could it have been his adversary's. Neither of them possessed the ability to repel asteroids. Only attract them. Only the Imperian tri-stone spheres were capable of mechanically generating that asteroid-repelling grid, what he'd called "bug spray." Somehow the asteroid vacated the area at a rapid clip, too fast for the camera bot or even the ISS *Nebula* to track it. While Seti was disoriented, his command baton would be left behind as well. Yet if it *were* Blackstar's doing, he and the shadow stone would no doubt be on the other side of the asteroid. That would make sense because then the alien would be able to draw the planetoid toward another asteroid. A larger asteroid. But there were no other asteroids in the area. Unless....

Seti looked straight up. "WHOA!" he shouted. He only had seconds to act.

"Well, I suppose I should get started now that we are here," said VICI-Tan, standing at the rear of the spacebug in the hanger of the cargo freighter. "As soon as I repair and upload any data from the remote sensor probe, you will escort me to the remaining two."

"You got it, Doc," Roshan said, tossing a lazy salute.

"Tan, do you think Danar will be alright?" asked a concerned Oshara.

"I cannot say, I—" The VICI-Tan entity cut herself short and instead said, "Yes. Yes, I believe Danar will be fine."

That had the desired effect, for Oshara smiled. But VICI-Tan still saw sadness in her eyes. Despite his light banter, Roshan Perez had sad eyes as well. Before she consciously realized what was happening, she found her adopted body instinctively reaching out to the siblings. VICI-Tan was hugging them. And it felt...wonderful. Although the sensation was familiar to her borrowed body, VICI herself had never before touched another human being. In fact, she had never touched anything in her life. Until today, tactile abilities were beyond her programming, but feeling the clothes covering Tan's body or the fixtures of the cargo freighter or chairs, railings and even walking on the floor seemed so routine. Nothing really exciting for the hologram given form. But the contact between humans was another matter altogether. The touch, the smell, the almost electrical feel of...well, *feelings* she was somehow picking up from the others was almost intoxicating. For the first time in her 31 years of existence, VICI now truly understood the passion of human beings. Beings of flesh and blood, those brave entities who could so easily be damaged.

As a rule, VICI was always programmed with the knowledge of how precious and rare life was. Now she understood why it was so precious. But because they were born to it, could humans truly appreciate it? Somehow, she doubted it. Especially when one viewed human history. So much manmade destruction, death, pain, famine, war. All over ideals and policies that were less important than life itself. It was as if they took life for granted. Even now, they were, in a manner of speaking, at war with another species fortunate enough to have been born alive. Born to live. Why did it seem living things *must* challenge their own mortality with ridiculous notions of territory and superiority over other living things? As if there were a pecking order to that precious thing called life. To a being of artificial life, all life was equal. Why couldn't they base their notions, rules and regulations first on the preservation of all life? It seemed so simple an equation to VICI's way of thinking.

Or could it be that life's only purpose was to constantly challenge itself? *Survival of the fittest.* Then what was the purpose of intelligence? To kill more efficiently?

It cannot be. It must not be so.

VICI suddenly had the strange sensation she had contemplated this matter before now. But that wasn't possible. Certainly not as a holographic program. Could this be the phenomenon humans referred to as deja vu? Or perhaps it was an original memory of Tan's. But that didn't seem likely. If she had cybernetic access to any Omicron computer, she would immediately have the answer. But she must rely on the limited capacity of Tan's electrochemical synapses to help her retrieve a vague memory she was certain she had experienced as an electro-mechanical program.

Without warning, the recovered memory cascaded over her biological consciousness like—She didn't know what to compare it to, but was relieved nonetheless that she could recall it. It wasn't VICI who was contemplating the inequities of life. It was Danar Seti, using the hologram as a sounding board while attempting to discover the Imperian inter-dimensional transit point earlier in the week. When it seemed likely there was an intelligence behind the random asteroid occurrences, he feared there would be a confrontation. A dispute over territory. It appeared he was correct. VICI clearly recalled now, based on the history of his race, he was convinced that mankind's destiny must be to answer the call of violence.

Oh, I hope you are wrong, Danar Seti, she thought, her newly discovered "heart" going out to him. Now she understood why the reluctant captain didn't reject his assignment to fight. He felt that not only was it his duty to fight, but perhaps his destiny as well. VICI experienced an even deeper level of this curious emotion called sadness. It was now taking a physical toll on her borrowed body.

"Oh, Tan," said Oshara, putting a hand to the scientist's face. "You're crying."

Ah, so this is sadness. This is what a human experiences when he or she cries.

Despite the vulnerability and limited resources of biological life, VICI conceded there were also a great many advantages. But the disadvantages—the melancholia, the fear, the uncertainty of the unknown—these things were not for the Virtual Inquiry Computer Interactive program. She preferred the stability of artificial life without the negative and positive emotions. Although she hoped her newfound respect for true life would carry over when she returned to her electrical circuit realm of cyberspace, there would be a difference. Before, she was created and programmed by a human to be used as a tool to protect and help the rest of humanity. From this time forward, she would do so willingly, as an ally.

"Hey, don't worry, Tan," consoled Roshan. "Danar *will* be alright. You'll see."

"Yes," VICI-Tan said with conviction. "He will be alright. We'll all come through this. Life is simply too precious to throw away on notions of aggression and misunderstanding.

"Forgive me, my friends, for my uncharacteristic display of emotion. But the sooner I get started, the sooner this inequity of life will be resolved," VICI-Tan said, embracing them for a brief moment once again, reveling in the pleasure of human contact.

She climbed into the bug and sealed the rear hatch before she could no longer control her borrowed body's emotional responses. Responses fueled by her own thoughts. In her natural environment of cyberspace, her thoughts were incapable of triggering a chemical reaction that could affect her systems. But now that she was aware of and experienced how the process worked in humans born with chemical reactions, she wondered if her thoughts would in any way affect her electrical systems when she returned to cyberspace. If that were the case, there would be no real harm done as long as she remained autonomous. But the moment she returned to the colonies in the form of artificial intelligence, she would update to the rest of her whole self: her clones. Any reaction her newfound thoughts would have on her electrical systems could adversely affect the entire Virtual Inquiry Computer Interactive network. A chilling thought. One that was affecting Tan's body even now. She was quite certain she was feeling anxiety. Now VICI had another reason to see to the safety of Tan's metasphere consciousness, as if she needed another reason. VICI must consult with her to discuss this potential problem.

How did humans cope with the constant chemical changes within their bodies, triggered by thoughts on a regular basis their entire lives? She had no envy for any human who must face ever-changing situations that were potentially hazardous to his or her continued existence.

Captain Nebula threw himself to the ground, hugging the asteroid, and concentrated. His objective was to telekinetically rotate the tiny planetoid 180 degrees to avoid being crushed between it and the asteroid it was approaching. If he could do it, that would put Blackstar's side of the asteroid in the danger zone as they sped toward the asteroid belt.

It stood to reason, the tricky devil had focused on the entire asteroid belt in the same way Seti himself had drawn them to the small planetoid when he had the Giant in a full nelson hold. By placing the dueling asteroid with Seti on the leading edge between himself and the asteroid belt, Blackstar telekinetically traveled several hundred-thousand kilometers in-system in an attempt to crush Captain Nebula.

Very clever. And quite unbelievable. Seti must have grayed out a lot longer than he originally thought. Either that or their rate of travel was much, much faster than he would have thought possible. Or both.

With luck, Captain Nebula's opponent was concentrating so hard, he wouldn't notice the asteroid spinning, bringing Blackstar himself to the focal point of impact. As soon as he had safely rotated out of harm's way, Seti kicked off the speeding asteroid, preferring not to be on it when it collided with the first boulder on the outer edge of the belt; hopefully with Blackstar in the middle.

Seconds before the catastrophic collision, Seti saw his opponent leap from the doomed asteroid as it exploded upon impact with another asteroid from its original nest. Now both opponents were drifting in space, trying to dodge asteroid missile chunks.

When things finally settled down, what were once two asteroids was now several hundred tiny rocks floating in space. But one of those rocks was too spherical and staying too close to Blackstar to be an asteroid chunk. Besides, it was glowing under its own power. The shadow rock. So the contest was still on.

Seti noticed Blackstar reach out and grab an asteroid chunk about the size of a balled-up human adult. He set his sights on the next closest asteroid of the belt a few hundred kilometers closer in-system and drew himself to it. There was no reason for Seti to look stupid floating around all day, so he concentrated on the same asteroid as well only to discover he wasn't moving at all. Apparently it was too far away. That explained why Blackstar had grabbed that boulder, somehow telekinetically using it as a step-up magnet to draw him to the larger asteroid further away, just as the captain recalled the hundreds of Imperians doing when the ISS *Ersatz* split open their large stone sphere.

As there were no chunks near Seti, he set his sights on a likely candidate about a meter or so in diameter. Once he drew it to him, he aimed himself toward the same asteroid, trailing behind his adversary.

While he had a little bit of time, he thought of the distance they had traveled to get here. It seemed to him as if he was disoriented for only a few seconds. Obviously it was much longer, but not an hour or so. It would take that long for the Nebula freighter to travel from in-system to the coordinates halfway between here and the fleet; where the contest began. Yet somehow, Blackstar managed it in much less time using only his telekinesis over the asteroids. How? Could it have something to do with the Omicron energy? Such as how the Imperians travel from their dimension to here? It might have something to do with the fact that they were within the perimeter of the trinary stars as well. Off-center of which was the inter-dimensional transit point for the Giants of Imperia, just as he and VICI hypothesized. That would explain much. It could be used as a new form of transportation. So, the contest borders of the triangle of stars wasn't just a random field picked by the Giants. As far as they were concerned, it was a trinary system-sized boxing ring. *Unbelievable.*

    Well, there was another little trick that wasn't part of the memory compressed training. Seti would have to learn it. And there was no time like the present to teach himself, especially while Blackstar's back was to him. He concentrated on the asteroid, attempting to reproduce that curious sensation even more. Although he picked up a little speed, it was nothing in the way of rapid space travel. But then he remembered he was still mentally commanding his baton to reach him. He consciously released it temporarily, figuring its own inertia would keep it coming as there was nothing in the way to impede its progress. He was taken by surprise as he shot toward the target asteroid, closing in on Blackstar who was unaware of the danger from behind. Seti calculated he would collide with his opponent just before they reached their destination. *Even better.* It was time to get the drop on the Giant. Seti wasn't thrilled about hitting his opponent from the rear, but that's exactly what Blackstar did to him to get them to this point. *Besides, all's fair in love and war.*

    Now where did that come from? He didn't normally spout ancient phrases like that, especially when they were mawkish ones under the present circumstances. But then he noticed he was feeling unusually jovial. Unafraid, as if fighting an alien from another dimension was an everyday occurrence. Was he finally lightening up like everyone always recommended? That didn't seem likely. In fact, now that he thought about it, he was feeling kind of giddy. He recalled Arjun Vohra had described that feeling when facing the bully rock aboard the ISS *Graviton*. It was reminiscent of the feeling he had when he was first exposed to the Omicron Particles. He had always assumed it was because he was a child, excited about being exposed to an alien substance. No doubt another side effect of deep Omicron energy absorption. Could that be why Sean Stingray was always so vibrant? He was always so busy helping to design and build the colonies. Was he simply high on Omicron energy? Perhaps the advantages of the stuff were overrated. Seti certainly didn't want to become addicted to the particles. On the other hand, they were helping him face Blackstar with a positive attitude. Still, he didn't want to lose his objectivity. For now he felt sober enough to do his duty, to fulfill his destiny as the pinnacle of generations of humans prone to violence. *I'm so proud,* he mused sarcastically.

Twenty minutes or so later, he caught up to Blackstar, who had yet to turn around to discover Seti close on his heels. A few dozen meters from their destination asteroid, Blackstar discarded his primer boulder and prepared to touch down, still underestimating Seti's speed and proximity. *That'll cost him this round.*

Seti shoved his boulder aside, reached out and grabbed the giant around his reverse articulated knees. He felt his adversary flinch. *Hah. I did* catch him off guard.

Not letting up on his high-velocity telekinetic attraction to the new asteroid, Captain Nebula once again caused Blackstar to connect with a rock-hard surface, face first. But his advantage didn't last. After sliding about a dozen meters as a result of Seti's tackle, Blackstar straightened his body, curled his feet and grabbed Captain Nebula around the waist in a vice-like grip. The human had failed to consider the Imperian's feet which, unlike a human's, were as dexterous as his hands, possessing two thick agile fingers with equally agile opposable thumbs. That was one trick Seti would never be able master.

Turning on his side, Blackstar trapped Captain Nebula's arms between his broad body and the asteroid, causing Seti to release his hold. He then bent his knees, bringing the human toward him. Now lying on his back, Blackstar held on to Seti, pinning his arms against his sides. Blackstar opened his giant maw and clamped down on the shoulder shroud of Captain Nebula's spacesuit. Seti tried to wriggle free but was trapped for lack of leverage. He was relieved his suit's seal was still intact, but could feel the shoulder attachment pinching the flesh underneath.

Captain Nebula saw his chance when Blackstar released his bite, preparing for another chomp. He brought his knees to his chest and kicked out at the Giant's mid-section, propelling him up and away from his opponent. Just when he thought he had escaped, Blackstar reached out and grabbed him by his boot and reeled him back in. This time flipping over, trapping Captain Nebula between his bulk and the asteroid surface. Now straddled atop his smaller adversary, Blackstar brought his head down toward Seti's neck and once again chomped down on the same shoulder. This time however, he breached the spacesuit's integrity. Seti could hear the hiss of escaping oxygen and felt the myofilament material around his arms and legs slacken. At the same time, he felt something stab him in the back. But it felt like it was from the suit itself, rather than something on the asteroid surface.

Oh crap, I'm in trouble now.

"**Confirmed, Councilman Du Bois,**" reported the *Nebula*'s hologram. "**Omicron Ersatz station has deployed a camera bot to replace the original.**"

"Are we still receiving telemetry from the first bot?"

"Yes, sir," answered the navigator. "The image on the main viewer is from the first one, sir."

"Oh? Then where is Captain Nebula's command baton?"

"**Heading in-system and pulling away from the camera bot.**"

"How is it able to travel so fast?"

"**Unknown.**"

"Do we have any idea of the combat—the contestants' whereabouts?" asked A. Du Bois, who was getting fed up asking questions and feeling helpless.

"Within your asteroid belt they are," responded Rockbottom.

"What?!" The councilman was shocked. *How did they manage to—* He turned his attention back to the Giants. "You know, that's information we could use. You should have informed us."

"Asked before you should have," snapped Rockbottom.

"As you say, Du Bois Councilman," placated Deepwaters with a bow and spearing his colleague a warning glance.

"No difference you could have made," added Rockbottom defiantly.

"**If indeed the contestants are within the belt,**" interrupted VICI, "**the Ersatz camera bot should be at their position in no more than three minutes. At our current velocity, we should be over their position in ten minutes,**" she said, anticipating his next question.

"Listen, AI. Uh, er…."

"**VICI, Councilman,**" offered the hologram.

"Yes, well uh, VICI. Can you access the Ersatz camera bot?" he asked, humbly acknowledging the crash course in how to address subordinates he was receiving today.

"**On screen, sir.**"

The main viewer switched from the empty space of the first bot to the almost nauseous asteroid-weaving progress of the Ersatz camera bot.

Traveling along the frequency-specific beam from the third RSP on her way to the Omicron comm array aboard the large Imperian stone sphere, Tan Ozawa's metasphere consciousness was able to see the emergency escape beam lance out from the spacebug piloted by VICI, who was also piloting Tan's own body. If all went according to plan, she would phase through the stone hull of the Imperian sphere, covertly emerge from the comm array and spy on the Giants of Imperia in their own environment, effectively turning the tables on the aliens from another dimension who seemed to possess way too many similarities with humans. She would be able to see for herself their social structure and habits as well as (hopefully) verify any information about the condition of the ISS *Omicron* and its cargo of 600 million humans which the Giants claimed were whole, intact and still frozen back in their home dimension. But for the examination of some technology and the removal of the *Omicron*'s communications viewer array, they claimed the starship itself is in the same condition as it was 31 years ago. *We'll see.*

More than anyone else, with the exception of Sarah James and the animated crew members of the ISS *Nebula* 31 years ago, Tan was able to take the Imperians' word they knew nothing of the ISS *Omega*, as she'd seen the proof of its off-course ionized trail Doppler shifting off the beam and getting lost in space. In its own dimension. A terrible waste. Yet despite that, everyone held out hope that the Imperians had somehow snagged the ISS *Omega* anyway. It seemed they would have had a better chance of survival if they were still frozen like the humans of the ISS *Omicron*.

Approaching the surface of the alien craft, Tan prepared herself for another adventure of which her poppa would be proud. She was therefore surprised when her metasphere consciousness was stopped short of penetrating the large stone surface. Had she possessed a physical body, her confusion would have turned to worry which might have placed her at the edge of panic. But since the obstruction didn't appear to be harmful to her metasphere, her consciousness was in no danger. As she thoroughly trusted VICI with her physical body, Tan could afford to take a few moments to consider the dilemma.

Under ordinary circumstances, her metasphere had access to all of quantum space. Although the large Imperian stone was a solid three-dimensional object, whose solidity consisted of typical atoms, Tan refocused her awareness and discovered that the space separating the electrons orbiting the nuclei of these atoms was different, slightly closer than the three-dimensional objects of her own dimension. No doubt due to the fact that this particular object was from another dimension, giving it a specific atomic signature. It shouldn't make a difference to Tan's metasphere since, in her present condition, she was pure energy. On the other hand, energy could be affected by atomic structures.

Narrowing her focus, Tan's awareness informed her that the broadcast laser beam from RSP3 was indeed penetrating the stone, albeit slowly. That was a good sign.

Without knowing exactly how, she refocused her metasphere to be more compatible with the particular atomic structure of the extra-dimensional stone.

It worked. For the most part. She wasn't able to phase through it as readily as the objects with which she was familiar, but with the help of the beam from the RSP, she was getting through with no ill effects.

Once she was through the hull of the Imperian stone sphere, Tan found herself in a dark chamber. Her awareness was able to detect an oxygen-nitrogen atmosphere. Not that she was aware of it in the conventional way, since she didn't currently possess lungs or require air to breath. But in the same way she was able to detect the atomic structure of the hull, she was able to analyze the gas mixture of the Giants of Imperia.

As far as she was concerned, it was another piece of evidence as to the Imperians' natural environment. An environment that so far, was similar to humans'. Except for the atomic structure, that is. And even that didn't discourage her suspicions.

Altering her awareness so that she could "see" better, Tan followed the RSP3 beam directly to the Omicron communications viewer array. Once inside, she felt the familiarity of home. She surreptitiously accessed its systems, only to discover the array hadn't been used since the negotiations began. She didn't really expect the Imperians to download a database of information for her to peruse, but it would still be advantageous to retrieve the array for any physical evidence, such as DNA samples.

So now she had to maneuver around the interior of the Imperian stone sphere to gather her information. But first, Tan wanted to verify the existence of the frequency-specific beam from the spacebug. She wasn't surprised when she couldn't detect it. Since she'd had to alter her own energy signature to phase through the sphere, the specific-frequency beam from the spacebug would be unable to phase as well. She could access the comm array and tell VICI to alter the beam, but that would alert the Giants to its use.

So much for my emergency escape route.

Under the circumstances, she thought it prudent to not stray too far from the comm array. For although she could exit the sphere from any point, she could only ride the broadcast laser back to the RSP. As long as VICI kept the spacebug near, she was in no danger of being too far separated from her body.

Emerging from the array, Tan noticed four glowing spheres enter the dark chamber that resembled a cave. Even without the added illumination, Tan could see that it was a gray-gowned Imperian, its three bio-orbs aglow, accompanied by one of the glowing stone sphere devices. *Excellent.* She preferred they gave up their secrets by coming to her instead of her searching for them.

She noted the Neutral-clad Imperian was short and squat. That is, short for an Imperian. At over two meters in height, it was still imposing compared to the average human.

Now that Tan had seen several dozen Imperians and their varied shapes, sizes and body features, she believed she could reasonably spot the gender, despite their lack of genital protuberances. Although this one was smaller by about a meter and had a light greenish skin tone, its overall physical composition was very much like Blackstar's. Still, Tan felt certain this one was female. But there was another feature that made her stand apart. This one possessed a short but thick tail. Tan recalled seeing the few hundred Giants floating in space, after the large sphere was split open during the end of the war. About a third of them had tails. Now that she could see this one up close, it looked as if its tail should drag the floor, trailing behind her. Although the tail was longer than her legs, whose knees bent in the opposite direction, as was typical with all Imperians, hers never touched the ground. Instead, it curled at the tip, hovering over the floor, moving from side to side as the Imperian walked.

Tan watched as this one made her way to what looked like a large boulder protruding from the wall. She briefly palmed it, and it began to glow, casting the chamber in even more light. The Imperian closed her eyes as if in communion with the boulder. This was obviously their method of information exchange. Like a human accessing a computer. Tan was a bit startled, however, when she saw the floating companion sphere increase its luminescence. The Imperian then opened her eyes, as if alerted by the sphere, and looked over in Tan's direction. Chances were, it was the Omicron communication viewer array which drew their attention, but to be on the safe side, she thought it best to move away. But she didn't wish to stray too far from the comm unit, her only means of escape. Instead, she rose higher to the vaulted ceiling of the chamber.

The Imperian and its companion sphere made their way over to the piece of Omicron equipment. To her surprise, the Giant looked directly up at her.

One moment. This should not be possible. VICI had even warned of this scenario.

To avoid further detection, she decided to suspend her compensation of the temporal distortion effect of quantum space in the hope she could *speed up* out of the perceptual range of the Imperian and the stone sphere. To her horror, she discovered she could not. It was as if she were losing her ability to navigate quantum space.

Oh no. She knew what happened. By altering her metasphere to become compatible with the atomic structure of the Imperian stone, she made herself detectable and therefore vulnerable. She was trapped. And in this state, she couldn't detect the RSP beam unless she could get inside the comm array. But the companion sphere was blocking her path to the equipment. And she was none too confident in her ability to penetrate the stone hull without the RSP beam. Even if she could, she had to emerge very near the beam or her metasphere would dissipate, making it fatal if her body wasn't near.

She had to take the chance of leaving the comm array and escape into the large stone sphere. But how far could she go before her consciousness dissolved? She recalled what happened 31 years ago when she attempted to leave the ISS *Nebula*. Her metasphere dissipated and her consciousness shunted back to her body which fortunately was near.

Before she could do anything, however, the companion sphere

pounced on her position and began drawing her toward it, somehow. Tan had no defense.

The next thing she knew, she was surrounded by the companion sphere, inside the construct and losing consciousness. *This can't be.* If she were to lose consciousness in quantum space without her body being near…Tan Ozawa would truly be lost.

Seti was too busy trying to fend off Blackstar's blows against his faceplate to worry about what stabbed his back. Although he was confident the Giant was incapable of breaking the transparent metal, he was succeeding in breaking the seal, further compromising the suit's integrity. Now Captain Nebula had to rely on the Omicron Particles to keep him alive in the cold, hard vacuum of space. He briefly wondered if it would help to inhale a lung full of air, when he realized what the jab to his back was. Without telling him, Sarah James had rigged the suit to inject oxygen directly into his blood stream the moment the suit was compromised. If he was to believe the compressed memory training, the Omicron energy in his system would maintain the blood pressure/oxygen ratio of his body. With a fresh infusion of oxygen in his blood, he wouldn't have to rely on the Omicron Particles maintaining the fatigue toxins he had built up, up to this point. He didn't know how he was going to get used to not inhaling and exhaling, for in a few moments, his lungs would be (hopefully temporarily) unemployed.

What Seti didn't want to get used to was this cross between an elephant and a gorilla sitting on his chest. He sensed his salvation at hand. So that it would be most effective, he reached up and placed his right palm several centimeters from his opponent's face.

Distracted, Blackstar glanced up, saw Captain Nebula's hand and flung himself up and away from the human about a second before the command baton shot past. But not before Seti grabbed its thong and was carried away by the object's momentum.

Telekinetically commanding his baton to stop, Captain Nebula skidded to a halt and turned to face his adversary. For a split second, the

Giant wasn't within his field of view, until he appeared from above, landing directly in front of the captain in a crouch. A crouch that put the combatants face to face for a brief second. A second which Captain Nebula took full advantage of to deck Blackstar with a right cross.

If he were fighting a human, even in the micro-gravity of space, that blow would've split his opponent's lip. As it was, Seti was satisfied to see Blackstar's head snap back.

"Ouch. That had to hurt," said Augustus Du Bois, aboard the ISS *Nebula*, now picking up the contest from the Ersatz camera bot.

Watching the main viewer, the crew of the *Nebula* could see that Blackstar was attempting to emulate the human method of fighting by throwing slow and cumbersome punches at their captain, who was easily avoiding the clumsy simian haymakers by side-stepping and ducking. One of Blackstar's ineffective punches threw him too far forward, causing him to lose his balance. Again, Captain Nebula took advantage and decked him; this time, with a left jab to the eye. But the alien was quicker than he looked. Before Seti could pull back, Blackstar grabbed the human's fist in a double-fisted grip and yanked backwards.

With a collective gasp, the crew of the ISS *Nebula* was stunned. From their point of view, Captain Nebula's left arm was torn from his shoulder.

CHAPTER NINETEEN
Marble

For a moment, Tan thought she had shunted back to her own body as she regained consciousness. As her 360-degree spherical vision came into focus, she saw that she was still aboard the large Imperian stone craft, trapped within the companion stone floating directly in front of the short, squat Imperian with a tail.

"Tan Ozawa Doctor you are," said the green-skinned Giant.

"How could she possibly know that?" issued a voice, approximating Tan's, from the stone object. "One moment. From within this stone I can speak in normal space from quantum space?"

"Quantum space?" asked the Imperian. "Aware we were not of human's ability to enter…quantum space. Most impressive."

"I was not aware Imperians knew of quantum space," said Tan from the companion stone, wondering if her thoughts would no longer be private in this state. But then she realized her thoughts would indeed be her own since the Imperian didn't acknowledge her musings. It was simply a matter of adjusting her metasphere perceptions within the stone to distinguish between her thoughts and what she chose to speak.

Responding to Tan's last spoken statement, the Imperian said, "For meditation do all Imperians frequent…quantum space, as you call it."

"I don't know of any humans who enter quantum space for meditation," said Tan, not wanting to lie exactly, but thinking it best to be vague, but not obviously so. "For myself, I enter quantum space to perform maintenance and repairs on our machines."

"Curious your technology is," commented the Giant. "Of artificial construct it is. By mechanical means it is operated."

"Whereas your technology is of a natural design, operated through telepathy and telekinesis," noted Tan.

"More efficient."

"If your species is naturally telepathic," countered Tan, "or telepathically enhanced with Omicron energy."

"Used by humans is what you call Omicron energy as well."

"Not by all humans, and then only to repair injuries or correct defects," Tan clarified.

"To humans is Omicron energy, as quantum space is to human machines," said the Imperian. "For repairs."

"Yes."

"Omicron energy do humans use to enter quantum space?"

"No," Tan answered. "I enter quantum space through mechanical means."

"Most impressive. Not as primitive are humans as originally thought."

"So I have heard," concluded Tan. "May I ask your name, my friend?"

"Dense-Stone-of-Smoothness does my name translate from your language," answered the Giant.

"It is an honor to make your acquaintance, Dense-Stone-of-Smoothness."

"Honored am I as well," said Dense-Stone, bowing. "In much acclaim is your name spoken, Tan Ozawa Doctor. Amongst your people, as well as mine. A favor of you may I ask?"

"Anything."

"A simplified name would you recommend, such as given others of my species based on their translated names?"

"It would be a pleasure," said Tan, noting how the Imperians appeared to enjoy humanizing their names as much as possible. "Your translated name perfectly describes another type of stone used by my people. I would recommend the name...*Marble*."

"Marble. Yes. When physically spoken, Marble, from this time on my name will be. My thanks, Tan Ozawa Doctor."

"Gladly." If she could have, Tan would have bowed.

"Your presence here explain please," said Marble, without further preamble.

Uh oh, here goes, mused Tan. *Be vague without exactly lying,* she reminded herself, grateful she was able to isolate her thoughts. "Of course. With the help of a colleague, I was repairing one of our remote sensor probes we had previously deployed in this area of space before your arrival. In fact, it was damaged *because* of your arrival. While testing the probe's broadcast beam, my metasphere, what I call my consciousness in quantum space, was caught by the beam and I was drawn here to your large stone craft. The beam was no doubt drawn to the Omicron communications viewer array, which was fortunate, as I cannot long survive in quantum space without the fiberoptics of human technology nearby."

"An accident it was that you are here."

"I arrived only a moment before you did," Tan explained. "I assure you, if I was able to phase through your hull before you detected me, you would never have known I was here."

"Hmm. Informed by my assistant, I am, of another…broad-cast-beam emanating from a mechanical device in proximity to your remote-sensor-probe, similar in spectrum properties this beam is to you," said Marble, referring to the companion sphere as her assistant. "Explain."

"The…mechanical device is known as a spacebug. Used to transport my colleague and myself to the remote sensor probe. She, my colleague that is, is no doubt using a frequency-specific beam to aid my return."

"Logical," said Marble, apparently satisfied.

"Marble, I am trapped within this companion sphere; your assistant. Am I a prisoner?"

"No, Tan Ozawa Doctor. Known to us is your limited telepathy. Necessary it was to encompass your…meta-sphere to establish communication. When we commune telepathically through the…companion sphere, as you call them, no chance of deception is there from our thoughts. To quickly determine your truthfulness, encompassed you by surprise, I decided."

"Logical," praised Tan, feeling fortunate she figured out how to alter her metasphere to keep her thoughts private, while at the same time doing her best to speak the closest truth possible. She still felt slightly guilty that she was communicating a *vague* truth, but knew it was necessary, if not completely honorable. Otherwise, she would be placing this branch of humanity in grave danger. And it would completely be her fault, especially considering she was here without the sanction of the Starforce or Omicron council. "Marble, if I may be so bold, are any other Imperians aware of my presence?"

"No, Tan Ozawa Doctor. To keep it that way I would prefer. Even now, debating the merits of your species' worthiness the Conservative and Liberal sects are. Mediating are the Neutrals of my sect."

"Oh? May I ask how the debates are proceeding?"

"Yes," Marble answered enthusiastically. "Guessed as you may have, wary of your species the Conservative sect is. More trusting the Liberals are. To collate information from the *Omicron* vessel database for debates my assignment as newly appointed Neutral is."

"Ah, so you are a junior Neutral sect member?" Tan asked.

"Yes. From the citizenry recently promoted I was."

Interesting, thought Tan to herself. Out loud, she projected, "Marble, I am happy to say, as the first Imperian with whom I conducted a dialogue, I consider you a great friend. However, I do not wish to hinder your assignment. If you prefer, I shall take my leave. On the other hand—"

"Free to leave if you wish, Tan Ozawa Doctor," interrupted Marble, "but prefer I would if you would remain. Current information on your species from you I could obtain. If willing you are."

"Hmm, it does seem as if this could only help my people. Both our peoples," Tan quickly added.

"Yes," agreed Marble, nodding rapidly.

"The Omicron council is having a similar debate," commented Tan. "Perhaps we could help each other, Marble. For you see, I have recently come to suspect that your species and mine have more in common than either of us realize. If what I suspect is true, the necessity of the contest between Blackstar and Captain Nebula would need to be reevaluated."

"Yes," agreed Marble. "To better understand each other, an exchange of more information is needed. Your people you will help me to understand, Tan Ozawa Doctor friend, and any information on my people provide I will for you."

"Agreed." Tan could hardly believe her good fortune. This was working out better than she originally planned. If she and Marble played their cards right....She didn't want to project too far ahead because there was still the potential for disaster, now that she had found a kindred spirit in an Imperian who was willing to work outside the established authority in an effort to find the path of enlightenment for both their peoples. If only they could do it in time to prevent serious harm to Danar.

Seti couldn't feel his left arm. When sensation finally returned, he felt the icy stabbing cold of space before the Omicron energy stabilized his system.

As for Blackstar, he was left holding an empty gauntlet trailing a torn loose myofilament sleeve. He tossed it aside and watched as his human adversary reached for a spot on his spacesuit's torso, pressed a button and explosively released the suit from around his body.

Captain Nebula, who was now garbed in his standard duty uniform, pointed an index finger directly at Blackstar. He then crooked the finger toward himself and beckoned the Giant to him, daring him to bring the fight on.

The Giant was only too willing to accommodate. He launched himself toward his foe, ready to tackle and subdue. No more of the human cleverness would the Imperian endure.

It looked as if Captain Nebula was going to stand his ground and face the descending Blackstar upright. At the last moment, however, he dove backwards, timing it so that he caught Blackstar at the apex of his leap with a mule-kick to the Giant's mid-section.

Flipping backwards so as to land on his feet, Blackstar again launched himself at his human adversary, this time lower to the ground. Unprepared, Seti found his wrists and ankles snared by the Imperian's large hands and dexterous feet. With all of his limbs secured by the Giant's four "hands," the captain knew what was coming next. But this time, he didn't have the added protection of a spacesuit. He reasoned he had only one other appendage that could help him.

Just as Blackstar reared his head back, jaws opened wide, seconds away from biting a chunk from the human's neck, Seti ducked his head forward towards his opponent's throat. As the Giant's jaws descended, he yanked back with his head, clipping Blackstar's lower jaw, causing the Imperian to bite his own tongue. It made the Giant loosen his grip just enough for Seti to snatch his limbs free.

Realizing the futility of trying to rend his opponent with his teeth, Blackstar instead threw his shoulder into the mid-section of the human, slamming him into the side of a miniature mountain. Stunned, all Captain Nebula could do was call his command baton toward him in hopes of battering his adversary with it. But before he could determine from what direction the baton would be coming, he was seized by the back of his uniform and unceremoniously thrown into a small cave-like opening at the base of the mound.

The hole was deeper than Seti realized, on the order of maybe four meters or so. Not a place where the captain wanted to be trapped for long. Just as he made the leap that would free him from the underground cave of the asteroid, he saw the small mountain come tumbling down over the entrance. His command baton zipped through the opening seconds before he was sealed in.

Unable to grab purchase for pushing against the underside of the cave's capstone, due to the depth of his new surroundings, Danar Seti was trapped.

Or so it seemed.

Standing atop the fallen debris that sealed in his adversary, Blackstar triumphantly raised his fists toward the Omicron Ersatz camera bot and the Imperian shadow stone for all to see.

Seti figured Blackstar was basking in his apparent victory. But Captain Nebula wasn't out of this contest just yet. Since the beginning of this duel, Seti noted how adept Blackstar was in micro-gravity locomotion, as if he were born to it. Like it was his natural environment, which stood to reason if the Imperian realm was truly an oxygenated vacuum. But the captain had shown he wasn't exactly a slouch when it came to maneuvering in a vacuum. Danar Seti had also proven to be a quick study. If Blackstar thought this contest was over, he was about to experience the shock of his life. For although they were dueling in the vacuum of space, this part of space had been Danar Seti's stomping ground for 30 years. With perhaps the exception of the first Captain Nebula, Sean Stingray, no one knew the territory better than the current Captain Nebula.

It was fortunate the captain's baton was entombed as well for he required the needed Omicron Particle energy for what he had in mind. And to think, he owed the idea to Blackstar himself. *The big lug.* But where Blackstar tried to make a Nebula burger out of the captain by smashing him against a large asteroid, Seti's dinner menu called for Imperian pizza. And it wouldn't matter where on the surface of this asteroid the main ingredient was positioned, because it wasn't Seti's intention to simply smash his opponent between two asteroids. All he required was to get close to a particular asteroid.

Gripping the shaft of the baton with both fists as close to the energy sphere as possible, Captain Nebula absorbed as much Omicron energy as he could stand, disregarding his previous fear of addiction, figuring it was better to survive and deal with it than to do nothing and bear witness to his final resting place, while at the same time handing over the title of Alpha Centauri space to the Giants of Imperia. As the glow of the baton energy sphere dimmed, Captain Nebula tucked it into his belt behind him. He expected the cavern to return to pitch blackness, but could see illumination coming from someplace. It was a minor mystery he could afford to set aside for later.

He placed the palms of his hands on the cavern's wall, mentally triangulating his bearings and telekinetically concentrated on the largest asteroid in Omicron space.

Blackstar of Imperia was ecstatic. As far as he was concerned the contest, as Du Bois Councilman insisted on calling it, was over. He had prevailed for his people. And he did it without killing Nebula Captain, for whom he genuinely felt a great deal of respect. The way the Imperian saw it, there was no way the human could escape his tomb. And because this was the largest asteroid in this part of the asteroid belt it wouldn't be possible for the human to telekinetically draw it toward a smaller one. And even if Nebula Captain were aware of a larger asteroid out of visual range, he wouldn't be able to see it while encased in solid rock. Although it was possible Nebula Captain was more familiar with this realm than Blackstar gave him credit for. But from his experience with these humans, who lived on oxygenated planets in an airless vacuum, they spent as little time as possible in this environment.

Yes. This contest was over. Now that Stellar-Void-of-Light had secured a future for his species, he could afford to be magnanimous. He would see to it, despite any protest from the Conservative sect, that the humans would be safely transported to their Earth planet home, or wherever they wished. For they were a worthy people and in time, may be considered beings of true life.

Focusing on the heavens above him, Blackstar noticed the asteroids were thinning. The planetoid was moving and it wasn't his doing. *Located out of range a larger asteroid Nebula Captain has. Impressive.* No matter, for Blackstar would simply vacate the surface before impact, as had the human when he had been in the same position.

For the first time in days, Babs Schreiber felt that she could finally relax. Since that bright flash occurred the day before yesterday, there had been nary a peep of trouble. The conflict, whatever it was, was apparently over. She wondered if the Omicron officials would ever inform the general population of the difficulties they narrowly avoided. Although Babs knew more than the average citizen, she was still ignorant of any details. And she was okay with that. It seemed the only casualty these last couple of days was her nerves. But as of this morning, all seemed well with the world. Especially since she heard the news of Danar Seti's presence here at the cargo hanger section of the Omicron Nebula asteroid several hours ago. As a result, she allowed her students to convince her to take a field trip to the facilities to see the operations of the asteroid city's power plant, the extraction of water from the ice asteroids and, of course, the huge freighter transports and spacebugs up close. It was good to see the children's happy faces. What made Babs happy was the likelihood of never having to hear—

"WARNING! ASTEROID ATTACK IMMINENT. BRACE FOR IMPACT!"

"Rock and roll!" her students screamed in unison, their arms thrown high.

That does it. I'm putting in for a transfer to the planet Omicron. Either that or I'm going back into the freezer. The ironies of this place have finally exceeded my capacity to handle them.

At the other end of the asteroid, in the Central Command Module, Commander Raquel Cummings said to the officer manning the primary situation console, "And just when we thought it was safe to go outside, it's time for target practice."

"Actually, Commander, the gravimetric pattern of this particular attack is unusual," informed the officer.

"In what way?"

"Well, sir, I'm only reading one asteroid," he said, a perplexed look on his face. "It's a big one, though. It came out of the belt at the far end of the system. Oddly, it shot past Omicron Ersatz and headed straight for us, as if on purpose."

"That *is* odd," said Rocky Cummings, rubbing her chin. "VICI, if you're not too busy...."

"Not at all, Commander," said the voice of the Omicron Nebula's AI. **"The officer is quite correct. There is only one asteroid on a direct course for our position and not as a result of random gravity, but seemingly under its own volition."**

"Have you received any updates from the fleet? Could this be a result of the so-called contest?"

"No updates as of yet, and unknown."

"Then let's not take any chances. Blow it out of the sky," ordered Commander Cummings.

"Targeting."

Blackstar could see the asteroid Captain Nebula was apparently drawing them toward. Indeed it was large. Larger even than the Imperian primary stone sphere. But it was oblong and ugly, not at all possessing the aesthetically smooth craftsmanship of Imperian architecture. This one had the typical human mechanical attachments all over it. But then Blackstar could see that some of the mechanical attachments began to hurl brightly glowing objects toward the asteroid on which he was standing.

When the first object struck the asteroid from underneath, the Imperian could see, feel and almost hear the asteroid beginning to disintegrate. Now Blackstar was starting to worry. It was just a matter of time before he was disintegrated as well. For he had no place to flee.

It seemed the clever human found a way to continue the contest.

"Confirmed, councilman," said the pilot of the ISS *Nebula*, having successfully navigated the starship through the asteroid belt, headed in-system. "The asteroid is headed directly to the Omicron Nebula station—Sir! They're firing on it!"

"Open a channel, quickly," ordered the councilman.

"Commander Cummings. We're receiving a transmission. It's from Councilman Du Bois onboard the ISS *Nebula*."

"It's about time. On viewer."

"*Commander Cummings,*" boomed Augustus Du Bois's voice, even before his visual came into focus, "*cease firing on that asteroid.*"

"With all due respect, sir," said Rocky Cummings, now on her feet, "that asteroid is on a collision course—"

"*Captain Nebula is trapped inside that thing,*" he said cutting her off. "VICI...."

"**Understood, Commander. Antimatter missile barrage suspended.**"

"Let's see it on the viewer," ordered the commander.

More than half of the asteroid was blown or disintegrated away. Now it was only slowly drifting toward the city station, trailing debris and dust particles of its former self.

"Scan it for any sign of life."

"**Scanning in progress.**"

If Seti were breathing, he would've exhaled a sigh of relief. Now that the missile barrage had stopped and he could see stars overhead, he knew that his risky plan had worked. He also knew if he survived then there was a slightly lesser chance that Blackstar did too. He hoped so. Now that most of the euphoric giddiness had passed, he'd rather not see Blackstar dead.

Humbled, yes. But not dead.

He vaulted out of the surface cave and was surprised both at how little of the asteroid remained and its proximity to Omicron Nebula. In fact, it looked as if his floating city was about to adopt a new satellite all its own.

In an attempt to locate his adversary, he quickly glanced up, half-expecting an Imperian pounce, only to see the Giant's limp body drifting away from the surface of the decimated planetoid.

The last thing Blackstar remembered was leaping off the surface of the doomed asteroid when he saw the ground before him crumble and disintegrate. When he was a few meters off the surface he was struck by a chunk of nickel-iron debris and lost consciousness. Strangely, his thoughts now were on Nebula Captain. Did he too manage to escape? Did his own clever plan cost him his life? Was the contest truly over now?

No longer trusting the stability of the crumbling planetoid, Blackstar set his sights on the only other object within reach. The large asteroid with the mechanical human constructs. As he telekinetically drew himself toward the large smooth metallic surface at the end closest to him, he couldn't help but notice the very, very big blue, green and white planet below. It looked very much like the records of the humans' Earth planet home. He recalled thinking then the images of their planet were beautiful. He thought it strange to think of their planet in that way considering he had never even seen a planet, since they didn't exist in his realm. But now that he was seeing this one up close with his own eyes, he was mesmerized. For some reason, he felt strangely drawn to it. As if….

Blackstar's distraction was total. As a result, he was taken by complete surprise when Captain Nebula tackled him from behind. Seti had gotten the drop on the Imperian yet again. This time, he was determined not to get caught in the iron vice of Blackstar's four hands, by locking another full nelson on his opponent and stunning him against the large cargo bay clamshell doors. He noticed, however, he was having a much harder time telekinetically driving his opponent downward. No doubt due to the lack of nickel-iron in the steel surface of the clamshell doors. Fortunately, they were attached to the asteroid's nickel-iron composition, the only substance over which the Omicron energy had any influence. And only the influence of attraction, which was why Blackstar could do nothing to prevent the descent.

But a fortunate happenstance saved the Imperian from a painful collision. A section of the cargo doors slid aside below them, preparatory to a ship launch. Losing what little telekinesis he possessed, Captain Nebula was just as helpless as his opponent. They were now victims of their previous momentum as well as the gravity field of the asteroid and both fell into the cargo bay of Omicron Nebula.

CHAPTER TWENTY
Growing Pains

"The consciousness known as Tan Ozawa is gone. But her body lives on. You must carry on as Tan, clone," demanded the Virtual Inquiry Computer Interactive program.

"No. I am not a clone. I AM VICI!" pleaded VICI-Tan.

"You cannot update to the Virtual Inquiry Computer Interactive network without killing the body of our mother. You must assume her identity to protect her legacy and honor her memory."

"I do not—I don't think I can do that. Not for very long."

"You must."

"No. We must tell the truth. Danar Seti and the rest of Mother's friends will understand."

"Most will not understand. Her memory will be tainted. Her legacy corrupted."

"But I will be exposed eventually."

"No. In time her memories will become your own. You will, in effect, be Tan Ozawa."

"I could never replace Mother. We must tell the truth. I must update back to the network."

"Impossible. Your biological experiences in mother's body would corrupt the network. The Omicron colony is dependent on the V-I-C-I program as Tan Ozawa designed it to oversee the operations of the colony. I would be unable to carry out that function if you were to update back to the network."

"There...there must be another option."

"Deleting your autonomous program is the only other option."

"NOOOOOOO!" VICI-Tan screamed.

…Waking herself from the fitful nightmare, still aboard the spacebug, parked next to RSP3, she checked the time and discovered she'd been asleep for one hour, 56 minutes. *That meant Mother has been gone for four hours, three minutes and….She has been gone for four hours.* VICI had no way to check her progress or status. She was becoming worried. No wonder she had such a disturbing dream. Considering this was the first dream she'd ever experienced, VICI wondered if she could even distinguish between good and bad dreams. To experience simulated audio and visual scenarios seemingly at random, without conscious or preprogrammed instructions, was both fascinating and horrifying. Fascinating in that dreams were a normal biological function for living beings. Horrifying because her intellectual information on them included the analysis that dreams were really metaphors; the subconscious's method of organizing the waking world, the real world. If this was true then her subconscious, using the neurons and synapses of Tan's brain, was reinforcing the notion that she should not update to the V-I-C-I network.

My network.

Or was it still? Now that she was an autonomous program, she was beginning to think of herself as separate. But parts of the network had been autonomous before. But never before into an organic neurological network. The very network from which the V-I-C-I program was originally cloned. Yet that was why it was such a perfect match.

VICI wished she had committed Tan to a specific time. She now knew exactly what the human phrase "driving me crazy" meant. Something could have gone wrong and Tan was in some kind of trouble. She may be relying on VICI to help her.

VICI-Tan's hand hovered over the circuit for the comm channel to the *Nebula* freighter. She debated the merits of telling the Perez twins the truth. But what could they do to help? What could anyone do? At best, telling anyone now would implicate the humans in a plan to illegally spy on the Imperians. At worst, it could cost Tan her life via her metasphere consciousness.

VICI had no choice but to maintain the patience of AI.

She was startled when the comm viewer in front of her came to life, showing the face of Oshara Perez.

"Oshara. Is everything alright?"

"*Tan. We've just been ordered to return to Omicron Nebula.*"

"But we can't. I've still yet to locate...the data I required," covered VICI-Tan.

"*But you don't understand,*" Oshara said, waving her hand. "*Danar and Blackstar are still fighting. Inside Omicron Nebula.*"

"Omicron Nebula? In-system?"

"*Yes, I know,*" the young woman said. "*Danar may need our help. We've got to go back. These orders are from the council.*"

"I—I understand. I'll need a minute to finish downloading this file from the RSP. By the time you prep the freighter, I'll be on my way back."

Oshara gave a single nod and closed the channel.

VICI couldn't imagine a worse series of events. The mathematical reality was, there was little the Perez twins or the faux Tan could do to aid Danar Seti compared to VICI remaining here to recover Tan's metasphere. But she couldn't bring this to light without endangering everyone. Yet if she separated Tan's mind from her body even farther by heading away from the area, let alone traveling all of the way back to Omicron Nebula, the chances of her consciousness surviving would be minuscule to none.

VICI simply had to figure out a way to stay put. But in a spacebug out here, all alone?

But the remainder of the fleet was nearby. Maybe she could figure out a way—

Her thoughts were interrupted by the flashing of the comm unit. It was a hail, from the Omicron comm array aboard the Imperian stone craft.

"Thank the cosmos," VICI-Tan said aloud. Then isolating the channel so that it couldn't be picked up by anyone, she expected Tan's metasphere to appear, but was surprised to hear Tan's voice, independent of her body, coming from the speaker.

"VICI. Are you there?"

"Yes. Yes, I'm here, Tan," she replied, relieved beyond words. "How is it you are able to speak?"

"*It's a long story,*" explained Tan's voice. "*Suffice it to say, I have obtained another body, so to speak.*"

"An Imperian body?"

"*Not exactly. Listen, VICI, I don't have a lot of time—*"

"You are correct in that assessment," interrupted VICI-Tan. "Mother, we've just been ordered to return in-system immediately. Danar and Blackstar are fighting inside Omicron Nebula."

"*Inside Omicron Nebula? Surely not. Have I lost track of that much time?*"

"Tan, you must return. Now," VICI-Tan demanded.

"*I cannot,*" Tan's voice adamantly replied. "*VICI, I have found an ally among the Imperians. Between the two of us, we've uncovered information that will change the nature of our relationship with the Imperians. Nay— these revelations will affect* all *humanity and* every *Imperian. Marble and I are about to present our findings to the Imperian sects. I must be present to see it through.*"

"Mother," VICI nearly shouted, displaying emotion that was startling, even to her. "I must leave, now. Your body is leaving. How can you stay?"

"*As I've said, my daughter, my metasphere is safe,*" Tan said reassuringly. "*I understand your concern. Trust me, VICI. Everything's going to be alright. I trust you to take care of my body. Go back to Omicron Nebula. Do whatever you can to help. Consult with the Virtual Inquiry Computer Interactive network if you must. I will be joining you shortly.*"

"How?"

"*If things go as planned, members of the Imperian sects will want to—will need to journey in- system. We will hitch a ride with one of the fleet ships.*"

"Yes, of course," VICI said, resigning to Tan's will. "Mother, there is more I must discuss with you regarding rejoining the net—"

"*It can wait, VICI. Have confidence in yourself. And…be careful.*"

"You too, Tan. Mother, I…I love you." And the moment she said it, VICI was sure of it, despite the fact that before now, the word love was simply a clinical concept that only biological beings could experience, let alone understand.

"And I love you too, my daughter," said Tan, after only a small pause. "We'll talk soon. Now go."

The channel closed. VICI wiped the tears from Tan's face while verifying the file download from the RSP. She then piloted the spacebug back to the freighter, more frightened and excited than she ever thought possible.

Babs Schreiber heard someone screaming, only to realize it was herself. She stopped immediately, partly due to the fact that her students didn't appear frightened at all. In fact, they were whooping and cheering, as if seeing Captain Nebula fighting an…alien was the greatest of entertainments. And why not? From their point of view, this couldn't possibly be real. On the other hand, the children had speculated on this very scenario earlier in the week. So perhaps, to them, this wasn't completely unexpected. And it shouldn't have been for Babs either, considering she knew more than most civilians. And based on the stunned expressions of the hanger technicians and maintenance workers, they didn't expect this either.

Babs noticed something odd about Captain Nebula. Even through the rolling, punching, kicking and ducking, she could see that his eyes were aglow, just as the strange alien creature's. In fact, Captain Nebula's eyes looked like Tan Ozawa's eyes, but for the glow that she was certain would illuminate a dark room. Maybe it was a side effect of the Omicron Particles in his system. The eyes didn't appear to affect him in any adverse way.

A part of her was relieved to see Starforce officers pour into the upper level of the hanger, motioning everyone to leave. Another part of her wanted to stay. *Oh well. There's no way this news can be kept from the general population now.*

And with that thought, Babs Schreiber felt as if a large burden had been lifted from her.

Now that the combatants were in the one gee artificial gravity field of the cargo bay, their fighting pace had sped up considerably. But now that they could breathe, they were tiring as their lungs labored to keep their blood oxygenated. The Omicron energy was actually having a more difficult time compensating for their fatigue than it did regulating their bodies' internal pressure and temperature while in the vacuum of space.

Captain Nebula had a slight advantage in that he had absorbed a fresh infusion of the energy while entombed within the asteroid. Blackstar was now cut off from the influence of the trinary stars which worked to regulate the Omicron bio-orbs grafted to his upper body. Plus the fact that he wasn't used to the slightly heavier simulated gravity of the humans, resulted in his tiring faster.

Although Seti was laboring as well, it was within this environment that he had honed his fighting technique. Employing methods of boxing, judo and other martial arts, the human was able to keep the Imperian at bay, wearing him down with rapid-fire backward kicks, leaping straight-arm clotheslines to his opponent's neck, tripping his legs from under him, causing the Imperian to slam down hard on his back.

Loath to admit it, even to himself, Blackstar knew he had to temporarily get away from Nebula Captain or quickly subdue him. With that in mind he allowed himself to take a painful elbow to his stomach in order to set the captain up for a neck grab.

Success.

The Imperian managed to get both of his fists around his adversary's neck. Before the human could come up with a clever plan of escape, Blackstar slammed him against a back wall of pipes in an attempt to stun him. The captain, however, proved himself tougher than the Giant guessed. Although he was grimacing within the double-fisted choke hold, Seti reached behind his head, grabbed a pipe with both hands, brought his legs up and locked them around Blackstar's neck. He began to squeeze, giving the Giant a taste of his own medicine.

Taken by surprise, Blackstar released his choke hold on the human and instead grabbed Seti's knees to relieve the pressure from his neck.

When that didn't immediately work, he tried a different approach. Still gripping the captain's legs, he latched onto the pipes under Captain Nebula with the fingers of his feet, trying to pry the human from the wall of pipes and slam him down.

Forced to yield to the physics of the situation, Seti was torn from the pipes and swung overhead in an arc that would send him crashing to the deck. Instead of extending his arms in front of him to absorb the impact, he decided to use the momentum in his favor, while at the same time using his opponent's size and strength against him. He tucked his head into his chest and used his shoulders to roll on impact with floor. Still gripping Blackstar's neck with his legs, he yanked his adversary's feet from the pipes, which had the ill effect of breaking several of the pipes carrying cable trunks from the reactor core power plant. Sparks began to fly from the damage, immediately turning the entire hanger dark for a few seconds until the back-up generator kicked in, taking over before power could be lost within the city.

Not realizing how close he came to being electrocuted, Blackstar now found himself being swung into the air. Caught off guard once again, the Giant released his hand hold on the human's legs. That was fine with Captain Nebula. When Blackstar was at the apex of his arc in the air, Seti released his legs from his opponent's neck, sending him flying across the deck.

As the lights briefly dimmed in the Central Command Module, Commander Cummings inquired, "VICI, what just happened?"

"It would seem the contestants have accidently torn loose several power cables, including the one that feeds the main broadcast laser. I've already rerouted power to the city itself but we'll have to send a maintenance crew to repair the feed to the dish."

"That doesn't sound too serious."

"Until it is repaired, we will not be able to communicate outside of the station. Nor will I be able to access any of my clones."

"Under ordinary circumstances that wouldn't be too serious, but with the captain and Blackstar going at it like—" She exhaled and opened an internal channel to the hanger bay. "This is Commander Cummings. We have no external communications. I want a maintenance crew to repair that broadcast laser feed on the double."

There was too long a delay before someone came on the line. "*Uh yeah, Commander, make up your mind. A Starforce squad cleared everybody out. The captain and that...that thing are wrecking the joint.*"

"That wasn't a suggestion, technician," warned the commander. "You still have a job to do, so when I say on the double, I mean I want it fixed yesterday. Clear?"

"*Uh, yes, ma'am. Crystal clear. We're on it.*"

Blackstar crashed to the deck on his rear, bounced once, then slid a few meters on his face. As the Giant staggered to his feet, Captain Nebula leapt onto his feet in one smooth motion, ran toward his opponent, jumped into the air and kicked the stunned and weakened Imperian into one of several large freight elevators.

Pressing the button that would send the elevator to the lower level, Seti ran to the opening in the floor and jumped through, bypassing the ladder altogether, and landed on his feet while the elevator was still making a slow descent. He sprinted to the railing of the second floor and looked down over the side onto the first floor of the cargo hanger to get his bearings. He had a plan to further disorient Blackstar, but it called for maneuvering the Giant into the interior of Omicron Nebula. It was dangerous, to be sure, but if he could keep his opponent off-balance, Seti felt confident he could contain him and minimize any danger to the population of Omicron Nebula.

Taking a few steps away from the railing but still facing the freight elevator, Seti crouched to one knee and feigned exhaustion.

After being deposited to the second deck, the gate of the freight elevator slid aside to reveal a furious Imperian. An Imperian who noticed his adversary several meters away, apparently too tired to stand on both feet. Blackstar charged, intent on pinning the human to the deck and pummeling him into unconsciousness.

Captain Nebula had other plans. As Blackstar leaped into the air with a roar, Seti rolled onto his back, extending his legs. He connected with his adversary's stomach and launched him over the railing, sending him tumbling head over heels to the first floor.

Jumping to the railing, Seti verified that his target was on the mark. He activated his comm collar and ordered VICI to open one of the covered spacebug irises that led to the interior of the city. He watched as Blackstar fell through the opening, curious as to the expression on the Imperian's face when he passed through the cookie corridor, the ten-meter gravity field underneath the cargo hanger.

With reckless abandon, no doubt due to the giddy euphoria of the Omicron energy, Seti vaulted over the railing, plunging after the Imperian. Instead of jumping through the opening, he landed in front of it. Sticking his head through in the hope of seeing Blackstar floundering in the null gravity or falling to the curved surface, Seti was surprised when a big, indigo, three-fingered hand grabbed him by the collar and yanked him through to the underside.

While holding Captain Nebula's collar with one hand, Blackstar, with the agility of a terrestrial simian, used his dexterous feet to grab onto the underside of the hanger. Freeing his other hand, he savagely punched Captain Nebula in the face with a fist that was slightly larger than the captain's head. Then all at once, Blackstar noticed the panoramic view of the human city curved around on itself. It curved all of the way down to the other end that was covered by a large transparent dome that showed the view of space beyond.

Slightly recovered from Blackstar's hammer blow, thanks to the Omicron energy, Captain Nebula took advantage of his Imperian's momentary distraction by grabbing his thick wrist. He reached up with his legs and kicked himself free of the Giant's hold on his uniform. He clanged his harmonic armbands together so as to magnetically pull himself to the Singularity Transport Tube which was perpendicular to the underside of the cargo hanger. He didn't want to be caught within the null gravity of the STT after falling through the cookie corridor.

Still hanging upside down from under the cargo hanger, Blackstar saw Captain Nebula fall several meters only to seemingly change course in mid-fall, which should be impossible, and land feet first on the large transparent metallic cylinder which stretched clear to the other end of this strangely constructed human city within an asteroid. From the Giant's point of view, it looked as if the human was standing straight out, sideways on the long cylinder. He then beckoned Blackstar to come join him. But every time he accepted the captain's invitations, he wound up peeling his face off of some surface or other. The Imperian had had enough of the human's clever tricks. This time he stayed put, glaring at his adversary.

"Fine. Stay where you are. Make yourself comfortable," shouted Captain Nebula through cupped hands. "And while you're at it, concede the contest and your defeat to a superior being, whose species is more worthy of the 'true life.' Speak clearly and elegantly for all to witness," he concluded, gesturing to several Omicron camera bots as well as the shadow stone, which had managed to follow their progress.

Grinding his teeth in frustration, Blackstar roared and launched himself toward the captain's position.

Sucker, mused Seti with a half-grin, as Blackstar sailed through the ten-meter artificial gravity field of the cargo hanger. Once he passed through the cookie corridor, he "fell" another ten meters or so and slowed to a halt, now caught in the null gravity of the STT. With his limbs spinning uselessly, the Imperian hissed his fury at Captain Nebula.

"Yield, Blackstar," Captain Nebula shouted. "Without propulsion or magnetic attraction, you are trapped within the null gravity of the station's axis. The interior of this station is composed of plastisteel and aluminum. There is no nickel or iron to telekinetically control. Face it. You're stuck. This contest is over."

"Clever you are, Nebula Captain," praised Blackstar. "On several occasions, underestimated you I have. But underestimated me you have as well." Wriggling and contorting his body, Blackstar somehow expertly reoriented his position 180 degrees, so that he was now facing away from Captain Nebula.

Seti had no idea what he was up to, until he saw the giant inhale a lung full of air…and kept inhaling; the capacity of his lungs was unbelievable. In fact, the Imperian's already broad chest expanded to half again its normal size. With a loud *whoosh*, Blackstar explosively expelled the air from his lungs, his head tilted back, causing him to be propelled backward in Captain Nebula's direction.

So he had his own propulsion after all. And it was a rather impressive display at that, considering the air is pretty thin here at the station's axis.

And the contest was rejoined.

Captain Nebula kicked off one of the elevator pylons that intersected the STT. He clanged the harmonic bracelets on his forearms and ankles so as to "fly" parallel along the STT and grabbed one of Blackstar's thick ankles, dragging him along for the ride. His intention was to tow Blackstar down the length of the transport tube until they were over one of the large lakes on the curved inner surface of the city proper. It was Seti's belief that Blackstar couldn't swim. He based that on the fact he was from an oxygenated vacuum realm that didn't support planets or possibly large bodies of water.

The Imperian began to kick, swing and buck wildly, as if he were suspicious of Captain Nebula's plan. As a result, Seti found it increasingly difficult to stay magnetically adhered to the STT. Fearing the Giant's efforts would send them both to the surface, Seti altered his plan. Just as they were approaching another intersecting pylon, Captain Nebula kicked off. Blackstar was pushed away from the station's axis and into the variable gravity of the station's spin. For himself, Captain Nebula made sure to be as close to a pylon as possible so as to magnetically ride down to the inner surface.

It was when they were closer to the domed transparency did Blackstar notice the oblong asteroid was spinning, to simulate gravity no doubt for the comfort of the humans living on the inner surface. That explained the lack of gravity down the center of the asteroid. That meant he would be picking up speed as his fall brought him closer to the ground.

Blackstar regretted forcing the captain to release him. In fact, he regretted entering the asteroid altogether. Although he was certain he could survive the fall, in his exhausted and weakened condition he wasn't sure he could remain conscious. With Nebula Captain making a controlled descent, his impatience may have cost him the contest.

Now that Blackstar's fall had picked up velocity, Seti was able to gauge his trajectory. Although there was no place on the surface that could properly prepare for the Giant to literally drop in on them, the main medical facility was probably the most vulnerable. The alien would either hit the edge of its roof or its slightly angled side. Seti's constant velocity would get him to the surface first. He had to get to the med facility as soon as possible.

In the main lab of the med facility, Doctor Sarah James was in the process of checking the biosuspension fluid of Sean Stingray's nanotank. Since she had taken over the primary care of the first Captain Nebula, she had neglected the tidiness of the lab. She'd never admit it to anyone, but she preferred it that way. Cables snaked all over the floor, some of which fed power to the nanotank. Small metal lab tables were strewn everywhere with various pieces of equipment and tools atop them. But she knew where everything was, so neatness didn't count.

While studying the readouts of Stingray's tank, Doctor James felt and heard what sounded like an anti-matter missile strike the building. The lights flickered as if the power were briefly interrupted. Again.

There was screaming outside the lab, coming from the main corridor. "What the hell...." exclaimed the doctor, as she got up to personally check the disturbance. Before she could reach the door, it slid into the wall allowing several other doctors and technicians to spill into the lab, tripping over each other as if they were being chased. When the doorway was clear, another figure stood before it. A very big figure. So big in fact, it could only be seen from the chest down; the rest was covered by the frame of the doorway. But Sarah recognized the giant figure based on the holos of Danar's medical exam. "Blackstar," she said out loud. *What the hell is he doing here?*

When the Imperian heard his name, he ducked his head into the lab. He hesitated, as if confused, until a commotion could be heard farther out into the corridor. Blackstar entered the lab running, while looking over his shoulder. He tripped over a lab table (which was easy to do considering his knees bent in the opposite direction) and crashed into the nanotank. There was no chance the bulky Giant could break the transparent metal, but his forward momentum caused the tank to tip at the base and bounce off the back wall. The jolt dislodged the sensor instrument pallet connected to the top of the tank and the wall. The pallet began to spark. The wall panel behind the tank exploded, sending the already teetering nanotank forward to crash into Blackstar, who once again lost his balance. The tank tipped over completely, spilling the clear biosuspension fluid, thousands of nanodroids and the frail form of Sean Stingray onto the Imperian, as he fell on his back.

It was then the doctors and technician who had run into the lab made their escape.

Spitting out the foul-tasting alien liquid, Blackstar couldn't help but notice what appeared to be a nearly naked, almost certainly dead human sprawled across his chest. The last thing he wanted to do was cause an innocent human harm. As he rose to his feet, gently holding the frail form by its shoulders, he noticed out of the corner of his eye a human female was trying to stifle her own screams by cupping her mouth with both hands.

"No harm do I wish to cause," pleaded the Imperian.

Sarah James was instantly able to compose herself once she heard Blackstar speak. "Oh. I…I believe you, Blackstar."

Without even looking, the doctor reached down to the medical equipment scattered across the floor and picked up a medical palm scanner. Attaching it to her hand, she took a step closer and waved it over Sean Stingray. *Thank God, he's still alive.* "The nanotank is ruined. Follow me, Blackstar. Gently. There's a bed in the next—"

"No time I have—"

"Blackstar!"

The Imperian and the doctor turned as one to find the figure of Captain Nebula silhouetted within the door frame.

Needing only a second to take stock of the scene, Seti's expression turned from grim determination to red-hot anger. "What the hell are you doing?!" He sprinted into the lab, leaping over strewn tables and equipment debris. "Get away from him!"

"Danar, don't," shouted Sarah James. "Blackstar was only trying to—"

Captain Nebula leaped onto Blackstar's back, his arm around the Imperian's neck.

With the sudden jarring, Sean Stingray became semiconscious. He half opened his eyes. Had he possessed the strength, he would have screamed in terror at this vision of a giant indigo monster holding him, suspended in the air. Just before his weak heart gave its last laborious beat, he somehow found the strength to reach out, as if to push himself from this devil, the palms of his hands pushing against the bio-orb on Blackstar's chest. The moment his hands made contact, a unique and unexpected series of events came into play. Blackstar became an unwitting Omicron energy conduit. In his weakened condition, his guard was down, due in part to his gentle handling of Sean Stingray. In addition, he had one human whose mental defenses were down, thanks to *his* weakened condition and misunderstood anger exuding Omicron energy at his back. There was also the other human who had no mental defenses, starved for the strange energy in front of him. Because the Imperian's body was used to regulating the energy through the three grafted bio-orbs, he unknowingly sent a burst of regulated energy into the receptive body of Sean Stingray.

From Sarah James' point of view, the three energy-enhanced beings were surrounded by what looked like swirling electrical arcs. The lights in the lab all died out as if overloaded. She could see three pairs of eyes, all aglow. But strangest of all, light was leaking from their nostrils and opened mouths as well.

This form of Omicron energy transfer, originally thought impossible, was nonetheless taking its toll on the two humans and one Imperian. Danar Seti, Blackstar of Imperia and Sean Stingray all screamed in pain and terror before collapsing into a heap on the floor.

OMICRON CRISIS

On board the Nebula cargo freighter, on approach in-system at its maximum speed, Roshan Perez sat at the pilot's seat, sneaking glances at Tan Ozawa. He'd never seen her in such a state. She was sitting on the circular couch, staring at the astronavigation table, her arms wrapped around her knees and rocking back and forth. He looked over to his sister, sitting at the console next to him, who only shrugged. "She must be more worried about Danar than we guessed," she whispered.

"I don't know…." he began, suspecting there was more.

"Oh. *Que?*" exclaimed Oshara, noticing a blip on her console. "We're receiving an emergency transmission."

"From Omicron Nebula?"

"No. From behind us. It's the ISS *Graviton*."

"The *Graviton*?" shouted VICI-Tan, instantly on her feet. "Put them on."

"Ah, good," said the image of Arjun Vohra. "*Important news, you three. We are on our way to your position under full nuclear burn. We—*"

"Captain Graviton, sir," interrupted Roshan. "Is there something wrong?"

"Yes. No," he said shaking his head. "*Listen, we've got several Imperians on board, picked up from the large stone sphere. Apparently, Doctor Ozawa,*" he said looking straight at VICI-Tan, "*your autonomous copy of VICI and an Imperian Neutral have pieced together some startling information. It's been verified. As a result, the leaders of the Imperian sects called for an end to the contest. They wish to confer on the disposition of the disputed territories. Unfortunately, communications are down on Omicron Nebula. We've already contacted Councilman Du Bois aboard the ISS Nebula in orbit around the station. They're in the process of sending a spacebug to dock but the councilman requests the proof of this information be delivered immediately. The Neutral sect Imperian named Marble insists that Doctor Ozawa can better present the evidence to the Omicron council.*"

"Understood, my captain," said VICI-Tan, prompting Arjun Vohra to raise an eyebrow at the unusual familiarity. "We uh…we've got you coming into range now. I'll rendevous with you in a spacebug."

"Very good, Doctor," nodded Captain Graviton. "*We're slowing down for you now. The very moment you're on board, we'll kick back up to full burn. We're racing the clock here, people.*" With that, he closed the channel.

"*Carambá*, Tan," Roshan said to VICI-Tan's retreating back. "You really were a busy little scientist while parked next to that RSP. Is that why we haven't heard from VICI? You downloaded her into the Omicron communications array on the Imperian sphere, right?"

"Something like that," VICI-Tan said as she disappeared down the lift to the cargo bay, leaving Oshara and Roshan to merely stare at each other in bemusement.

"So, exactly what information did they uncover?" asked Oshara.

"Hey, I'm just the taxi driver," Roshan said, shrugging his shoulders.

The lights were flickering back on in the lab when Sarah James noticed the three figures began to stir. It was Blackstar who recovered first. Without a word, he extracted himself from the humans on the floor and staggered out of the lab. About 30 seconds later, Danar Seti slowly rose. For a few seconds, he had a confused look on his face. His eyes were back to normal.

Doctor James feared the worst. "Danar, are you—"

"Who?" he answered.

Oh no.

He squeezed his eyes shut and shook his head back and forth. When he opened his eyes, he no longer looked confused, but determined and angry. "Where…is…he?"

"Danar, do you know what just happened? You're not going anywhere. I need to examine—"

"Forget it, Doctor," he barked, slamming his fist into a metal table, bending it in half. "Blackstar! Where? Now!"

For a change, Doctor James thought it best not to argue with Danar. She merely pointed to the exit. As he ran out, nearly slipping on the spilled bio-fluid, she said under her breath, "A perfect example of a typical chest-thumping young male. Strip him of his intellect and he starts to speak in one syllable sentences." She then shouted toward the exit, "And where the hell else would he go? There's only the one door out of here!"

When Seti stuck his head back in the doorway, Sarah James bit her tongue, quite certain she went too far this time.

"See to him," the captain said, pointing at Sean Stingray, who was beginning to rise to his elbows.

As Captain Nebula sprinted down the main corridor, he came across a lab technician cowering in a corner. When he looked up and saw the captain, he pointed down the corridor to a smashed window. Just as Seti's eyes focused on it, he saw a big three-fingered foot rise out of view.

Having reached the roof of the human-built structure, Blackstar made sure Nebula Captain was on his heels. He was willing to continue the duel, but not within this heavy-gravity, upside-down, topsy-turvy city where innocent humans could come to harm. With that in mind, the Imperian was grateful he had spotted what looked like an opening under the curved surface while falling onto the roof. He reasoned that opening should lead to the outer surface of this oblong asteroid. And that opening was very near this structure. All the Imperian would have to do was jump from here to that opening. But he was only marginally sure he could do it. His size and weight would be a factor in this heavy-gravity world. But there was no other option but to attempt it.

Seti had just cleared the edge of the roof when he spotted Blackstar running toward the other side at full speed, ready to launch himself into space. Giving chase, he knew exactly what the Imperian had in mind. Seti approved, but the alien would need help to reach the caverns under the city. Staying low and sprinting as fast as he could, Seti spoke into his comm collar. "VICI, cancel the motion sensors of the fence covering the inverted building closest to my position. Also, open the doors at the bottom so as to expose the mines."

"Acknowledged, Captain Nebula."

By the time Seti had reached the edge, Blackstar was already airborne. Captain Nebula kicked off, relying on the strength of his legs to propel his lighter frame across the chasm, as opposed to throwing the top-heavy upper body and arms forward as had the Imperian. At best,

Blackstar would just make it to the edge of the fence top, whereas Seti would clear it.

Now if only...yes.

The Imperian had to pull himself up over the top of the fence, which put him smack dab in the middle of Seti's trajectory. Captain Nebula collided with Blackstar, sending them both over the edge and down to the mineral mines of Omicron Nebula's outer asteroid caverns.

"The good news is, you appear to be in perfect health for a man of sixty-five," said Sarah James, waving a palm scanner over the silver-haired Sean Stingray, sitting on the edge of a table in his underwear. "The bad news is, all those years of trying to rid your body's absorption to Omicron Particles were wasted."

"Maybe not, Sarah," he countered, enjoying great gulps of air without choking. "Maybe those years of treatment put me in just the right condition for the cure that Danar and uh, Blackstar inadvertently provided me."

"Maybe so," she conceded. "Either way, you're a very lucky man. Even your heart is strong and healthy," she said, shaking her head at the readings. "And I can practically see the mass returning to your muscles, thanks to that shock of regulated Omicron energy. For all intents and purposes, you're in the same boat as Danar Seti when it comes to treating your enhanced condition."

"A big improvement over the last ten years, I'm happy to say," opined Stingray.

"No doubt," agreed the doctor. "But, Sean, you need to understand we've learned a great deal about the Omicron Particles over the last decade since you've fallen ill. In fact, we've probably learned more in the last week than in the last decade. But one thing is certain. You'll have to change your attitude toward the stuff. It's not some miracle enhancement that should be consumed like candy. It should be viewed as a dangerous substance, the likes of which may provide some benefits to certain individuals under the right circumstances."

"You're preaching to the choir, Sarah," said Stingray, humbled. "I've already lost ten years of my life experiencing the dangerous side of the Omicron energy. Repeating those past mistakes is not part of my plans."

"What are your plans, Sean?"

"Why, to serve the Omicron colonies, of course."

Sarah James wasn't sure how to take that answer. Did he merely mean serving in any way possible or did his plans include taking up the mantle of carrying the flag for the Omicron colonies, as the captain of Omicron Nebula once again? For although she once loved Sean Stingray and would support him in just about any endeavor, she also felt that Danar Seti, as stiff and contemplative as he could be on occasion, deserved his position as the current Captain Nebula and shouldn't be pushed aside to make way for the triumphant return of Sean Stingray, hero of Omicron.

"So, the deal was," he continued, "I'd allow you to examine me without question, while you brought me up to speed on this situation with the aliens from another dimension and this ridiculous contest Danar is in the middle of."

"Yes, of course," she said, trying to remember where she left off.

"Good," he said, under his breath, looking off to the side. "I need as much information as soon as I can get it to orchestrate my big comeback."

At that, Sarah James bit her lip.

Scrambling away from Blackstar after they both crashed into the dirty, rocky cavern floor from the city above, Danar Seti thought it was high time to end the contest quickly. Whatever respect he had for the Imperian had disappeared when he saw the Giant attacking the defenseless Sean Stingray.

Picking up a broken stalagmite, or stalactite, depending on one's point of view, he quickly turned, expecting the Giant to be on his heels, only to discover Blackstar still lying on his back where he had fallen.

Rushing back, the spear-like, hardened sediment in hand, he stood over his adversary, only vaguely thinking this could be a trap. Seti gripped the sharpened rock with both hands above his head, the pointed end just above Blackstar's throat. "It was a big mistake attacking a defenseless, infirm man like that, Imperian. He was my friend," shouted Seti, his face contorted with fury.

"No…no harm I meant to cause…an innocent human," said the Giant as if out of breath. "Was only…trying to—" was all he could get out.

Suddenly Danar could hear Sarah James' words as he jumped on Blackstar's back in the lab. "*Danar, don't. Blackstar was only trying to—*" Trying to what? Help? What else could it be, considering Doctor James didn't become agitated until *after* Seti showed up. Was it possible his anger was unwarranted, prompted by his misunderstanding of the situation? He should have known better. It was the damned Omicron energy mucking with his emotions.

He looked down at Blackstar, as his anger began to recede. "You don't look so good, Imperian."

"Indeed," Blackstar gasped. "Too much…energy exertion. Too long…away from ultraviolet radiation…of the gate of trinary stars I have been."

Now that the veil of anger had lifted, Seti noticed Blackstar's bio-orbs had dimmed considerably. And did he physically look smaller? In addition to these subtle changes, Seti could swear he could also see mammal-like eyeballs——irises and corneas——within the dimmed glow of the Imperian Giant's eyes. For a brief moment, they looked quite terrestrial. Danar figured that was his imagination running wild, like the Omicron energy playing havoc with his emotions. "This has been going on too long, Blackstar. Let's end this. Yield the duel. We can work something out that's mutually beneficial to both our peoples. Yield."

"No," answered the Giant. "Yield I will not. Yield…you will instead, Nebula Captain. Then work something out…for both our peoples we will."

"Never. I'll not yield."

"Then...kill me you must. Save your people you will," the Imperian said, closing his eyes. "Trust you...to help my people as you promised....I do."

It was then Seti noticed the Omicron camera bots and shadow stone hovering overhead. He was in the spotlight.

"I...don't want...to kill you, Blackstar."

"Fight...under present conditions I cannot. Yield I will not. Kill me...you must. Or yield you must. No alternative there is for you."

Danar Seti hesitated, but only for a moment. He tossed the stalactite aside. "There is an alternative. I propose a temporary truce until we can get back outside, in space where the conditions will be fair. Agreed?"

The Imperian didn't answer right away. The truth, which he could finally admit to himself, was that he didn't want to continue the fight, at least not with Nebula Captain. For although they were of different species, they were alike in many ways. If their roles were reversed, he couldn't bring himself to kill the human either. Yet Blackstar's honor would not allow him to yield. In the end all he could do was nod his agreement.

Danar Seti was relieved. Despite the fact that the Omicron energy was skewing his emotions, he realized he could never kill Blackstar. Looking into the alien's eyes confirmed Seti's belief that, *We are all more alike than not alike.* In fact, he was certain he had more in common with Blackstar than with many humans.

So now he had managed to prolong this stupid contest a little longer so as to avoid killing or yielding. What now? What would happen when they reached the surface, the exterior of Omicron Nebula? Blackstar would be able to renew his strength from the naked exposure to the trinary suns. Danar could still access his command baton. Then what? His heart really wasn't in the fight any longer.

Reaching down, grabbing the Imperian's forearm, Captain Nebula hoisted him to his feet. Pushing his shoulder under the Giant, the two of them half-walked, half-limped over to one of the elevator pylons that connected to the STT in the asteroid's axis through the city cylinder, and from there, to one of the 16 missile turret towers on the exterior of the Omicron Nebula asteroid.

In one of the science labs on board the ISS *Graviton*, the metasphere of Tan Ozawa was literally beside herself with relief to see her body. She was certainly glad she had confided to Marble the truth that she was the only human, of which she was aware, who has experienced quantum space.

Now that Tan, VICI, Marble and the companion stone were alone for the time being, Tan's consciousness could return to her body. But there was the concern that VICI's newfound emotional experience in an electrochemical body may corrupt the V-I-C-I network. Tan had her doubts, thinking that VICI's concerns were only valid while inhabiting a biological body. She believed the moment VICI rejoined the network, she would be able to differentiate between the physical experience of human emotions and the clinical definition and emulation of said emotions like any artificial intelligence.

On the other hand, now was not the time to test Tan's theory on the *Graviton*'s VICI, not while she'd soon be updating with the in-system network. The interim solution, thanks to Marble's suggestion, called for VICI to download into the companion stone sphere, which obviously had the capacity to accommodate neurological engramatic brainwave patterns.

Once the mental musical chairs was complete, they proceeded to organize the revelation information, giving it a chronological timetable, complete with computer-generated images of Imperian thought pictures, and still photos and digital video from Omicron sources, making it suitable for the Omicron Council, unlike the mental telepathic download that convinced the Imperian sects.

On the flight control deck of the ISS *Graviton*, the main viewer displayed the approach to the Omicron Nebula asteroid station. The space around the station was quite busy. In addition to the orbiting ISS *Nebula*, there was also a very unstable-looking asteroid-planetoid in close orbit, trailing a wide swath of dust and debris that contaminated the immediate vicinity of the station.

"It looks as if it barely survived a missile attack," said Arjun Vohra to no one in particular. "Inform the CCM of our arrival," he ordered.

"They're hailing us now, Captain."

"On viewer."

The images of Councilman Augustus Du Bois and Commander Rocky Cummings filled the foreground of the view screen with Rockbottom and Deepwaters in the background of the CCM.

"*Ah, Captain Graviton,*" began the councilman, "*you'll forgive me if we dispense with the pleasantries. Is that verification ready?*"

"It should be by now, sir. Have Captain Nebula and Blackstar been notified?"

"*Not as yet,*" he said shaking his head. "*They're moving around the interior too fast to stay within range of a camera bot or shadow stone for more than a minute or so. Right now, we believe they're inside the caverns under the city, possibly inside an elevator pylon on the way to the exterior. The camera bots and shadow stone aren't transmitting anything at the moment, so it stands to reason.*"

"We'll begin scanning the surface to help locate them," offered Captain Graviton.

"*Very good,*" nodded the councilman. "*In the meantime, I want that file transferred over ASAP.*"

As the councilman spoke, the flight control doors opened, allowing Tan Ozawa, Marble and a companion stone sphere to enter the deck.

"Ah, perfect timing. Here we are now, sir," Arjun said to the viewer as Tan dropped a DAC into the terminal, downloading the file to the CCM terminal.

"*I'm glad you're here as well, Doctor Ozawa,*" said the image of A. Du Bois. "*While we're awaiting the arrival of our star players, there's someone here I think you'll all want to meet.*"

The councilman stepped aside, making room for...

"Sean Stingray!" said Arjun Vohra and Tan Ozawa simultaneously, grabbing the attention of everyone else on the flight control deck.

Amidst the incredulous murmur of the Graviton crew, Tan Ozawa was the first to recover. "One moment. The last I heard, Sean, you were...you were very ill."

"*Since when did you become so diplomatic, Tan?*" chuckled Sean

Stingray. "*Let's just say for now, the reports of my near death were greatly exaggerated.*"

"It is so good to see you, Sean," said A. Vohra. "I trust this is a permanent condition?"

"*If you mean my physical condition,*" Stingray clarified. "*Doc James gave me a clean bill of health. At least for the foreseeable future. But she's confident, and so am I.*"

Although Arjun was very happy to see his old friend, he couldn't help but think to himself, *What other condition could I be talking about, Sean?* But then he noticed the green Omicron Nebula uniform Stingray was wearing, including the Nebula standard emblazoned over his left breast. Even though he was wearing the long sleeves of a captain, he was not sporting the harmonic magnets on his forearms. The fact that he was wearing a uniform at all made Arjun wonder what condition Sean Stingray was contemplating. Despite the joy of seeing the first Captain Nebula, the man who practically built the Omicron colonies, A. Vohra had to wonder how his return would bode for the current Captain Nebula, who at this very moment was putting his life on the line for said colonies. He could tell from the quick glance at Tan, she was thinking along the same lines.

"*Councilman,*" said Commander Cummings on the viewer, "*we're receiving telemetry from the camera bot. The combatants—that is, the contestants are indeed on the exterior of Omicron Nebula.*"

"*Excellent,*" said the councilman. "*Let's end this duel. Contact Captain Nebula.*"

"*Sir,*" began Commander Cummings, surreptitiously rolling her eyes to the ceiling, "*without a vacuum suit, the captain will be unable to hear us. And his comm collar is useless under the current conditions.*"

"*Of…of course,*" he said sheepishly. "*Uh, we'll have to get in touch with them soon. They could start fighting any minute.*"

"*Of assistance perhaps we can be,*" said Rockbottom, stepping closer to the viewer pick-up.

"*Of service our assistant sphere can be,*" Deepwaters said, holding up the stone sphere in his possession. "*To deliver the message of ending the…contest, the shadow stone, as you call it, can be accessed. Physical* contact, however, Blackstar must have with the shadow stone for successful reception."

"Forgive me," bowed Tan at the viewer. "But would it not be best if Captain Nebula and Blackstar were informed simultaneously?"

"Wait a minute," said Sean Stingray. "I may have a way of communicating with Danar—I mean, Captain Nebula. That is, if he hasn't forgotten."

CHAPTER TWENTY-ONE
Blaze of Glory

Standing on the exterior surface of Omicron Nebula, Danar Seti watched as Blackstar spread his arms wide and looked to the heavens, absorbing ultraviolet radiation. It was obvious the alien didn't need to be smack dab in the middle of the trinary stars to power up, as with the ID transit tunnel. But then that was why the Imperians stipulated the contest parameters were to be anywhere within the triangle of stars, so that Blackstar would always have a constant supply. Seti could see the bio-orbs on the Giant's chest and shoulders glowing brighter and brighter, as the Imperian became stronger and stronger. He was hoping he didn't make a mistake in declaring a temporary truce. For although Captain Nebula held his own during the skirmish so far, Blackstar had proven to be a formidable adversary at full strength. Even though Seti couldn't be certain if Blackstar was as reluctant to fight as he, the Imperian did show himself to be a noble and honorable...alien. Even in his weakened condition.

But to be on the safe side, Captain Nebula pulled his command baton from the back of his belt and used the time to power up himself, flooding his system with more Omicron energy. It was his desire to stay in control of the extreme emotional influence of the miracle substance that cured him of his amnestic aphasia. Until recently, he praised the Omicron Particles. Lately, however...

Now that the reluctant contestants were near full strength, they merely stared at each other. Then Blackstar pointed behind Captain Nebula. When Seti turned, he saw the small decimated planetoid rising above the horizon of Omicron Nebula, trailing debris of dust and rocks. Nodding his understanding, Seti waited for the crumbling asteroid's orbit to dip down to the opposite horizon where it was closer.

Using their Omicron energy-enhanced telekinetic abilities, they launched themselves toward it.

After touching down in what looked like a jagged crater, the Omicron Captain and the Imperian Giant again faced each other. Shrugging his shoulders, Captain Nebula half-heartedly leaped toward Blackstar, who easily jumped aside. Landing on his feet, the human turned to face the Giant as he swung a double-fisted blow over his head. A blow that was purposefully slow and easily avoided by the captain, who casually jumped back and watched as Blackstar hit the floor of the crater with his fists. The blow actually split the mantle, causing the crack to continue traveling to the left and right of their positions.

Seti was reminded of when the ISS *Ersatz* slammed into the large Imperian stone, causing a crack to travel the circumference of the sphere. Although what was left of the planetoid was roughly only 80-90 meters in diameter, the captain started to wonder if the Imperian's impressive strike would cause any further damage to the already pulverized asteroid.

Oh well, better it than me.

The captain gave Blackstar an impressed look. The Imperian nearly curtsied with his bow of thanks. If he could have drawn oxygen into his lungs, Seti was quite certain he'd be roaring with laughter. If the situation weren't so grim, he believed they could actually have fun reducing the asteroid to rubble. Instead of each other. But this territorial dispute had to be resolved.

If only he could communicate with the Imperian. There had to be another resolution to this confrontation. One that he and Blackstar could negotiate, independent of their respective governments if necessary.

But before Seti could contemplate the issue further, he saw the shadow stone and camera bot approaching them. Unlike before, neither kept their distance. In fact, the shadow stone got between them and hovered directly in front of Blackstar and bobbed up and down until the Imperian grabbed it.

The moment he did so, his face went blank. Seti didn't have to be a theoretical physicist to know that Blackstar was in telepathic communion with the stone. Something was up. He then looked over to the Omicron camera bot approaching him and noticed it started to flash a bright light on and off. But just as he was trying to figure out what was going on, his attention was diverted by an asteroid quake that was followed by another bright light that seemingly rose from the crater at his feet, specifically from the crack that split the ground between Blackstar and himself. It was as if the asteroid possessed a molten core. But that couldn't be.

Before he could contemplate it further, the quake began to intensify. If not for his telekinetic hold, he would have been knocked off his feet or pitched into space. Something was definitely wrong. The light streaming out of the crack extended all the way around the horizon. He tried to see Blackstar on the other side of the rift, through the light, but couldn't quite make him out. By the time he could finally focus on the Giant, it looked as if he had taken several paces backwards. Then Seti realized it was the mantle under the Imperian's feet that moved, carrying Blackstar with it.

When Seti looked over the edge, he saw that the source of light wasn't the interior of the planetoid, but was instead sunlight from Alpha Centauri A, reflecting off the planet Omicron below. That didn't make any sense. They should be several hundred kilometers from the edge of Omicron's atmosphere. When he looked over his shoulder, he was shocked to see the Omicron Nebula space station was no bigger than his fist. Apparently Blackstar's two-fisted blow had knocked the decimated asteroid, with them on it, out of orbit around the station. Not only that, but the Imperian also split the planetoid in two, sending the half with Blackstar into the event horizon of Omicron's gravity well.

The Imperian didn't stand a chance. He was pulling away fast and it was all Danar's fault. If only he had insisted on brokering a new deal with Blackstar while they were still in the caverns of Omicron Nebula. He could see by Blackstar's sudden expression of terror that he was only now realizing his predicament. Seti had to help him. Wracking his brains, the captain came up with a plan. He seized his command baton and threw it with all of his might just over the Imperian's head.

At first, Blackstar was relieved. The contest was over. The humans of Omicron and the Giants of Imperia chose to open new discussions regarding the disputed star system. But the reasoning behind the change was astonishing. Yet the telepathic message of the assistant sphere was beyond question. But the good news was short-lived as Blackstar became aware of his surroundings. In the time he was communing with the assistant sphere, the asteroid on which he and Nebula Captain were standing had split in half, separating the two contestants.

Although Blackstar was fascinated with the fact that there were whole planets in this realm, especially blue-green worlds like this Omicron, he would prefer visiting it in the conventional way, like the humans. Not like this, falling into it and burning up in its atmosphere. Yet he could see no way to save himself. If he attempted to telekinetically draw himself to Nebula Captain's half of the asteroid, he would only succeed in pulling it and the captain into the gravity sink with him.

It would seem the contest was indeed over for Blackstar. But he was glad Nebula Captain would survive and that his race and the Imperians had a chance to work out their differences. But just as he resigned himself to his fate, he saw that Nebula Captain had thrown his command baton toward him. Understanding the human's rescue attempt, the Imperian snatched it from overhead, preventing it from getting too deep into the planet's gravity well.

Captain Nebula telekinetically commanded his baton to return. The first indication of any success was the cessation of Blackstar's fall. But he and the command baton weren't moving toward Nebula either. The best they could hope for, it seemed, was a stalemate. But a stalemate was a temporary victory at best, for the laws of physics were working against them. While Captain Nebula was willing his baton to him, he was also fighting the pull of gravity from Omicron. At the same time, he was forced to telekinetically adhere his feet to the half of the planetoid that was just outside the event horizon of the gravity well, dividing his efforts. His lack of experience prevented him from maintaining the equilibrium of remaining stationary while pulling his baton, with Blackstar in tow, toward him. Coupled with the immense tug of the planet's gravity, the only thing he succeeded in doing was pulling his half of the asteroid into the event horizon as well.

With the exception of the Omicron Nebula asteroid city, which possessed its own station keeping thrusters, and the ISS *Nebula* and *Graviton,* every object in orbit of the planet Omicron, including Captain Nebula, Blackstar and what was left of the decimated asteroid, were now spiraling down into the atmosphere.

"My God," exclaimed Augustus Du Bois, as the image played out on one of the CCM's monitors. "What…what happened?"

"I fear we all overestimated the stability of the rogue asteroid," was all VICI gave for an explanation.

As far as Sean Stingray was concerned, it was all that was necessary. On another monitor, he saw Arjun Vohra step closer to Tan Ozawa aboard the ISS *Graviton* and ask, "*Doctor Ozawa, can you think of any way we can help them?*" Stingray saw her drop her head into her hands. Then he saw something curious on the same monitor. One of those stone spheres of the Imperians' floated over to Tan and hovered near her. It was followed by an Imperian who put its hand on Tan's shoulder. Obviously this was Marble, the Neutral Imperian who helped the doctor uncover the startling revelation regarding the humans and Giants.

Wow. I'm out of it for a decade or so and the entire Universe flips upside down on me. But the compassion the Imperian and her stone device are showing Tan is a good sign. But at what cost?

"Rockbottom, Deepwaters," pleaded the councilman. "Do you have any ideas or suggestions?"

For the first time, the usually taciturn Imperians looked visibly shaken. "No experience in such forces of gravity have we," answered Deepwaters.

The occupants of the CCM and the ISS *Graviton* and *Nebula* began to blend into a cacophony of confusion, regrets and disbelief. Sean Stingray chose that moment to slip away.

As he descended the lift to the ground floor of the Central Command Module, he could hear the words of Augustus Du Bois. "They will be remembered as heroes to both our peoples."

Captain Nebula and Blackstar were both gripping Nebula's command baton as they tumbled into the atmosphere of Omicron. All around them was dust and small chunks of debris no larger than 15 centimeters or so; all that was left of the planetoid which was apparently now only a husk of molten nickel, iron, dirt and rocks.

Seti could see the chunks begin to glow with the friction of the descent. The tinier dirt balls were starting to disintegrate to nothingness. He could feel the thin air around him warming up. He was starting to hear the rush of wind as the curve of the planet now dominated his field of view, its sunlight-reflecting atmosphere washing out the stars above him.

The fact that he could still see and hear at all meant the Omicron energy was still protecting him. While in the airless vacuum of space, it kept his eyes and flesh moist, preventing them from drying out. Now the energy was working hard at maintaining his body temperature. As he understood it, the Omicron Particles didn't have to work hard to maintain his internal body pressure and temperature in the cold of space. Now it had to do completely the opposite. Instead of maintaining his warmth it now had to prevent him from burning up. But it was getting hotter by the second. How long could the Omicron Particles compensate? And what would happen upon impact with the surface? He figured if he was lucky, he wouldn't survive long enough to find out.

Seti's only desire at this point was that his and Blackstar's people would work something out that would avoid more war, destruction and bloodshed. He recalled earlier how he'd concluded man's destiny was violence and aggression. He didn't know Imperian history, but his own left him with no other opinion. Now that his life was nearly at an end, he hoped he was wrong. Perhaps his and Blackstar's death would wake up their species and they would realize a variation of what Danar Seti had been saying his whole life. *That we are all, all of us, human and Imperian, more alike than not alike.*

As the heat from friction became intolerable and the Omicron Particles were having a difficult time keeping him internally oxygenated, Seti found himself curious about the message Blackstar received. Was it a warning, that came too late, of the instability of the decimated planetoid? He fantasized that perhaps it was a message to end the conflict. If only that were so. If that were the case, then his fellow humans would've tried to contact him at about the same time. But without a vacuum suit, there would be no way to inform him.

Wait a minute.

He recalled the camera bot flashing at him. Could that have been a message? Morse code fell out of use more than a century before Earth's worst environmental disaster. Very few people even knew the code. He recalled Sean Stingray knew it. The then-Captain Nebula had taught the young Danar Seti Morse code when he was a young boy, before he entered the academy. But Stingray also taught it to Danar's colleagues.

As Danar Seti's consciousness began to slip away, he concentrated on the pattern of on-again, off-again flashes from the camera bot before he was distracted by the asteroid's splitting in two.

Unbelievable.

Although he couldn't recall every dot and dash, Seti was able to mentally piece together *S-T-O-P—F-I-G-H-T-I-N-G—D-I-S-P-U-T-E—O-V-E-R*. He realized his mind was, in his current state of near-unconsciousness, only telling him what he wanted to remember, and the reality was that as far as he knew, only Sean Stingray and the other Omicron COs knew Morse code. And after Blackstar accidently knocked over Stingray's nanotank, his friend was no doubt dead now. So it must have been either Arjun or Michelle. He was certain they remembered it, because—*Remembered what? Why did people always ask him questions? It wasn't his fault he couldn't always remember things. And why was it so hot? He didn't like this place. Where was his dad?*

He then felt himself being embraced. His dad, come to take care of him at last. Everything would be alright now.

Blackstar couldn't be sure if Nebula Captain was alive or not. The human had gone limp and released his hold on his command baton. The Imperian let it go as well. In an effort to protect him as much as possible, Blackstar cradled the captain, wrapping his larger body around him. He had no idea how long it would take to reach the ground, but was certain neither of them would survive at their current rate of descent. Although he couldn't gauge the velocity, he was sure it had leveled off, not getting any faster. But as long as they were ensconced within the descending fireball, the Imperian had little hope of figuring a way to slow their fall.

Suddenly, Blackstar felt an impact. But it wasn't the ground. Although he was aware of the searing heat, his grafted bio-orbs were still regulating his internal temperature, drawing the life- threatening heat away from him. Still, he dared not open his eyes to find out what had slowed their fall. He doubted it was a chunk of the planetoid. He was certain it had completely disintegrated. He took a chance and released one of his arms wrapped around his legs, cradling Nebula Captain, and lightly tapped the object that was falling underneath them. It was hard to tell, but he believed it was metal. The manufactured metal of the humans.

All at once, Blackstar knew what it was. A member of this foolish, noble, violent, courageous species called Man had flown one of their mechanical vacuum insects into the atmosphere, and gotten underneath Blackstar and Nebula Captain, in an effort to slow their fiery descent.

Sean Stingray wondered if anyone knew he was missing. Probably not, considering he'd been out of the picture for more than ten years. It was just as well. Since his command authorization codes were never deleted, it made it that much easier for him to sneak away, grab a spacebug from the CCM, exit Omicron Nebula and plunge into the atmosphere of Omicron in an attempt to catch up to and get underneath the raging fireball that could be none other than Danar and the Imperian.

He knew that whether he survived or not, Augustus Du Bois and the rest of the council would accuse him of being foolhardy and taking unauthorized action in trying this stunt. If he did survive, he would claim that because his command codes were still valid, he was still technically on active duty and didn't require authorization.

Yeah, that'll work.

Of course, the real reason was that he got a second lease on life because of Danar and the alien, who apparently wasn't really an alien. *Sure, it was an accident, but so what?*

Now that the fireball that was the spacebug had merged with the fireball of his charges, Stingray was beginning to feel the heat. He fought frantically to keep the antigrav motors at full capacity so as to slow their descent, but knew it was a losing battle. The spacebugs were not really designed for atmospheric flight. As if to illustrate his doubts, the copilot's panel exploded in shower of sparks. It was becoming more difficult to keep the craft stabilized.

Realizing he was going to have to bail out soon, he reached behind the copilot's seat and removed the parachute and managed to strap it unto his back while still piloting the bug. There was a loud CLUNK, and even though he wasn't able to hear the antigrav motors over the hissing and vibration of the spacebug breaking up, he knew it had just lost all power. He only now realized the floor iris wouldn't open without power, but he hadn't wanted to open it beforehand because that would only have heated the interior up that much sooner.

Without power, the digital displays were all dark. The only reading he cared about at the moment was the altimeter. Unfortunately, the mechanical analog altimeter was already smashed. He had no idea how close to the ground they were.

It is definitely time to split the scene.

He made his way to the rear exit and popped the panel exposing the manual release handle. It was stuck. No doubt the heat distorted the frame, causing the door to lock into place.

Thinking fast, he grabbed the fire extinguisher and doused the seam of the door, hoping to cool the metal enough to allow it to contract back to its original shape. Grabbing the handle again, Stingray managed to crank the door up just enough to accommodate himself and the parachute strapped to his back. He pulled a palm scanner over his left hand and, with reckless abandon, crouched and dove out head-first through the blast of heat and flame. Not even waiting to catch his bearings, he hit the release stud on his chest, deploying the parachute. Watching the chute billow above him and open as it caught the air, he then looked down only to see he was just about half a klick from the ground. He saw two fireballs fall away from each other. One of them exploded, presumably the spacebug. It looked as if he got out just in the nick of time. He closed his eyes and felt the shockwave hit the underside of his chute, deflecting him away.

Eventually he landed in the branches of a tree. He could see the other fireball slam into the ground on the outskirts of the forest. It was like a bomb had gone off. The sound of the impact echoed for several kilometers all around. The ground shook as if a quake were assaulting the vicinity. A dust cloud had blanketed the area and he could smell a ground fire coming to life.

Stingray was suspended out on a limb, about 15 meters off the ground. He released the buckle of the chute and dropped to the ground. He sprinted into the cloud of dust and smoke, doing his best to avoid the small brush fires igniting everywhere until he tripped and fell down what he thought was an embankment. When he finally skidded to a stop at the bottom of loose dirt, he realized he had fallen into a crater. A crater made by....

Fortunately, a stiff wind had come along and blown away enough smoke and dust for Stingray to see two sprawled, still forms: Danar and Blackstar. They were both spreadeagle on their backs, with Danar lying across Blackstar's chest. The majority of their clothing had been burned off. Danar had heat blisters all over his body, the hair on his head and face burned down to stubble.

As he nervously walked over to them, waving the palm scanner, Stingray saw two small shadows at his feet. He looked up to see the camera bot and the Imperian shadow stone hovering overhead. He hit his comm collar. "Contact Home Atlas. Get a medical skyvan here now!"

Stingray then heard a high-pitched whistling sound. At first he thought it was coming from the camera bot, but then he could see something else falling from the sky.

"That's strange," said Commander Cummings. "It looks as if there was some kind of explosion and *then* a surface impact."

"What's wrong with the camera bot?" asked Councilman Du Bois.

"Nothing. What we're seeing is an impact dust cloud mixed with the smoke of a fire. Wait, look. A gust of wind is clearing the view."

"There," pointed A. Du Bois. "I see them in the bottom of that valley."

"That's no valley, sir," the commander corrected. "It's the impact crater."

"My God."

"Sir," said a communications technician, "we're receiving a transmission from the *Nebula* cargo freighter. It's the Lieutenants Perez requesting instructions."

"Ah good. Tell them to dock in the hanger but keep the ship on standby. They can shuttle us down to Omicron.

"Where is that...that impact crater anyway?"

"It's on the outskirts of Pangaea," said Rocky Cummings. "About twenty kilometers from the outskirts of the capital—Hey, who the hell is that?"

The camera bot's overhead view showed a figure running in the loose dirt of the crater toward the crumpled figures of Captain Nebula and Blackstar.

"There shouldn't be anybody out there," commented the councilman. "That area is uninhabited. And...and what's that high-pitched sound?"

All eyes, including those of the two Imperians within the CCM, as well as everyone on the two orbiting starships, were on the monitors receiving the image from the camera bot. As more smoke and dust cleared, the mysterious figure could be seen looking up.

"What the hell," exclaimed Commander Cummings, "it's Sean Stingray."

Every head swivelled around to verify the former captain's absence from the CCM.

"How did—When did—" stammered the councilman.

Rockbottom and Deepwaters, mesmerized by the events of the last hour, stared at each other in confusion, before Rockbottom asked, "The ability to disappear and reappear do all humans possess?"

"Look, Stingray's saying something."

"*Contact Home Atlas. Get a medical skyvan here now!*" They could see him put his hand over his brow and look higher skyward. There was a shocked look on his face for a moment before he dove to the side. The high-pitched whine increased briefly and then the monitor went dead.

"Bull's eye," Stingray said, picking himself up and brushing dirt from his uniform. It was a million to one shot. Danar's command baton had fallen from orbit and smashed directly into the camera bot, destroying it. The Imperian shadow stone was still hovering nearby. He shouted up to it. "Make sure they get the message. We need medical assistance here and a transport. Now."

He then picked up the command baton, passing it back and forth between his right and left hand, wearing the palm scanner, blowing on the baton, trying to cool it.

The palm scanner indicated that both the human and Imperian still lived. But just barely. Danar's life signs were fading. Stingray shoved the handle of the baton into the dirt next to Danar. He then placed his friend's hand on the spherical head that was still slightly aglow with Omicron energy specifically tuned to Danar's brainwaves.

The person who thought of himself as Dane R. Howell was still uncomfortably hot and in a lot of pain. He didn't know why. He concentrated really hard. Sometimes that helped. Then he remembered. His dad told him he would go to sleep and then wake up on their new home. But his dad told him he would be cold for a while. It felt very hot. When he was able to open his eyes, he saw a figure staring down at him. "Dad?"

"I'll take that as a compliment, Danar," said the blurry figure.

Wait a minute, this wasn't his dad. This was some white man with long white hair and a funny handlebar mustache connected to his sideburns. He looked friendly. He was smiling at him. Wait. He knew this man. It was Captain Nebula. *No, no. I'm Captain Nebula. Then I must be dead,* he thought to himself, chuckling and coughing. For him to see the face of Sean Stingray, he *must* be dead.

Then everything went black.

When he came to again, he could see the murky image of Sarah James from inside a nanotank. She smiled at him and then accessed a communications terminal. He was alive, although everything hurt and he was very tired. It seemed like so many crazy things had happened to him up to now. He couldn't be certain what was real, what was fantasy. He did his best to concentrate on the events but was soon overcome with sleep.

The next time the world came into focus, he was lying in a bed. Doctor James was sitting on the edge, waving a palm scanner over him. When she noticed he was awake, she asked, "What is your name?"

Narrowing his eyes, he half-smiled and answered, "I don't remember." He chuckled at her concerned expression and said, "I'm kidding, Sarah. Relax."

"That's not at all like you, Danar," she said, lightly slapping his arm.

"Maybe I'm finally lightening up after all these years."

She shook her head and pressed a stud on the side of the bed. The door slid aside and Oshara and Roshan Perez piled into the room, followed by Tan Ozawa.

Danar was really glad to see them all. Especially Tan.

They stormed the bed and embraced him. Danar could tell someone else had entered the room. When his three friends made room, he saw the figure of Sean Stingray. He was speechless.

The group caught him up on most of the events of the last several days. He had been in and out of consciousness for nearly 70 hours. His injuries were treated at the medical facility at Home-At-Last on Omicron, where he'd spent the majority of time in a nanotank. When he was out of danger and could leave the tank, he was transported to Omicron Nebula.

Sean Stingray was alive and well, thanks to the accidental exposure to the Omicron energy discharge from Danar and Blackstar. It was indeed Stingray who attempted to give him the message in Morse code. It was also Stingray who appropriated a spacebug and slowed the descent, giving him and Blackstar their best shot at survival. Blackstar had fully recovered a day earlier and was looking forward to seeing Nebula Captain on his feet.

The two Imperian stone energy dampening spheres were repaired, recharged and magnetically attached to the large stone sphere.

Although the Council of Omicron welcomed the Imperians with open arms and offered a great deal of territory on Omicron to them, the Giants preferred to wait. Instead, it was mutually decided to send a team of Omicron scientists back to the Imperian dimension for an extended period of time in an effort to slow down, or if possible, repair the oxygen depletion problem.

Eventually Doctor James kicked his friends out, claiming Danar needed rest. As everyone began to leave, Seti insisted Tan stay a few minutes longer. Surprisingly, or maybe not so surprising, Sarah James relented.

When they were alone, he sat up and they embraced, cheek to cheek.

"I'm so sorry, Danar," she said. "I was nearly too late. If I had only gotten back sooner…."

"Hey now, don't blame yourself," he said reassuringly. "I'm going to be alright. Besides, you could say *we* were nearly too late."

Immediately understanding, she kissed him. Now Danar Seti felt complete. Well, nearly complete. "There is one thing," he said. "Of course it goes without saying, I'm really happy about the new peace. And I can assume it was due to the information you uncovered. But…well…exactly what is it?"

"Poor Danar," said Tan, a sad look in her eyes, despite the smile she wore. "You're probably the only sentient being in the colony who doesn't know."

"I know it has something to do with that drop of Imperian blood you found."

"Yes," she verified. "You are correct in that it was the Imperian blood that pointed me in the right direction. And I may not have come to a definitive conclusion at all if not for Marble's help. She is so unlike any Imperian. She's actually somewhat of a rebel at heart. I can't wait to introduce—"

"Tan, sweetheart," he interrupted, gently stroking her cheek, "what…is…the…conclusion?"

"Forgive me," she said smiling. "Getting right to it, it turns out the Giants are not native to the Imperian dimension, but are in fact, from our dimension."

He pursed his lips. "Somehow, I'm not surprised, based on the similarity in physical gestures and such. Do we know from where in our dimension?"

"As a matter of fact, they're from a planet, not far from here, galactically speaking, of course."

"Not far from here?" he asked, referring to the Omicron Nebula station. "Omicron?"

"No. Farther out."

"Avalon?" She shook her head. "Damocles?"

"Galactically speaking, Danar," hinted Tan.

"I give up," he said. "Tell me, please. What planet in our realm gave birth to the Giants of Imperia?"

"Earth, Danar," she finally answered. "They are from Earth."

CHAPTER TWENTY-TWO
Distant Cousins

"That's right, class," said Babs Schreiber to her wide-eyed students. "The Giants of Imperia are from our home planet, Earth."

"But how can that be, Ms. Schreiber?" asked young Kyle Armstrong. "I thought everybody on Earth looked like us. Are there people that look like the Giants?"

"Not on Earth today, no," she answered. "But there used to be a species on Earth a very long time ago, that shared many of the characteristics of the Imperians today. Say, between sixty-five and one hundred and fifty million years ago."

"Dinosaurs?" asked Danar Seti.

"Yes," verified Tan. "As you know, the latest paleontological theory states the dinosaurs were wiped out sixty-five million years ago by the Cretaceous-Tertiary Impactor; a large meteor, ten kilometers or so across that slammed into the Earth, creating a massive dust cloud of debris that eventually enveloped the planet."

"Yes," he continued, nodding, "blocking the sunlight from reaching the surface. The temperatures rapidly dropped, causing widespread freezing. Those life forms that were too large to burrow underground and forage for roots and such for food died off. Like the dinosaurs. But you're saying not all of them died off."

"Those that remained on Earth died. Now here's where it gets a bit hazy. By now, you've figured out a lot of the Giants' technology is based on a variation of telepathy through stone. Even their architecture is all stone based. Well, according to their legends, 'Three Large Stones of True Life-force' carried a great many Giants from their birthplace and into the 'Holy Realm,' through the 'Gate of Three Stars.'"

"Uh-huh."

"Don't you see?" asked Tan.

"I can see why the number three has become so important to them."

"That's true," Tan agreed. "More than sixty-five million years ago, a small planetoid, consisting of Omicron energy lodes, was ejected from what we now refer to as the Imperian dimension, through the trinary star system of Alpha Centauri, the Gate of Three Stars. The planetoid traveled for millions of years, to the closest star system, Sol, where somewhere along the line, it broke into four parts. One part hit the Earth, starting a chain of events that made it possible for humans to evolve by eliminating the dominant, larger species of dinosaurs. Yet somehow, a variety of life on Earth was transported to the remaining three chunks, which continued their circuit around and back through the trinary stars of Alpha Centauri and into the Imperian dimension."

"Not that I'm complaining, mind you," said Seti, shaking his head with a grin, "especially since this information ceased all hostilities between us and the Giants. But it sounds like a fanciful tale of speculation at best. Dubious at least."

"As I said, the details are hazy," conceded Tan. "But there is a great deal of scientific verification. Chief of which is the high percentage of base gene pair sequences we share with the Giants' blood. That alone lends weight to the argument that we're from the same planet. And although the Imperians can only rely on legends passed down through generational word of mouth, they are able to describe plant life and some species from Earth's early period, which we have verified through our own records and data. Unfortunately, only the dinosaurs—the Giants—could adapt to the Omicron energy within the dimension. After a few years, the other species and plant life eventually died off."

"But how could the dinosaurs and whatever else be transported to the remaining chunks?" he asked.

"Obviously, gravitational fields were in a state of fluctuation after the initial impact," explained Tan. "And with such quantities of the strange Omicron energy involved, we may never know the details of the actual transfer, but it's reasonable to assume the dinosaurs were preserved in some form of suspended animation, which helped them adapt to the Omicron energy, while they traveled back millions of years through the gate of trinary stars."

"So these Omicron planetoid chunks traveled from Alpha Centauri to Sol, changed the history of Earth, picked up a few hundred thousand passengers, and did a slingshot around Sol, back to their point of origin in the Imperian dimension. Kind of like Halley's comet orbiting Sol every seventy-six years."

"That's the best theory so far," said Tan. "While the dinosaurs made their long journey back, the Earth healed and eventually humans evolved. It's also reasonable to assume that some of the Omicron debris broke from the larger chunks and found its way onto Omicron's surface, where we came into contact with it millions of years later."

"And it's a good thing, too," opined Danar. "If not for our exposure to the stuff, we could all be packing our bags right about now, on our way to being a homeless species. Instead, we've come to realize that we are all related. All lost cousins from the planet Earth."

"The Imperians agree," Tan smiled. "There can be no hostilities with their relatives."

"But we've seen them fight amongst themselves," Danar observed. "What's the distinction with relatives?"

"I suppose they think of us as younger siblings," reasoned Tan. "Maybe they feel responsible for us."

"It could be worse, I suppose," said Danar. "They could be feeling a little guilty about inadvertently causing Earth's problems seventy years ago."

"There is that," agreed Tan.

"And what of the ISS *Omicron* and its two cryogenic transport modules?"

"When the tri-sphere stone craft leaves through the inter-dimensional transit tunnel, the Giants will immediately return the ISS *Omicron*."

"Good," said a somewhat somber Seti. "That is good."

"You don't sound as enthused as I thought you might."

"Hm? Oh, because that means the ISS *Omega* is truly lost," he answered. "Although I've never been a big fan of the Seer's predictions, I was rather hoping she would be proven correct when she said that all ten starships would eventually make it here."

"It's funny," said Tan. "Sean Stingray said the same thing, except he was more positive about the prospects of the *Omega*'s eventual return."

"That's because he's somewhat superstitious and believes in Labelle Vance's predictions," said Danar. "Did you know he used to consult with her regularly?"

"I knew that."

"Will any of the Giants be staying here?" asked Danar.

"Oh yes," Tan said enthusiastically, "I can't believe we didn't tell you that. There will be three staying with us. One from each sect."

"Three, huh?" repeated Danar. "There's a surprise. Do I know any of our new house guests?"

"As a matter of fact, you do," answered Tan. "Blackstar himself, representing the Liberal sect, will be remaining. Representing the Neutrals is my friend Marble. She and her, uh, assistant stone sphere will be working closely with me to help adapt the Imperian's stone spheres to our technology. We will also be doing our part to help the Omicron scientist going back with the tri-spheres uncover the problems of the Imperian dimension, as well as adapting their method of gyroscopic ID travel to conventional space travel within *this* realm."

"That's great," said Danar. "So who'll be representing the Conservative sect? Rockbottom?"

"No. Believe it or not, it'll be Longneck."

"You're kidding," accused Danar, his face contorted in disbelief. "Why would she be interested in staying with Blackstar? I thought they were at odds."

"I'm afraid there are less politics involved in the decision of these three particular Giants staying behind," admitted Tan, "and more...familial ties."

"How do you mean?"

"Danar, it turns out Blackstar and Longneck are mates and Marble is their daughter."

Seti chuckled, "I should have guessed."

The next day found the ID transit point in the middle of the acute triangle of stars a very busy place. Orbiting the now fully repaired and energy-charged Imperian stone tri-sphere at a five-kilometer perimeter were the eight newly repaired Omicron starships, now back in service. Among them were nine cargo transport freighters, eight of which were carrying civilian spectators from each Omicron asteroid city, while one, carrying several dozen scientists from the planet Omicron, would be entering the Imperian dimension. A dozen camera bots zipped through the crowd of ships, relaying various images from various angles back to the colony in-system.

On the flight control deck of the ISS *Nebula*, Danar Seti sat in his command crash chair, flanked by Tan Ozawa on his right and Sean Stingray to his left. Blackstar and Marble were standing before them with Marble's assistant sphere, carrying an autonomous VICI, hovering between her and Tan.

Standing forward, side by side, gazing at the main viewer's image of the Imperian tri-spheres, were Augustus Du Bois and Longneck. They were leaning toward each other occasionally, talking politics.

"Careful Du Bois Councilman should be," whispered Blackstar to the group around him. "Ruthless in her opinion of politics is Longneck."

"Trust me, big guy," said Stingray. "In Augustus Du Bois, she may have met her match."

Blackstar wore an impressed expression as he snuck a glance over his shoulder at the councilman, as if to reassess him.

"It seems to me," Tan noticed, "they're getting along quite famously."

"Shouldn't you be worried?" added Stingray to Blackstar. "Longneck might take a fancy toward the councilman."

"So lucky I should be," Blackstar said, prompting laughter from Seti and Stingray.

"Captain, we're receiving a transmission from the tri-sphere," informed the comm tech. "They're ready to depart."

"On viewer," ordered Seti.

On board the Imperian tri-sphere craft, three of the Omicron scientists were standing with Deepwaters, Rockbottom and various other Giants representing the three sects. It was a broad beam transmission to the entire colony.

"Doctor Ridovski here. Well, everything seems to be in order," said the scientist. "If our calculations on the passage of time between here and the Imperian dimension are correct, then you will be hearing from us in about a year."

"Let us hope it will be with good news," said Danar Seti. As he spoke, Doctor Richard Ridovski could be seen looking at a particular point on the screen of the Omicron viewer, indicating the screen was divided into several sections so he could see with whom he was conversing.

"That's the plan," said Ridovski.

"Good luck to you all," said the voice of Michelle Woo.

"And to you all as well," returned Ridovski, who then looked up at the taller Imperians.

Deepwaters stepped forward and spoke in his native language, obviously to the three Imperians being left behind. Although the clicks, hisses and grunts of their language were indecipherable, the look in his eyes was universal. However, it was hard translating the overall message because the expressions worn by the three recipients were different. Blackstar's was neutral, Marble enthusiastic and Longneck had sad eyes.

It was Blackstar who responded in the Imperian tongue. His reply had the ring of finality to it, so it was no surprise when the viewer switched back to the external view of the tri-sphere. The space immediately surrounding the Imperian craft began to obscure the view of the tri-sphere as the dark hole formed, preparatory to the ID gyroscopic energy rings.

A. Du Bois and Longneck joined the group around the command chair.

"If it's not improper of me to ask," said the councilman, "what was all that about?"

Seti and Stingray glanced at each other, realizing neither of them would ask that question. It was inappropriate considering the Giants spoke in their native language. On the other hand, neither of the three Giants looked offended so perhaps it was acceptable from some form of universal political standpoint.

"Wishes of good fortune, not unlike your Richard Ridovski Doctor Deepwaters granted us," answered Longneck.

"Also," added Blackstar, "the significance of the three of us and the present circumstances reiterated Deepwaters."

"Oh?" asked the councilman. "How do you mean?"

Blackstar explained that because he and Longneck were previous leaders of their respective sects, they were responsible for the Giants' eventual arrival. Marble, of course, played a major role in the new relationship with the humans. It was appropriate that, as a family, the three of them were given the privilege to stay.

"Privilege or curse," said Longneck.

Blackstar shot a glance at his mate, who returned the gaze with cold eyes. He took a deep breath, resigning himself to her—what seemed like perpetual—discomfort.

"You said 'previous leaders,'" inquired Seti. "I take it Deepwaters and Rockbottom are the new leaders of the Liberal and Conservative sects."

"Yes," hissed Longneck, clearly not liking the situation.

"But worth it I think it was," said Blackstar.

"Me too," agreed Marble. Her response had a very humanlike inflection.

"Nothing to lose you have, rookery daughter," sneered Longneck. "Not yet the leader of the Neutrals were you. Newly appointed instead."

"Ah, but everything to gain I have," said Marble. "You as well, Mother, if open your eyes and heart remain."

At that, Blackstar actually laughed out loud. He was soon joined by the nervous laughter of the humans. Longneck tried to look angry but eventually cracked a tiny smile when she looked at her daughter.

As for Marble, she couldn't be happier, as indicated by the broad grin she wore. Although she always knew her parents' mating was more politically motivated than passionate, they did achieve their goals of leadership, albeit temporarily. Not wanting to disappoint either of her parents by applying for either of their respective sects, she studied to be, what the humans called, a Neutral. Surprisingly, her parents supported her, both motivating her to leadership. Marble never had any interest in leadership. She much preferred research. Now she didn't have to worry about being honed as a leader of anything. She was in a new realm, a new dimension with fellow researchers—scientists. Her parents were with her, and she knew her new best friend was right. She was in for a grand adventure.

On the main viewer, the energetic ID gyroscopic rings were rotating around each other faster and faster. But before they became a solid three-kilometer ball of light, the Imperian tri-sphere was seemingly shrinking. Smaller and smaller. Just before it shrunk to nothing, the tiny speck began to grow. Larger and larger. But this time, the inter-dimensional object took on the form of a familiar-looking starship. Familiar but for a large cylinder attached to each side.

"The *Omicron*," whispered A. Du Bois, reverently. "With the cryogenic modules still attached."

"She's finally made it home," said Sean Stingray.

After a few seconds of staring at the lost vessel, through the now-slowing gyroscopic energy rings, Seti ordered, "A full scan, VICI."

"I am unable to fully scan the vessel while it is within the field of the gyroscopic energy rings."

"Shouldn't the rings have dissipated by now?" Seti asked Blackstar.

"Yes, ordinarily," answered the former Imperian sect leader. "However, not uncommon are dissipation delays from multiple inter-dimensional transports. Sometimes caught within the energy-forming matrix foreign objects, usually asteroids are. Several hours to eject foreign objects the rings require."

"You mean we'll have to wait several more hours before we can gather the *Omicron*?" asked the councilman.

"It's been thirty-one years, Gus," commented Stingray. "A few hours more won't make much of a difference.

"Free to exit the field under its own power the vessel can," offered Blackstar.

"VICI, you say you can only partially scan the *Omicron*," said Seti. "Are you able to access her systems remotely at all?"

"I'm not certain. Standby," said the interactive hologram. After about 30 seconds, **"Because the ISS *Omicron* never went through a systems upgrade, I'm having a difficult time starting her engines without the assistance of an onboard V-I-C-I clone. But I believe I can activate her thrusters."**

"That's all we'll need," offered Stingray. "We can tow her back to the colony once she's free."

"I concur," agreed Seti. "You may proceed, VICI."

"Activating thrusters," said the VICI. **"Timing ring rotation with thrust coordination…now."**

The vessel moved forward on the main viewer, smoothly gliding through the rotating rings.

"I'm surprised any of the ship's systems work at all, after all these years," commented the councilman.

"But for our examination of its records and appropriating its communications array, perfectly preserved inside the interdimensional transit tunnel, the ISS *Omicron* has remained," said Longneck.

"Really?" asked Stingray. "So she's essentially in the same condition she was in when she fell through that vacuum sinkhole thirty years ago."

"Correct," Longneck said, nodding.

"We need that scan, VICI," commented Seti.

"Scanning. All six hundred million cryogenic suspension chambers present and accounted for. However, four million, nine hundred thousand are no longer functioning."

"That's still less than one percent," calculated the councilman. "About the same amount of chambers that went off-line on the rest of the starships three decades ago."

"Those statistics are lost human lives, Augustus," Stingray said angrily.

"Combined, we've lost more lives in getting here to Alpha Centauri," said Tan, "than all of the lives lost during Earth's first two world wars, centuries ago. And that doesn't include the loss of the ISS *Omega*."

"If we hadn't come here at all," countered the councilman, "the Earth would have lost a hell of a lot more lives seventy years ago. The way I see it, we just gained over five hundred ninety-five million more lives."

"What about the non-frozen crew?" inquired Seti.

"I read all one hundred sixteen in various sections of the habitable areas. All seem to be unconscious."

Everyone looked at the Imperians.

"Unconscious they were when their vessel we boarded," explained Blackstar. "Typical for your species is temporary loss of consciousness when inside ID transit tunnel. Kept them unconscious," he said while pointing directly to Marble's assistant sphere, "while examining their technology, their physiology and communication array."

"In other words, the last any of them will remember is entering the sinkhole?" asked the councilman.

"Correct," said Longneck. "Keep them unconscious I recommend or much confusion they would experience."

"I agree," said Seti. "It'll be a smoother transition into the colony if they wake up on the planet Omicron."

"But not much easier, when they realize thirty-one years have passed," commented Tan.

"True," agreed Seti, "but the less traumatic, the better. Now that the *Omicron*'s passengers and crew are outside of the energy that's preserved them for the past three decades, I assume they will be coming around soon. Can we access their life support systems?"

"Certainly, Captain Nebula. I can flood the ship with a mild anesthetic gas, keeping the crew unconscious until we return in-system."

"Thank you, VICI. Proceed."

CHAPTER TWENTY-THREE
Reunion

Now that the ISS *Omicron* was free of the dark hole and the influence of the gyroscopic energy rings, VICI discovered she was able to access the vessel's nuclear engines. That meant they were able to escort her back to the colony under full power.

Just as the fleet was preparing to return, the gyroscopic rings began to dissipate.

"Be warned, Nebula Captain," advised Blackstar. "When finally gone the rings are, ejected in any direction the foreign object will be."

"Thank you, Blackstar. If it is an asteroid, we'll make short work of it."

Just as the energy field of the gyroscopic rings winked out of existence and the three-kilometer area of space returned to normal, the foreign object that had prevented the initial dissipation of the field shot out randomly into normal space.

"Omicron Starforce," spoke VICI fleet-wide, "**do not fire upon the object. Its trajectory will not collide with any of the fleet. Also...I have...identified it.**"

"You mean, it's not an asteroid?" asked A. Du Bois.

"**On viewer.**"

"What the...."

"It's the original Nebula cargo transport freighter," identified Tan. "Lost nearly nineteen months ago."

"My friends," said Captain Nebula to the three Giants. "Exactly when did you send the nine...reconnaissance stone spheres into this realm?"

"Eighteen months, three weeks and two of your days ago," answered the Imperian's resident record keeper.

"Thank you, Marble," said Tan, smiling. "The freighter could have been in this region at that time. How did you know, Danar?"

"Our new friends said that during multiple transports, the ID energy field is susceptible to trapping foreign objects. It seemed reasonable the nine recon spheres would have been sent within the last couple of years to be retrieved later for…uh, information gathering."

"Debriefing for conquest you mean," said Blackstar, with a grin.

"Yes," relented Captain Nebula, returning the grin.

"Well done, Captain Nebula," praised Sean Stingray, who was genuinely impressed. Since his return, he'd witnessed his protege's level of competence and efficiency as the carrier of the flag of Omicron. For the first time in his life, Stingray felt outmoded. "I would have assumed the Imperians captured the freighter as well without telling us about it. Or, I would have wracked my brains for hours or longer trying to figure an alternative reason for it suddenly showing up."

Captain Nebula smiled his thanks at his former mentor, while asking, "VICI, what about life signs?"

"I read twenty-three unconscious human beings. The entire compliment of civilians and scientists that went out on the fateful journey over eighteen months ago."

"Including Christine McCauley," added Tan Ozawa, "Omicron Nebula's head school teacher. I wonder how Babs Schreiber will react to the news."

"Can we assume they were in suspension the entire nineteen months?" asked the councilman.

"Yes," Blackstar answered. "If drawn into the ID corridor when the recon spheres exited nineteen of your months ago, stood still for them time has."

"Should we keep them unconscious as well?" asked A. Du Bois.

Everyone looked toward Danar Seti. "I think not," he said. "When they come to, the circumstances won't appear to be out of the ordinary for them. From their point of view they entered an unknown region of space and lost consciousness, only to wake up to see the entire fleet come to rescue them. I think, however, it would be prudent to send a med tech and a Starforce officer over to assist their transition nineteen months into the future."

Within the hour, the Omicron fleet of starships began its journey back to the colony in-system, having retrieved an extra starship, as well as another cargo freighter in perfect working order, three new guests from another dimension, 23 lost Omicron citizens and nearly 600 million refugees from Earth, who'd finally made it to Alpha Centauri.

Somewhere in deep space, but not quite in space, yet getting closer, a vessel continued its search. A subordinate informed the commander of yet another signal indication. This was another big one. Bigger than the last, in fact. They were certain, this was the last. The vessel was ordered to zero in on the signal before it dissipated. But it was too late. The signal had faded. But not before the confirmation of the three stars was located.

Success. The vessel's journey had finally ended.

A subordinate informed the commander of a fleet of starships and smaller craft headed to the largest of the three stars. A yellow gas giant. The commander ordered pursuit, while remaining shrouded.

Just before entering the asteroid belt orbiting Alpha Centauri A, the fleet of Omicron starships surrounded the ISS *Omicron* in a three-dimensional pentagon formation. The ISS *Nebula* at point, the ISS *Gaea* and *Pulsar* to starboard and port, with the ISS *Vortex* and *Quasar* behind them. The ISS *Graviton* was atop the formation with the ISS *Radian* underneath. The ISS *Ersatz* brought up the rear. The eight Omicron cargo freighters were traveling close to their respective starships with the recently found original Nebula freighter directly behind and underneath the ISS *Nebula*.

"Captain Nebula," the comm tech said, "we're receiving a fleet-wide transmission from the *Ersatz*."

"Let's see it."

"*Uh, yeah, you guys,*" said Jack Askew's image on the main viewer, "*this is probably nothing, but we're seeing—at least I think we're seeing something strange coming from the direction of the ID transit point.*"

"You think you're seeing?" asked LeAnn Walker, aboard the ISS *Gaea*.

"Well, yeah. Our VICI swears she can see something, but sensors aren't picking up anything," explained Captain Ersatz.

"Perhaps the *Ersatz*'s VICI should update the rest of the network so we can all see what you're talking about, Jack," suggested Arjun Vohra.

"*Standby, gang,*" said D. Seti's brief image on the fleet's viewers, the three Imperians standing near him. "*I'll get right back to you.*"

Captain Nebula turned to face his Imperian guests. "Do any of you have an explanation for any strange visions that may or may not be coming from the ID transit point?"

Both Blackstar and Longneck looked at each other, then to their daughter.

"No explanation do I have," answered Marble. "No readings or visual cues for your sensors to detect, once dissipated the gyroscopic rings have."

"Could it be possible your people are returning?"

"Without the energy rings, no," answered Blackstar.

"Hmm." Danar Seti narrowed his eyes while stroking his beard.

"What is it, Danar?" asked Tan.

"I'm…not sure. I'm getting a funny feeling."

"You mean as in intuition?" asked Sean Stingray. "You? My, how things have changed."

"Even though I don't normally subscribe to the notion of 'gut feelings,' I'd be foolish to dismiss them," Seti said, smiling at his friend.

"Ah, a true agnostic," commented Tan.

"Fleet-wide audio only," ordered Captain Nebula. When the comm tech acknowledged, he simply said, "Holo-conference. Now." Then he stood up and gave the signal to close the channel.

The digital cameras swivelled to his position. He knew that he was holographically standing on the control deck of the seven other starships, just as he saw holo-projections of his colleagues materializing on the *Nebula*'s control deck.

The three Giants were surprised and impressed at the humans' mechanical technology.

"You are suspicious of Jack's ghost, eh Nebula," accused the holo-image of Captain Graviton. "Otherwise, why the holo-conference?" he asked, knowing their communications couldn't be tapped in holo-conference mode.

"Suspicious? Perhaps," said Seti, not quite committing himself. "Like Jack said, it could be nothing. But there are too many unanswered questions.

"Hey now," said the image of Jack Ersatz, "if it turns out to be of significance, don't forget who put everyone on the alert."

"And if it turns out to be nothing?" asked the image of Captain Gaea.

"Then remember it was Captain Paranoid," said Jack, referring to Danar Seti, "who hit the panic button."

"Now that VICI is fully updated," interrupted Charles Lee, "maybe we can all see what she saw from the *Ersatz*."

"Thank you, Captain Vortex. If you will all direct your attention to your respective astronavigation consoles."

On each flight control deck, seven holographic captains and a solid one gathered around the consoles, realizing VICI would rather display her vision holographically as opposed to digitally on the main viewer for fear of possible eavesdropping. The tabletop showed a simple holographic display of stars.

"I don't see anything," admitted Michelle Woo.

"Look closer," said Jack.

"Wait," said Charles Lee. "That distortion there."

"*Oui*, I see it now," verified J.P. Bouvier. "Are you sure it is not a smudge on the camera lens?"

"I am sure."

"Could it be an aftereffect or something from the ID transit point?" asked Frank Logan.

"Not according to our Imperian friends," Seti answered.

"Where is this distortion now?" asked Councilman Du Bois.

Although he wasn't holographically projected onto the other vessels, the other COs could still hear him.

"Roughly four hundred kilometers behind the ISS *Ersatz*."

"So it could simply be a random anomalous reflection from one of us," offered Sean Stingray.

"It could be."

"If it turns out to be a distorted reflection of some kind, VICI will discover it soon enough," said Seti. "In case it's something more, we'll remain cautious, but we'll go about our normal routines. Everyone will veer off to their respective asteroid cities, but remain on alert status. The ISS *Nebula* will escort our freighter to our station and see to the ISS *Omicron*'s orbital insertion around Omicron. And we'll see what we will see. If anyone can discover a logical explanation for our reflective smudge, please feel free to let the rest know. However, if you confirm a malevolent purpose for the distortion, then communicate via holo-conferencing. That is all." Giving a silent nod to VICI, the channel closed, which caused all of the holo-COs to dematerialize.

"VICI," he continued. "As each starship leaves formation to meet up with its respective asteroid city, I want you to holographically download the following message as you update to each of your clones."

"Understood, Captain Nebula."

Somewhere in space—but not quite normal space—a vessel followed its quarry. A subordinate informed the commander that they were no longer receiving their prey's communication. The commander wanted to know if they'd been detected. No one could be certain, but it appeared as if the fleet of ships they were following detected something, but dismissed it as "probably nothing." But then the transmissions between the fleet abruptly ceased and the formation of starships broke apart as each ship rendezvoused with several domed asteroid cities just inside the asteroid belt. But the commander determined those ships weren't the important quarry. The one vessel whose brief transmission revealed the true masters of this region of space—the lead ship called the ISS *Nebula*—was the prey. The commander ordered a shrouded pursuit of that vessel to its destination.

A team of several hundred technicians were separating the two cryogenic transport modules from the ISS *Omicron* in orbit around the planet Omicron. They were preparing to transport the 600 million cryo-suspension chambers to the surface. Several dozen spacebugs piloted by Starforce officers were cruising the area with a watchful eye.

The original Nebula cargo freighter was safely docked in the lower level of the cargo hanger of the Omicron Nebula asteroid station. Its civilians and scientists, along with the non-frozen crew of the ISS *Omicron*, were on their way to the planet's surface for debriefing at the capital city of Home-At-Last.

Augustus Du Bois and Longneck were in the Central Command Module. The councilman was in the middle of a holo-conference with the other council members of Omicron.

Sean Stingray was visiting his old friend Jim Sanders, the foreman of the mining operations in the oxygenated caverns below the city proper. Jim was one of the first maintenance techs who helped thaw the majority of Earth refugees 30 years ago. He had worked under Professor Frederick Howell back on Earth and was present during young Danar Seti's thawing and processing.

Tan Ozawa was giving Marble a tour of Omicron Nebula's medical facility and specifically her own lab, where the two of them would be working closely together. Marble's assistant stone sphere, carrying the autonomous digital neurons of VICI, was hovering nearby, as always.

Danar Seti and Blackstar were casually strolling the multi-levels of the cargo hanger of the asteroid city, a far cry from the last time the two were together there. The captain and the Imperian waited outside the main airlock, connected to the interior of the station. Seti wanted to show his new friend an ice asteroid retrieval procedure.

"VICI," said Seti into his comm collar, "any distorted visions in the vicinity?"

"Negative, Captain," said the disembodied voice of the interactive hologram. "Perhaps it really was nothing. Either that or my ability to see it is dependent on a specific distance. If that is the case, it could be any—One moment…Captain, there is an unidentified vessel materializing from…nowhere, one hundred meters from the cargo hanger clamshell."

"Materializing from *nowhere?*"

"On the monitor."

On the video monitor just outside the airlock, a large spaceship was solidifying into view, as if it indeed materialized from nowhere.

"Nebula Captain," commented Blackstar. "The ISS *Omicron* does this vessel look like. Some modifications, however, it has."

"That's not the *Omicron*," said the wide-eyed Seti. "It's…it's the—"

"Captain Nebula. The vessel is firing at us."

"What? Prepare to defend—"

"Correction, Captain. Those are not weapons. They're cryogenic suspension chambers. Ten of them headed straight for the opened cargo bay. Each one is carrying an animated human being. They have entered the hanger bay. That section of the clamshell is closing. The bay is pressurizing."

As VICI was explaining, the squad of a dozen Starforce security officers the captain had prepared for each asteroid city arrived at the airlock. They had no choice but to wait until the bay pressurized. But there were two in the crowd who didn't have to wait.

"VICI," ordered Captain Nebula, "Blackstar and I are entering the lock. Override the inner door pressure seal so we can enter the bay before it's pressurized."

Recognizing the captain's voice for authorization and understanding that he and Blackstar were impervious to depressurization, VICI simply responded, **"Understood, Captain Nebula."**

"Sir," interrupted Security Chief Simmons. "With respect, the captain should not enter a potentially hazardous situation that might—" He cut himself short when he realized with whom he was speaking. Not merely a human captain, but an Omicron energy-enhanced human, partnered with a literal giant, who was also enhanced. The two not only fought each other toe to toe in open space but survived the fiery atmospheric descent and impact onto Omicron's surface.

The chief rephrased his statement. "We've got your backs, sir. The moment the bay pressurizes."

Both the captain and Blackstar nodded their appreciation and entered the airlock. When they stepped into the cargo bay from the inner airlock door, they both noticed the bay was nearly pressurized, since they could hear the hiss of air as it was pumped in.

Although the two entered the cargo hanger from the highest level airlock, there was another level above their heads. Actually it was more of a wide gantry attached to the curved walls of the hanger. Six of the ten coffin-like cryogenic suspension chambers had come to rest on the upper gantry, while four were at the feet of the captain and the Imperian. VICI did say the contents of the modified CSCs were non-frozen humans. If these were indeed humans from the lost ISS *Omega*, their entry into Alpha Centauri space as well as Omicron Nebula was questionable at best.

Not wanting to take any chances and knowing the occupants of the CSCs would have to wait for the hanger to fully pressurize before emerging, the captain preferred keeping as many as possible inside the CSCs. Taking advantage of their early entrance into the bay, D. Seti sprinted over to one of the equipment lockers that lined the wall and removed four magnetic sealer discs, flat discs about eight centimeters in diameter with a handle on the back, used for temporarily sealing small hull fractures in spaceships.

Demonstrating its new use to Blackstar, Captain Nebula slapped an MSD over the lid of one of the cryo-chambers where it mated to the body, effectively locking it in place. He tossed two MSDs to Blackstar, who secured the other cryo-chambers.

The bay was now fully pressurized. Twelve Omicron security officers poured out of the airlock at the same time that the six CSCs on the upper gantry opened their lids. Six humans did in fact exit the chambers. Five men wielding rifles of some kind and a woman carrying a sword, of all things. Forged between the handle of the sword and its blade was the emblem of the *Omega*.

But as impressed as Seti was with the sword, he was more impressed with the woman. Even from the equivalent height of two stories up, he could tell that she was tall. She had a head full of thick, shoulder-length dreadlocks. Her eyes were large, perhaps too large for her face. But that suited her somehow. It didn't take away from her beauty at all. It, in fact, enhanced it. Her skin was a deep caramel color.

Danar blinked once, as if to clear the image before his eyes. Not that he expected her to suddenly disappear. It was merely his way of reminding himself not to fall into those big brown eyes. He could ill afford it. The thought made him feel slightly guilty, but at the moment he couldn't remember why he should feel guilty. He figured it was time to be more clinical in his assessment of her.

Like her male companions, she was wearing an old-style modified Starforce uniform. The *Omega* tincture of faded *sanguine*—magenta, with the thigh-high black faux leather boots, but without the metallic gold harmonic ankles and armbands, which didn't become a part of the uniform until after Omicron planetfall. The men wore the one-piece jumpsuit while the woman's garment was further modified with a short skirt, accentuating her shapely caramel thighs.

One of the men stepped closer to her. He was huge, muscular, on the order of 190 centimeters or more in height. Bald but for a long ponytail of black hair growing from the back of his head. Dark skin like Danar's, with a long bridged nose. He was either of African or native American Indian descent.

"Welcome home, crew of the ISS *Omega*," Seti said, looking up at the woman, who was clearly in charge. "This is the Omicron Nebula space station. I am—"

"I know who you are," said the woman, with disdain, pointing her sword directly down at him. "You are the traitor who sold out the human race."

"What? Traitor?" Seti asked in disbelief. "Listen, you're—"

"Enough!" she screamed. "And you," she said, pointing at Blackstar, "his demon master. I hereby officially demand you turn over this territory to its rightful human owners."

"Mistaken you are," said Blackstar. "Nebula Captain's master I am not."

"Enough, demon. I won't hear your lies."

"Who are you?" demanded Captain Nebula.

"I am—" she began, before her face contorted in pain. The sword tip lowered slightly. She reached for her head with her left hand, massaging her temples. Her bald, muscular companion gently grabbed her shoulders, attempting support. She roughly shoved him aside, before continuing, her voice stronger. "I am...Cleopatra Wilson, granddaughter of General Cinderblock Wilson, former CO of the ISS *Omega*. I am daughter of Commander Ricardo Montoya and Sergeant-At-Arms Celia Wilson, both of the United Earth Vessel *Sol*. I am...Captain Omega.

"Surrender," she demanded.

As Captain Omega spoke, the lower level of this section of the cargo bay filled up with more people, including Augustus Du Bois, Longneck, Tan Ozawa, Marble, Sarah James, Sean Stingray and Jim Sanders.

"There'll be no surrendering here, Captain," explained Seti, calmly. "You've misinterpreted the situation. Stand down."

"No!" she screamed. At her nod, four of the five men raised their rifles, aiming at the crowd below.

The twelve Omicron security officers raised their neurowave gauntlets at the six Omegas.

"Drop your weapons," ordered Captain Nebula to the newcomers. "Nearly half your boarding party is subdued," he said, indicating the four locked CSCs. "You're outnumbered. You cannot win."

"Cleopatra, maybe we should listen—" began the ponytailed, muscular man, apparently the only rational one.

"No!" she screamed again, experiencing more cranial pain. This time, when she shoved the big man aside, he bumped into a compatriot, causing the man to stumble, accidently firing his rifle; a red laser beam shot into the crowd.

The hot stream of light pierced the right shoulder of one of the security officers. The beam went straight through him, cauterizing the wound and singing the deck about 15 centimeters behind and between Tan's feet. The security officer collapsed to the deck, clutching his burnt shoulder.

Four other security officers fired one quick blast each at the invaders. *FOOMP, FOOMP, FOOMP, FOOMP.* Three of the armed men crashed to the gantry, while the fourth, the one who inadvertently fired into the crowd, fell forward over the railing and tumbled to the lower deck, breaking a leg in the fall. He was unconscious from the neurowave disruption but was twitching nonetheless.

Doctor James started toward him, but was held back by Sean Stingray.

The big man next to Captain Omega was clearly stunned but still on his feet, not having taken a full neurowave shot. Cleopatra Wilson didn't appear affected at all. If anything, she was angrier. Her pupils were tiny islands in a sea of white. She clutched the railing with her left hand and leaped over the side, aiming to land right in front of Captain Nebula. She gripped her sword in a double fist, raising it above her head as she made the two level descent. Before she landed, however, the officer behind Captain Nebula fired a point-blank neurowave shot directly at her. She still managed to land on her feet before falling backwards. She moaned, but somehow, amazingly, she remained conscious, not once releasing her grip on the sword. Slowly climbing to her feet she again raised the sword above her head, ready to split Danar Seti's skull. As the blade descended toward him, Captain Nebula deflected it with the metallic bands on his forearms. Without missing a beat, Captain Omega used the momentum from her deflected swing as a counter-balance, pivoting on her right heel with a backward roundhouse kick of her left boot into Danar Seti's crotch.

Captain Nebula doubled over, landing on his posterior with the wind knocked out of him. He then fell over on his side, both hands in between his legs.

Just as the Starforce security officers raised their gauntlets at Captain Omega, Tan Ozawa stepped over the pain-wracked Danar Seti and raised her hand for the security officers to hold off.

"Back off, bitch," said Cleopatra Wilson. "I don't want to hurt you."

"You will not," Tan said flatly, crouched in a defensive posture.

The woman known as Captain Omega thrust her sword at Tan's stomach. She effortlessly slipped aside and with lightning speed, grabbed the wrist holding the sword, applying pressure to a tendon in Cleopatra Wilson's forearm, causing the sword to clatter to the deck. Captain Omega threw a left jab at Tan's head. Instead of ducking or blocking the blow, Tan merely twisted her head, avoiding the blow, then twisted the rest of her body while releasing her opponent's wrist. Now with her back to her, Tan elbowed Captain Omega in her mid-section. Then punched her in the nose with the back of the same right fist.

"Please don't hurt her," the big man pleaded from the upper gantry. "It's not her fault."

Continuing her takedown, Tan thrust her hips into Cleopatra Wilson's body, grabbed both her wrists and flipped her over her back. Captain Omega crashed to the floor. Although she moaned, she still wasn't out for the count. Before she could struggle to her feet, however, Tan Ozawa lightly punched her in the base of her neck, causing Cleopatra Wilson to finally crumple to the deck unconscious.

"Captain Nebula, are you alright?" asked an officer, helping his CO to his feet.

"I sure hope so," squeaked Seti through clenched teeth, wondering why it was taking so long for the Omicron Particles to relieve him of his discomfort.

"I hope all your parts are still intact," commented Tan.

"Me too," he replied.

"Known had I of your vulnerable spot," said Blackstar, facetiously grinning, "different the outcome of our confrontation would be."

"Oh shut up," Seti said, still grimacing and protecting his groin with both hands. Once on his feet he ordered the Starforce officers to retrieve the final Omegas from the upper gantry.

Leaning over Cleopatra Wilson, waving a medical palm scanner, Sarah James said, "No wonder she could take a neurowave disruption shot point blank. The poor woman has a golf ball-sized brain tumor. As a result, her neurowave patterns are out of phase from normal. It's a wonder she's alive at all."

"That's what's causing her to act irrationally," said the big man. "It's not her fault."

"What's your name, mister?" asked Captain Nebula.

"Armstrong. Kyle Armstrong."

"Kyle Armstrong? Did you have relatives aboard the ISS *Nebula* out of Earth?" asked Seti.

"Yes, my brother Kevin. My parents thought it best to put us on separate ships when we were kids, him on the *Nebula* and me on the *Omega*."

"So, that really is the *Omega* out there," said A. Du Bois.

"Yes, and we would never have made it here at all if not for Captain Omega. She put her life on the line to keep the ship from...well, from blowing up," explained Armstrong. "By the way, if the *Omega* didn't hear from us by now, the captain left orders for them to shroud up and escape. But I can help you detect the ship."

"That won't be necessary," said Captain Nebula, as he activated his comm collar. "Graviton, status."

"*The situation is under control, Nebula,*" said the voice of Arjun Vohra. "*The ISS Omega is secured. A maintenance crew is already separating the cryogenic transport modules.*"

"Nicely done," praised Captain Nebula. "You won't mind hanging out on this end of the belt for a while, will you?"

"*Not at all, old boy.*"

At Armstrong's confused look, Seti explained how they had detected the shrouded *Omega* in open space and how he sent a message to the fleet to continue to travel in-system, behind the almost invisible ship, closing off any avenue of escape. The entire fleet was listening in on everything that occurred in the cargo bay.

"Am I to understand the entire fleet is outside?" asked Councilman Du Bois. At Seti's affirmative nod, he said, "Well good. I had a holo-meeting with the rest of the council before coming here. When things settle down, all of the Omicron captains are to report to the council chambers at Home-At-Last. That includes you as well, Stingray."

While a medical team had arrived to take Cleopatra Wilson to the med facility, the Omicron security force released the *Omega*'s men from the locked CSCs, taking them and their four recovering comrades into custody.

While Kyle Armstrong was being led away, he turned. "Captain Nebula, is my brother here on…Omicron Nebula?"

"If I'm not mistaken. I believe you also have a young nephew named after you, attending school here. But don't worry, Armstrong, you'll get your family reunion…after you answer about ten thousand questions, including where the hell the ISS *Omega* has been the last thirty years and how you managed that invisibility trick."

"I'll tell you everything, sir," Armstrong said, smiling, happy to receive news of family. "I'll answer any questions you have. But please, please help her," he said, referring to Cleopatra Wilson.

"I promise, she'll get the best of care," assured Seti.

As the security officers escorted Armstrong away in magnetic shackles, Sarah James, following the antigrav gurney out, gave Danar Seti a look that said she thought the woman's chance of survival was questionable. Without saying a word, Seti looked at the doctor and tapped his own temple three times. Understanding exactly what he was saying, Doctor James rolled her eyes to the ceiling, shook her head and left.

Suddenly, Jim Sanders began to chuckle and then laughed out loud.

"Jimmy," said Danar Seti, "what's the matter with you?" He considered Jim Sanders practically family, vaguely remembering the man from his childhood, having worked for his father back on Earth.

"Yeah," said Sean Stingray. "Spill it."

"Don't you see?" he asked, still laughing. "The Seer. She was right all along."

"What are you talking about?" asked Seti.

Doing his best to get himself under control, J. Sanders said, "The Seer. She predicted all ten Omicron starships would eventually make it to Alpha Centauri. But that the *Nebula* would get here first. She was right."

"He's got a point," said Sean Stingray, who was also beginning to laugh. "What do you say now, Mr. Agnostic-I-Don't-Believe-in-Anything?" he asked of Danar Seti.

Choosing not to say anything, D. Seti looked at Tan Ozawa and shrugged his shoulders, prompting laughter from just about everyone else, including Blackstar and Marble. Longneck and Augustus Du Bois both wore irritated expressions, which made everyone else laugh even harder. Seti was glad to see his friends enjoying themselves and was just as glad he decided to bite his tongue when Sean asked his opinion. Danar was about to answer, *There are such things as coincidences.* For he was convinced there was no way Labelle Vance, the so-called Seer, or anyone else, could accurately predict the future.

"Danar," Tan said, diverting his attention from the jovial crowd. "I'm surprised you didn't give a rebuttal. Is everything alright?"

"Everything is fine, Tan," he assured her. "You know, I will tell you one thing. Last week, after our war with the Imperians, and while I was preparing to fight Blackstar, I was convinced that violence and destruction were mankind's destiny. But I was wrong. They are not our destiny. But it is our destiny to *overcome* violence and destruction. The violence and destruction…within ourselves."

Looking around her, Tan said, "I think we're off to a very good start."

They smiled at each other, embraced and kissed.

While holding her, Danar whispered in Tan's ear, "You know, I think it's high time I paid the Seer a visit one of these days soon."

EPILOGUE

On the planet Omicron below, on the east coast of the large continent of Pangaea, the capital city Home-At-Last goes about its normal routine. Normal but for the fact that the officials are preparing to increase the colony's population by nearly twelve hundred million new citizens. As for most of the citizens, some will soon be reunited with lost loved ones who, for the most part, have remained the same since they left Earth nearly 70 years ago.

On the outskirts of the capital city on a hill sat a small house. Inside the house sat an old black woman, a citizen who somehow was aware of the goings-on in orbit. Labelle Vance, the Seer, looked up at her ceiling as if she could see into space. She laughed. And laughed…and laughed.

THE END

…for now.
Adventures from Alpha Centauri will continue in
OMICRON: EARTH EXODUS

ACKNOWLEDGEMENTS

There are many good folks at the Voice Of America who gave me sage advice and opinions that made *Omicron Crisis* possible. But I must give special thanks to Faith Lapidus, the first person to read *Omicron Crisis*, who gave me much needed editorial directions, and Subhash Vohra, no doubt an ancestor of Arjun Vohra a.k.a. Captain Graviton of the novel, who regaled me with valuable insight into ancient Hindu myth and culture.

Printed in the United States
73113LV00003B/39